PRAISE FOR THE NOVELS OF CECILIA TAN

WILD LICKS

"A rock-and-roll love song to erotic romance readers and music fans... An outstanding example of the erotic romance genre."

—*Publishers Weekly* (starred review)

"Emotional angst, drama, and a seemingly impossible romance are just the tip of the iceberg for a couple whose dark erotic desires can either bring them together in the ultimate salvation or drive them apart forever."

—Heroes & Heartbreakers
"Erotic Romance Best Bets, July 2016"

"This one is great for those of you looking for plenty of smoking hot consensual BDSM sex."

—Bustle "Ten Romance Novels for Steamy Afternoons"

"Cecilia Tan's second Secrets of a Rock Star novel starts off with a bang and doesn't let up." —*RT Book Reviews*

TAKING THE LEAD

"Veteran Tan kicks her Secrets of a Rock Star series off with a sultry start... With a satisfying plot and an engaging cast of characters, the only thing slowing readers down will be their refractory period." —*Publishers Weekly* (starred review)

"4 stars! An emotional whirlwind romance. Axel is as strong and sexy as readers expect in a rock-star hero without being an overly brooding jerk. The length he goes in order to win over emotionally closed-off Ricki will melt your heart."

—*RT Book Reviews*

SLOW SATISFACTION

"Cecilia Tan has a way to seduce you into her stories . . . you can't put her books down because she's that great a storyteller."

—RakesofRomance.com

"*Slow Satisfaction* is everything I expected it to be. The perfect closing of the curtains to a story that had a fantastic ending."

—SinfulReads.com

"This couple always finds new and interesting ways to raise the heat index." —*RT Book Reviews*

SLOW SEDUCTION

"The sex scenes here are once again as hot as they are imaginative." —*RT Book Reviews*

"5 stars! *Slow Seduction* was a tasty treat to say the least. I cannot wait to get my hands on book three. If you are looking for erotica, stop whatever you are doing and get this book." —DivasDailyBookblog.wordpress.com

SLOW SURRENDER

"4½ stars! This is the BDSM novel all the other millionaire dom heroes want to star in. Tan takes an overused trope and turns it into a dreamy, erotic fantasy that draws the reader down the rabbit hole along with Karina. The sex scenes are lush and erotic... Readers will be clamoring for the next book in the series." —*RT Book Reviews*

"Move over, EL James. Cecilia Tan's *Slow Surrender* is sinfully sweet and sublimely erotic. As with sipping a superb single-malt scotch served neat, you'll savor the slow burn as it builds to a deliciously unanticipated... climax."

—Hope Tarr, award-winning author

"Loved, loved *Slow Surrender* and am waiting on pins and needles for book two... another brilliant outing from Cecilia Tan... her characters are full of life and emotion, and so believable. Definitely a keeper!" —NightOwlReviews.com

"If you are a fan of the billionaire dom, you should not miss *Slow Surrender*. Cecilia Tan weaves a compelling and red-hot tale that will have readers eager for more."

—RomanceNovelNews.com

ALSO BY CECILIA TAN

Taking the Lead
Wild Licks

Slow Surrender
Slow Seduction
Slow Satisfaction

Black Feathers
Daron's Guitar Chronicles
The Hot Streak
Initiates of the Blood
The Incubus and the Angel
Mind Games
The Poet and the Prophecy
The Prince's Boy
The Siren and the Sword
Telepaths Don't Need Safewords
The Tower and the Tears
The Velderet
White Flames

HARD RHYTHM

CECILIA TAN

FOREVER

New York Boston

Forever
Hachette Book Group
1290 Avenue of the Americas
New York, NY 10104
forever-romance.com
twitter.com/foreverromance

Printed in the United States of America

LSC-H

First Edition: January 2017
10 9 8 7 6 5 4 3 2 1

Forever is an imprint of Grand Central Publishing.
The Forever name and logo are trademarks of Hachette Book Group, Inc.

Library of Congress Cataloging-in-Publication Data is available upon request.

ISBN 978-1-4555-3367-1 (trade paperback edition)
ISBN 978-1-4555-3366-4 (ebook edition)

HARD RHYTHM

CHAPTER ONE

MADISON

"Are you sure about this?" I asked Gwen as I swung the short whip back and forth, getting the feel of it. The whole thing was about as long as my arm, the braided black leather making it look like a cobra with one long loose leather piece at the tip. The catalog had called it a "quirt" but it was a whip for sure, a mini–Indiana Jones number, made for driving people, not cattle.

"Oh, Maddie, it couldn't be worse than the leather belt Mal likes to use," Gwen said, her eyes lighting up like a cat's as I flicked the whip in the air.

I chuckled. "I think it's *you* who likes the belt."

She blushed with a glowy smile. "Yeah. My favorite." She and Mal had been engaged for a couple of months and they were the cutest sadomasochists I knew. She loved pain, he loved her, and they doted on each other. I handed her the quirt and she ran her fingers down the length. "I ordered one for each room. You think they'll be too harsh for people?"

"I guess it's just that it's an actual whip." Visions of cowboy justice being meted out by sadistic sheriffs ran through my mind. I'd been playing at BDSM a long time. Not only had I worked here at the Governor's Club for a few years now, ever since I'd moved to LA ten years before I'd always been involved somehow with kink or with sex-related jobs. Even my volunteer work had been on the margins: staffing a domestic violence crisis hotline. It wasn't like I hadn't seen a whip before, but the big ones were typically only attempted by people who trained to use them for years. This one was small enough to be dangerous in some amateur's hands. I trusted myself to use it responsibly but I wasn't sure I trusted the members of the club not to hurt themselves, especially with all the new ones we had been bringing in lately. "Maybe we should test them out before we just put them in all the playrooms."

Or maybe I was worrying too much. "Ooh, I really want to find out what it feels like," Gwen said dreamily, followed by a sigh, oblivious to my concern. "But Mal won't be back for another week. What else is in the box? I ordered some stuff for the dungeon and some to kick-start your new column."

I looked up from digging in the box. "You did? You didn't have to do that, Gwen." I was due to start a weekly sex toy review column for the PlayPeople Network next week, partly writing and partly video blogging. It was a high-profile, well-paying gig, and I was a little nervous about it. Working in a sex toy store was one thing. Putting up videos of myself for the whole world to see was another. Well, it's not like I was going to run for office, right? "Sex toy manufacturers will send me plenty of stuff once the word gets around."

She grinned. "I'm worried you'll just get ten knockoffs of

the rabbit pearl vibe and nothing interesting. I want to get you started off right, you know? I know how important the opportunity is to you."

"Aw, thank you." I gave her a quick hug. Gwen and I had gotten really close since her grandfather had died. I'd been giving her BDSM and boyfriend advice and she'd been wanting to help me with my stalled journalism career. I still wasn't sure if reviewing sex toys for one of the biggest "adult lifestyle" media companies was a great career move. I had a strong feeling my résumé being heavy with sexual topics was already the reason editors didn't take me seriously; becoming a well-known video blogger was probably going to be the final nail in that coffin. Every time I did something sex-related, I seemed to succeed, while all my attempts to do "serious" journalism had been stymied. With my thirtieth birthday on the horizon maybe it was time to give up on doing something my parents could actually tell their neighbors about and just go with what had always worked.

Being what my own mom called "a busty bombshell" had gotten me plenty of attention over the years, and while that attention might have been necessary—even welcome—when I was trying to get dancing gigs, it had mostly negative consequences in the journalism world. If you wanted to get into political reporting your best bet was to be a tall man with a square jaw.

I dug into the box to find a new set of leather paddles. They were black with silver studs set in them: very punk rock meets the Inquisition. Under those were a few sets of shearling sheep–lined leather wrist and ankle cuffs and some other useful bondage items. Then I pulled out something white with that molded high-tech look. "This must be a vibrator?"

"Oh, yes. You can remote control it with a phone app. I don't know how that one is to play with solo but I've worn it while Mal's had the control." She grinned and bounced off to check the sheet and towel supply for the evening.

I set about distributing all the new toys into the playrooms of the dungeon before the party guests could arrive. Gwen and her sister Ricki were the official hosts since the dungeon was in their family mansion—the family secret—while I was a mere employee, one of three paid hosts who kept an eye on the guests and, when necessary, kept things interesting. I made the rounds, checking on the safe sex supplies and plugging in one of the other new pieces of equipment Gwen had recently acquired, the Rotorvator.

Everything seemed ready, so it was time to get dressed myself. As I entered the employee dressing room I was startled by someone rushing out: Paul, Ricki's assistant. Inside the room I found one of my fellow hired hosts sitting on the shoe-changing bench, looking a bit sheepish. "Brad," I scolded. "Aren't you straight?"

"Not completely," he said with a shrug, and followed his—paramour? conquest?—out of the room. I hoped for low drama with whatever was going on there and opened my own locker. As I pulled my bag out to stash the toys Gwen had bought for me, my phone buzzed with a new voice mail message. I picked it up to see who it was from and cursed silently: a guy I had tried to land a writing gig with a year or two ago. Back then he'd been an editor at a big newspaper. Word was he'd been recently fired. What was he doing calling on a Friday night? No doubt trying to hit on me again. *Loser.* I made sure the ringer was off and stuffed my bag back into my locker. I got quickly into my usual work attire: an overbust leather corset, matching knee high boots, leather "tennis" skirt, and badass attitude.

The attitude was second nature to me now. It was all about maintaining professionalism; before this I'd worked in plenty of sexually charged situations, including as a showgirl, model, and cashier in a sex toy emporium. Here at the Governor's Club I did demonstrations of techniques and equipment with Gwen and Chita—getting naked from time to time—but I wasn't technically there to have sex with party guests. Well, unless I really wanted to—and I typically did not want to. Everything went more smoothly if they remembered that. They were here to have fun; I was here to do a job. It wasn't as if working in the dungeon actually got me aroused.

Guests began to trickle in and I went to play hostess at the front door for a bit. I greeted Conrad Schmitt, one of the oldest members of the club, and inquired after his wife, who wasn't with him. She'd caught a cold and had stayed home, he said. Lately it seemed fewer of the older members were attending, as more people who had been recruited by Gwen and Ricki joined. Next to arrive was Sakura, a close friend of Ricki's who was also a part-time fetish fashion model and performance artist. "Maddie, so good to see you. Help me tighten my corset, would you?"

"I was about to ask you to do the same for me," I said with a laugh.

After we'd helped each other tighten our laces in the guest changing room, Gwen caught up to us. "Sakura! Come see the Rotorvator! No one's tried it yet."

"I'm sure if you keep showing it off, someone won't be able to resist," I told her as she led Sakura to see the contraption. I went behind the bar to pour drinks while people were still in social mode. Done in polished wood and red velvet, the bar ran along one wall, while a sectional sofa and some low, leather-covered seats lined the main socializing area, and the Catherine wheel dominated the far corner.

I was startled to see Chino Garcia come in. I'd assumed if Mal was away that all the members of The Rough were out of town, but apparently not. Chino strutted into the dungeon like the cock of the walk. Or as my dad used to call it, *the walk of the cock.* "A bad boy like that just wants to stick it somewhere warm," he had warned me.

When I was younger I hadn't heeded that warning. Bad boys were my catnip, the thing that made me roll on my back and yowl. But after years in Hollywood, years of cheaters and losers whose only redeeming quality was how good they were in bed, I was jaded to the tattoos and the macho saunter. Maybe if I'd spent less time being derailed by attempts at relationships with those guys, I'd be something more than a dungeon hostess and sex toy expert now.

I watched Chino cross the room to greet Sakura and Ricki, and I saw Sakura look him up and down. Was she trying to figure out if that strutting attitude translated to dom or sub? I know I was. Since Axel's bandmates had joined the club, I hadn't seen Chino play. Oh sure, he joined in happily enough when it was Ricki's birthday and Axel made her crawl through "the paddy-whack machine" like a kindergartner, or that time when one of the older executives' wives had wanted all the men to do a circle jerk onto her. But being sexually adventurous didn't reveal whether he was a sadist or a masochist, a top or a bottom, a dom or a sub. Usually anyone who came into the club identified themselves right away so they could find a partner. Chino hadn't, and that bugged the hell out of me. I was used to doms being bossy and subs being needy and Chino was neither. My bet was he was just a poseur who liked hanging around with his kinky friends.

He slipped off his leather jacket as he greeted Axel and Ricki. He was wearing nothing but leather pants and tattoos underneath. I felt as if a cool breeze had just blown across my own bare shoulders, goose bumps rising and my fingers itching to touch his ink all of a sudden.

Stop it, I told myself. *He annoys the fuck out of you and you're better off steering clear of him.* I didn't appreciate how he turned everything into a joke. But when he threw back his head and laughed at something Sakura said, I found myself adjusting my corset as my nipples hardened against the supple leather. I stared at the long line of his neck, leading down a buff, well-inked chest. Playing drums kept him in ridiculously perfect shape.

My hormones must have been peaking or something. I made myself tear my eyes away from him and went to do a rounds check of the rooms, to see which were in use and whether any of them needed a resupply of condoms or lube. It was still early in the evening, though, and while Kresley Palmer had strapped his wife over the new padded spanking bench in the Inquisition Room, everyone else was still socializing and warming up.

When I came back Gwen was showing the new paddles to the group. "Can't wait to find out what these feel like," she enthused, "but I have to wait until Mal gets back."

Chino picked one up and swung it in slow motion like a tennis forehand. Then the annoying fuck made eyes at me. "Hey, Madison, aren't you the one who usually shows off new things around here?"

"You bet I am," I snapped, holding out my hand for the paddle in challenge. *Let's see how fast this joker backs down.* "I'd love to see how many you can take before you beg for mercy."

He twirled it by the leather loop on the handle instead of handing it over. "Is that right? Who do you think could take more, you or me?"

Sakura's eyes lit up and she came between us. "If you wanted a fair test, I could paddle you both."

Chino's eyes were locked on mine, though. Not backing

down at all. "Naw. I think the only way it'd be fair is if we take turns beating each other. You think you can take ten at a time? Twenty?"

"Twenty per set, no bondage, hands on the wall, drop hands and you lose," I said, staring right back at him. Oh, I was so on fire to put him in his place, to make him lose that smirk.

"Agreed," he said. "Should we flip a coin to see who goes first?"

I clucked my tongue. "*Tsk*, no. You can beat me first to make sure this contest isn't over too quickly."

He raised an eyebrow as if to say *touché*, and Sakura chuckled, looking back and forth between us. "Oh ho. And what does the winner get from the loser, hm?"

"How 'bout fifteen minutes in private to do whatever we want," Chino said.

"Does the Rotorvator work on men, too?" I asked.

"Definitely," Gwen said.

"Then I know what my fifteen minutes of entertainment will be," I said with a wicked grin. "Lube up, drummer boy. Sakura, will you be the judge?"

"Surely," she said with a wicked grin of her own.

Chino sketched a bow in my direction and then gestured toward the empty area of wall across from the Catherine wheel. "If you'll assume the position, please."

I took my skirt off, revealing my thong underneath, and placed my hands on the wall. There was no way I was going to lose this contest. Gwen had nicknamed me "Iron Butt" after the first time she'd tested new hardwood paddles on me. I was sure Chino was either going to be all bravado and turn the scene into a joke, like he did every conversation we'd ever had, or he was going to turn out to be a secret sub who was going to *love* being paddled... which might be more fun than winning. How long would it be before he was actually begging me to spank him?

Either way I couldn't wait to beat the smirk off his face. Those thoughts entertained me while I waited for him to start. I imagined his ink-black hair plastered to his neck with passionate sweat while he looked up at me from his knees...

What was taking him so long anyway? I glanced back: he was gathering a crowd of spectators.

And he'd stripped down to nothing. My jaw dropped. The real thing was even better than my imagination. His entire body was lean, hard muscle, not the chunky bulk of a weight-lifting nut but the powerful form of a man who actually used his muscles for something. He'd even stripped off his leather pants, revealing the dragon tattoo on his leg, but I found my eyes drawn to the graceful curve of his cock—already hard. Just from anticipation of paddling me? If so, there went my theory that he was a closet subbie.

* * *

CHINO

I could feel the stiffened leather of the paddle in my hand and smell the leather of her corset, but the taste in my mouth was the rush of anticipation. *Finally.* I'd been trying to find a moment, an opening, an opportunity to play with Madison ever since I'd met her on the orientation tour of the dungeon. She put up a strong front—sexy independent woman—so I knew it had to be the right moment. And now, after months and months of waiting, she was finally right where I wanted her, submitting to me.

Well, not exactly *submitting,* since at this moment—despite readying herself for an ass-beating—she wasn't acting submissive in the slightest. "You ready?" I asked.

She sneered. "Waiting for you."

Perfect. This was going to be fun. "So that's how it's gonna be." I tucked the paddle under my arm so I could run my hands over her bare buttocks. Ample and round, ripe for a beating, and all mine to feel as I wished at this moment. She kept her hands against the wall and let me have my way. Apparently she didn't mind being touched or I was sure I would've heard another comment from that smart mouth. She didn't flinch and I wondered if I could get away with kissing her.

Later.

"I'll count," I said, and stepped back to take aim. Twenty strokes, eh? She had plenty of real estate down there: ten on each side was barely going to cover each cheek from all angles. But my intention wasn't to just beat her all to hell. I wanted to make it last. I wanted to make a connection. I'd been biding my time for so long, I wasn't going to rush through it like some newbie.

I didn't hit particularly hard, just hard enough to wake up her skin, to pink it up. The sound of the leather smacking her bottom was more arousing than the dirtiest dirty talk I'd ever heard, and the sight of her back arching as I laid on the blows made my cock strain upward in response. Oh, yeah. That was what I wanted. Seeing Madison take what I could dish out made every dom instinct in me sit up and roar.

Frankly, being a dom is a lot of work. In my time in the scene I'd tried everything and everyone—after all, it was practically a rule of being a rock star that the "purity test" was your to-do list. Unless you're some kind of control freak, there are easier ways to get off than domination. It takes the right partner to be worth it, which was why I didn't just play with anyone available. But right then, reddening her ass and hearing the paddle go *smack*, I had no questions about whether Madison was worth it. I wanted to rope her hands and drag her into a private room. I wanted her. Not "for sex," not for "a girlfriend,"—it wasn't on that level of thought. It wasn't a thought at all, in fact. It was pure desire.

And she wasn't even acting "submissive." That only made me want her more. A lot of the control freak male doms of the world can't handle that kind of woman.

But I can.

* * *

MADISON

Chino seemed determined to spread the redness all over my butt. He'd barely gotten one good swat in on each part of my bottom before it was time to switch places.

He handed me the paddle with a little bow and put his hands on the wall. I imitated him, rubbing my hand over the peach fuzz of his buttocks before I took to swinging the paddle. Unlike me, he had hard, tight buns, easy to hit both at once. I swung upward slightly, catching the tender underside with each swat. He gritted his teeth and by the time I neared twenty he was grunting on each blow.

His turn again. "Remember, Madison," he said as he ran his hand over the striking zone, "all you have to do to make the pain stop is put your hands down."

I could feel the warm spot on the wall where his hands had been. "Not likely."

"As you wish." He stepped back.

This time he hit much harder and it was me who grunted. Apparently he'd gone easy on me for the first round, but since I hadn't gone easy on him, now the gloves were off. He was putting a full swing on each blow and leaving the paddle against my skin so the studs would dig in. Still, I'd suffered worse. This wasn't that bad...

Until he got to eleven and I felt my palms prickle with sweat. What was going on? All of a sudden there wasn't enough oxygen in the room, but as I sucked in breath after breath the feeling only got worse instead of better.

I felt his hand on my shoulder, solid and warm. The blows had stopped and his voice was calm in my ear. "You all right?"

"Of course I'm all right." I blinked. Wasn't I? I let out a breath. It was just a little adrenaline rush, I told myself. *No big deal.*

He sounded amused. "Because it's your turn."

"Oh." I stood straight, my heart still pounding but my head high. "I lost count."

That smirk again. "Good thing I'm honest, then." He held out the paddle and I took it, remembering my goal. To wipe that smirk off his cheeky poseur face. His flushed, exhilarated face. That wasn't the only part of him that was flushed, either. The eager curve of his cock beckoned, a glistening bead of precome at the tip catching my attention. I gave his shaft a couple of quick tugs to surprise him—sometimes a little attention right there would drop a guy into subspace once he realized someone else would do him—but not Chino. He growled low in his throat.

I started paddling him as hard as I could, taking the full backswing and really laying into him. But did he scream? No! The bastard started barking like a dog on each swat!

When I got to twenty I almost threw down the paddle in aggravation, but I took a breath, thinking if I lost my cool I lost the contest. Keep calm and carry on; isn't that what they say? I gave him a glare as I handed over the paddle and put my hands against the wall again.

The pain of the paddle radiated from my buttocks down my legs and up my spine. But it wasn't serious enough to be the cause of the tightness in my throat or the stone in my gut. I forced air in and out of my lungs, my eyes clamped shut, trying to figure it out. Maybe I should have eaten more than a granola bar for lunch. Maybe I hadn't remembered to drink water for a while. I clamped down on everything, knowing all I had to do was outlast him. I focused on that goal.

I felt his hand at the small of my back. His voice was low and firm in my ear. "Your turn."

"Thank you." I snapped my eyes open and grabbed the paddle again.

This time I laid into him without a pause between blows, *bam-bam-bam,* and this time there was no dog barking or cheeky waggling of his ass. This time he threw his head back, his teeth gritted, a long grunt or growl erupting just as I got to twenty.

"Whew," he said as he let his arms down slowly. "Remind me never to make you mad."

My jaw dropped. Couldn't he tell I was mad already? I put my hands against the wall, my thoughts whirling, but it was difficult to think through all the freaking out my body was doing.

The first blow came quickly and I suddenly focused: What exactly was I doing? I shook my head. I knew better than to hit someone in anger. That went against everything I knew and everything I'd been taught about BDSM, against everything I counseled victims of abuse about on the hotline. My knees began to shake as the realization sank in along with the next few blows. I was really out of control. And why? Because Chino was annoying? That was not a good reason to hit someone, even if he did volunteer for it.

A sob caught in my throat as I realized he was slowing

down, smoothing his palm down my buttocks between each hit, and then giving me a sharp, corrective swat with the paddle before soothing the sting again. The unexpected feeling welled up that I deserved it, I deserved to be corrected, punished, in front of everyone. How could I have let my emotions get the better of me like that? I was supposed to set an example. I was supposed to enforce the rules, not break them.

"Fifteen," he said, keeping the count aloud. "Sixteen."

I swallowed hard, trying to keep all my emotions bottled up. I would not cry. Not in front of everyone. "Chino," I forced through my tight throat.

He swatted me sharply again. "Seventeen. Remember, Maddie. If you've had enough all you have to do is drop your arms."

I pressed my palms flat against the wall. Could I do it? Could I bring myself to give in?

"Eighteen." After this one he didn't soothe the skin and a new sob tried to erupt. Why? Because having that small dab of forgiveness taken away was abruptly soul-crushing.

What the hell was going on in my mind, my heart?

"Nineteen," he said from right beside me as he swung the paddle . . . but this time he only placed it lightly against my skin, as if he knew I'd had enough, as if he knew it was only going to take a feather to knock me over. As if even one more gentle tap would be too much.

I dropped my arms and fell into his.

CHAPTER TWO

MADISON

In the BDSM how-to books and SM 101 seminars they always talk about how people can get blindsided during scenes by unexpected emotions or sudden memories. It had never happened to me before but as Chino led me to a private side room—to collect his "prize" of fifteen minutes to do as he wished—I realized that must be what was going on. Every emotion I could imagine was zinging around inside me like ping-pong balls: anger, shame, fear, sadness, confusion.

And lust. Most confusing of all, I was dripping wet and didn't know what to do about it.

Well, maybe Chino was going to have his way with me, if his comments to the spectators as he half carried me away were any indication. Axel and Ricki and Sakura had all congratulated him as we'd left the scene. The door closed behind us as he took me into a private room. He swept me literally off my feet then—and I am not a petite girl—picking me up and then laying me down on a bed. I expected him to start unlacing my corset, but I heard him rustling around beside me. Was he getting lube or something?

No, a bottle of water. He cracked it open and encouraged me to sip from it. I concentrated on swallowing, on not spilling it, on handing the bottle back without dropping it. We were in the "princess" room, the one with the four-poster canopied bed. The posts each had pairs of leather cuffs attached, hidden by the canopy. I wondered if Chino knew they were there. I decided not to tell him.

Instead I said, "Thank you. Um, I mean, I'm sorry." I couldn't even figure out what I meant; that's how jumbled my thoughts were.

He climbed onto the bed beside me and I noticed he'd wrapped a towel around his waist. That was odd, I thought. He held his arms open and it felt right to settle against him. The warmth of his body and the sound of his heartbeat were soothing. Grounding. I felt my pulse slowing from the frantic flutter it had been.

Then he spoke. "What are you sorry for?"

"Nothing. I don't know." I was sorry for freaking out, but since that had led to him winning I supposed there was no reason to apologize for that. Wait, that wasn't what I meant at all. "I mean, I'm sorry I went at you so hard. I'm not usually like that. I got a little out of control."

He stroked my hair and it felt like forgiveness. I felt the lump in my throat again and had to ask, "Do you forgive me?"

"No harm done, sweets," he said and kissed my hair. "No harm done."

Relief so intense it bordered on euphoria flooded me, my guilt blown away by that gentle kiss. "Can I do anything to make it up to you? I'm yours for the next fifteen minutes."

He let out a long sigh. "Are you sure you're up for *anything*?"

I steeled myself. Having already let down my own standards for conduct once tonight, I wasn't about to disappoint myself again. "Anything. That was the deal."

"Okay, because this might sound kind of weird."

"I've seen and done a lot of weird shit in my time, Chino." A lot weirder than being paddled almost to tears by some rock star.

"Yeah? How weird?"

"Like the time I tried 'exotic dancing.' There was one guy who paid for a lap dance but only if I'd wear a *lucha libre* wrestling mask."

"Really?"

"Really. Actually he was one of the nicer guys. He wasn't the reason I quit after a month."

"No kidding. Well, my request is a different kind of weird."

I was starting to feel more like myself again and I raised my head so I could look him in the eye. "Okay. What is it?"

His eyes were a deep brown ringed with black and I felt like I was looking into his dark depths—dizzying, disorienting. Like my world was shifting. Especially when I heard his voice catch as he said, "I want to talk. I... need to talk to somebody."

I found myself reaching up to touch his cheek, brushing the side of his lips with my fingertips. Was it the serious, pained look on his face that made him look like a different person, or was it that I was seeing him with new eyes? "Are you all right?"

"I'm fine." He met my searching stare with his own. "But I had a bit of a flashback, I guess you'd call it? A realization, anyway. You seem like you know what's what with BDSM. And there are some things I can't talk about with the guys in the band."

I sat up a little more, surprised, intrigued, and wondering

what on earth he was about to tell me. "You can talk about it with me."

He hitched himself up all the way and rearranged the pillows so we could lean against them, but he could still hold me close. He didn't start speaking right away. He stroked my hair, pushing stray locks of it behind one of my ears with his fingertips. The deliberate gentleness was such a contrast to the savage energy I'd beat him with and reminded me again of the way he'd brought me to my moment of surrender.

"I realized something while we were playing. Maybe something I'd suppressed or maybe you just don't think about things as a kid," he said.

I stroked his hair with my own fingertips now, emulating him, encouraging the words to flow.

"My parents split when I was ten," he said. "And you know, I considered myself the man of the house after that. Ten going on thirty, you know what I mean? We had a couple of tough years then, until this rich dude swept my mother off her feet."

His eyes were distant as he said this, focused on the far wall—the far past. I tried to imagine him at eleven years old, thinking he had to be the man of the house. A far cry from the irresponsible gadfly I'd pegged him as.

"They got married, and we moved out of LA and into his place, a huge house in a good neighborhood outside Toledo, six bedrooms, three-car garage. But that's not what I should be telling you. The thing is after they split, I never saw my father again."

I counted his breaths while he thought about it. His eyes looked troubled. "What did you realize?" I asked.

"I was not a good kid. I was a hellion. One time, I must've only been five or six, Flor was a baby and Vicente wasn't even born yet. Mom was at work, and I did something bad like knocking over my father's beer when I ran through the TV room. Dad wasn't a particularly big guy but times like that it was like he got huge. His hair was thinning but he wore it in a long ponytail and when he got mad it looked to me like his whole face and scalp got red, and with the patches thinning it was like his face was devil-shaped. Scary as shit when you're a kid, you know? Anyway, this time, instead of just reaching out and swatting me like he did when I was a toddler, he roared 'how many times have I told you no running in the house?' and ordered me to stand in the kitchen holding on to the back of a chair."

I held my breath while Chino felt his way through the memory. One of his hands trembled slightly.

"I'd completely forgotten about this. What came to me during the paddling was this: He told me to stay still, that I was a big boy now and if I wasn't going to act like one I had to learn to take my punishment like one. And then he went to the bedroom, came back with a paddle, and paddled the shit out of me."

"Oh, no," I said, feeling the guilt about how hard I'd hit him again. "I made you have a flashback to being abused as a child. I'm so sorry. You know I used to volunteer at a domestic violence hotline, right? You can tell me about it—"

"No, no, that's not even it, Madison." He laughed, gently but genuinely. "It wasn't like that. It didn't become a regular thing. It was really nothing to a snot-nosed tough-guy like six-year-old me."

I didn't really believe that, but he went on.

"No, the thing I realized is this. *He went to the bedroom to get a paddle.* As a kid it never occurred to me that it was hidden in there for any reason but to be brought out when I was bad." He raised an eyebrow. "But think about it. Why did they have it? It's obvious."

Aha. "Your parents were kinky."

"Apparently. What a thing to realize, eh?" He looked thoughtful. "Kinda challenges the idea that my sexuality is some kind of rebellion or breaking the mold or something."

"Do you think of it as rebellion?"

"Given how religious my mom got—yeah, I guess I do. It never occurred to me she wasn't *always* like that." He moved his jaw as if trying to swallow the idea. "Until now, that is."

"No one really wants to think about the sex their parents have."

"True. And things changed so drastically when we moved in with my stepfather. The total opposite of my dad. This guy was a straitlaced, church-going, tie-wearing type who wanted dinner on the table every night at six and the kids in bed by nine. It meant my mother didn't have to work anymore, though, and we went to a fancy suburban school."

"Was that . . . good? You don't sound very happy about it."

"I hated it. I hated the suburbs, I hated the Midwest, I hated my stepfather. He and I fought constantly while my mother begged me over and over to be good. But I wasn't good at being good. I got into trouble at school, with the local authorities, with the police. Finally my stepfather had enough. He threatened to throw me out when I was sixteen because I was getting into so many fights. I saved him the trouble and left on my own." Chino moved my hand to his chest and I could feel his heart pumping. "And here I am, beating you black and blue." He turned to look into my eyes. "Making you have a flashback of your own."

His gaze pinned me where I was, my tongue frozen in my mouth, my heart starting to flutter like a trapped bird. Now that the scene was over I wanted to retreat to my safe illusions and not face the truth about what I was feeling. Chagrin and embarrassment flushed my cheeks.

"You want to tell me about it?" he asked.

I closed my eyes, but I could still feel the heat of his gaze. "I didn't have a flashback." I felt his hand massaging the back of my neck, then his fingers working their way into my hair.

When he tightened his grip slowly I felt a sudden rush of my arousal, like he'd turned on a tap. *Oh, shit.* I tried to tell myself that being dominated couldn't possibly be what I needed, but I was more turned on than I'd been in years. "I've still got seven minutes left," he said, his face very close to mine. "Are you sure? Tell me what was going on with you, Madison."

"There's nothing to tell, really," I insisted, but the lie was making my insides twist. Since when was I so interested in obeying a dom? Since never, that's when. But okay, here was the truth . . . or at least *a* truth: "I don't know what happened. I just went out of my head for a bit. No big revelations. No memories. Endorphins. That's all."

"How do you feel now? Be honest."

I felt my cheeks flush as if he had caught me lying and maybe he had. Was he trying to get me to admit that I had dropped into subspace and that I was sliding inexorably toward it again now? Or was it just dirty talk? Somehow it was like he held not just my body but my will, and I couldn't outright lie to him. "I'm hot," I said. "Very hot."

"Oh, really."

If he made a joke I swore I'd get revenge later.

He didn't make a joke. "This is probably the wrong time to fuck you until you lose your mind, though." He growled a little as he said it, then forced himself to speak as calmly and rationally as a possible. "I think that scene turned out more intense than either of us intended."

True. But calm and rational was not what I was yearning for. I couldn't believe the words that came out of my mouth.

"Maybe that makes it the perfect time to fuck until we lose our minds," I said. "I mean, we lost our minds already."

"Hush." He dipped his mouth to my neck, kissing and sucking gently and sending waves of pleasure through me. *Nngh,* when was the last time a man made me feel like that? Like every kind of pleasure could be had in his hands if I would only let him have his way, if only I'd surrender. Surrender never ended up being as good in real life as it sounded in books, but inside I was burning to test that theory again. *Maybe Chino's different, maybe it'll work this time.* Or maybe I just was too horny to think clearly.

I clutched at him as he let me go and started to withdraw, though. It felt like he wasn't just withdrawing physically, but emotionally, and I'm not sure which ached more. "Chino."

"Maddie."

"You can't . . . just leave me like this."

"I've got four minutes left in charge," he said, pulling away and sitting on the side of the bed. "If we're going to fuck I'd like to be thinking about something other than asshole father figures the whole time."

"Maybe if we fuck," I said, surprising myself with not only how much I wanted him but how hard I was pushing him, "you'll forget all about them. For a little while."

He looked back at me. "I didn't think you liked me that much."

I don't, I wanted to say. *But I want you anyway. Hormones. Horoscope. Something out of my control is going on here.* I felt guilty now not just for hitting him too hard but for judging him so harshly before. I tried to put it back on him, though. I pinched the corner of the towel and edged it slowly aside, revealing a raging red erection. "Your cock doesn't seem to care what I think."

He let the towel drop and crawled on top of me, dragging

the hot hardness of his length up my thigh. He slipped a hand between my legs and discovered how utterly lush I was. "Neither does your pussy," he said.

I thrust my hips upward. "Fuck, it's... it's stupid how"—*much I want you*—"horny I am right now. I'm... not usually like this." I was racking my brain trying to figure out what I could say that would make him give in.

"Uh huh," he said. "That's why we're not going to do the fuck-and-Velcro thing."

I was about to cry foul—I wanted him so much—but then he buried his head between my legs, one hand pulling my thong aside and keeping me spread while his tongue went to work. I writhed against him, so aroused already that I didn't think it would take long to come. Which was fortunate. When he paused for a breath he said, "Two minutes," and I wasn't sure if it was a threat or a promise.

His mouth was beyond talented, a true connoisseur of woman-flesh, and as he slipped two fingers into me I peaked, the orgasm rocketing up my spine and sending my already spinning head into outer space. He didn't let up, either, stroking me from the inside and continuing firm sweeps of his tongue until I'd ridden out the full glory of my climax.

He raised his head and looked at me from between my legs, his eyes feral, licking his lips. Then he threw his own head back and let out a kind of roar, like a tiger or a lion, and I realized he'd been jerking himself off with his other hand. He came onto the sheet covering the bed and then hung his head, panting hard.

I was stunned but my entire body was feeling so languid and delicious that it was like no negative emotion could get through the cocoon of pleasure I was wrapped in. Fifteen minutes ago I'd been feeling every bad thing possible and now I couldn't imagine feeling disappointment, or shame, or fear or anger or sadness. "Chino."

He lifted his head at the sound of his name and my cocoon was pierced by the look of pain on his face. He hid it quickly with a smile, but I had seen it.

"Hey," he said. "Thanks."

"Um, thanks," I said back, which felt ridiculous. "You seem like you could use some cuddling."

He raised an eyebrow. "Do I? You sure it isn't you who needs some cuddling?"

"Shut up and cuddle me," I mock-ordered and he laughed and moved up to hold me again.

"Let me ask you one more thing," he said as he put his arms around me.

"Sure. Anything."

He paused, maybe for dramatic effect, maybe just to make me wait, then said, "House hunting. I need help house hunting."

"Seriously?"

"Seriously. Real estate agents ignore single guys and pay way more attention to couples. There's a bunch of open houses in Laurel Canyon. We don't have to hold hands or anything, just come around with me."

I laughed. Maybe it was that I was still softened up from the scene and all, but I agreed right away. Besides, it might be fun to see what kind of house a rock star could afford.

* * *

CHINO

Well, that wasn't how I thought tonight was going to go. We emerged from the playroom to applause from our friends, which made Madison blush and me pump my arm in triumph. Seemed they approved of our apparent hookup and I kind of wondered if they'd been waiting for it to happen. I thought I had kept my interest in her pretty close to the vest but Axel knows me well and nothing gets past Sakura's notice.

In my line of work—especially at this level of success—I meet a lot of top-shelf gorgeous women and some of them are quite smart: what struck me about Madison was that unlike most of these gals she didn't try to hide how smart she was. I liked that even more than the way her corset framed her luscious hips. I hadn't missed a party since we'd met—except for the month when The Rough tour took us to Europe—but somehow the opportunity to invite her to play had never come up. In fact sometimes I had the feeling she was avoiding me, but the question was whether she was avoiding me because *I* was interested in *her* or because *she* was interested in *me.*

I would say, given what had gone down tonight, I now had that answer. She was more than interested, but if all the mood swings she went through during our scene were any indication, the woman had issues. Serious issues. *Well,* I told myself, *I guess I'll find out if those issues are deal breakers or if we have something going here.* Something was going on in that gorgeous red head of hers. Madison was obviously a lot more complicated than I'd first thought.

I was always a kinky fucker. The whole idea of slave girls and bondage and whipping has always turned me on, even when I was a kid and had snuck a look at my dad's magazine collection. Some guys had *Penthouse* or whatever, right? My dad had these wild European and Japanese and American underground and indie comic books hidden in a locked drawer in his office, full of drawings of corsets and boots and rope bondage and weird shit. European artists with names like Moebius and Milo Manara and Americans like Michael Manning and Frank Gary. After I left home and moved to the city I found one of those Frank Gary comics at a flea market and had matching "Bondage Beauties" tattooed onto my upper arms. My first tats. I could barely afford food, so spending the money on tattoos might've seemed crazy, but right then it had been more important to me to grab hold of who I wanted to be than to eat.

I met Axel and Mal shortly after that. If you want to be superstitious about it, I think those two tattoos were like a magic spell, summoning the two people I needed most at that time of my life.

The ink was still fresh on my latest tat, a pair of guardian eyes on the backs of my shoulders. Maddie commented on them as she scrubbed my back in the shower. She'd taken me not into the huge suitable-for-six-people dungeon shower but to the still-quite-large one in the employee dressing room. "You're peeling."

"Yeah, the ink will shed for a couple more days," I said. The heavy black would leak right out of my skin, forming a layer which would then flake off. "What about you? I don't recall seeing any ink on you."

"Never got around to it," she said. "Couldn't ever decide on something I wanted to keep forever, you know? Do all of yours mean something?"

"Yeah," I said, but I wasn't in the mood to describe them. I decided to stick with the ones she was looking at. "The eyes are the only ones on my back because when I started getting tattoos I wanted them where I could see them myself."

"Why is this one different, then?"

I shrugged and ducked my head under the water. When I emerged I swapped places with her, drinking in the sight of the water rushing over her pale skin and voluptuous curves. Gorgeous. I really hoped this wasn't my one chance with her and that she wasn't going to shut me down the second we got dressed. She was still looking at me expectantly, so I answered the question. "It's supposed to be... this sounds corny."

"So?"

"I put the eyes there so there'll always be someone watching my back."

"Axel and the guys—?"

"Don't get me wrong. The guys in the band are my brothers. I know they'll always have my back and yet, you know, they're pairing up, thinking about starting their own families—" I broke off, not wanting to talk shit about my brothers-in-arms. "Well, it's like you said. A tattoo is forever. I guess it's my reminder that I need to always look out for myself, ultimately."

The truth was that although the guys loved me and we'd been through a lot together, there was a lot they didn't know. And if I had my way, they wouldn't find out. Mal was rich as hell, came from old money. Ford, too—his dad had made millions in the music business. Axel hadn't always had it easy, but he'd never gone hungry, or been yelled at for throwing away a yogurt container because his mother needed a cup and couldn't afford one.

Those were my first drums. Overturned buckets and coffee cans, shoe boxes, plastic Easter eggs filled with rice. Anything I could make into a percussion instrument, I would. When other boys were playing with toy cars, toy soldiers, or toy dinosaurs, I was playing with my homemade drums, banging along with my dad's stereo, singing and dancing in the living room. My father had been an artist, a cartoonist, and my mother cleaned houses, but I had been too young to understand why art didn't pay better and why my mother couldn't get a better job. When my sister was born, my mother had to stop working for a while and Dad couldn't make up the difference. He went hungrier than me—at least I got lunch at school. My brother followed a year later, when I was in second grade, and things went downhill from there. The split had come not long after that.

Axel had bought his mother a house with his share of the money we'd made from the first album. That had got me thinking about doing the same thing myself. I hadn't talked to my mother much since I'd left home over ten years ago, though not for lack of trying on my part. The few conversations we'd had were mostly her telling me it wasn't too late, that Jesus would always forgive no matter how bad the sin. I still called her, though, on holidays and birthdays, even if all I'd get was a lecture. I guess I hoped someday she'd come to her senses and talk to me like a human being again. *Grow up, kid,* I told myself, and the voice in my head sounded a lot like my father. *If your mother doesn't love you, buying her a house won't change that.*

"Chino?" Maddie was brushing my wet hair off my forehead with her fingers. "You done?"

"Let me just rinse one more time," I told her, shaking water from my head and trying to clear it. That memory was clinging to me like a bad dream. Maddie stepped out of the shower while I made sure all the soap was off me. I might be a sinner but at least I was squeaky clean on the outside.

I shut the water off and slid the glass door open and there she was, holding a thick, luxurious towel at the ready for me, her head slightly bowed. Like some kind of serving girl. I'd never seen her give anyone this kind of deference before.

Madison, what's going on in your head? I hadn't gotten the impression that she was one of those women waiting around for a big bad dom to put her in her place. Something had changed during our scene.

I let her wrap the towel around me. Maybe she was just being courteous. After all, she knew where everything was in the employee area and I didn't. "Thanks." I swabbed myself down and then tried to get a look at my butt in the mirror. "Hm. I can see a little bit of bruising coming up." I poked at it. Didn't feel particularly sore.

She joined me. A pattern of black marks on her own bottom was blossoming into dark purple where the studs had impacted. "Yeah, figures," she said and didn't object when I ran my hand gently over the marks. "I guess if I do any demonstrating in this week's video blog I'll definitely keep my undies on."

"Which blog is that?"

"I'm starting a new feature for PlayPeople, reviewing and demonstrating sex toys." She sighed. "They didn't explicitly say they want me to ream myself on camera but I kind of get the feeling they're hoping I will."

"What makes you think that?" I asked.

"Well, for one thing, they sent me their standard porn performer contract rider and rates." She shrugged. "I'm thinking I'll start slow anyway, though, and then work up to being more graphic later, if it seems warranted."

"Rates?"

"Yeah. They pay more the more you show, plus bonuses if clicks go over certain thresholds."

I pulled her against me, naked and damp. "You think they'll dock you for showing unsightly bruises?"

She snorted. "If you don't like bruises, you shouldn't have put them there."

I dug my fingers into her buttocks, making her grit her teeth with pain as I pressed us together. "Oh, I like the bruises. Maybe too much. I think they should pay you more for those. Call me when you have paddles to review, eh? I'll help you out."

Her eyes went misty, her lips parting, as I loosened my grip and massaged her marks instead. If I didn't know her better, I'd have said it was the quickest drop into subspace I'd ever seen. But surely sassy, borderline-domme Madison didn't roll over that quick, did she?

I tweaked a nipple, thinking that would zing her back to life, but she only gasped and moaned. *Well.* Every instinct in me was screaming that I should push her down on the floor and stick my cock into her to lay my claim. She'd asked with words in the playroom and I'd said no, but her body continued to beg for it with every move she made. I had a feeling if I fucked her there would be no going back. We'd be welded together and separating would wreck us. Good reason to get to know her better, right? Good reason to slow down and take care of us both instead of giving in to how much I wanted to fuck her. I was a little surprised how strong that feeling was, given that my cock hadn't recovered yet from the ball-wringing I'd given myself while eating her. That proved it wasn't just my cock and balls that wanted her, I guess. It was something deeper in me that wanted to claim her.

I let go and patted her cheek instead, a pantomime of a slap. "Come on, Maddie. You've got a party to work."

She shook herself. "Right. Yeah."

"You want to tell me what's going on in that gorgeous head of yours?"

She sparked the fire I was used to seeing, wrinkling her nose at me and cocking her hip. "Nothing. It's nothing. Stop pretending you don't know that women fall at your feet when you snap your fingers."

I laughed. Being a rock star had some definite perks. But

Madison had never struck me as the fall-at-your-feet type. It was probably why I had been so interested in her since we met. My usual charm hadn't seemed to work at all. But maybe she had just hidden her interest until now.

I still wanted to know what had happened to her while we were playing; I didn't believe it was "nothing" for a second. But until she was ready to tell me I wasn't going to force it out of her.

She gave me a rich purple bathrobe—it matched the towels—to wear, and rather than putting the corset she had been wearing back on, she changed into another party-appropriate outfit, a black velvet catsuit with black leather waist cincher. The velvet transformed her already voluptuous curves into something nearly irresistible, the waist cincher accentuating them like gold on a lily. I wanted to fit my hands against the leather and then run my palms over the velvet forever.

I caught her sneaking a look at her phone and murmuring "damn it."

"Something wrong?" I asked.

She shoved the phone into the locker. "No," she said and then repeated the lie of earlier. "It's nothing."

I was sure it wasn't nothing, but right then there was nothing I could do about it.

CHAPTER THREE

CHINO

I called Axel the next day for a reality check. I went out on the back balcony of the place I was renting and looked down at the body shop where they built custom motorcycles. This part of Koreatown was rough around the edges but I liked that. The tattoo shop on the corner had a couple of Frank Gary "Bondage Beauties" in the window and that had been why I'd checked out the street in the first place, then discovered the handful of apartments on the upper floors above the bike shop and the screen printing place. I suspected the buildings weren't zoned for apartments but the landlord was okay with me going month to month so I didn't ask too many questions. Axel's phone rang twice before he picked up, sounding groggy.

"H'lo?"

"Dude, it's almost noon. You still in bed with your heiress?"

"Still in bed. Heiress is on the patio doing yoga or Pilates or something. I have to literally tie her to the bed if I want morning sex." He yawned. "What's up?"

"You've been dating Ricki how long?"

"About a year," he said. "Why?"

"How well do you know that redheaded hostess from their club?"

"Madison? Pretty well, I guess. I mean, not in the biblical sense. We've hung out a bunch. Nice gal. You guys put on quite a show last night."

I guess we made an impression. "Tell me, though. Is she single? Married?" I kept wondering about the text she'd gotten. Was she worried I'd freak if she told me she had a boyfriend? I didn't know what to think.

"Single," Axel said, making me breathe a sigh of relief. "And, I would've put my money on her being more interested in women than men until you made her putty in your hands." He chuckled.

"Yeah, well, maybe I'm special," I bragged. "But you're sure she's single?"

"Hang on a sec." I heard him get out of bed and then yell to Ricki. When he came back he said, "Yep, single. And you know how fanatical the family is about keeping the dungeon a secret. They did background checks on all the employees, her included. If there was a husband, or wife for that matter, we'd know."

"Okay. I just..." I trailed off, trying to figure out what to tell Axel, and what not to tell him. "Just making sure everything's cool. You know, that some spouse isn't going to be pissed at me for the marks I left on her last night."

"You mean it's cool she's available to be pursued, right?"

Damn Axel for twigging to my interest right away. "She's a club employee." I downplayed it as much as I could. "I don't think she's that into me. She helped me have a good time but I don't think she really meant it."

Axel chuckled. "That didn't look like a woman just doing her job. Did she give you her number?"

"Well, yeah." I didn't tell him it was because she'd agreed to come house hunting with me.

"Then why do you sound so stressed about it? Talk to me, bro."

Play it cool. Play it cool. "I'm not stressed. Just trying to get the lay of the land before I go trekking across it, you know? Neither of us was looking for anything but some kinky fun."

I was expecting him to bust my balls over getting serious with a club girl and part of me felt almost superstitious, like talking about her was going to jinx my chances, but to my surprise Axel said, "I know. But you guys are good together."

I hoped he was right but at that moment I felt like pushing back against his pat reassurances. "I'm sure she'll be tired of my shtick soon enough," I said. "Talk to you later, Ax."

"Sure thing. See you at the listening party, if not sooner."

"Right." The next time the whole band would be together in one spot would be at a record company event after Mal got back to town. Until then I had nowhere I had to be, officially.

Which was why this was a good time to try to reach my mother. No distractions. It sometimes took a couple of days for her to respond and I never knew when she might.

But when I picked up the phone I found myself looking up Madison's number instead.

* * *

MADISON

I dreamed that I was in some kind of Vegas revue, like Siegfried and Roy except instead of tigers the guy who was the star of the show had me and a few other girls on leashes, and we danced and pranced as he put us through our paces. When the show was over, instead of going to a dressing room he walked us back to holding pens, where the secret was that we were actually tigers in disguise.

He scratched me behind the ears and I purred.

When I woke up my ginger tabby Morris was kicking me in the head and purring as he tried to take over my pillow. Some tiger. The man in the dream had looked suspiciously like a certain drummer I knew, though. Ink-black hair, dark eyes . . .

I stretched in bed and felt the soreness of my glutes. Instead of being angry I'd let him do that to me, I felt strangely proud of myself. The memory of his hand gliding over my skin, the intense look on his face as he examined the marks, made me feel warm all over. And thinking of how he'd buried his tongue between my folds only cranked up the heat level. I had no regrets about getting down with Chino Garcia. None.

I pulled my vibrator out of the drawer beside my bed and clicked it on. Morris leapt down immediately; he didn't like the humming noise it made or the way I sometimes shouted when I came.

I pressed the nub of the vibrator to my clit and squeezed my legs together, letting the memory of Chino's hands, his voice, his skin against mine, play through my memory. Mm, yes, I still wanted him. No getting around that. A dildo wasn't going to satisfy that craving. Not even close. Not after the gorgeous sight of him naked had been imprinted in my brain, and not after the incredible sensual touch he'd demonstrated. I wanted to feel that again, this time in complete privacy...

I came suddenly, bucking against the vibrator trapped between my legs, and I kept jerking my hips until two more orgasms had wracked me. Then I clicked the vibrator off but something was still buzzing.

My phone. Thinking it must be Chino about house hunting, I grabbed it from the side table, the orgasmic aftershocks still ricocheting through my body. "Hello?"

"Maddie. Been trying to get through to you. It's Price Lawson. Remember me?"

As if I could have forgotten that Lawson was the former editor of the arts and entertainment section of *LA Newsday*, a man I'd tried several times to get a writing gig with. The closest I'd gotten was the time he'd asked me to come to a business lunch. That morning he'd called back and said something had come up and would I mind changing it to dinner?

Ladies, let me tell you something. If a businessman *ever* changes a lunch date to dinner, it's because he wants to hit on you. At least I didn't feel the slightest bit bad about sticking him and/or *Newsday* with a very expensive food and beverage bill, but he definitely had no intention of offering me a job.

I confess I had cheered a little when I'd read the announcement earlier this week that he'd been let go from *Newsday*. I'd assumed his call last night was a booty call and had ignored it.

And here I was talking to him. "Yes, Price, I remember you." I used his first name on purpose, to make a point. If I was being overly familiar, it was his own fault for forcing that familiarity in the first place. "How could I forget?"

"Now, Madison, don't be like that. You're an attractive woman. Surely you can't blame a man for trying."

I was in no mood to be polite. "For trying to get into the pants of a prospective employee while you were in marriage counseling trying to salvage things with your wife? If I can't blame you for that, who should I blame?"

He didn't rise to the bait, his voice staying jocular and light. "Now now, that counseling stuff was just a hoop we had to jump through before we could finalize the divorce. But funny you should bring that up when a sex scandal is just what I want to talk to you about."

"I'm—"

"What you don't know is they didn't fire me from *Newsday.* I left because I'm starting a new, edgy publication, a website with a multimedia smartphone magazine app and a premium newsstand edition, a mix of arts and politics the way the old *Village Voice* and classic *Rolling Stone* used to be. It's called *Pop-litico.*"

I don't care if it's called "Pop Goes the Weasel," I thought, but I was starting to wonder why he was telling me this. It didn't sound much like a new ploy to get into my pants. "Congratulations," I said neutrally.

"It's going to be better than both the gossip rags and the pundit blogs. It'll be groundbreakingly investigative."

And he'd said he wanted to talk about a sex scandal. The hairs prickled on the back of my neck and I sat up. "Price. You'd better be calling me because you want to hire me to be the next Woodward and Bernstein." I hoped I was getting the names of the Watergate guys right.

"Well, funny you should say that. Have you heard of Conrad Schmitt?"

He obviously wasn't asking me just by sheer coincidence about someone from the Governor's Club, but I couldn't very well admit that, could I? "And what if I have?"

"He's a big-time shareholder in CTC, senior partner in a top entertainment law firm, and one of the richest men in SoCal. Also, as it turns out, one of the biggest donors to ultraconservative political causes and candidates."

I can't say I was surprised about that. A lot of rich guys were conservatives at heart, even the kinky ones. I tried to keep my poker face. "You don't say."

"I don't just mean Republicans. I mean the serious nutjobs who want to criminalize birth control, outlaw extramarital sex, and kill gays. Four so-called Purity Values candidates could be vying in the upcoming gubernatorial race here in California."

"Price, why are you telling me this?"

"Because I know you met Schmitt last night at the Hamilton estate."

I sat in stunned silence, stunned because I couldn't believe he'd come right out and said it, silent because I was racking my brain for something to say that wouldn't be incriminating. "Bullshit," I finally said.

"Nice bluff, Maddie, but I have proof. I didn't call you today to accuse you of philandering, though. I know you're not into married men because you told me so yourself in no uncertain terms."

"How nice of you to remember."

"I'm going to ignore the bitter, sarcastic tone in your voice, Maddie, because even though you don't know it, I have a lot of respect for you. That's the real reason I'm calling. You proved when you turned me down that you are a woman of integrity and principles. I fully admit it was my mistake for thinking big boobs and a liberal attitude about sex meant you'd be easy. I apologize."

I kept silent. What universe was I living in right now?

"And I've thought of you fondly and respectfully since then. The thing is, if you're involved with Schmitt—who's married in addition to being a secret Purity Values supporter—I figure it's probably not because he's good in the sack. I figure you're either being blackmailed into it, or paid off, or something that's probably not in line with your principles, and if so you might be looking for a way out."

He must have tailed or tracked Schmitt somehow. Maybe they had photos of license plates entering the Hamilton gates? "What do you mean, a way out?"

"Now now, Maddie, play nice. I can't give you everything without you giving me a little something back."

"Let's just say I might have a certain amount of access to Mr. Conrad Schmitt. What exactly are you trying to pin on him?"

"Don't you think it would do some damage to the Purity Values Party if one of their top donors was revealed to be an adulterer? And I know you're not a fan of theirs. That website you used to write sex articles for: Didn't they get it shut down? Think about this, Maddie. *You* write the Schmitt exposé, you have the byline, we back it up with our fact-finding, we blow the lid off this creep with your help. I'm talking Pulitzer material. You finally get the journalism career you always wanted, I launch my new venture with a bang, and we nail a political scumbag who I strongly suspect is taking advantage of you, all in one swoop."

I have to admit, Price Lawson was a pretty good salesman. If it had been the pitch for a screenplay I bet he would have got the film produced in no time. But one problem was that, well, I *wasn't* having an affair with Conrad Schmitt. I was an employee of a secret BDSM club that Schmitt had been a part of for fifty years and which I had sworn not to betray. Even if I'd wanted to take Lawson's offer, there was no way I could.

I didn't particularly trust Lawson, either. I had to try to play for more time, to try to figure this out. If he sniffed around much more, he was bound to find out about the club, I was likely to be implicated, and not only did I not want to betray the Hamiltons, Schmitt could be downright scary. People said if you crossed him you might as well leave LA because you'd never work again. I'd always assumed that only meant in the entertainment business, but if he was heavily politically connected, who knows. There were stories about politicians who would send a SWAT team to terrorize an opponent's family, change their records so their cars would be repossessed, and worse.

I shook my head. None of those things were happening right now. I needed to focus. "You have proof of Schmitt's political contributions?"

"Yes. If it'll help convince you, I'll show you the proof. In person."

I had to bust his balls. Had to. "I dunno, Price. Last time I agreed to an in-person meeting with you, it didn't work out so well..."

"I've learned my lesson. Maddie, we can help each other. Tell me you'll meet me today. How about for coffee, in public. You pick the place, even."

I needed time to think this over. "Five o'clock," I said, figuring that would give me all day. "There's a drive-through Starbucks off Highland at Willoughby." It was one of half a dozen within a mile of my house. By that time the place wouldn't be busy.

He repeated the location to me with pauses as if he were writing it down. "Starbucks, drive-through, Highland, Willoughby. Got it. See you at five, Maddie. You won't regret it."

I sighed in relief after he hung up. *Not* talking to him was so much preferable to talking to him. Even if he was "reformed" it was still draining to have to put up with him.

And now I had agreed to meet him. I had to figure out my story before then or it was going to be a disaster. I decided to brush my teeth and get dressed before I did anything else, though. Maybe it'd all seem more doable once I was prepared for the world.

I'd brushed my teeth but was still in my bathrobe when the phone rang again.

Chino this time. I considered sending it to voice mail, but my fingers had answered before I thought it all the way through. "Hey."

"Good morning."

I checked the clock. Just barely. A few minutes until noon. I needled him: "You sleep all right? Or did your bruises keep you up?"

He laughed, a genuine, full laugh. "You're a piece of work, Maddie."

"Yep. So are you." I found myself smiling. We'd never talked on the phone before but I suddenly felt like I was talking to an old friend. "What are you doing today?"

"House hunting, remember? You still up for coming along?"

"Can't. Something's come up," I said automatically, cursing Price Lawson and the trouble he was clearly bringing into my life.

"You sure? I really don't want to go by myself."

I clucked my tongue. "You don't have some other woman friend you could call?"

"Well, I could, but I may as well confess, the house-hunting idea is one hundred percent just an excuse to spend some time with you," he said. I could almost hear the boyish shrug I imagined him making. "You know."

Charmed. *When was the last time you were charmed, Madison?* "You don't have to make an excuse to see me," I said quickly.

"Are you sure? Because it kinda sounded like you were making an excuse *not* to see me a minute ago."

"I know. Something really did come up. Although I don't have to be there until five o'clock . . . " I pressed my knees together, wondering if I had the guts to ask Chino to just *come over and have sex.* What was the point of being a sexually forthright "babe" if I couldn't? But somehow I couldn't. "Were you serious about what you said last night?"

"Which thing?"

I felt shy all of a sudden, which was not like me. Why was Chino suddenly the one guy who could make me blush? "About, um, helping me with my sex toy videos."

"Totally serious. But that's all the more reason you should help me with real estate. You help with the houses, I'll help with the toys. We'll just eyeball some places. I won't keep you longer than your meeting," he promised.

He made it easy to agree, like that logic was irrefutable. "All right. Come pick me up."

I gave him my address and then sat down at my computer to take notes on the conversation I'd had with Price. I wanted to make as detailed a record as I could just to keep it all straight.

That took longer than I thought it would and the next thing I knew I was rushing around trying to throw on something that looked decent and that didn't have any holes but that wasn't *too* too square. What did rock stars wear to go house hunting, anyway?

As it turned out, Chino wore a variation of pretty much what I'd usually seen him in: black jeans, black engineer boots, and a gray tank top that showed off his ink when he took off his leather jacket and slung it over his shoulder. I had put on blue stretch denim jeans and a scoop neck cotton tunic. Laurel Canyon was a mix of celebrities and hippies so I hoped we'd fit right in.

If I'd been thinking that maybe I'd have one of those "what was I thinking?" moments when I laid eyes on him, nope, that was not the case. If anything my heart did a little skip when I realized he looked even better in the light of day than expected.

He held the car door open for me and I gave him a funny look. What did he mean by that? Was he just being polite because he was the driver, or was it my imagination that there was some old school protectiveness in the gesture? He ignored the raised eyebrow I gave him and got in the driver's side, carefully backing out from where he'd parked behind my downstairs neighbor's car. The driveway was flanked by high stone walls around the small courtyard patio in front.

"Nice place," he said with a glance up at the Spanish-style building before he turned to look behind the car.

"Yeah, it's a two-family. I own both units and rent out the first floor."

"Even nicer," he said with a nod and then a sidelong look at me, as if he were wondering how I could afford to own something so nice right in West Hollywood.

"I got lucky," I said, which was true. "My grandmother left me a pile of money at the right time to buy this place as a fixer-upper. Rents have skyrocketed so much that what the guys downstairs pay covers the whole mortgage plus a little extra. I'd have to move to the boonies now if I didn't own." Or get much better paying gigs than I'd been living on for the past ten years. "Where do you live?"

"Oh, nowhere special," he said, brushing the question off, which seemed a bit odd. Did he have something to hide? He slipped his sunglasses on as we pulled into the main flow of traffic. "They say owning is the way to go now that I have money in the bank. It's better spent on a house than most other things. Right? Assuming no mudslides, earthquakes, wildfires..."

My instinct was to dig deeper to try to find out what he was hiding, but I told myself to let it go. "Is there a part of the country where they don't have any of those things? I keep hearing how Seattle is going to get destroyed by a volcano. Tornadoes, hurricanes, floods? There's always something no matter where you go, I think."

"Probably true." He was wearing some silver rings and had an assortment of leather and bead bracelets on his left wrist. As he turned the steering wheel my eye was drawn to them, flashing in the sun. They looked like he'd been wearing them for so many years they were part of him, like his tattoos. "You hungry? My coffeemaker broke this morning and I need to fuel up."

"Turn here and there's a drive-through Starbucks a little ways up," I told him, figuring I'd check the place out before meeting Price.

We pulled through the drive-up window, and both ordered the largest iced coffees allowable by law. Chino also asked for a handful of food items, chocolate croissants, muffins, graham crackers, enough stuff that I was starting to laugh a little by the end.

"Something funny?" His own smile was kind of sly, kind of self-deprecating.

"We're going to pull up and they're going to wonder where the carload of hungry ten-year-olds is," I said.

"And they're going to see a pair of red-blooded American twentyish-somethings...how old are you, anyway, if I may ask?" Before I could answer he went on to add, "I get the feeling you're like me. All the other guys in the band are like, twenty-four, twenty-five tops. I'm about to turn thirty and sometimes it feels like there's a much bigger gap between me and them than you'd think."

He glanced sideways again.

"I'm about to turn thirty, too," I told him.

"Wow. You don't look it."

"Neither do you."

"I had the feeling you were more...experienced in life than Ricki and Gwen." He lowered his window to hand his credit card to the cashier. "I'm glad."

"Glad about what? That we're the same age?"

"That I was right and it wasn't just wishful thinking on my part." He flashed me that smirk as he handed me my coffee and it seemed a lot less annoying than I remembered. Maybe remembering how good that mouth was at other things biased me somewhat.

We chatted about inconsequential things for a while, and I started eating one of the croissants so I'd have something other than coffee in my stomach.

"Give me a bite of that?" he asked.

I tore off a piece. "I'm getting crumbs all over your car," I said with mild alarm.

"Don't let that get in the way of your enjoying it," he said, then opened his mouth like a baby bird.

I popped the piece of the croissant in and felt the soft edge of his lip skim my finger as he took it. *Purrrr.* He settled back into the bucket seat with a sensual ripple of his spine. Was it my imagination or was every move he made pure sex?

I decided to ask. "Are you always like this or are you being a sexy beast just for me?"

"Always like this, sweets," he said, "though maybe thinking about last night ramps it up a little. *Mmm-mm.* Have I mentioned how glad I am you're coming with me today?"

"It was at least implied." I grinned. I liked his easy, breezy manner. It made it easy for me to relax around him even though underneath I had all these questions simmering. Was this going to turn into something more serious and how much did I want—or not want—that to happen? It made him easy to like.

"So, how long have you lived in Southern California?" He turned the car stereo down a little so he could hear me better.

"Most of my life," I said. "I was born in San Diego when my dad was still in the military. We lived in Las Vegas for a little while after he got out of the service, and then various places around Southern California."

"Are your folks still here?"

"They moved to Arizona a couple of years after I finished college."

"Oh, yeah? Where'd you go?"

"Cal State. Long Beach."

"So you really know this area." He took a sip from the straw, holding his cup in one hand and the steering wheel with the other. "Your cred as a house-hunting companion gets better all the time. I lived here as a kid but it's changed a lot since then. We lived in Los Feliz then but now that's gotten pricey."

"What made you want to look at Laurel Canyon? Lots of celebs up there?"

"Ford's dad has a house there so I've been up there a lot. Seems nice." He slid his coffee into a cup holder by the gearshift. "And it's really not that far from everything, even though it sometimes feels like it when you're up there."

I took a good gulp of my coffee, holding it for a moment in my mouth before swallowing. In iced coffee I liked the interplay of the dark and bitter flavors vying with their opposite, cream and sugar. I wanted to ask him more about his background but wasn't sure where to start, so I stuck with geography. "Where'd you live when you weren't in LA?"

"Ohio mostly, with stints in Detroit and Cleveland." He shrugged. "Best thing about the band making it is moving back here."

"Is Chino a nickname?"

"Oh yeah. Got it as a kid for two reasons. My real name's not a practical, everyday name by any stretch."

"You mean it's something like Mergatroid?"

"Something like that," he said with a smirk and I knew he wasn't telling me on purpose.

"What's the second reason?"

"It's a pretty common nickname for kids with black hair and chubby cheeks—you know, kind of Chinese-looking—but my dad liked to watch Bruce Lee and Jackie Chan movies and I liked to jump around and pretend I was a kung fu fighter." He let loose a Bruce Lee battle cry—*wasssaaaaaaaah!*—and then chopped the steering wheel before laughing. "So he started calling me Chino and it stuck."

"Huh! I've known a couple of Chinos and I never realized it meant 'Chinese' in Spanish."

He chuckled. "It's that or those guys were known for wearing khaki pants."

We pulled into a driveway in the hills where a woman was just planting an OPEN HOUSE sign into the ground at the side of the road. Four other cars were already parked in the curved driveway, every one of them a luxury model of some kind.

The front door was open, and we walked into a split-level, ultra-modern house that looked like something out of a furniture catalog. Everything was sleek and spacious to the point that there were bookshelves but almost no books on them.

I found myself more curious about the other people checking out the house than I was about the house itself. Maybe Chino was right: They were all couples—at least I was pretty sure they were—including the two men who were walking around together and pointing at various spots discussing where their furniture and art might fit.

Chino took a prospectus sheet from the coffee table and then gave me the high sign we should slip out. We got into the car without talking to anyone and drove on. I looked at the sheet as we headed uphill toward the next place he had on a list on his phone.

"Six million dollars!" I stared at the paper in disbelief. "That wasn't even two thousand square feet. Were the toilets gold-plated or something and I didn't notice?"

"Looks to me like the price doubles on anything that has an actual view," he said. "I guess that's what happens when you have a bunch of people with more money than sense."

We looked at three more places in quick succession, ranging from a three-million-dollar, three-thousand-square-foot mansion to a hundred-thousand-dollar shack.

"An actual shack," I said incredulously as we drove away.

"The listing did call it a 'cottage.' I guess now we know that's Realtor-speak for 'built by back-to-nature types with a bare suggestion of interior appliances and plumbing.' But it sure was cheap."

"I'm sure anyone who buys it wants to tear it down. How much you want to bet there's some kind of a problem, like a neighbor who can block new construction or something. That's the only reason I can think it hasn't been snatched up by someone already."

"Or it's haunted," Chino said with a laugh. "No, thanks. Let's look at one more before I drop you back home."

"Okay."

I caught a glimpse of the HOLLYWOOD sign as we drove around a bend and then turned up a way we hadn't yet gone. Cars were parked along the side of the road and we pulled in behind another sports car. There was a bit of a gully on my side of the car so I climbed over the gearshift and emerged from the driver's side. Chino held the door open and helped me out with his hand.

There it was again, that hint of something that felt like his manners were beyond simply polite, something darker and more possessive underneath. Something in the way his eyes followed me, in the curve of his arm and the firmness of his fingers. If I weren't attracted to him, would I have even noticed it?

But I did notice it. And I found it strangely attractive. Strange because if a guy was solicitous toward me usually my reaction was to bust his balls. I guess I liked Chino's balls just the way they were.

CHAPTER FOUR

MADISON

The final house was another split-level, built into the hill. The top floor had a patio, most of the bedrooms were on the middle floors, and the garage sat at the bottom.

As we entered the foyer we ran into the real estate agent, another woman, this one middle-aged. Her suit was dove gray, her scarf a riot of pinks and yellows like an Easter basket. "Welcome," she said, and held out her hand to shake ours. "Mr. and Mrs. . . . ?"

"Jones," Chino said with a broad smile before leading me away to explore the property.

One of the bedrooms was built into the hill and only had one tiny window. As we took a turn through the room I said, "Here's where we'd build the private dungeon, don't you think, Mr. Jones?"

He slid up behind me, his hands fitting around my hips. "Would we? What would we furnish it with?"

"With all this wall space you could have a St. Andrew's Cross over there, hang all the floggers and whips here, a sling there—"

"A sling?"

"Definitely," I said with a knowing nod.

He slid his hand up my body until two fingers were holding my chin. "I like your...taste in interior decoration," he said as he turned my head to the side. His grip tightened suddenly and I realized he had my other arm by the wrist, effectively trapping me in his embrace while he took lush liberties with his tongue in my mouth. He tasted dark and sweet and fresh all at once, and as I sucked in a breath I could feel how tightly he held me, the heat of his skin soaking through his shirt and warming my back. I could imagine us in the room outfitted as a dungeon, getting ready to play in it for the first time, and all the unfulfilled desire from last night flooded me once again.

We separated quickly when the Realtor brought another couple into the room. I was flushed, my breath heaving, my lips tingling, but the Realtor just smiled and the male half of the couple gave Chino a wink.

"Picking out drapes is my kink," Chino said to the guy, as he slipped his sunglasses on.

He led me back to the car by the hand. It took me an unsteady moment to climb into my seat.

He started the engine but didn't pull away, turning to me instead and saying, "So. This sexual chemistry thing."

"Yeah?" I said, still reeling in a happy, hormonal daze. "I mean, yeah."

He smiled. "Not just me, then."

"Fuck no."

"*Tsk.* You're supposed to say fuck *yes.*"

"You're the one who said no to fucking me last night." I

couldn't resist needling him about it since I couldn't outright complain. I knew he'd done the responsible thing, the right thing, but I wasn't used to being strung along and hunger for him gnawed at me.

He looked at the beads and silver on his arm and I realized he had a watch on, too. "When I fuck, I like to take my time. And we've got to get you back to town before five o'clock."

I made a frustrated noise. "This is torture, you know, getting me hot and bothered like this."

"You're the one who said you wanted a torture rack in our dream home," he joked, and put the car into gear. We pulled away from the shoulder and he eased the car down the winding, hilly road. "Tell me seriously, though, what are your kinks?"

"Oh, you know, the usual," I said.

"Uh huh. So you're into . . . uh . . . baked beans? Clown makeup? Boiled doll heads up the butt? Pineapple soda?"

As each thing he named got more nonsensical, I laughed harder and harder. "Pineapple soda?" I squeaked. "*Pineapple soda?*"

"That's a serious heavy-duty kink," he said, shaking his head. "I'm not sure I can go that far. Might be my limit."

I wiped carefully at my eyes, which were tearing up, trying not to smudge my eyeliner. "Okay, point taken. I'll try to be more specific, but I guess it really depends. I'm not into any specific toy or activity, you know?"

"You're not that into toys . . . but you're about to launch a video blog about them?"

"That's not what I mean. I mean, you know, when it comes to specific kinks, I've had good and bad spankings just the same as I've had good and bad sex."

"Okay, that makes sense," he said. "I guess I'm similar. There's not one specific thing that gets me off. I've been trying to take that as a healthy sign."

"Healthy how?"

"Like a healthy appetite. It's not like I can't get off unless I spank you or you wear a clown mask because I was spanked by a clown as a child or something. I just mean it's not that I'm broken somehow. This is just who I am."

"Right," I said, wondering just how much experience with kink and dominance and submission he actually had. Over the past six months at the club I had been assuming he was a newbie, but between the way he'd handled our scene and the way he was talking now I knew I'd been wrong. He was more experienced and much more of a dom than he'd let on. "I had a boyfriend once who could not get off, literally, unless his thumb was in my mouth."

"Really? I've heard of people who sucked their own thumbs but that's a whole 'nother level." Chino snorted.

"Exactly. It got really weird. Like even if he was masturbating at night he wanted to put his thumb in my mouth."

"That's someone unclear on what self-love is all about, don'tcha think?"

"This was in college. I had an early morning class and would be trying to sleep and he would be like 'just ignore me, honey, I'll take care of myself so you can sleep, but oh by the way could I stick my thumb in your mouth?' We didn't have one of those 'I own your body' kind of relationships, either. It was more like he was just . . . just . . . " I flailed for an adjective suitable for what a loser he was.

"Weaksauce," Chino said.

"Yes. He was the king of weaksauce. I might've respected him more if he'd just said, 'Shit, honey, I'm horny, can we have a quickie before we conk out?' "

"Did he ever say that?"

"No. It was always passive-aggressive bullshit with him. Which was probably a much bigger deal breaker than the thumb." I shrugged and picked up what had been my iced coffee and was now just ice. I slurped out the last of the melted water and rattled the remaining ice around in the bottom of the cup.

"Speaking of horny," he said. "On a scale from one to ten, how horny are you right now?"

"I don't want to give you the impression I'm easy," I said, squirming luxuriously back against the leather seat, "but I'm at a seven right now."

"And it's all my fault you're so hot, is it?"

"One hundred percent your fault. Picking out drapes is not my kink." *But kissing you might be.*

He turned us onto another road, this one going up the hill, and I got the feeling he was driving around aimlessly now rather than trying to get back to the main drag. "I guess it's my job to cool you down, then. Fish an ice cube out of your cup," he said. "And then rub it against your clit."

"Is that an order?"

"It's a suggestion," he said, but over the tops of his sunglasses his gaze bore into mine. "A very strong suggestion."

I swallowed, my throat going dry as it felt like all the blood in my body surged between my legs. How could he make me so hot with just a few words and a look? This was a different kind of domination than most guys would throw at me, rousing my curiosity as much as my lust.

My fingers trembled a little as I got the lid off the cup and I tipped one of the larger remaining pieces of ice into my mouth. I took it between my fingers. It was flat on one side and curved on the other. I popped open the button on my jeans and undid the zipper. Thank goodness for stretch denim: I could just get the ice and my fingers in there if I slid down in the seat a little.

The ice was cold but my flesh was hot, so hot, and the

throbbing of arousal only increased as I moved it up and down on my clit. I moaned as the ice melted down to nothing and then my fingers were stroking up and down.

"Oh, sweets," he said. "I can smell you."

That comment sent a flush of heat to my cheeks, making me feel like such a naughty girl at heart. "I'm sorry."

"Don't apologize. It's the best scent in the world. Hot woman. Very distracting, though. Get a fresh ice cube. Do it again."

I did it again, whining as my arousal mounted and I jerked my hips, but the ice was frictionless. I would never be able to come from it.

"Again," he said.

I picked out a third piece of ice, this one with a "rough" texture, but within seconds it had melted down smooth.

"Is it working, sweets? Are you cooled down now?"

"Ah, fuck you, Chino," I said through clenched teeth. "I'm at eight or nine now."

He laughed his evil laugh. "When you reach ten what happens?"

"I don't know. Maybe at ten I go crazy from the need to come?"

"Crazy enough to do anything I tell you?"

Now I laughed. "You don't have to wait until I'm at ten for that."

"There you go again with the 'anything.' Well, I haven't told you about the doll heads in the trunk yet," he said with a grin. "So. It would seem the hornier you get, the more pliable you get."

"Doesn't everyone?" I asked, squirming with my fingers sliding down as far into my pants as I could go.

"Get your jeans off." He checked in the rearview mirror. "I want you to spread that pussy wide. Let it breathe."

I kicked off my shoes and peeled my panties and jeans off.

"Now," he said. "I need to keep my eyes on the road, so I want you to take my phone and take pictures of yourself fingering yourself for me."

"Oh, fuck," I said aloud.

"Is that a problem?"

"No! That was a general 'oh, fuck' of enthusiasm," I said. "Chino, you are one hot and twisted individual."

"Yep," he said with a nod. "See, the thing is, I'm not into sex toys... except that anything can be a sex toy, you know?" He gave me the code to unlock his phone. "Right now, Maddie, you are my sex toy."

Nngh, those words, the rush of desire I felt when he said them was like drinking a shot, heat flowing deliciously through my whole body.

"Spread yourself with the fingers of one hand and hold the phone with the other," he directed. "Take plenty. I've got lots of memory on that phone."

I unlocked the phone and caught a glimpse of his "recent calls" log. Were those women's names I saw? Flora, Christina, Penny... I switched to the camera quickly, telling myself they were probably the names of real estate agents. I was wholly entranced by the Chino Garcia sex god spell and didn't want to burst the bubble. *Don't be paranoid,* I told myself. *Stop it and enjoy the ride.*

I took about a dozen shots from various angles. I hadn't examined myself so closely in a long time, not since college when I'd been worried I had caught herpes. (I hadn't. Thank goodness.)

"Now put some fingers in for me."

"How about some video?" I suggested. I slid a finger into myself. "Oh, fuck."

"Was that the 'oh, fuck' of enthusiasm?"

"It was." My own fingers sliding in and out of me felt far better than they had this morning. I was much more aroused, I guess. I took some photos of my middle finger planted deep, and then some video of my index and middle fingers drilling in and out of me.

"One more suggestion," Chino said, his gaze resolutely on the road ahead. "I want you to put something else in you. Something you choose."

"Something else?" I glanced around the car, trying to come up with something. "Like the straw that was in my mouth?"

"For example. Unless you've got something in your purse you'd prefer."

There wasn't much in this purse, I didn't think, except... "I've got mascara." I pulled the container out of the bag and held it up, a gold and black tube about six inches long and about the width of my thumb.

"Ever fucked yourself with it before?"

"Nope."

He made that purring sound. "Excellent. Do it."

It wasn't very wide and I was gushingly wet, so the hard plastic cylinder slid into me easily. I took both photos and video of it going in and out of me.

"Thank you, sweets," he said, when I turned to him expectantly. "You can put my phone down now and make yourself come. Unless you're really *really* into delayed gratification, in which case you can wait till you get home."

"I... I..." I was already fingering myself furiously, so impatient to come that I didn't even pull the mascara tube free.

"Don't scream," he said mischievously just as I neared my peak. I clamped my jaw shut—my eyes, too—as I came so hard I saw stars.

* * *

There was just barely time for Chino to drop me at home so I could change into not-damp panties and jeans and get to my rendezvous.

Price Lawson looked much the same as he had a few years ago, the cut of his suit and his hair a tad more chic than when he'd worked at a daily newspaper, but otherwise same former-athlete-prone-to-pack-on-weight build, same rakish hunch to his shoulders. I saw him waving from inside while I pulled into the drive-through. I got myself some hot tea at the window—after all, I might need something calming—then pulled out the other side and parked on the street at the curb, motioning him to follow.

Mine wasn't a glamorous car by any stretch, a hand-me-down from my father, but not only did I feel safer in it than out in the open, I'd also hidden a voice recorder in the glove compartment. Just in case.

Price didn't object to my choice of meeting place, getting into the passenger seat without hesitation and perching a backpack on his knees. "Thanks for meeting me," he said.

Having spent the afternoon with Chino, I hadn't exactly given a lot of in-depth thought to the situation, but somehow I felt clearer now about what to say. In fact it was suddenly obvious: "I decided it was best to tell you off in person, Price. How dare you make accusations about me having an affair while simultaneously pretending to be some kind of dream-job-dangling knight in shining armor?"

He cringed sheepishly. "I, ah, you're right. I'm sorry."

"Now give me the dirt on Schmitt and I'll decide whether I'm going to deign to help you or what."

Price pulled a sleek laptop out of his backpack and shoved the bag into the footwell. Before he opened the laptop, though, he said, "Maddie, I want you to know I really do think you have writing talent. And I really do think a story like this would have much more virality if told by a woman."

"Is 'virality' the new term for sensationalism?"

He cleared his throat, pretending I hadn't called him on it, and opened the laptop. On the screen were spreadsheets and images of statements showing deductions from Schmitt's bank accounts that exactly matched the income from the Purity SuperPAC. It looked as though Schmitt hadn't even tried to keep the contributions secret and I told Price that. "I don't know if your plan is going to work."

"What do you mean?"

"I mean, if you're going to try to discredit Purity Values, will showing that a donor doesn't adhere to those values actually make any difference? What if Schmitt gives to *all* the candidates because he's hedging his bets? He's a power broker. He gets in everyone's pockets. Do you know if he gives to liberal PACs and candidates, too? What then?"

Price frowned. "Hm."

"Or another thing: What if the only reason he gives to these guys isn't because it's his beliefs so much as a smoke screen in case he ever does have something quote-*unsavory*-unquote come up? He doesn't even look like he's tried very hard to hide it."

"Huh."

"Your scenario only makes sense if Schmitt is in fact having an affair with me, but unfortunately he isn't." I gave Price a pointed look. "I know you're looking for a huge exposé or story to make a big splash, but Schmitt carrying on with me isn't it."

"What were you doing with him at the Hamilton place, then?"

"That's private and yes, I'm going to be an ass about my privacy because it's payback, Price. But I will tell you normally he has his wife with him; that's how off base you are. She just had a cold and stayed home."

"Damn." He closed the laptop. "I was so sure I was onto something."

I gave him an innocent-looking shrug. At least, I hoped it looked innocent. "Got anything else you'd like written? I'm sure there are plenty of feature article topics I could tackle. Sexy ones, even. How about the explosion of male exotic dance revues in the wake of *Magic Mike XXL*? I could totally do that one justice."

"Sure. Yep. I'll think about it. Thanks for meeting me, Maddie. Sorry again. Bye." He got out of the car so fast it was crystal clear to me he wasn't the slightest bit interested in my story idea. Although, granted, I'd picked the topic to needle him, so I wasn't too surprised that he couldn't get away from me fast enough. Now that I'd thought of it, though, I decided I should pitch that as a story to some other online magazine. Meanwhile, I hoped I'd thrown him off Schmitt's and the Governor's Club's scent. The exposure of the playground of Hollywood's kinky elite would truly be a massive, massive scoop, but Price would never know it. Not if I could help it.

* * *

CHINO

My phone rang shortly after I dropped Madison off. It was sitting on the dashboard of the car and I answered it, putting it on speaker while I drove. "Yo."

The voice of Ford, my partner in crime in the rhythm section of The Rough, came from the phone. "You still house hunting? Or are you ready to come and jam?"

"I had to run a quick errand in West Hollywood," I said.

"But I'm heading back into the hills now. I'm probably fifteen minutes from your place."

"Cool. Actually, if you're still down there, pick up some burgers? There's nothing to eat here but the crap flavors of Campbell's soup."

"No worries. In-N-Out is only five minutes out of the way." I hit my blinker and turned toward the nearest burger place.

"Bring me two Double-Doubles? One for later?"

"You know, when you house-sit for your dad you are allowed to actually *leave* the house to do things like, oh, shop for groceries and have some fun, like, for example, attending super-secret sex dungeon parties that you're invited to."

"Oh, don't you get on my case about last night," Ford said.

"I'm not on your case, bro. But you and Samson did miss a good time."

"Oh?" Curiosity made his pitch go up. "What happened?"

The most amazing thing happened. "Tell you when I get there." I hung up and then chuckled to myself, feeling gleefully evil.

A short while later I made my way up to the Cutler house. Ford's dad was something of a legend in the music business, sort of a Tom Petty or John Mellencamp type who'd made his name with American roots rock in the eighties and nineties and still toured regularly. He'd bought the house in the eighties and while it wasn't an over-the-top luxury mansion like some of the places here in the Hollywood Hills, it was extremely nice and well kept. The main section of the house was a great room with dining area, sunken living room, and kitchen. One whole wall was windows and sliding glass doors onto the pool patio overlooking LA.

The front door was unlocked, so I let myself in and locked it behind me. Ford was standing by the pool table leaning on a cue and staring at the balls on the table. I held up the bag of food to get his attention, and he looked up like a hunting dog picking up a scent.

I set it down on the counter island of the kitchen area and got out plates. I was as familiar with this kitchen as I was with my own. I'd crashed here a lot when Ford had first joined the band and we hadn't made any money yet. At first I'd felt a little weird about it—though extremely grateful for a no-cost place to lay my head at that point in my life—but it eventually sunk in that taking in strays was something the Cutlers did regularly. When Remo was in town there was often a revolving round of houseguests, and having his son's bandmates camping out for weeks or months at a time was par for the course.

Ford had grown up here, nestled in the hills so close to the star-making machine that was Hollywood. As the son of a millionaire musician he'd never known what it was like to miss a rent payment, never had to decide between paying the gas bill or buying new shoes, never gone hungry.

Well, except for times like this. "I had an egg for breakfast but there was no bread and then I went into the studio and man I'm *starving.*" He picked up a burger and bit into it over the sink so the juices could drip. After he'd swallowed he said, "Thanks. There's probably a grocery delivery service I could use on the Internet, but I haven't gotten around to it."

"Probably," I agreed, putting the plates back into the cabinet and joining him at the sink with my own burger. I was ravenous, too, but if I couldn't have what I was craving most—Madison—then this would have to do to take the edge off.

A good jam session would do that, too. Ford and I were working on some songs together. Some might turn into songs for The Rough, or maybe we'd end up recording a side project, or who knows—our A&R man might funnel one or two of them to other artists. We were having fun with the music and trying not to be too concerned about what was going to happen with it. After how stressful working on the last album had been, we needed to put some fun back into things. Sometimes a little stress helps creativity flow, but sometimes you just need freedom to experiment and see what happens.

Thus, jam sessions. Ford could play most of the usual stringed instruments: guitar, bass, mandolin, banjo, dobro, pedal steel, plus he could get by on a lot of others. Me, I played some guitar, too, and in addition to my drum kit in the studio I also had a portion of my ever-growing collection of percussion instruments. Indian, African, Latin American, Japanese—if a drum or percussion instrument sounded interesting to me, I wanted it. I tried to exercise some restraint because part of me kept saying it was a waste to buy a bell or a shaker or whatever that I might never use, but on the other hand now that I had the money, why not buy it? I was trying to sock away as much as possible in savings but my entire "percussion of the world" collection probably still cost less than a single one of Mal's custom guitars.

"I have a riff for you to hear," Ford said. He'd already inhaled his food and had washed his hands in the sink.

"Good," I said, or rather grunted, since my face was full of burger. Almost done.

I had just washed my own hands when my phone rang. I dried them on my shirt before answering. "Yo."

"*Tú*," my sister, Flora, said with a huff. "I saw you left a message."

"I did. I tried to call Mom and she hasn't answered. I just want to know if everything's okay, you know?"

The next voice that I heard was my brother Vincent's. "Like you have a right to be concerned."

Flora: "Hush, Vincent. Chino's trying to be a good son."

"He'll never be that."

"Don't speak about your older brother that way," she chastised.

I waited for them to stop bickering before I tried to say anything else. When it was silent for a moment, I went on. "Is she not calling me back because she doesn't want to or is something going on with him?"

"If you won't call him Father, can't you at least have the respect to call him by his name?" Vincent insisted. "I swear you're just doing it to piss me off."

"No, if I wanted to piss you off I'd call him by the names I use for him in private," I said. "Like 'motherfucker.'"

"You think because you're a big-time rock star now you can use bad words? That doesn't make you free. It makes you low-class trash," Vincent sneered.

"What are you going to do about it, spank me?"

Flora interrupted us. "Stop it, stop it both of you. Were you just calling to say hi to her?"

"And if I was?"

"I could give her a message," Flora said. "Or give her some time."

"How much time should I give her, Flor? Two days? A week?"

Vincent jumped back in. "Did you ever think maybe she doesn't want to talk to you because she's ashamed of you—"

"Shut the fuck up, Vicente."

"Don't call me that! When are you going to learn!" He had been a strident child, and now he was a strident twenty-two-year-old. "You're never going to get anywhere in life if you don't straighten up and fly right."

"Do you hear yourself? You sound like something from a 1950s high school film."

"You're impossible." I heard the click as he hung up.

"Flor, you still there?"

"Yes."

"Is V off the line?"

"Yes."

"Okay, listen. The reason I've been trying to call Mom is I want to buy her a house. If she'll move to LA, that is."

"You're what? Where'd you get the money for that?"

I took that to mean that they were still living under the ban on "corrupt" television, radio, et cetera. "If you'd just stick your heads out of the conservative bubble you've been living in, you'd see my band is at the top of the charts. I'm famous now, Flor. I've got money in the bank."

"What about Vincent and me?"

"You're both welcome to come, too, if you want."

"And our stepfather?"

I was counting on the fact that man would never, ever deign to live in a house I owned. Plus he'd often railed about how Los Angeles was Sodom, a land of fornication and sin. Come to think of it, he was right. But so *so* wrong about everything else in life. "You know he'd never come here."

"So you're trying to break them up over money."

"Ma told me once that she married him for his money, to give us a better life." I had been maybe twelve at the time, and I sometimes doubted the memory because she never said anything like that to me again. He'd punished me for saying something in Spanish and I wondered if she'd only said it to try to make me feel better somehow. "I want to know if it was true. Can you tell me, Flor? Can you tell me she's truly happy with him? If she is, I'll give up and go away."

My sister didn't answer my question. Instead she said, "You know Vincent thinks the reason you're such a moral degenerate is because you were already too old and rebellious before we moved in with Dad. That if you'd only learned to do as you were told, you'd be happy now."

"I am happy, Flor. Very happy. Is Vincent happy?"

"He's fresh out of college, already engaged, and has a full-time job, so, yes."

"So, soon to have wife, two-point-five kids, and a two-car garage, and go to that fucking church on Sundays." I was not a fan of our stepfather's newfangled church. I hadn't liked it as a kid—when we'd gone from being Christmas and Easter Catholics to his brand of joyless midwestern Christian—and I didn't like it now. Religion is one thing; brainwashing is another. "Okay, fine. If that's Vincent's definition of happy I won't shit on it. But it's not mine, Flor." I waited a moment for her to respond, and when she didn't, I added, "And I don't think it's yours, either."

"You don't know what life is like for me," she said.

"No, I don't. But if you're waiting around in a nothing town for big daddy to arrange you a marriage—"

"You really mean I could come, too?" she blurted suddenly.

"With Mom? Yes, I really mean it."

"B-but what if she doesn't want to go?"

God. My baby sister. I could hear the quaver in her voice. "Do you want to come to LA, Flor?"

Silence again, and then very quietly she said, "I want to . . . go back to school. But it's expensive and I'm saving up the money very slowly."

"How much money do you n—?"

"I have to go," she said quickly, and then hung up.

I stared at the phone in my hand. My family lived in an alternate universe where rock and roll was the devil, sex was only for procreation, and women were supposed to be literally subordinate to men. This was the first hint I'd had that maybe Flora really wanted to break free. I realized my hands were sweating and it wasn't because I was in the sun.

I stuck the phone back in my pocket and saw Ford was sitting on the edge of the pool, his feet in the water. His blond hair was bright in the sun and he was squinting at me. Up until now I'd kept the guys in the band in the dark about my family. I didn't know what to say.

Ford did. "Family shit is complicated shit," he said with a knowing nod.

"Yeah."

He climbed to his feet. "So what happened last night that you had to wait until you got here to tell me?"

"Oh. Yeah. I... hooked up with Madison."

"The redhead? The one whose eyes always follow you around all the time?"

That was news to me, but welcome news. "Uh, yeah. That would be the one."

"'Bout time," he deadpanned.

We went into the studio then. He took that riff he'd been working on, married it with something I'd said on the phone, and I beat on the drums like a wild man while he improvised lyrics on top of it. The result was a song called "Nothing Town" so at least something good came of it.

CHAPTER FIVE

MADISON

I spent a restless night, dreaming about Chino while I was asleep and fantasizing about him when I was awake. It was like being haunted by a very, very sexy ghost. I woke up exhausted and horny. *Fuck. A major crush is the last thing I need distracting me right now.* But regardless of what my mind thought, my body and heart and soul were already set on him, apparently. I kept imagining the dark depths of his eyes, the silky honey of his voice making wicked "suggestions," the firmness of his fingers on my hip, or around my waist, or on my shoulder...

I groaned. I had a strong feeling that even spending the morning in bed with my vibrator wasn't going to sate me.

Stop it, Madison. You know better than to crave a hot bad boy. You know how this story ends and it's never pretty.

I reached for my phone to check the weather and glance at e-mail. There was a message from Gwen, checking in on me. Since when did Gwen check in on me? I was the one who was supposed to check in on her. I took a sip of water from the glass I kept on my nightstand and Morris leaped up on the bed to get petted now that I was awake. He snuggled under my arm while I called Gwen back.

"Hey." She sounded out of breath. "How are you?"

"I'm fine. How are you?"

"On the exercise bike. Don't mind me. Quick, say something to distract me from the burn in my thighs. Speaking of burning thighs, how's Chino?"

"He's fine, I'm fine." I waved my hand in the air and Morris made a noise of protest. "I wasn't expecting the class clown to suddenly get all intense on my ass, but it was okay."

"Just okay? When you came out of the room I thought you guys were getting along better than okay."

"Then why the check-in, Gwen? I can take care of myself."

Gwen clucked her tongue. "Maddie. I'm an expert on big sisters who think they never need help. I *know* you can take care of yourself. But you always call me after I have an intense time in the dungeon and I figured it was time I returned the favor."

I rubbed my butt against the bed. Still sore. "Sorry, didn't mean to sound ungrateful. I really do appreciate it. But I don't know, Gwen."

"Don't know about what?"

"About me and Chino." I liked the sex. I liked him. But I was avoiding the gut-dropping place the scene had taken me like an acrophobic avoiding cliffs. Plus every previous experience with bad boys, rock stars, or musicians really hadn't worked for me. What made this one different?

"Well, if you're trying to figure out if employees and club members are a no-no, you know that's how my parents met, right?"

"What?"

"My mom was a hostess. It was relatively a secret I guess, but Dad told Ricki last year. So there you go. He's cute and it's obvious he likes you."

"Chino's a red-blooded male who likes anything with two legs and two breasts." Even as I said it, though, I realized I'd never actually seen him hit on any of the other women at the parties, not even the other hostess. I'd been assuming that he was like other guys I'd known, that the flirtatious jokes he'd flung my way were how he treated everyone, but it was starting to sink in that maybe that wasn't the case.

"That's what Ricki thought about Axel, too, but he's turned into a real one-woman guy. I think Chino's just been waiting for the right time to make a move on you."

Maybe I argued because I was hoping to be convinced otherwise. "He's an opportunist. Come on, Gwen. Until yesterday I couldn't even tell if he was a dom or a sub."

"Or a switch, like you, you mean?"

She had a point. "I guess."

"I think the reason Chino never seemed like a dom or a sub is because you go back and forth yourself, Maddie. I think he's been waiting to find out how you two could fit together. So which is it? When the two of you were alone, *ugh*"—she grunted—"sorry, just started a hill interval—did he come out on top?"

"He did," I said, thinking about his hand at the small of my back...and the intense need for his forgiveness that had sprung up in me during the scene.

"Oooh. And how much of a dom is he, really?"

"He's totally and completely a dom when he's with me. But don't get the wrong idea."

"Wrong idea? Why so defensive?"

"I'm not being defensive." I cringed as I said it. The only people who ever claim they're not defensive are people being defensive, and I knew it. "I guess I'm defensive because I don't know if I'm ready to jump into a relationship with Chino Garcia." *Especially one where I'm the sub.*

She was silent—well, except for the huffing as she pedaled her way up the virtual hill.

"Do you know him, Gwen? Do you really know him?"

"Not much better than you do, but I'm not getting any red flags about him, if that's what you mean. I know you've got trust issues with guys, but—"

"I do not have trust issues with guys!"

"If you say so," she said warily.

"I'm just not ready for something heavy, that's all," I went on. "That's just not my scene right now. Sure he's hot. Sure he's got a great body. Sure he's probably amazing in bed. That's like... 'that mountain over there is beautiful.' Doesn't mean I have to climb it."

"I'm under the impression this mountain will come to you, though," Gwen said.

I didn't say anything. I wanted to climb the mountain. I was aching to. But I was about to turn thirty; this was supposed to be the year I got my act together like a real adult, wasn't it? The last thing I needed was to fall back into my bad-boy habit.

But the memory of the way he'd kissed me on the house-hunting trip sent a pussy-melting wave of heat down my spine. Even more than getting off in his front seat, that was the moment that my brain kept coming back to. How'd he trap my hand like that? How did he hold me so securely, and taste my mouth so surely? *Nnnf.* I wanted to taste that again.

"Tell me I can have some fun with him without it ending in tears," I said suddenly.

"Oh, Maddie, of course you can. The guys in the band are

really good guys. He's not pushing you to make some kind of a commitment, is he?"

"No. I'm just... you know how guys can get." *What the hell are you talking about, Madison?* This had nothing to do with fear of commitment on either of our parts. It had everything to do with me avoiding what that scene had dredged up. I wanted the sex, I wanted the play, but I skirted away from whatever was going on with that forgiveness bullshit. It was bullshit, right? I didn't need some guy's approval to be happy with myself or my choices, and it was freaking me out how good it had felt.

That little taste was like having a "little" hit of cocaine. Some people only had to try it once to be hooked for life; wasn't that what they said? I was not going to let myself be reduced to a crawling, pathetic mess who needed her man's constant assurances to function. Just no. But I couldn't say that to Gwen without it possibly coming off as a criticism of her own relationship, even though I knew it wasn't like that for her and Mal. Their mutually worshipful master/slave thing really worked for them. What was going on in my head was... something else. I didn't even want to think about it for fear I might start wanting it even more.

I settled on a safe bet about why I was holding back. "I guess I'm still gun-shy after the past couple of disasters, that's all."

"It was hardly your fault that one of them was married and didn't tell you, one was on the lam, and one couldn't keep up a conversation outside the bedroom."

And that was only the ones I'd bothered to tell Gwen about. "I don't know. After a while I start wondering if the common denominator is me." Me and my thing for bad boys. "Why do I keep finding these guys who are great at sex and terrible at life?"

"Maybe concentrate on the sex, then, if it's good? I've been kind of worried that with you sex always turns into a job."

"I like working. Working keeps me focused."

"Uh huh. But if you're leery of getting in too deep, Chino seems like the fun type."

"True." And he had kind of backed off, if you considered making me finger-bang myself in his car backing off. He hadn't pushed to dig deeper emotionally, anyway.

And I wanted him too much to push him away entirely. "I'll be fine, Gwen. Look, speaking of work, I asked him to help me out with some of my sex toy reviews and he said he would. So, see? I'll multitask. I'll do some work and have fun with Chino at the same time."

"Aha! Let me know how it goes."

* * *

CHINO

I arrived at Madison's freshly showered after a workout at the gym. The place I went was not one of these yuppie hamster farms with a window full of gleaming treadmills, but a boxing gym in a run-down neighborhood not far from where I was renting, a place with peeling paint and a practice ring in the back. No one made stock trades from their phone while on the exercise bike at this place. I had a good lock for my locker and thus far no one had bothered my car or me. None of the guys there gave me much of a second glance, either.

My hair was still wet as I went up the stairs to Madison's second-floor entrance.

She opened the door, revealing to me the delicious sight of her in a white tank top and pink shorts. Her feet were bare and she smiled as she stepped back to let me in.

"Thanks for coming," she said. "This is all kind of new."

She could've been talking about our mutual attraction, but then she went on about her new gig, leading me to her couch without even letting me say hello. The ceiling was vaulted with a few overhead fans turning gently, circulating the AC. "They sent me all these portable cameras. I'm still figuring out what they want. All I really know is they—"

I kissed her. I caught her around the waist and swung her toward me and kissed her. "Well, hello," I said. "May I come in?"

"Hi, Chino," she said, blushing prettily. "Sorry. I didn't mean to be rude."

"It's okay, sweets," I told her. The kiss had revved my already humming engine, and all I really wanted to do was tell her forget the video, it's time to fuck. But I was enjoying riding the high that came from wanting her. It was like every time I didn't give in to the urge to just get right down to the "good ol' in-out" I got another hit of the drug. Besides, I really had promised to help her with the video. "I'm taking it as a sign that this gig is really important to you. You nervous?"

"I guess?"

"I know it's not because of the sex," I said, thumb on my chin. Let's see if I could lighten her up. "Compared to dungeon hostess or, what was it you said? Something about a *lucha libre* mask?"

She laughed softly. "Yeah. My attempt at 'exotic dancing.' And there was burlesque and selling sex toys. And abuse counselor. You're right. Nothing should faze me. But it'd be easier if they'd told me more about what they want. Less guessing."

"Maybe they want you to discover what works for yourself." I took a seat on her couch and pulled her down beside me. She smelled delicious and I couldn't help but assess whether the couch would be a good one for sex. Yes. It had a nice wide back—good for bending her over—and firm cushions. "What toy are you doing today?"

She got up from the couch and crossed to the computer desk in the corner of the room to retrieve a box. I watched her the whole way, her well-sculpted dancer's legs crowned by curvaceous hips. So fine.

"I've got a bunch of things to choose from." She upended the box onto the couch between us and several smaller packages and boxes tumbled out. I started picking through them. "This dildo looks like a giant gummy worm," I said, holding up a bright green translucent thing in a clear plastic box.

"It's supposed to feel amazing, though," she said. "According to the hype."

I pulled out another package, which from the picture appeared to contain a matched set of a blindfold and thong panties.

"Definitely not that," she said.

"Yeah, a bit boring," I said. "Although it could be kind of funny. 'Hello, everyone. I'm trying out this blindfold and I can say very definitely it is dark under here.' "

She laughed a little at that and threw the package back into the box. "How about this?" She broke the seal on another package and held up something curved and sleek hanging between two loops of black elastic. "It's a vibe controlled by an app. You'll have to download it."

I was already pulling out my phone from my leather jacket's inner pocket. I slid the jacket off and while I fussed with that Madison went over to her computer and fired up her video software.

"Hello and welcome to Madison's Mad World of Toys," I heard her say. "Where I'll be introducing you to new and exciting toys that are definitely for adults only. I'll be trying out each toy personally, sometimes with the help of a friend. Today we're exploring the V-Curve, a special vibe that a woman can wear under her clothes and which is controlled by a smartphone app."

I moved quietly to stand beside her desk, showing her my phone and giving her a thumbs-up. She held the toy in front of the camera on top of her monitor. "Apparently these adjustable elastic straps are supposed to hold it in place."

"They're like the ones you're supposed to adjust on airplane oxygen masks," I said.

"That," she said, with her eyebrow raised, "is my aforementioned friend."

"Adjust your own vibrator before helping others," I said, in my best imitation of a flight attendant voice, making her crack up a little.

She clicked pause on the recording. "You want to introduce yourself or stay anonymous?"

"Well, as our manager would say, helping out a friend with her sex toys is definitely 'on brand' for The Rough. But why don't you just say 'my friend Chino' and we can let people figure it out."

"Okay." She clicked the mouse again. "My friend Chino is going to use the app to control the vibrator. First, though, let me see if this thing fits."

She kept right on recording as she dropped her shorts. The camera couldn't see that—it could only see what was above the desk—but she bent over and put her feet through the loops, then wiggled it all upward. "Chino, would you get me a little dollop of lube?" She pointed back toward the pile of things we'd left on the couch. "Part of it's designed to go inside me."

"Glad to be of help." I tipped her head back and gave her a devouring sort of kiss, my hand slipping under the toy, teasing her, spreading her with two fingers and flicking her clit with a third. As I felt her swell, the same thing was happening in my own pants, as if we were connected. When she moaned into my mouth I slipped that finger into the sweet spot and let her go. "There. Plenty of lube."

She looked up at me, her cheeks flushed, her mouth slightly open like she wanted to say something but hadn't quite got the words for it yet. "Thanks," she finally said, and then resumed fitting the toy into place. *You're welcome, sweets. You're more than welcome.*

Raking her hand through her hair, she looked into the camera and tried to focus. "Well, it's in. Part of it's inside and part of it curves up to touch my clit. It's not the most comfortable while sitting in a chair but I could probably get used to it."

"How is it if you're walking around?" I asked.

"Let's test it."

She handed me another small digital camera on a strap. "Here, you wear it and follow me while I walk."

"Wear it?"

"You can put the strap around your head so wherever you look, the camera will record."

"All right."

Madison slipped her shorts back on while I strapped the camera to my head. I felt like a bit of a dork wearing it, but hey, she had just given me permission to stare at her beautiful ass. "You want to walk back and forth in the living room?"

"How about we walk down the block and back?" She slipped her feet into flip-flops by the door.

"I think this video thing is bringing out your exhibitionist side." I adjusted myself in my jeans before going out the door, wondering who was going to walk funnier, Maddie with her sex toy or me with a boner the size of Baja. I started the camera going as we went down the stairs to her driveway.

"Oh, hi, Maddie!" said a man in the front courtyard. He had a neatly groomed mustache and appeared to be bringing a tiny schnauzer in from a walk. I kept the camera focused on the dog, who happily came to sniff and lick my hand when I offered it. Probably tasted like Maddie's vagina; if so, the pup approved of it.

"Jim! Didn't realize you were home in the middle of the day."

"It's a Sunday, Maddie."

"Oh, that's right. I forgot."

"That's because you work too hard," Jim said. "I get up in the middle of the night sometimes, you know, dear, and I can see the glow of your computer screen and hear the *tap tap tap* of your nails on the keyboard."

"Um, yeah, work. In fact, we're in the middle of filming a vlog right now," Maddie explained. "Talk to you later, Jim?"

"Sure thing, dear. Don't let me interrupt."

I tried not to snicker as we walked away.

"What's so funny?" she asked.

"Oh, just, you know. He's taking his dog out for a walk, you're taking your sex toy out for a walk..."

She huffed and mock slapped me on the arm. "Okay, I guess let me walk ahead of you so you can film it."

"Sure thing, sweets."

I let her saunter ahead, staying focused on her ass. Fine. *Mm.*

She turned around to walk backward, saying to the camera, "It's interesting while walking. I can feel it but I think you're supposed to. Even if it didn't have the vibrating function, walking definitely provides a certain amount of stimulation."

She turned around and kept walking, setting a quicker pace now. We went to the end of the block and then turned around.

As we were walking back, I pulled my phone out of my jeans. "Let's see how easy it is to connect the devices now," I said. The app blinked green when it was connected. I filmed the control panel that appeared on the phone screen, or at least I hoped I did, and then I thumbed one of the sliders from left to right.

She let out a sudden squeak and whipped around. "Chino!"

"What? You said you wanted me to control it." I moved the slider further to the right. "How's that?"

Madison made a Y of her legs like a girl having to pee. "Can you wait until we get back ins—"

I flipped it all the way and she threw her head back and began to sink to her knees on the sidewalk. "Whoa, whoa, whoa," I said, dialing it back a little. "Come on, let's walk."

I took her by the arm, camera be damned, and walked her back to her place and up the stairs. I steered her to the couch.

"Okay, Maddie," I said, sitting across from her. "Why don't you tell the viewers what you're feeling when I do this?"

I eased the slider toward the right again and she sucked in a breath. "That's the clit vibe. It's much more intense than I was expecting for a battery-powered toy."

"And now?" I upped it again.

"The intensity goes up. If you're not careful I'll come from that in like two minutes."

"Okay." I lowered that slider and tried the next one. "And?"

"And, oh, God, the internal vibe just started. It's right on my G-spot."

"Huh, okay. So if this one does the clit"—I aimed the camera at the phone screen again while I manipulated the sliders—"and this one does the G-spot,"—I jumped it up momentarily and she squealed—"then what's the third one do?"

I began sliding it upward very slowly. She groaned. "*Ungh.* It starts to pulsate. Both parts of the vibrations together."

"Slowly?"

"Yeah."

I gradually moved that slider and it felt like I was controlling her breathing. Her breaths came faster and faster as I pushed it, then slowed if I reversed it. Ultimate control. My cock throbbed with no stimulation at all, other than the knowledge I had such command of her body.

I began to play the three sliders—and Madison—like a high-tech musical instrument, changing the combinations of sensation and listening to her moan, groan, gasp, and sigh.

"I'm so close now," she said breathily. "So close."

"Well, let's show the people what it does," I said, pushing all three controls to their max and making Madison scream. Her hips jerked, her head flew back and forth, and she kept her hands on the back of the couch as she rode out her climax. "I'd say it works just fine," I said, lowering the power again and coming closer, straddling her legs so I could zoom in on her face, which was now rosy and ecstatic-looking.

I turned the camera off and set it on the coffee table, with my phone still in my other hand. "I like this toy."

"You can buy one—"

"No no, sweets. Not that toy. You. You're my toy."

Her eyes looked huge as she opened them, trying to read the emotion on my face. I had put on the stone cold, faux-cruel expression. "You're my toy and I'm going to play with you, doll," I said, thumbing the control again.

"Oh, God," she whispered, every muscle tense. Seeing her like that, feeling the tension pouring off her in waves was making me hot as hell.

So was playing with her. It felt diabolical that I could make her come so easily, with just the flick of a finger. It made me feel like a god. How could anyone not be turned on by that? I dialed up the internal vibe all the way and then pulsed the clit slider by hand, flicking it up and down and making her hips pump in time.

"Oh, fuck, oh, fuck!" She reached for her crotch but quickly put her hands on the back of the couch again when I gave her a sharp glare. Wow. She was so deep under my command that I didn't even have to say anything. I only had to *think* it, to glance at her, and she not only knew right away what I meant, she obeyed.

Hot as fuck.

I pegged the controls again and she convulsed back against the couch, her eyes squeezed shut and her jaw clenched. She breathed in and out through her teeth until she peaked, letting loose a full-on cry from her throat.

Her voice was a little rough when she spoke next, as I dialed the power back down. "I . . . I . . . I need a break."

"Are you sure? I'm pretty sure you can take a lot more than this thing can dish out," I said, waving the phone across her vision.

"I g-guess so," she said, biting her lip.

"Come on, Maddie. You can't be in that much of a hurry to edit the video."

I saw her eyes flick toward the computer, though, and I realized that was exactly what she was thinking, that we should wrap this up so she could get to it.

Ha. Oh, no, sweets. "I'm not done playing with my toy yet." My voice was low. I began sliding the controls up and down randomly, sending pulses of pleasure and sensation through her in unpredictable patterns. When her cheeks were starting to look flushed again, I turned the camera back on.

"Tell the people what you're feeling," I said as I began moving the controls again.

"*Nngh.*" She whipped her hair forward as she tightened her abs and thighs, curling around the humming device in her shorts. "That's the clit vibe again, so intense. It's like being stung by the pleasure bees."

"The *pleasure bees*?" I repeated with a little laugh.

"Yeah. You'd know what I meant if you tried this yourself."

"Alas, I haven't got the right plumbing," I said, switching the controls again. "How about now?"

"*Mmm.* That's the G-spot vibe inside. It's like..." She closed her eyes and pressed her hands against her stomach. "Like..."

"Pleasure gophers? Pleasure piranhas?"

"No!" She started to laugh, though, at the same time she started to come, her laughs continuing loud and long as the orgasm swept through her. "Oh my God, Chino! *Ah ha ha!*"

I switched the camera off and pulled her up into a kiss, molding one hand around her ass as I ground my rock-hard erection against her and the toy. "Wow. That does feel like pleasure bees."

"Told you," she whispered breathily.

"You know what I want next?"

"Me?" She gripped my collarbones hopefully with her fingertips, as if she might be able to climb onto my dick.

"You," I said. "You seem really eager to fuck."

"That's because I am." Her eyes were wide and gorgeous and I seriously wondered what was wrong with me that I wasn't just going to plow into her like any red-blooded male should. A chuckle escaped my mouth and I felt another heady rush as I knew I was going to deny her again. "I love giving you pleasure," I said, upping the vibrations again. "But your hole's stuffed right now. I'm going to use the other one."

A moment of surprise shone in her eyes and then she said, "All right."

"*All right?* What kind of answer is that?" My twisted side

came all the way to the fore and I gave it free rein. "Say 'yes, sir.'"

Her mouth fell open—in surprise, not protest—hanging there for a moment before the soft syllables slipped free: "Yes, sir."

I gave her cheek a light slap. "That's for being surprised. The sooner you get used to reality, the better."

Her eyebrow went up. "Reality?"

I ground against her again and the added pressure on the still-vibrating toy made her moan. "That I'm in charge."

This time the "yes, sir" came out quick and easy, and that made my blood surge even more, not only because I wanted to stick my cock in someone—hell, that's me 24-7—but because I felt the way she was softening, opening, blossoming into the surrender she had been holding back from ever since the party. *That's my girl.*

"This'll be the third time you've more or less asked me to fuck you and I'll have said no," I commented as I pushed her back a half step, my hands on her hips telling her to freeze where she was. I pulled her shorts down to the middle of her thighs, exposing the toy strapped to her. I admired the view, then rucked up her shirt so that her tits were staring at me, too, curvaceous and soft. Her body was always sexy as hell but somehow her clothes exposing her that way was far hotter than when she was just plain naked. "I'd say that's a pattern, wouldn't you?"

"Yes, sir," she said, sounding a bit plaintive.

I laughed my evil laugh. "Your ass will satisfy me for now."

The lube was still on the coffee table with the other stuff. I circled around behind her to pick up the little bottle and then leaned her forward until she was bent over. With her feet a foot apart she was so limber she could put her palms flat on the floor—a beautiful pose but not practical for fucking purposes.

"Hands on the back of the couch. How many times have you come so far?" I asked, marveling at the desire slicking her folds where the toy disappeared into her.

"Um, five? I think?"

I gave her a slap on that beautiful, round ass. "Answer properly when you're about to get fucked."

"Y-yes, sir. Four or five, sir. I've lost count."

"Better." I used my fingers to spread her natural juices around, not to get her ready but just to feel her, smell her. "I take it you've been fucked in the ass before."

"Yes, sir. Um."

"Um?" I warned.

She mumbled the next thing, as if embarrassed to be saying it. Embarrassed? Brazen, bold Maddie?

I gave her another sharp downward slap on the ass. "Speak properly when you address me. Repeat that. Clearly."

She took a breath before answering. "Never by someone as big as you. Sir."

I took that as my cue to drop trou and stroke myself a little. I love the feeling of a hard-on, especially when it's about to get taken care of. "I'm not particularly big."

"For a porn star, no. For a human being, yes." She turned her head to look over her shoulder at me. "Sir."

"Are you telling me to take it easy on you, sweets?" I ran the head of my cock up and down her silky thigh with my hand. "Because I'm not good at getting hints."

She swallowed. "No, sir."

"If you want me to take it easy on you, it's on you to say so, you hear me, girl?" I uncapped the lube and drizzled some on her rosy hole, massaging it gently. "It's on me to decide whether to go easy or not, but it's on you to tell me what you're feeling. All right?"

"All right, sir." She braced herself with her hands against

the couch, letting her head hang as I worked the tip of my index finger into the tiny opening.

Lube, work, lube, work. Eventually I got in past the first knuckle but it took time. "I'd tell you to relax but I kinda like that you're so tight. I'm going to work this ass until I'm balls deep, sweets. Even if it takes all day." I gave an evil laugh as that little speech only made her clench even more before she started really trying to let go.

Once I had worked up to drilling her with that finger, twisting it as I pushed it in and pulled it out, she started to moan. The vibrator was still on low and I could feel it in my whole hand. She moaned again as I slid my finger in more quickly this time. *Oh, yes, sweets, you make me feel like no one else.*

"I'm going to work in a second finger now," I told her.

"Yes, sir," came the answer.

"Mm, yes, that's my toy." When her voice sounded like that, like her answer came from deep inside her, so sweet and hungry, so at peace with her role, the twisted devil inside me wanted to wrap her up and never let her go. "Give yourself to me. That's my girl."

I hadn't meant it literally, but she pushed back, driving herself onto the wedge of my two fingers. Awesome and gorgeous. I dripped lube onto the trough of my fingers and fucked her slowly with them, delivering as much of the fragrant, slippery goop into her as possible.

I was trying to get a third finger into the mix when she raised her voice again, hesitantly this time. "Sir?"

"Yes, sweets."

"I... You don't have to do that much. I mean... I'm ready for you." Her head was hanging down but I could hear the words quite clearly.

"Are you sure, Maddie? Because you're still tight as hell."

"I know. I—" She hurriedly murmured the next bit and this

time I didn't hesitate, I gave her seven, eight, nine, ten hard spanks on her buttocks, making her cry out and yelp in pain and surprise.

"I warned you about that," I said. "Now say it again."

Again she took a breath, two, before she spoke, but the words came slow and clear: "I like it to hurt a little. I like the ache."

"Ohhhhh, very nice, sweets. Now that's a truly lovely thing to hear. Why'd you try to hide it from me?" I caressed the reddened flesh of her butt cheeks, soothing her. "You like the ache, huh. That means you like it slow, but deep."

She nodded.

"Your reward for telling me is you'll get it exactly the way you like it. Let's move. Either all the way over the back of the couch or to your bedroom, if you've got a bed a good height for this."

"My bed's a good height for this."

"Come on, then. Let's go."

She stood up straight and started to pull her shorts up.

"Uh uh, sweets. Leave it all hanging out for me. Take baby steps if you have to. I'm in no hurry." In fact I hung back and watched as she made her way across the great room. She turned and looked back at me when she reached the hallway.

I made sure I had my phone and the lube and prepared myself for heaven on earth.

CHAPTER SIX

MADISON

Chino's voice was soothing and winding me up at the same time. "Just relax," he was saying, and I was trying to do just that, facedown on my bed, telling every muscle in my body to let go, but I couldn't really when his red-hot cock was poking me in the thigh like a brand and I knew the next place it was going to poke was my ass.

The last time I'd been ass-fucked was by a really sweet guy I'd tried to date named Jerry. He had all kinds of sex fantasies he was continually surprised I was willing to try out—butt sex being one of the main ones—but he'd been so timid and worried about his own kinks that sometimes I had to remind him it was his idea. I'd dominated him a couple of times, but his unenthusiastic obedience had made it not that much fun for me—and on the other hand when he was in charge it was like he didn't know what to do or say.

Chino was certainly not having that problem. "Reach back and spread 'em," he said. "Just because it's hot."

Yes, it was. *Nngh*, whenever he said something like that the fires in me burned like crazy. I wondered what my ass looked like when I was ready to be fucked. The skin was so slippery it was hard for me to hold on. He slid his cock up and down in the valley between my butt cheeks and then put his fingers into me again.

"Okay, sweets. Hold on to the bed now, because the ride's about to start."

I took two handfuls of the bedspread, breathing hard in anticipation as the crinkle of the condom wrapper reached my ears. Then I heard cloth rustle—was he getting all the way undressed? Yes. I felt bare skin along my back as he lay down on top of me, kissing my neck and rutting.

The rocking motions of his hips gradually brought the spongy head of his cock to center on my rear hole. He knocked on the back door firmly but gently, smoothly, until the muscles gave in and the angle was just right and *oh*.

The first inch of him had gone in, and he held in place a moment before pumping gradually. "Holy fuck you're tight. Is this the ache you like, sweets?"

"Yes, sir." My own voice sounded strange to me, low and guttural and flat against the bedspread.

"Open up a little more for me now."

He pushed in another inch, still rocking and rolling his hips and spreading the ache from there all through my legs and extremities. So good. When anal is done badly it can make you swear it off forever. When it's done right, though, it's like a perfect delicacy, rare and precious and memorable.

"How's that, sweets?"

"Good. Oh, fucking good," I said, melting into the sensation.

"Good," he said, and then I felt him shift to one side.

He'd reached for his phone. "I wonder how many times you'll come during this," he said with a casual, offhand manner that was borderline cruel. It made me feel so deliciously dirty to be treated like a plaything by him.

As the power on the vibrations inside and out went up, he began to thrust into me harder. The full length of him driving deep pained me sharply for a moment before it was obliterated by the pleasure vibrations. And then the orgasm started building, this one from deep in my bones, shaking me like an earthquake. I screamed into the bedspread, beating my fists, barely even feeling how hard he was pounding me now. His fingers gripped my hips so hard they might bruise but all I could feel was wave after wave of release.

And it didn't stop. The harder he fucked me, the more it multiplied the vibrations, like the heavy tide coming in, wave piling on top of wave, pounding against the shore. I ran out of screams and panted as I rode them out.

"You. Feel. Amazing." He grunted between deep thrusts. "I can barely hold back."

"Don't hold back," I heard myself say.

I earned another sharp slap for that one. "Who's in charge here, Madison?"

"You. You, sir," I said quickly.

"Maybe I should just pull out now, go take care of myself. My right hand does a pretty good job of wringing the sperm right out of me, you know. Years of practice."

"No! No, please, sir." Don't ask why, but the thought that he'd finish himself off instead of inside me just broke me, like the threat of taking away a child's favorite toy. "I promise I'll be good. I promise."

"Oh, Maddie, you're very good," he murmured, nosing

through my hair as he thrust deep again. And then again on each word: "Very, very, very good."

His approval was like a new drug, a new sensation, a new setting on the vibe, kicking off a new wave of pleasure and setting me to screaming again. This time he joined me with a roar, coming at last and continuing to thrust as he milked every ounce from his climax. Chino seemed to know how to maximize his pleasure and I lay as still as I could to let him have his way.

Then he slumped atop me and the vibrations finally stopped as he switched off the app. After having them on for so long it felt weird to be without them now.

What didn't feel weird at all was Chino on me like a blanket, skin against skin, comforting and protecting me at the same time. "Mmmmmm." I wasn't ready for words yet, but my whole body was humming with pleasure and so humming I could do.

"Mm-hm," he agreed. "You okay?"

"Mm. Fantastic. Terrific. Wonderful."

"I know I am," he said, and I could hear the smirk. "But really. How are you?"

"I'm fine."

"See if you still say that when you can barely sit later," he said and pulled gently free. "Bathroom?"

"That way," I pointed toward the hallway, aiming my finger to the right. "I'll come with you."

"Okay." He stood up, one hand on his junk, keeping the full condom in place, the other hand reaching toward me.

I tried to stand up but my legs weren't ready for that and I sank down onto the carpet next to the bed. "Wow, jelly legs. I haven't been fucked that hard since college."

"Stay there," he said, bending down to plant a kiss on my forehead.

When he returned from the bathroom he had a couple of warm, wet washcloths and a towel. He spread the towel on the floor and I scooted onto it.

"Lie down." He knelt and eased the toy out of me, detaching the straps and setting it aside. "Got to take good care of my toy," he said, and wiped my pussy softly with a cloth. I felt as warm inside as out. He put one of my legs on his shoulder and continued cleaning my ass and folds. "You can take care of the vibrator."

"Yes, sir," I said, to see how he'd react to me saying it now that the scene was over. I knew how I felt about it: strangely attached, like I wasn't ready for that security blanket feeling to end.

He seemed to feel the same. "Good girl," he said, and knelt down to lick my pussy like a lioness licking her cub. The sensation was amazing, even though I didn't want to come again. And the feeling of being cared for was even more amazing. He lifted his head, his dark hair hanging in his eyes as he looked up at me from between my knees. "There you go. Nice and clean."

"Thank you, sir." I was definitely going to have some stuff to tell Gwen after this. What was happening to me? Whatever it was, I liked it. But was I still going to feel that way after he left and I returned to my senses? *How about worrying about how you feel now instead of how you might feel later?*

Right then I wanted to curl up with him and go to sleep...except that I really wanted to get to reviewing and editing the video. I wasn't going to do that with him here, though.

A phone began ringing from up on the bed. "Is that yours or mine?"

"Mine." He climbed up, looked at it, and switched it off.

"Who was that?"

"Nobody important," he said, too quickly, and I knew he was hiding something. Huh. I wondered what he could be trying to keep secret from me. A girlfriend? Wouldn't be the first time, but I had thought Chino was better than that. The nagging feeling about how he had brushed off my question about where he lived resurfaced, too. I didn't even know his real name.

The fact that the next thing he said was that he was going to leave only deepened my suspicion. "I'm gonna get out of your hair now," he said. "Let you get to editing that video. I know you're anxious to."

He knows me that well, already? But I wasn't ready for him to leave yet and if there was some other girl or three out there, I wanted to keep him for myself a little while longer. "But I'm starving now, and I'm going to order a pizza from Vito's. I can never eat a whole one myself, so if you could stick around just a little longer—"

"All right. Pizza and then I'll scram." He gave me a quick, affectionate kiss on the cheek. Then he opened his mouth as if to say something, thought better of it, and kissed me hard and passionately again instead. I'd confront him about my suspicions later. Right now everything was too sweet for me to let bitterness in.

* * *

CHINO

I took the stairs from Madison's door down to the driveway two at a time. As I unlocked my car door I caught a glimpse of something—a flicker of sun glare reflecting off the side window of a car parked across the street. I slipped my sunglasses on not because of the glare but because I'd been coached that type of light reflection usually came off a camera lens as the camera was lifted or put down. Paparazzi? If they'd followed me to Madison's they'd been waiting a long time for me to come out. It didn't seem likely. The tabloids weren't really interested in me. Axel and Mal got the brunt of the attention both by dint of being frontmen and also the high profile of who they dated. I had let our manager fix me up with a fashion model from time to time to attend awards ceremonies and premieres, but I didn't really draw press. They were rarely interested in talking to the drummer. You might think, given the band's image, that they would be sniffing around us for a sex scandal but if anything it was the opposite. As if by being in-your-face kinky we took all the fun out of exposing our sex lives. Maybe my luck had finally run out on that score. I decided to cross the street and find out if it was my imagination or if there really was a paparazzo there.

I know that's not what I should've done. Our band manager, Christina, always said not to encourage them or confront them. But I've never been good at following orders.

There was a guy in the car. He looked suddenly worried and rolled up his window, but he hadn't started the car yet by the time I knocked on the glass. "Hey."

"Uh, hey," he said. "Can I help you with something?"

"Maybe." I could see the camera on the seat next to him. "You better be careful with that thing."

"Oh, this is just, um, I wasn't—"

I suddenly recognized him. "Isn't it a little weird for the editor of the arts page to be on photo assignment?" I couldn't quite remember his name but the band had met him more than once at press events.

"Er, uh, did Madison send you out here to beat me up or something?"

Wait, what? Did Madison have a problem with this guy? It occurred to me then that the guy didn't recognize me. I flexed a little muscle and looked at him coolly over the tops of my sunglasses. "I think you better move along."

"Um. Yeah." He started the engine. I stepped out of the way so he could pull out and he nearly cut off a minivan full of Little Leaguers. As the mom driving swerved around him I heard her shouting things Little Leaguers definitely should not hear. He sped away after her like a dog with its tail between its legs.

I got into my own car and called Madison from the road. I got her voice mail. "Hey, sweets, I know you're probably editing, but I wanted you to know I chased a guy away from your door. He was using a long lens camera and I thought maybe he was a typical paparazzi type, but I'm pretty sure he's the arts editor from *LA Newsday* or one of the papers here. I don't think he knew who I was so I think he was watching you. Kinda freaky. I ran him off but call me ASAP if there's actually something freaky going on and you need to get away."

I wondered if he'd been there when we went out for our "walk" with the vibrator and I hadn't noticed. Or had he showed up later? I felt stupid for almost making her come while we were outside. Maybe that had been riskier than I'd thought.

Although, risky in what way? If the guy was some kind of stalker, was that different from the risk of, what, getting caught doing something sexy? I wasn't afraid to get caught and I don't think Maddie was, either. I put it on my list of things to talk about next time I saw her.

Then I tried calling my sister back, but I got her voice mail, too. I should have just called while Madison and I had been waiting for the pizza, and asked her not to eavesdrop. Would she do it? I wondered. I really didn't want her to overhear what I had going on there. Flor's message ended and I didn't leave one of my own.

CHAPTER SEVEN

MADISON

If I thought things were moving fast with Chino, what with the party having been a Friday, the house hunting on Saturday, and the vibrator testing on Sunday, they were about to start moving even faster. On Monday Sakura called with a proposal.

"I have something you might be interested in." Her voice was always a kind of purr, perfect for a sultry voiceover, even when she wasn't insinuating something erotic. Although in this case she was. "Private party in Palm Springs this weekend. Very exclusive."

She and I had known each other for a couple of years, having crisscrossed on everything from fetish modeling gigs to her being a loyal customer when I worked at the store and she was giving professional domination a try. The first time she'd shown up at the Governor's Club I hadn't been surprised to see her there. What had surprised me was that instead of being some elderly executive's arm candy, she'd been invited to join as a full member by her old college roommate: Ricki Hamilton herself. "More exclusive than TGC?" I asked, using our code for the Governor's Club.

"Yes, just five or six couples and a triad. Some friends of mine. They're renting a place for the weekend. Cost is a share of the rent and kick in for food if you feel like it."

I was making dinner at the time, trying to sauté kale with shallots but it just didn't seem to want to cook down. "This weekend?"

"Yes. Ricki had to go up to Silicon Valley for business meetings, so she and Axel backed out. To keep it affordable for everyone it's really best to have all the bedrooms filled. I thought you and Chino might enjoy it."

I upped the flame under the pan. "What made you think that?"

"Oh, come on, Maddie, you were melted on him like cheese on a burger Friday night."

"Yeah, thanks to you, you instigator," I joked.

She cackled. "That's me. Both exciting and inciting. Aren't you seeing him now? I thought for sure that was the start of something beautiful."

"I...we're still feeling each other out," I said, though the feeling that swept through me as I said it was a shivery ghost of the deep, deep backdoor orgasm Chino had given me.

"I thought it might be good for you guys to get away from TGC for a bit. You know."

I pushed the kale back and forth in the pan with a wooden spatula. "I know. So I won't have to feel like an employee; is that it?"

"That's exactly it. Although correct me if I'm wrong, I've been feeling like the club has become a lot more like a good time for the employees than it used to be?"

"That's true," I said. "Now that there are a lot more members our age, and they're all Gwen and Ricki's friends and acquaintances, it feels a lot more like, well, like a club. I like that but at the same time I'm not sure it's the best thing."

"Why?"

"Oh, just the whole professional distance thing." But honestly was there ever truly any professional distance between the hosts and our employers? "Anyway. You're right. It would be nice maybe to get away with him. Who are you bringing?"

"I've got a friend I do performances with, Helene. I think you've met her before? We might come do an opening scene, or maybe we'll just play together. We're still negotiating."

"Makes sense. Would it be all right if we just came in for Saturday night? I'm not sure I'm ready to spend a whole weekend with people I don't know that well." Or with Chino, truthfully. I was feeling my way along a tightrope where if I went too fast, I might get hurt, but if I went too slowly I might lose him. The kale still seemed rather stiff and tough. I tried drizzling some more oil into the pan.

"It'd be great if you guys wanted to come in for Saturday. The official party will start around sundown, of course, but people will be playing whenever the mood strikes."

"I'll ask him if he wants to go. But let me ask you something else while we're on the subject of TGC."

"Sure."

"Did you know about the club before Ricki told you about it?"

"I knew that something like it existed. I had no idea it was in Ricki's basement."

"Hm. There's a guy in the press who's been sniffing around me lately. I've been trying to work out the best way to tell Gwen and Ricki."

"Oh, honey, they have a PR firm at their beck and call if necessary."

"I know, but the PR firm would have to know what they were dealing with, and currently the club is still a secret from everyone except the direct household staff. I don't want them to fire me just because a reporter is inappropriately interested in me."

"Tell Schmitt and he'll scare him off. He'll put the fear of God into him."

"Here's the thing, though. The guy isn't afraid of Schmitt."

"But he should be?"

"He's dumb enough to not know what's good for him," I said. "But Schmitt's a target, too. I guess I should just tell Gwen and Ricki everything I know so far."

"What do you know?"

"This member of the press—he tried to inappropriately get me into bed a while back. And now he's sniffing around me and Schmitt and I'm afraid he'll figure out about the club, basically."

Sakura sighed. "Ricki's out of town this week. You know they won't discuss the club by phone at all. Ask them to meet next week. Maybe by then you'll know more."

"True. Maybe I should voluntarily recuse myself from the next party? Throw him off the scent?"

"Maybe." Sakura's voice became distant. "I'm texting you the info about the weekend party. Talk to Chino and let me know, okay?"

"I will. I'm talking to him tonight about helping me with another video review."

"Is that gig working out well?" Sakura asked.

"I uploaded the first one today and they really liked it, so . . . so far, so good," I said. "They want me to get a backlog of three in queue before the first one launches."

"Fun." Her voice was a pleasant burr. "I'm looking forward to seeing it."

I got off the phone and finished making dinner, then sat on the couch with Morris and ate while watching clips of Jimmy Fallon and celebrity lip synch battles from the Internet. And yes, I wished Chino was there. But every instinct in me said I needed to slow down. I'd seen him three days in a row. If nothing else, my body needed a rest.

But I didn't want to rest. Even thinking about him idly made heat start to rise.

Next thing I knew my phone was in my hand.

"Madison." He sounded delighted. "How are you?"

"Sore as hell, thanks to you."

"Excellent. That means you're thinking of me."

I squirmed on the couch. "Yeah. Meanwhile, I sent in the V-Curve footage and write-up today and they loved it. They said they want to get three vlogs in queue before they launch the first one, so I should do two more ASAP."

"By ASAP, do you mean tonight?"

"Well—"

"Because I could come over."

His hunger seemed to pour right through the phone and my own surged to meet it, obliterating common sense. "How fast can you get here?"

"Oh, you want me that bad?"

"Yes, and you know it."

He chuckled.

A flicker of self-preservation shone through. "But I'm sore. I... thought I should warn you."

"Oh, I bet you are. I really jackhammered your ass."

"This time they want me to review a kit a sponsor sent."

"There better not be a giant butt plug in the kit, then," he said.

I laughed. "I think it's a beginner flogger set."

"Oh, much better. I'll be there in an hour, okay, sweets?"

I rushed into a whirlwind of cleaning and tidying. He'd been here just yesterday, so it wasn't like he hadn't seen the place, but I suddenly wanted to make sure not only that the area we were filming in was neatened, but that the dishes were all cleaned up and the cooking smells were aired out. I lit a sandalwood candle in a jar and moved it to a shelf so Morris couldn't bat the flame.

My editors wanted some variation, so every vlog didn't look like it was in exactly the same place. Maybe this time the bedroom would be better?

I rearranged the lights so that the bed would make a good spot for filming. I lay a maroon suede hide over the bedspread to give us a solid background color. I was just fluffing the pillows when the doorbell rang.

It was Chino. "Come look what I did to the bedroom," I said, pulling him into the house. "I think we should do this one in there."

He pulled me into an embrace before we got across the great room. "Hey."

"Hey?" I gave him a quizzical smile.

"You skipped the hello kiss again." He locked his hands behind my back.

I blushed. "Oh."

"*Tsk.* I'll have to punish you for that." He leaned in to kiss me and bent me back as his mouth met mine aggressively. I resisted instinctually but he did not let up, one hand making its way into my hair and trapping me as his lips and tongue ravished mine. This was no coaxing, teasing kiss. This was Chino taking what he wanted and sending me instantly into subspace, my knees weakening.

While one hand stayed in my hair, ensuring that my mouth

could not escape his, the other snaked down my front and his knuckles rubbed up and down my mound. Could he tell how instantly inflamed I had become? I levered my hips to give him better pressure against my trapped clit. On the next downward pass of his hand he reached under my sundress and pulled it upward, then dug his fingers under the waistband of my panties.

His fingers found wetness equal to his tongue and I whimpered, wordlessly begging him to fondle me, fingerfuck me . . . anything.

Two fingers slid in and his palm vibrated against my clit. My knees couldn't hold me anymore but I barely registered that we were sinking to the floor. My entire universe was impaled on his tongue and fingers, the only gravity that mattered the weight of his body beside me. I don't think I'd ever had a lover who was as good with his hands as Chino.

He was pushing me so quickly toward orgasm I thought I was about to set a new record. Two minutes? Definitely not three . . . But then he jerked his hand free and I cried out in loss and need. "No!"

"Yes," he murmured against my cheek. "Tell me how much you want me, sweets."

"Fuck, Chino! I . . . I . . . need . . ."

"Told you you needed to be punished. Well, maybe if you're good from here on out I'll let you come later."

"Yes, sir!" His dominance closed around me like a fist. "Whatever you say, sir."

His smile was brilliant and devious. "Exactly right. Now, what do you need to do to get ready for this video?"

"Oh. Um." My loins were on fire, my clit throbbing, aching with the need to come. But I forced myself to focus. "I should do my makeup."

He slapped me lightly on the thigh. "Get to it, then."

I hurried into the bathroom with my makeup kit and then stood there with my legs shaking. I wanted him so badly I could barely stand.

I stripped off my clothes, washed my hands and between my legs, then started on my face. My hands were unsteady, though, and I couldn't do my eyeliner without getting it everywhere.

I sat down on the toilet and took some deep breaths. When was the last time I'd felt lust so strong that my entire body shook with it? Never, maybe. I stole a peek through the cracked open door into the bedroom.

Chino was setting up the computer and cameras. He was whistling merrily to himself.

I grinned. He really enjoyed torturing me like this. He was having a blast.

And so was I, if I was honest with myself. That felt special and rare.

Okay, Madison. Get your face on and get ready for whatever he's going to dish out next.

* * *

CHINO

"Okay, Maddie, should we do the full unboxing of the kit?"

"Sure," she said, kneeling at the center of the bed. She looked perfect against the earthy color. She was naked and wearing a set of heavy glasses that doubled as a camera, making her look like the sexiest librarian you can imagine. She faced the camera on the side table first. "Hi, I'm Madison and welcome to my toy reviews. Today we're doing a product placement."

"Is that what the kids are calling it these days?" I joked.

Maddie made a face. "That'd be funnier if it was a dildo."

"What is it, then?"

"It's some kind of BDSM for Beginners kit. Let's find out what's in the box, shall we?" She tore into one of the packages we'd ignored yesterday and pulled out a toy with gray leather tails. "First up... nice flogger." She ran her fingers through it. "Very nice. And here's another one just like it but suede and... aha, a third one made of rubber." She swished them around in the air. "And under that?"

She pulled up a set of Velcro wrist straps and ankle straps. "I sense a theme. It used to be that all sex toys were either black or pink. Now everything's gray."

Next came two short gray cylinders with eye hooks at each end. She quickly figured out they were portable expandable spreader bars and how to extend them to their full length, about three feet.

"And... oh, of course," She pulled a gray thong panty from the bottom of the box.

I slipped the camera from her face and put it onto my own. "Okay, sweets, let's see you wear the thong."

People think it's sexy watching a woman undress. That's nothing compared to the way Madison looked putting one pointed foot through the thong, then the other, and shimmying it up her thighs and over her hips. The lacy gray strip almost disappeared between the globes of her ass. It looked enticing on camera, but the camera couldn't capture the way my blood surged, the way my hands itched to touch her, the way I wanted to pin her down and possess every inch of her. She lay back on the bed like a classic pinup girl, full-bodied, luscious, glorious. Knowing that she'd obey my every command made the sight even hotter.

I pulled the box off the bed so it wouldn't be in the shot and realized she had left something in the bottom. Weird. She must have missed it. I plucked the last gray item out: a blindfold with elastic straps.

I stretched it out with my hands. "Maddie, come here."

She looked up and froze, an *oh no* look caught in her eyes. Because she'd made a mistake and forgot the last thing?

I tried to smooth it over. "One more thing. Or should we save it for later?"

"Yes, please," she said, her voice rich and sweet with submission and relief. I was very conscious that this was all being captured on video. Maybe she just didn't want to stop to explain what was going on.

"All right," I said, going with the flow. I set the blindfold aside. "Why don't we try getting you into these spreader cuffs?"

I encouraged her to lie facedown and then spread-eagled her across the bed with her wrists locked to the ends of one of the expandable rods, and her ankles to the other. She made a giant X, her rump an inviting target smack in the middle.

Smack in the middle. "You'll have to tell the viewers how each of these floggers feels," I said. "I think we should start with the suede one."

"Yes, sir," she said, craning her neck to watch me twirl it in the air. The handle was about six inches long and the suede tails were maybe a foot long at most. I gave her a swat with it. "Well?"

"Hardly feels like anything."

"Really? How about now?" I put more *oomph* into the downward stroke. She flinched but then said, "I suppose it's nice for a warmup, but it doesn't hurt at all."

"Let's see how it feels after a while." I began flogging her steadily, alternating swipes at her right cheek with her left, crisscrossing in an infinite loop—no, really, the motion traced the infinity symbol in the air. My patience was finite, though. "Your skin is looking nice and pink now," I said.

"The suede feels almost soothing, like some kind of exotic massage treatment."

"Massage. I like that idea," I said and rubbed my hands up and down her reddened skin.

"Oooh, now I feel it a little," she said.

"You should. There's still faint marks on your butt from the other night. Let's try the leather one next." I held it up so the camera could get a good look at it.

The sound it made when it hit her flesh was sharper, louder than the suede, and the sound she made was, too. She yelped but then settled down as I moved into the same crisscrossing rhythm, hitting her as lightly as I could at first. I gradually increased the pressure, the smack increasing in volume the harder I plied it. Finally I switched to snapping it like a towel, and she screeched on each one of those. A few welts began to come up where the snaps had caught her and I ran my palms over the spots before digging my fingers in.

"Now I'm really feeling it," she said with a moan, wiggling her ass in my hands.

"I think a couple of these welts might bruise a little, too," I added. "But if I hadn't really snapped it at the end there you'd have no marks at all."

"Good to know," she said. Then she let out a breath. "The rubber one last?"

"Yep. You ready?"

"As I'll ever be."

"Okay, folks watching at home . . . " I tested the rubber one on the underside of my forearm and whistled in appreciation at the instant welts that showed up. "Can you guys see that? And it stings like a motherfucker. Hey, am I allowed to say 'motherfucker' on this video?"

"I'm pretty sure if you're allowed to show my boobs you're allowed to say anything you want," Madison said with a laugh.

"So are you," I replied and then gave her a sharp smack with the rubber tails.

"Oh, fuck!" she cried.

"Like I said." I swatted her again and her head snapped back.

"Ow!"

"Ow? You make it sound like it hurts," I joked.

"You weren't kidding when you said it stings like a motherfucker!"

I gave her a third swipe and she began to pant, saying, "Okay, you know what? I'm not sure the people who made this 'beginner' kit knew what that thing feels like, because if you didn't know better and you started with that you might think 'nope nope nope, I'm not a masochist after all.' "

"Is it that bad?"

"It burns. It really burns. Maybe it's just me but it's not my favorite sensation all on its own."

I massaged her buttocks then, soothing her. "Well, that's useful to know." I meant for me, but it was probably good for the viewers watching at home to know, too.

I unstrapped her from the spreader bars. "Slide down. Put your feet on the floor and lean on the bed on your hands."

She did. Was her obeying me ever going to be less than utterly thrilling? I hoped not. It was one of the best feelings in the world.

I picked up the blindfold then and slid it over her head, covering her eyes and tamping down her hair.

"Chino," she said, but then she didn't say anything else.

I put my hand on her back. "You got something to tell me, sweets?"

She shook her head and I wondered what was going on in her mind. Maybe she didn't want to have to say the word "no" to me?

I lay the three floggers across her bare back as if she were a display table and filmed a panning shot. Then I pulled them aside. "I'm going to flog your back now," I said.

She said nothing, just put her head down in preparation. I could see the tension in her shoulders though, as she steeled herself.

I started with the suede and watched that tension go out of her as she realized, *oh, it's the soft one.* She realized she could take it, that she even liked it, and soon she was rocking side to side with soft moans as I whipped her into a sensual haze.

Then I switched to the leather one without breaking rhythm and she gasped, tensed all over again, and then went through a couple of waves of starting to relax into it only to tense up again suddenly each time I changed the pressure or angle of my stroke, gasping and flinching.

She thinks I'm going to switch to the rubber one without warning her, I realized. In fact, I was considering it. It was logically the next thing to do in the scene. If this were a porno movie that would have been the point of the earlier segment where we tested it out, right? The here-comes-the-one that really *really* hurts.

But this wasn't a porno movie—not exactly—and this wasn't just some actress. This was Madison. And I'd like to think I wasn't that stupid.

I ramped down the intensity and speed of the blows, slowing gradually, and saw that instead of ramping down with me she was getting more and more keyed up, her breathing quick and her shoulders shaking with anticipation.

With fear.

I turned the camera off, set the glasses aside, and closed the laptop on the side table. I laid my hand gently on the spot in the middle of her shoulder blades. I could feel her heartbeat and panic trying to rise. "Breathe, Maddie. I'm here."

"Oh, God," she said, struggling to contain herself, swallowing hard.

"You're so good. You look beautiful," I said, trying to give her some positive emotions. Did she think I was punishing her? That wasn't the vibe I was trying for at all.

It didn't help. She clearly thought I was just pausing to build her up to something terrible. "Oh, God," she said again. "Oh, no."

I knew she was freaking out and I didn't want that. The question was whether I should end the scene instantly, or if I should ramp it down slowly to a close. Sometimes too sudden an ending was traumatic, too, like yanking somebody with an injury out of a hole. Sometimes it was better to ease them out. I put my hands on her shoulders again, massaging firmly. "Breathe." I squeezed her tense traps as she exhaled, then worked my thumbs under her shoulder blades as she took another breath in. "Breathe."

She listened to me. She did as I said. *Oh, Maddie, you beauty, you angel.*

When she was breathing calmly on her own I kissed her on the back of her neck, rolled her onto her back, and slid the blindfold off. She opened her eyes, blinked like she was seeing light for the first time, and then I kissed her on the lips. "All done," I whispered, and kissed her again.

Her return kiss was sudden, passionate, almost desperate, and her arms wrapped around me like I was rescuing her from the depths of a dark, dangerous hole.

I kissed her and held her and rocked her. Some of her gasps for breath sounded like sobs and her cheeks were wet.

Oh, gorgeous, oh, sweetness, don't cry, don't cry. Don't you know Daddy loves you?

The bottom dropped out from under me as that thought rocketed through my brain. Now wasn't the time to drop a bomb like that on her. Time to show her how I felt instead of saying something she might not take the right way. I slid a hand between her legs and encountered the rough lace of the thong. I'd forgotten about the thong. "Tell me what you want, sweets."

She made an inquisitive noise and opened her eyes.

"You've been very good. A very good girl. Tell me what you want as a reward."

She blinked for a moment. "Can I ask for anything?"

"Anything short of my car," I said. "I need that to get around."

That made her smile. "Dork. You know what I mean."

"Do I? Come on, Maddie. When a dom asks a question sometimes it's because we really want to see what kind of answer you'll give."

"You know what I really want, though," she said, biting her lip.

"Hm, yeah, that would be, a top reporter position at the political news desk at the *LA Times,* world peace, and the best cheeseburger in Southern California. How's that for a guess?"

"You left your cock off the list," she pointed out.

"Well now, I wasn't going to presume." The piece of me in question was straining against my jeans so the reason I'd left it off the list wasn't because I wasn't in the mood. But I hadn't been sure she would be, after all that. "Is that what you want? Is there somewhere special you want it?"

She squirmed a little in my arms. "You know exactly where I want it. But…you seem to be saving it. I don't want to push."

"Maddie, listen to me. When the genie comes out of the bottle and grants you a wish, don't mess around. You have to just go for it. What I want most is the truth, not for you to try to figure out what answer I want you to give. If you want me to fuck you, P-I-V style, now's the time to play that card. If there's something you want even more than that, though, say that instead."

She mulled that over for a few seconds. "I don't know . . . "

"Then that's a no." I kissed her on the forehead. "At least that's what I've been taught. If she doesn't give you an enthusiastic yes when you offer cock, that's a definite no."

"It's not that I don't want you. I do! I'm just . . . my head's all a jumble."

I wondered if it was the same jumble as it had been during the paddling scene in the dungeon. I bet it was. "I know, sweets, I know, which is why we're talking about it instead of me just flattening you to the bed and fucking you all the way to Long Beach." I kissed her again.

"But that does sound kind of good," she murmured. And then she ran a hand up my thigh and discovered how hard I was. "I can't leave you like this. My pride won't let me."

"I think you could do with an orgasm or two to clear your head, too," I said. "Here you go, my girl, roll over, on your face. Get a hand under there so you can finger yourself. We're going to have the world's quickest quickie pseudosex."

"Pseudosex?"

"Yes." I eased the thong off her and then grabbed the bottle of lube she'd set on the side table. I drizzled it at the base of her spine and the settled my cock between her ass cheeks. "How fast can you come? Because I'm going to be done in five minutes, tops."

"It won't take me that long."

"Then come as many times as you can, and that's an order." I began to rut against her. Fuck, that felt good, her curves squeezing sensually and the hardness of her tailbone meeting my boner.

Maybe a minute later she was crying out like she was there, or at least very close, and I ramped up my own speed. Then her cries went to a completely different level and I knew she was coming. Sweet music to my ears. I let my own voice free, groaning and swearing as I rubbed against her. Some people would say this wasn't sex. Some people think it's only sex if the cock goes inside somebody else. Some people are stupid.

When I came I jetted all over her back. Does anything feel better than those seconds when your cock is coated in hot come and everything's throbbing and perfect and the head of your dick is like the motherfucking center of the sweet sweet universe? If anything does, don't tell me, because I think I found nirvana right there.

When I got my breath back and could tear myself away from kissing the backs of her perfect shoulders, I eased myself carefully off her. "Stay still," I warned her. I grabbed a hand towel from the lube drawer and wiped up most of the mess on her back. "Don't move."

I threw the goopy towel in the hamper in the bathroom and then returned with a damp washcloth and another towel. I sponge-bathed her and then rolled her over onto the towel, then cleaned a little between her legs.

"You're amazing," she said. "You didn't wreck the suede."

"Did you want me to? It seemed too nice to spooge all over." I lay down next to her on my side, propping my head up with my hand. "We need to talk about what was going on there."

"Going on where?" She gave me one of those naïve eyeblinks. "Everything's fine, Chino. Really. Everything's great. That was great."

"Yeah, but I want to know what was going through your head."

"Oh, you know how it is," she said. "Emotional stuff comes up sometimes. It doesn't mean anything. Really."

I toyed with her hair. She wasn't telling me the truth. But was it because she was lying to me or to herself? Was this what she was desperately trying to believe—that nothing was wrong and everything was perfect? "You sure seemed like you were going through something."

"It's nothing, Chino, really. Didn't mean anything." So much for gaining her trust and getting closer. This was the second time we'd been through a scene followed by her claim that nothing had happened. Her insistence felt like a door slamming on my fingers. "Yeah," I said, and was surprised how rough my voice sounded. "Totally meaningless sex. That's what it was. Meant nothing to me, either."

I pushed away from her, cursing myself. *You stupid shit. You're falling for her—no, be real, you already fell—and she knows it. That's why she's backpedaling so fast and shutting down on you emotionally. She doesn't want the L-word hanging like a ball and chain around her neck. No modern independent woman does. Not from a clown like you.*

CHAPTER EIGHT

MADISON

Oh, shit. I knew hiding my feelings had been a bad idea, but if I'd known *how* bad, would I have still done it? I'd only thought it would be bad for *me* and I'd be able to tough it out. It hadn't occurred to me it would hurt him. Not like that. *Oh shit oh shit oh shit.*

Chino had not struck me as a "sensitive" guy. He wasn't emo like Mal or an impulsive, flighty adventurer like Axel. I was sure he was a down-to-earth, down-and-dirty guy. Which meant if he was pulling back this hard, this fast, I'd really hit him where it hurt.

I tried to grab him but he slipped from the bed so quickly I missed catching his arm. He went to my window, the one that looked over my neighbor's back courtyard, but his eyes weren't focused. Was he looking into his past, or into the shreds of a future I'd just dashed?

I was scared to find out. "Chino," I said softly. But he didn't move, as if he hadn't heard me. My brain churned for a way to take back what I'd said, or to fix it, or for something new to say to bring back the joking, nothing-bothers-me man I thought I knew.

"I'm sorry," I tried.

"Don't be," he snapped.

His anger hit me like the burn of the rubber flogger. That wasn't something I could just take without snapping back: "Why, because you're in charge of my emotions now, too? Gonna tell me when to smile?"

"No, I'm not going to fucking tell you when to smile." He turned to face me, confusion twisting his features. "I'm just the . . . the . . . what do you call it. The catalyst for you to have your little revelations, your mind trips." He made a spiraling motion beside his head. "It's no concern of mine what the fuck goes on in your head, right? I'm only supposed to be interested in you for your body, is that it? I'm just supposed to show up when you call so you can make your videos and get it over with? It's not supposed to mean anything; okay, fine, I get it."

"No, no that's not it at all." I sat on the edge of the bed, folding my hands in my lap. "I'm . . . I'm not trying to shut you out."

He came a few steps closer to me, as if unsure whether it was safe to approach. "I need to know if you're still interested in doing this."

"In . . . playing? Testing out toys with you? Having a relationship?" There, I'd used the R-word. Time to find out if he was allergic to the idea.

Or if I was.

He pulled on his jeans and zipped them up, then sat down next to me. "Let me say it another way. Madison, what *are* you interested in?" His tattoos seemed to have a depth to them in the lights I'd set up, his skin a glow. I wanted to touch him.

I reached out tentatively for his hand instead and was bolstered when he didn't pull away. I realized it was going to be easier to answer his previous question—the one about what was going on in my head during the scene, than to answer this one. "I'm sorry. I should've said something about the blindfold."

I felt his pulse quicken in my hand.

"I…I left it in the box because I didn't want to use it."

His voice was gentle. Quiet. Confused. "Why didn't you just say so?"

"I didn't want to…make a problem. I didn't want to seem like I was a bad bottom or like I need special treatment."

"Special trea…" He trailed off, his confusion deepening. "You do realize I'm interested in playing with *you*, not some generic idea of a perfect sub?"

"I know," I said quickly. "But I mean, seriously, I didn't want you to…even know about the blindfold thing."

"Why?"

"Because blindfolds are supposed to be…easy. Basic." I gestured at the box on the floor. "I mean, they're even used by vanilla people to spice things up. It's why they're in a kit like that. Any beginner c-can do them—" My throat tightened.

"Maddie." He was squeezing my hand rather hard. "If they're a problem for you, there's nothing wrong with that. Every person's different. You should've told me."

"I…I know. But what if I'm just a b-bad submissive." My voice quavered and I felt myself suddenly on the verge of tears.

"'Bad submissive'? Who the hell told you that? Maddie, you're a dream, a—"

I couldn't hear what he said, as if the static in my mind

screaming at me that I'd fucked up was louder than his words. I started to hyperventilate instead of cry, trying to keep my tears in check at all costs. Why? I didn't know. Probably for the same reason I hadn't just told him in the first place.

"I'm afraid," I told him. Afraid to cry? But why? Was I afraid of what might happen if I did?

He put his arm around me carefully. "Because I scared you? With the blindfold?"

Right. That was where this had all started. Why did I avoid blindfolds? Could I even explain it? "I guess I'm scared to trust anyone with them."

His arm tightened almost imperceptibly. "I thought... I'd been doing pretty well earning your trust until then."

"You were! You are."

"You can always talk to me, Maddie. You can tell me to turn the camera off. I need you to talk to me. Or the only way for me to learn your danger zones is going to be by stumbling into them like this."

"I know." I really did know. But if it had been easy to say what the pitfalls were, they probably wouldn't have been pitfalls at all. "I want..." I tried to say, but the words wouldn't come. "I want to..."

"Want to what, sweets?" he encouraged me gently.

Want to kneel at your feet. Want to give you everything. But I can't. "I want to try," I managed. "I want to try to... submit." My heart spasmed as I said the word. "For real, I mean."

He pulled me close and kissed me on the hair, the gentle affection finally making my tears spill from my eyes. I blinked as they fell into my lap.

"You've never really done it before?" he asked gently. "You're so experienced."

"I've gone through the motions with a lot of doms but I

never really *felt* it, no," I said, my breath coming in shaky gasps. Admitting this to myself was as hard as admitting it to him. "Because I'm pretty sure a lot of guys will put up with me talking back or pretending to be obedient for the sake of the scene but the ones who are looking for 'true' submission get turned off and move on real fast."

"Okay, whoa, hold on. Anyone who is more concerned about whether you're a 'true' submissive instead of whether or not Maddie submits is an asshole as far as I'm concerned." The motions of his hands were soothing, even as his voice picked up some fire. "Especially anyone who only played with you because you were pretty."

I felt a spark of my own fire in response. "Oh, like you weren't attracted to my looks?"

"I am very, very attracted to your looks," he said sagely, kissing the tear tracks on my cheeks. "But I'm jaded to them, too. I'm a rock star, Maddie. I have supermodels throwing themselves at me constantly. Trust me, your looks were not what got my attention."

I blinked. Now I was curious. "What did get your attention?"

"That you stood up to me and pushed back whenever I made a bad joke or whatever. Most girls would have just giggled and glossed it over."

I felt a weight in the pit of my stomach, though. "But talking back has always been my problem. I can't just . . . lie there and take it the way doms want. I'm not that good."

He tipped my face up with his fingertips under my chin and I bit my lip to keep from blubbering at him. "You're not a bad sub because you can't take everything. You're not a bad sub because you want to see what's coming. Don't trust me yet? That's not a bad thing. That's not even disobedience. That's just you, sweets. That's just you."

He kissed my eyelids—one, then the other. "No wonder

you were so tense, if you were trying to just put up with it. No more blindfolds, okay? Should we get rid of rubber floggers, too?"

I forced myself to focus on the toys. The review. Yes, let's talk about that instead of me. "I . . . I was surprised how much it hurt. I don't think it's appropriate for a beginner play kit."

"Definitely," he said. "A lighter gauge of rubber maybe, but this was too heavy. Did I show you?" He held out his forearm where he'd given himself welts.

I ran my fingers over them in sympathy and his whole arm broke out in goose bumps. "I was . . . afraid you'd be angry if I couldn't take it."

"What? Why? I mean, I see why you might fear that but why would I be angry about that?"

"Some doms would be," I said with a shrug. My voice sounded a lot calmer now. Thinking about work helped me focus. "I can take a lot of pain, you know? But this one just wasn't for me."

"Good to know," he said. "You know, the submissive in a D/s relationship, not just the dom, is allowed to . . . no, is *supposed to* express some preferences and set some boundaries."

Well. Now he'd used the R-word, too. "I know. I guess I wasn't sure if we were in an actual relationship yet."

"It's starting to feel like one," he said. "But I guess I can see how you might think, four days . . . that's kinda fast."

I nodded. "I . . . I think we need to slow down."

"If it'll keep you from freaking out, I'm all for that," he said. "You tell me. When should I see you again?"

Oh. Right. Trying to get my brain in gear with real world stuff took a moment after being in scene space. "This coming weekend. Sakura invited us to a small play party in Palm Springs. They had a couple drop out at the last minute—Ricki and Axel, actually—and so there's a bedroom free."

"Oh, really." He couldn't hide his amusement and pretended to be contemplating it. "Sounds like fun. But are you sure going away together is slowing down?"

"It's almost a whole week," I said, and he didn't call me on it. "Besides, I thought it might be good for me to get away from the club."

"I agree with that thought." He yawned and stretched. "You feeling all right now?"

"Yeah." My little flip-out was over and I was feeling like I was on solid ground again. Like Chino and I were on solid ground. I wondered if the reassurances were going to stick this time or if my suspicions were going to creep up again. I still hadn't forgotten the way he'd switched off his phone or brushed off my questions about where he lived. He was holding something back from me, but I pushed it to the back of my mind. Chino was better than that. Better than the exes who had lied or cheated. Or at least I truly wanted him to be.

His voice was grounding. "What are you going to do about the other video you need to turn in ASAP?"

"These vlogs were supposed to be solo," I teased him. "I've got a couple of things I can try out in the bathtub, that sort of thing."

He took it well. "All right. I'll see you this weekend, then."

"You don't have to rush out, you know," I told him.

"Yes I do, sweets," he said with a laugh. "If I stay much longer we'll end up going another round, and you literally just said you want to slow down."

Right. Yes, I did. I wanted to slow down and at the same time I wanted to spend every waking moment with him. Which definitely meant it was time to slow down. Going overnight to Palm Springs with him was going to be a big enough step to take for one week.

CHAPTER NINE

CHINO

When I first got into the rock-and-roll business, I knew an older guy who had toured the world in a lot of famous bands. He was kind of a mentor and kind of a dick, so shall remain nameless, but one time he said to me, "Sometimes you get wild with a girl, but the next day you think to yourself: Was I the only one enjoying myself?"

"What do you do if you think that?" I asked.

"Leave town."

That bothered me a little when he said it, but a lot more as time went on. The Rough got famous, and more and more girls were throwing themselves at us. Each of us dealt with it in our own way. Mal had a roadie interview each girl about whether she was really into kink. Samson preferred taking on two or more at a time so there'd always be witnesses and no mix-ups about romantic pair–bonding.

Me? I made it up as I went along but I usually stayed far, far away from the really kinky stuff when I hooked up with groupies or random women. It was safer for everyone concerned, including me. It's one thing to have morning-after syndrome when all you did was have sex. When you tie her up and put bruises on her, though—man, if she didn't like it and only went through with it because you're a rock star and she was trying to please you? You're up shit creek without a paddle. Not only would something like that suck for her, it'd wreck me with guilt, not to mention open the door for some of the worst lawsuits, blackmail, or tabloid situations you can imagine.

But over the course of the week since we'd first played, I had to keep checking the temperature with Madison, trying to figure out how she was feeling. It wasn't that she ran hot and cold—not at all—but I could feel the swirling emotions around her, and something deep down that she wasn't letting loose. This was a woman who was trying to figure out her shit. Smart, beautiful, honest, special. It was easy to want a beautiful woman, but I liked her, too. I liked not just fucking her or dominating her; I liked talking with her, being with her, being near her. I liked her smile, her mind, her way of speaking, her attitude. Come to think of it, there wasn't anything I didn't like.

But that question had nagged the back of my mind. Was she only doing it because she wanted to please me? Did she feel like she had to because of my position in the club or in her world? I felt that push of resistance from her every time and then a surge of ecstasy when she gave in—was that my drug? That feeling of conquering her?

Any questions I was having about whether Madison really liked it when I held her down and ass-fucked her—or whatever else I did—were largely quieted not only by the conversation when she confessed she wanted to "try" to submit, but when she was the one who invited me to a private play party. That wasn't the sort of thing a woman who was just going along for the ride would do. How could I say no?

Not that I would have said no. Not at all.

The drive eastward took us through the wind farms into the desert. On the way there we chatted easily and discovered we liked a lot of the same music, which meant some of the time we didn't talk, we just cranked up the volume and flew down the highway with Primus and Cake and Jane's Addiction blasting.

The house was a ways from town, which made it nicely private. I'd been picturing a mansion but it was actually a small compound: a low, flat bungalow for a main house with two casitas flanking the swimming pool in back, and nothing but scrub and a sharp, rocky ridge behind that. We arrived late Saturday afternoon so we had some time to get to know folks a little before the official party time, grilling burgers and sausages at poolside.

The first couple we met was a male dom—a somewhat round guy with curly black hair and glasses who was a Silicon Valley executive of some kind—and his submissive, a very cute, vivacious Asian gal, introduced to us as Lion and Kittyn. The heart-shaped metal tag on her collar read KITTYN. He was the silent type, while she did the talking for both of them and he participated mostly by smiles, nods, and the occasional skeptical expression.

She was in the middle of telling us a story about the one time they'd decided to go to Burning Man, when the male sub who was manning the grill in a leather apron announced, "Burgers up!"

"Kittyn," Lion said, gesturing toward the grill.

"Yes, sir!" She hopped up from the lounge chair with a

huge grin. This was a girl who enjoyed serving her dom, apparently. "With ketchup and mustard?"

He nodded.

While she was gone, he continued the story briefly. "Trying to rent an RV anywhere in the state of California the month before Burning Man is pretty much impossible. But a friend of a friend said he'd lend us his. What we didn't know until we went to pick it up was that he had outfitted the interior as a . . . how should I describe it? Groovy psychedelic bachelor pad?"

Kittyn was back with two burgers on plates. She knelt down gracefully and presented one of them to Lion, and then sat down in her seat, picked up her burger, and picked up the story again. "Anyway, we go to pick up this friend's RV." She bit into the burger.

Lion let out an audible sigh and rolled his eyes.

Kittyn froze. "Ohmygod," she mumbled, putting a hand over her mouth while she hurriedly chewed and swallowed. "Sorry sorry sorry." She cringed and hid her face behind her hand for a second.

Lion sighed again. "What did you do wrong?"

"I'm supposed to ask your permission before eating anything. I'm so sorry, sir. I'll try to be better next time."

"You say that every time," he pointed out. "Are you very, very hungry?"

"No! I just forgot." She turned toward me and Madison. "I . . . I always forget when we're in public."

"How long has it been?" Madison asked.

Lion rolled his eyes again. "Almost a year. Funny. She never forgets to ask permission to come, but she never remembers the food thing."

"I'm really not doing it to embarrass you, sir! I really just can't remember."

"You *can* remember. If you're sufficiently aware of me and our relationship at all times, not just when we're having sex, you'll remember."

She sucked in a breath, the "trying not to cry" kind of sucking in a breath, and I looked around for a graceful way to exit the conversation.

Madison patted Kittyn on the leg. "Sometimes it takes time," she said. "Lion, your sub is really charming. I look forward to seeing you guys play together."

"I love her dearly," he said. "I guess I'll have to punish you for this tonight, Kittyn."

"Oh please, Master, please please." She leaned against him and snuggled under his arm, the plate and burger on her lap tipping precariously but staying put.

He stroked her hair and rolled his eyes at us one last time.

"A burger sounds like a great idea," I said. "I'm going to grab one. Maddie, you want?"

"I'll come with you."

We settled again to eat on the far side of the table loaded with condiments. "They seem nice," I said neutrally.

"They're cute." Maddie gave me a slight grimace, like she felt exactly like I did: like we weren't going to say anything bad about them when they were right over there. Cute or no, I got the feeling that what Lion and Kittyn had wasn't right for us, anyway.

Us. Was that just wishful thinking on my part or were we really as deep into this relationship already as I felt like we were?

"Should we have come up with scene names, you think?" I asked.

"For anonymity purposes?" She chuckled. "I don't think either of us is in danger of losing our jobs if our bosses find out we're kinky."

"Ha, true. I get the feeling it's not just anonymity, though. People pick a persona before they jump into the community. Neither of us seems to be doing that."

"Well, I'll confess one thing to you," she said, licking her lower lip as she looked out over the scrub desert. "Madison isn't my given name."

I laughed gently. "Well, you know Chino isn't mine."

She looked back at me and smiled. "Maybe our whole lives are one big scene, then."

"Oh, definitely." That came with the territory of rock stardom and celebrity. "Did you pick the name for anonymity purposes, though?"

"Initially, yeah, because I didn't want my parents to Google me and be shocked and appalled by what they found. But when I picked it as a name I had this feeling, too—that I was becoming my own person, I guess. Not that I wanted to disavow that I was their daughter—I'll always be that—but giving myself a name felt symbolic of being my own person. You know?"

"I know exactly what you mean." There had been a point where my stepfather had declared "Chino" to be too "Latin"—yes, he called it "Latin" as if he needed an extra-Anglo word for it—and had tried to call me "Al." He'd even tried to get my mother and my super-obedient siblings to do it. But none of them could get used to it. By the time I left home they'd simply stopped saying my name at all. "When I hit the street I could've used any name I wanted. I stuck with Chino."

"The nickname your dad gave you."

"Yeah." I hadn't thought of it that way at the time, but she wasn't wrong. "It felt right."

As the sun set I felt my energy rising like it did before a show. There was no arena here, no mass crowd of thousands of fans screaming, but the excitement was building nonetheless. I took Madison into the casita that was to be ours for the night.

I could feel the electricity rising on her skin, too. I moved her to stand in the middle of the throw rug between the bed and the dresser and ran my fingers lightly down her bare arms. "Are you nervous?"

"Yeah," she said with a huff of breath. "I…I don't know what's wrong with me."

I closed my hands firmly around her shoulders. "Nothing's wrong with you. You can sense what's going to happen. I'm going to do terrible, awful things to you, and no matter how much you enjoy them, there'll always be a part of you that fears what's coming."

"Oh." She sucked in a breath. "I mean, I *know* that. It's not like I'm some newbie."

"Maddie, it's okay. If you *weren't* buzzing with nervous excitement I'd be worried." I gathered her hair to one side and pressed a kiss against the back of her neck. "When you pretended to be submissive for doms in the past, did you not get nervous?"

"Not really. I don't know why this time's different."

I suspected what was different was how hard we were falling for each other, which reassured me, actually, even if she hadn't come out and said it. "Tell me if there's anything in particular you're worried about. Is it this crowd?"

"No. Everyone seems nice. Sakura's always introduced me to good people. I guess…I guess I'm just a little freaked that I have no idea what you're going to do or what you're going to want. You haven't given me any hints at all."

Aha. I had wondered if keeping her in the dark about what we might do would bring up the same kinds of feelings as the blindfold had, and it was nice to know I was right.

But then she said something that made me realize maybe it wasn't simply fear of the unknown. "If I don't know what you're going to do, I might not be prepared for it."

"Prepared how?" I asked. "You sound like you want to study up in advance or something."

I felt her stiffen, freezing up as the thought hit home. "I . . . I guess."

"Did you ever think that what would please me more than you being well-prepared for what I'm going to dish out is you being surprised by it?"

"I never thought of it that way before." I could hear the wheels turning in her head.

"There's a reason I haven't clued you in and it isn't that I haven't given a ton of thought to what we might do."

"A reason?"

"Yes." I stepped back and watched her posture. "I figured keeping you in the dark about what I want to do or what toys I brought would make you nervous."

She swallowed. "Well, you were right. So it's all going according to your plan?"

"Yes, sweets." She shivered as if the AC had just kicked on, which it hadn't. "You swear you didn't peek into my bag while I wasn't looking?"

"No, of course not."

"Because I did peek into yours." I ran my fingers lightly across her shoulders and goose bumps came up at my touch. I circled around to face her. "And I couldn't help but notice that you packed a leather paddle with metal studs."

Her cheeks flushed. "Yes. I . . . thought it might come in handy."

I ran my fingers over her eyebrows, down her lips until they parted slightly, taking in the beauty of her face with my hands.

"So does bringing the paddle that made you break down and cry last week mean you want that again?" I began to circle her, pulling the straps of her sundress off one shoulder, then the other.

"I brought it because . . . it was familiar. And you seemed to like using it."

"Ah. So you brought it for me?"

She seemed to sense a trick question. "For us," she said. "I didn't put too much thought into it. Just seemed like a good possibility."

I started unzipping her dress. "All right. How about the things you brought to wear? I found a couple of sexy negligees, thongs, stockings, two corsets . . . isn't that kind of overpacking for an overnight trip?"

The dress unpeeled from her body and then hung on her ample hips. "I didn't know what you'd like so I brought a bunch of things for you to choose from."

"Oh, that's interesting." It truly was. She'd clearly put a lot of thought into this, which was exactly what this little pre-scene warm-up interrogation was supposed to show me: her thoughts. "So you were actually trying to guess what I might like? And picked things trying to anticipate my taste?"

Funny how she bowed her head a little as she answered, sinking gradually toward subspace. "Yes, exactly."

I pushed the dress over her hips and it fell to the floor. She wasn't wearing underwear. I smiled. "Well, you got one thing right." I smoothed my hands over the curves of her ass. "The thing I like you wearing best is nothing."

I smacked her lightly and she made one of those sweet little girl-grunts.

I climbed onto the bed and leaned back against the headboard, crossing my ankles. "But go on. Try to prove to me I ought to choose one of these other outfits. Try them on.

Model them for me." I unzipped my jeans and let my junk out into the open air. "This'll be the judge." I was half-stiff already, so it was going to take a real effort on my part not to respond. But it was something to say, you know?

I lay back and watched my girl work her ass off to please me. Nothing could please me more than that.

* * *

MADISON

Good job, Chino, I thought as I picked up my dress from the floor and opened my suitcase. Between taking me into a private area and what he'd said, he'd managed to turn my nervous energy into a positive thing just when I'd been starting to think I might make some excuse for why we shouldn't play tonight. I'd known he was clever on the spur of the moment but I hadn't realized what a devious dom he could be when he had time to plan. He'd had all week to think about tonight.

And so had I. I put one of the black lace teddies on first and twirled on the carpet in front of him. You could still see my large dark nipples right through it, and I bent over facing away from him so he could see my ass revealed as the edge of the teddy rode up.

He waved his hand like a king telling his jester to get on with it. Okay, not the teddy, then. I went for the brown and brass corset our designer friend Dara had made for me next, with garter and stockings and a skirtlet that could be stripped off while leaving the corset in place. I put the edge of the skirtlet in his hand and then pirouetted away from him, leaving it behind in his grip.

"Very nice trick." He nodded. "But no."

And so it went through everything else I had brought. An electric blue leather corset with matching high heels, no. A sheer "slave girl" tunic, no. Thong and bikini top, no.

I stood beside the bed buck naked with my hands on my hips. "That's all I brought. What do you want?"

He gestured at his limp cock flopping out of his jeans and then crooked his finger to beckon me.

I crawled across the bed toward him.

He chuckled softly and joked, "Now remember, you have to ask permission before you can eat me."

I couldn't help but laugh. "Oh, master," I said, "may your slave please have the pleasure of your cock in her mouth?"

His eyebrows rose and he pointed at the fact that his erection was starting to rise. "Hm. Apparently Mr. Stiffie likes when you ask permission."

"He'll like this even better," I said, taking hold of his shaft and licking a wide stripe across the head. In my hand he thickened and swelled and I licked him once more before waiting.

He chuckled again. "Yes, you may devour me, my slave girl."

I took him all the way in and he began spouting the most lovely obscenities. Apparently that was the kind of blowjob Chino liked. Or one kind, anyway. So far I hadn't found much that Chino *didn't* like. Outside on the patio music began to play, some kind of techno, and I took that as a sign that the party was getting started.

He pulled me off him after a short while and gestured me back to the rug. I stood there waiting for his next command. I was so much calmer now that I wasn't constantly worrying about what was going to happen. I mean, I was still wondering—*constantly* wondering—but something about how complete his dominance was allowed me to let go. I felt like now that he had taken control it wasn't my job to worry about what to do next. He was giving me just enough leeway to let me express myself while following his orders but not enough that I felt anxious about what I did. That wasn't a dom style I was used to, but it was fun.

"Please me," was his next command.

"Sir?" I wondered if I'd missed something.

"Please me. However you think I might like to be pleased. If I'm not pleased, I'll punish you, and if I am pleased, I'll share the pleasure with you." He pulled slowly on his cock with two fingers.

I needed more to go on, though. "Would it please you to watch me dance?"

"Do you think it would?"

"I think you like to watch." I struck a pose. The music wasn't very loud coming through the window to the patio, but it didn't have to be. "And I like to dance."

He gave me a tiny nod of assent.

I wasn't warmed up, but this wasn't a full-on routine either. There were plenty of moves that showed off my body that wouldn't result in a pulled muscle. Flow it, stretch it, move it, shake it. Arms, legs, hips, boobs. I danced long enough to work up a light sheen of sweat.

He snagged me by the arm as a move brought me close to him and pulled me on top of him. "Rub your cunt on my dick."

"You're not wear—"

"*Don't* put it in. Don't you dare, girl." His voice was rough in my ear, as rough as the hand in my hair.

"Yes, sir." I rolled my hips, grinding my mound against his rock-hard erection.

"Get it wet. But not inside," he ordered.

I spread my legs and curved my spine, using one hand to

spread my folds so my natural lubrication—which was copious now that he was manhandling me—buttered him well.

"You want to know the real reason I haven't fucked you in the traditional manner yet?"

"Yes, sir." *You mean it isn't just to torture me with deprivation?* I wondered if what he was going to tell me now was actually a reason or if this was just an excuse to talk dirty. Either way, I was all ears.

"Most of the women I've been with, for a night, or for a relationship," he said, rolling me onto my back and pausing to suckle my nipples before he went on. "They come in two kinds. The kind who hold back because they believe their vagina is some kind of prize I'm supposed to win, and the kind who think my cock is some kind of prize *they're* supposed to win. And you know what? Neither one of those attitudes has ever worked out in the long run. It's lose-lose."

Okay, that was not a dirty-talk kind of explanation. "I don't think either of those things are true."

"I know, which is one of the things that intrigues me most about you, Maddie." He shifted downward between my legs and spread my folds with his thumb, admiring my clit. "It helps that you're not a twenty-two-year-old ingenue. You've been around almost as long as me." His thumb brushed across my clit and my hips jerked. "I've tried to develop a healthy appreciation for all the kinds of sex that aren't P-I-V."

"You're a connoisseur," I said as his mouth closed over my clit, his tongue making me tremble. "Oh. Oh! Oh!" His fingers slipped into me with the most delicious penetration and I bucked against them. "But you know, you're making me crave your cock."

He lifted his head, his chin glistening with my juices. "I know. So now that we've gotten the 'intercourse is a prize' thing out of the way, *now* I'm just holding out to torture you."

He laughed wickedly. "And torturing you is definitely a win-win situation."

I groaned while his fingers continued to work inside me and his tongue tip teased me to the edge of orgasm.

And then he pulled away, one hand massaging my thigh tantalizingly close to my pussy but no longer stimulating me directly. "So, ground rules for tonight. If you're really craving cock, what if I let Lion or one of the other guys fuck you?"

"No!" I said instantly. "I'm not actually interested in anyone touching me but you. I mean, if you would find it super-hot to have someone else play with me, we can negotiate that, but if you're asking me my preference? No. You or nobody."

He gave a slow nod, like the answer was satisfying to hear. "Good. And very good for expressing your preferences clearly. I won't have anyone else fuck you. I am going to torture you with not having my cock, but I thought you should know I'm not going to stick it in anyone else, either." His hand drifted northward and a finger slipped gradually into my swollen pussy. "That goes for in general, by the way. Not just while we're at this party."

I bit my lip as he slid a second finger in beside the first one. "I'm glad. Thank you."

"Thank you?"

Hearing him ask made me wonder, too: Why had I said that? "Most guys won't declare monogamy without being prompted."

"All relationships are a kind of bargain," he said, his dark eyes deepening as the night sky darkened through the window. "But I'm not offering it to you as a bargaining chip. I'm interested in you, Madison. We've obviously got a thing going on here. Even if it's just sex, just kink, I only want you. I'm going to be exclusive to you."

Hearing him say that made my heart jump and race. The cheaters and jerkwads in my past would never have dared to bring it up. I wasn't even sure if it was more scary or exciting. "And . . . and do you want me to be exclusive to you?"

There was that long slow nod again, but the words that came out of his mouth were, "There are a lot of things I want. But as I was saying after the thing with the blindfold, you shouldn't always give me what I want just because you're the sub."

"Do you think I should have a safeword?"

He grinned. "Well, yes, but you should also point it out if I'm asking for too much, you know? Because I have this feeling I'm going to go further with you, Maddie, than I've ever gone before."

The racing of my heart intensified, and I could hear the blood pounding in my ears. "I have that feeling, too. That's why I'm so nervous."

"Remember. I like you nervous," he said. "That'll be your signal to me that you've got a problem, all right? If we're in public and you don't want to say too much or you aren't sure what's bothering you, say 'I'm nervous.' That'll cue me to dig deeper, all right?"

"All right." I had never used a safeword that way before. I decided that might be relevant for him to know. "For me a safeword has always meant 'stop right now,' like an escape hatch. Like for emergencies."

He patted my knee. "So would saying 'stop right now, this is an emergency' work in that case?"

"Um, yeah, now that you mention it."

"Let's keep that in mind," he said with a grin. "Now, up you get, let's go out and mingle with the others and watch some scenes. You're going to be wearing nothing but the trickle of your desire. That means you better carry a towel with you to sit on or kneel on so you don't end up leaving wet spots everywhere."

"Yes, sir."

"I'm going to put leather pants on. I'll let you know when I want them to come off and if I want your help with that."

"Yes, sir." I found myself grinning with happy anticipation, even though I had no idea what we were going to actually do later. Something fun, I was sure.

* * *

CHINO

When someone says "bungalow," I imagine a shack in the jungle, or maybe on a beach somewhere, not a high-tech, luxuriously carpeted pop art house, but that's what this one was. No wonder the rent was kind of high. The casitas were nice but the main house was nothing short of swank, and when you added in the bondage furniture that had been brought in for the weekend, it was a decadent paradise. A standing frame in front of the fireplace, a leather-padded spanking bench where a coffee table should've been, a sling in a cube of gleaming steel pipes looking part modern art, part torture device.

A lot of couples—and triads and quads, let's be real here—have a pattern of scene that's pretty similar. The dom(s) puts the sub(s) into bondage, some kind of beating happens (sometimes an artistic flogging or a strict caning or a passionate spanking or a sadistic whipping), and then when the sub(s) are totally turned to jelly, the actual sex happens. There's nothing wrong with that any more than it's "wrong" for every restaurant to offer you appetizer, then main dish, then dessert. There are a million variations: all good. What kind of bondage? What kind of beating? What rules or twists do you put on it? And what kind(s) of sex?

The thing I've noticed is that for most of the people I seem to know, the beating is the main dish and the sex is the dessert. Which is great if that makes them happy. In fact we know some people for whom the bondage itself seems to be the point. But with me, if sex isn't the main dish, I don't get it. I mean, why tie someone up if it isn't so you can do wicked things to them? And no matter how much it floats my boat when I spank her or bite her or whatever, the beating and bondage only make sense to me as foreplay. I know not everyone's like that and that's cool, but for me, if there isn't a fuckload of orgasm at the end, something went wrong.

We sat on the sectional sofa, Maddie on her towel, watching a short woman with glasses flogging her man with great gusto.

"Jeez Louise," she said at one point, pausing to stretch her arm and shoulder. "Bry, I swear you've got Kevlar instead of skin."

He laughed.

"I mean, lookit." She gestured to his white ass cheeks and we spectators could see they were slightly pinked by her efforts but nothing more. "I'm switching to the paddle."

"Don't you dare," he said.

"Nope nope nope, this flogger just isn't doing it." She laid it down and picked up a wooden paddle with holes drilled in it. "Here it comes, baby."

She swung it with both hands and it cracked mightily on his rump. He howled and thrashed in the sheepskin-lined cuffs and she laid the swats on heavy and fast. I felt Maddie tense next to me, maybe thinking about how hard she'd paddled me a week ago.

When Jill paused to inspect her handiwork, she was disappointed. "Nothing. Barely a welt, Kevlar Butt. It's so unfair. I sneeze and I get a bruise! I'm getting the Top Saver."

"Don't you dare," he said again. "I mean it this time, Jill."

Maddie and I exchanged looks. This couple clearly had negotiated a very different kind of scene—or had a very different definition of limits than we did.

From their toy bag, Jill pulled out a small flail of some kind, with two thick leather tails hinged on a stiff handle about the length of her forearm. "Oh, come on, you'll barely feel it."

She snapped it a few times against his skin and his howls turned quickly to curses and profanity and then, in a move I didn't expect at all, he unclipped his wrist cuffs and grabbed her. "You minx! I warned you!"

A great deal of laughing and shouting and wrestling ensued, and eventually she twisted free and fled toward the pool, giggling maniacally. He unclipped his ankles and ran after her.

"Well, that was different," Maddie said, biting her lower lip to keep from laughing too hard.

"Here they come back again." I patted her knee and encouraged her to put her legs over mine. Watching Jill and Bry was stimulating to say the least, and I wanted some of Maddie's weight against my rising boner.

Bry carried Jill over his shoulder—her kicking and protesting the whole way but not enough to actually get free—and then laid her over the same bench where he'd been. He quickly had her tied to it and then picked up the paddle. "So," he said, swaggering up to her, smacking the wood against his palm, "the paddle isn't that bad, eh?"

"Oh, no no no, please Bry, no, not that."

"It's no more than you deserve, you wicked thing."

"I know, I know, I'm sorry!" Her eyes were wide and her voice squeaked as her pitch went up.

"Ten smacks with the paddle. Count 'em."

She slumped in her bonds and counted out her punishment, sniffling and weeping a bit at the end. "I'm sorry! I won't do it again!"

"You bet you won't. Now, what about this." He picked up the Top Saver and twirled it.

"No. No, no, no. I don't even know why we have that thing. We should throw it out," she said quickly.

"I'm pretty sure it was you who bought it—"

"No way, mister—"

"And you who packed it—"

"It was in the bottom of the bag! I thought you packed it, I swear—"

"And however it got there, you got a good three or four licks in before I stopped you."

She was silent, then, looking very contrite, her lip trembling.

"So I'm thinking four stripes," he said, bending down to put his face near hers. "On your inner thighs. The bruises'll be so dark they'll look like burn marks."

"No, please," she said, her eyes huge and round, her eyeliner running from the brimmed tears. "I'll do anything you want if you spare me that."

"Anything?"

"Anything."

"Four minutes of me fucking your face, then."

She blanched but said, "Okay. It's a deal."

He untied her and turned her over so that she was on her back lengthwise on the bench, her head hanging off one end.

It was one of the more impressive face-fuckings I've seen outside of professional porn. He wasn't small, and I swear we could see the bulge in her throat when he went all the way in. I was very tempted to have Maddie put her mouth on me, but I didn't want her to miss the show. I moved her hand to my bulge instead. A couple of times Bry held himself against Jill's face, waiting for her to gag or struggle, and then when she would he'd thrust in and out hard. He slapped her cheeks sometimes if he felt her teeth, but how could he not?

When the four minutes was up he hadn't come and he went right around to the other side, put a condom on, and fucked her the traditional way—well, as traditional as you can get while tied to a custom-built bondage bench in the middle of a group of voyeuristic pervs like us. She came three times before he did and when he finally did it was with the exclamation, "What a freakin' unbelievable wife Jill baby love you oh my freaking *ngggghhhhhhh*" which caused the rest of us watching to break into applause.

They were giggly as fuck afterward. The two of them got wrapped in blankets and joined us on the couch and then dissected their scene. Jill whapped him on the shoulder. "I almost lost it when you were like 'four, four licks, muahaha.'" She did her best impression of the Count from *Sesame Street*. "In my head I was thinking, *Four? Four is nothing!*"

"I was just trying to make your capitulation make sense, you know?" he said, cuddling her close. "I guess I should've let you go on a little longer before I busted out but man, that thing freakin' hurts."

"I know, dear. That's the point." She giggled and looked at Maddie. "Did you guys enjoy it? It's always more fun with an audience."

"Loved it," Maddie said. Her voice turned curious, which made me curious, too. "How long have you guys been together?"

"Twelve years in August," Jill said.

"Thirteen," Bry corrected. "But who's counting."

Jill wound her hand in his and held up their forearms. "Check out our tattoos."

The two designs were supposed to merge together into a single image but I wasn't at the right angle to really see it. Something circular like a geometric sunset or a flower, maybe?

Suddenly an ear-piercing sound like an extremely rhythmic pig squeal cut through the room. On the other side of the dining room Sakura was doing something to Helene that made her come with one of the most distinctive orgasm noises I've ever heard. We had to wait until she was done before we could continue talking. Not that we minded.

"Your tat is so cool," Madison said to Jill. "Have you guys been going to parties like this for a long time?"

"We met at one." Jill grinned at him.

Bry grinned back. "We flipped a coin to decide who got to top that time."

"You mean who got to bottom!" They both laughed.

"You should've seen it out there," Bry said, jerking his thumb toward the patio. "She almost slipped and fell in the pool. That would've been a very different scene."

"I know, right?" Jill sighed happily and snuggled down close. "Maybe next time."

A tall black man in leather pants and a leather vest approached. "You guys done with this?"

"Oh, yes, David. Let me clean it up," Jill said.

"No, no, you guys do your aftercare. I got this." He whistled and another man, this one in a leather hood shaped like a dog's head and leather short-shorts came hurrying over on all fours. Following behind him was Faisal, the guy who had been grilling the burgers earlier. David clipped the puppy's collar to an eyebolt on the bench and Faisal began wiping the bench down with the cleaning supplies on hand for that purpose. The puppy wagged his butt.

When the cleaning was done, Faisal stood aside with his hands clasped behind his back.

"Thank you, boy," David said. "You're released to go have some fun, at least until I'm done here." He gave the other man a quick kiss and then turned his attention to the pup, who was rubbing against his leg.

It truly takes all kinds. I enjoyed watching the other people playing, but the whole time I was wondering what Madison was thinking and feeling. She watched very quietly, very still, as if she wasn't going to let what she was seeing affect her.

"Come all the way into my lap," I said, and shifted her so she was leaning back against my chest. I wrapped my hands around her to fondle her breasts, my thumbs paying particular attention to her nipples until they stood out pebble-like. "You like watching guys with guys?"

"Yes," she said, her chest swelling as she sucked in a breath. "If you like cock, two is better than one, after all."

"So logical. Enjoy the show while I enjoy you." I let my fingers do the walking, so to speak, exploring her inner thighs, the soft curve of her belly, the sweet dampness under the curve of her breasts as what she watched heated her up and made her sweat, and the even sweeter dampness between her legs.

When I brought my sopping wet fingers up she licked them clean without even a single moment of hesitation. "I guess I don't necessarily have to beat you into submission," I murmured to her.

"No, sir," she whispered, and I felt a thrill go all the way to the tip of my toes, and the tip of my stiff cock. I'd thought I might have to work as hard as I had that night at the Governor's Club to turn her into putty in my hands in front of other people, but here she was as soft and pliant as I could imagine.

"Can I put you on display for these nice people?" I asked her.

"Aren't I on display already, sir?" Her legs were splayed wide, her folds wide open, her breasts free and loose—she had a point.

"Yes, but I was thinking something to show you off a bit more." In particular I wanted to explore what felt like a deepening D/s bond between us. How did it work? What made the engine run? Madison had played with lots of doms but had never actually felt deeply submissive to any of them. I was in a similar boat. I'd enjoyed playing the dom role for lots of women because it turned me on, but I'd never found one I wanted to keep. Lusting after each other was only the start. If there was something more to us, I wanted to find out what the limits were, how the inner workings functioned, what made us tick. That meant taking her apart and putting her back together: exactly what a scene is for.

CHAPTER TEN

MADISON

Chino brought me out by the pool where the night air was cooling off but the sky was beautifully clear and full of stars, something we didn't see often from the city. "Jill and Bry seem like they have a lot of fun, don't they?"

"Seriously," I said. "I wonder if they plan in advance when they're going to switch or is it totally freeform? I almost got a little worried a couple of times when they were saying 'no, I mean it' but they obviously know each other well enough to tell when the protest is serious and when it's part of the fun."

"Think we'll ever know each other that well?" Chino asked, looking up at the stars.

I looked at my own hands. "I suppose if we did as many scenes as those guys, we'd learn a lot."

He took my hands in his and turned me toward him. "Is that what scares you about BDSM? You're not afraid of pain, or of being sexual, like most people. Are you afraid I'll figure you out?"

His voice was gentle, making it a good-humored joke so that if I wanted to I could laugh it off, or I could answer seriously.

I wanted to laugh it off—or run away—but that wouldn't have been the mature thing to do. "Isn't that what everyone's afraid of?"

"I dunno about that. I think some people are desperate to be understood."

"Even those people might still be afraid, though . . ." I kept my voice from quavering, but it was probably obvious to him I was talking about myself. ". . . that once people figure them out, they'll stop liking them. They'll decide they're not worth it after all."

Chino pulled steadily on my hands until I was almost nose to nose with him, our hands in front of our chests as if we were about to start some kind of formal dance. He slipped one of his around me and rocked me back and forth, not to the beat of the soft techno coming from the living room but to the gentle sway of some song in his head. "I want to know you better, Maddie, and it's not so I can hurry up and decide you're not worth it."

I leaned my head on his shoulder, letting his words sink in. I felt like the better I knew him the more I liked him, too, but why was it so hard to believe that he was going to stay interested in me? Because no other guy had? "Do you want to ask me something? I'll answer any question you want, you know."

He ran his fingers through my loose and wavy hair. "No, sweets, I don't think an interrogation scene is on the agenda. After all, twice during scenes I've asked you what was going on in your head and you've refused to answer."

He was right and the knowledge that I'd shied back from whatever was brewing in there embarrassed me. "I wasn't... doing it to disobey you."

"I know. But how about we do an obedience scene."

"What do you mean?"

"I want to find out if following orders actually turns you on or if I need to tie you down to really get a rise out of you." His lips twisted in challenge and his eyes sparkled with amusement.

"Okay, sure."

"And what's the safeword?"

Right. He was being very responsible. "If I don't want to do something I should say I'm nervous."

"Good. And if you want to stop right away?"

"Then I'll say that." The truth was I was still nervous not knowing what we were going to do. He was right—I didn't fear what was going to happen physically. Been there, done that. It was not knowing itself that was the hardest.

He stepped back from me then and said, "Stay still."

"Will there be a punishment if I don't obey?"

He seemed wickedly amused. "Do you want there to be?"

"What? No. I mean, whatever you want. I'm just asking."

He held his hands palm up and I put mine into them automatically. "Maddie," he urged, "if you have a lot of questions, now would be the time to ask them, before we get started."

"How can I ask questions if I don't know what you're going to do?"

Chino's cheer was undeterred. "How can I answer them if I don't know what I'm going to do either? Go with the flow, Maddie. And do what I say. That's the test."

"Oh." Of course. "You didn't say it was a test."

"Well, now I did. Don't you feel every scene is kind of

a test? Some of them are a test of endurance, some of skill, some of love. This one, I told you, is a test of obedience."

"And what happens if I pass? Or fail?"

"If you fail I get to punish you by demanding the filthiest hot sex imaginable. And if you pass, I get to *reward* you with the filthiest hot sex imaginable."

That made so much sense I was surprised I was that concerned over success or failure. "So it doesn't matter."

"It matters because if you fail, you'll be disappointed in yourself." He let go of my hands and stepped back again.

And you won't be disappointed, too? I wanted to ask, but he was trying to tell me to "go with the flow" and me grilling him was starting to feel like too obvious a stalling tactic. Because that's what it was. I don't know why I was so self-conscious. It wasn't because I was naked. I was used to that.

"Go with the flow," Chino said, and took another step farther back from me. "First order. *Stay. Still.*"

I was about to nod my head when I realized that would be against the order. Shit, obedience was tricky. I didn't move a muscle and he nodded in approval. "Good. Right like that. Like you're a robot and you can't move until I give you the next order."

His approval was like a sip of cool water on a hot day, a momentary pleasure, but then it slipped away as he went into the main house through the patio door. Huh. Was he just going to leave me standing out here? Was it that kind of mindfuck? I felt the night air moving against my skin and where my hair brushed my shoulder blades it began to tickle. My nose itched. Did I dare reach up to scratch it? He was probably watching, right?

Chino emerged a few minutes later with Lion, each of them carrying a drink. Lion's appeared to be a margarita. Chino's was a curved glass of some amber liquid, cupped in his fingers. Scotch, maybe?

They sat down not far from me. "Maddie, walk to the far side of the pool, and then back to your spot," Chino said.

I turned and walked to the far side of the pool, trying to figure out what the exact right spot was to turn around. How far should I go? The pool was mostly rectangular with one curved end and a hot tub built off to one side. I decided making a full turn around on the other side, clearing the corner, was enough, and then I walked back to my spot and waited for the next order.

"Do it again," Chino said, "but this time a sexy walk. Walk like you want every guy in this place to be drooling by the time you get back."

Okay, I could do that. I retraced my steps, but I used the runway walk, putting each foot onto the imaginary balance beam in the center of my path, my hips swiveling. I swung my head, shooting sultry glances this way and that. Sakura and Helene came out onto the patio and settled in ironwork chairs at a small table. They were wearing matching silk robes and I wondered if they were finished playing or if they were just taking a break.

When I returned to my spot I resisted the urge to put my hand on my hip.

Chino took a sip from his glass and then licked the rim. Watching his tongue sent electric shocks between my legs, the memory of him eating me seared permanently into my nerve endings. "This time, all the way around the pool."

Okay, around the pool. I can do that. I assumed he still meant with the sexy walk, so I pretended I was in a Beyoncé video. When I had just reached the corner by the hot tub, though, his voice rang out. "Stop. Freeze."

I stopped where I was, both feet on the ground but my

hands splayed a bit to the side from the way I had been sashaying.

"Three steps forward."

One, two, three. I held my pose again on the third step.

"Good. Three more steps."

One, two, three.

"One step."

One.

"One more step."

One.

"Now continue around until you return to your spot."

I walked slowly but freely once again and was amazed to find how aroused I was. All from being ordered around like that? From obeying him? From everyone watching? Or from the way walking naked was affecting me physically? My clit was swelling and as I walked, my folds rubbed it. I could feel myself growing heavy with damp desire, and the more people drifted out to the pool area to watch, the more aroused I felt. This was very different from being tied up and flogged; it was pushing buttons I didn't even realize I had.

Faisal and the puppy, whose dog mask hood was now hanging down his back, walked over to stand behind Chino and Lion, sipping drinks of their own. "So is she a sex doll? Is that the idea?" Faisal asked.

"Basically," Chino said. "She can only do what I tell her and she'll do exactly what I tell her."

"Bend down and touch your toes!" Puppy yelled at me.

I stayed still and tried my best to keep an *oh really?* expression off my face.

Faisal clucked his tongue. "Weren't you listening? She only does what her master tells her."

"Just seeing if she was paying attention," Puppy said, and sat down on the stone patio next to Chino. "Will you make her bend down and touch her toes? It fascinates me the way big breasts flop around."

Chino chuckled. "Are you getting tempted to try being bi for a while?"

"No no no," Puppy insisted. "I'm one hundred and ten percent gay. But I can appreciate the fascinating variations and wonder of nature."

"Hello! You can't be one hundred and ten percent of anything," Jill yelled from the open patio door to the kitchen. "That's not how percents work!"

"Nerd!" Puppy yelled back, to general laughter.

"Madison," Chino said. "Come closer. Stand right there." He pointed to a spot a few feet in front of him.

I marched up to the spot.

"Lift up your breasts. Heft them. Show them off for this poor, deprived soul. Show him what he's missing."

I did as he ordered, and the orders kept flowing. "Brush your fingers over your nipples. Make them hard. Roll them. Pinch them. Harder. Use your fingernails. Now tug them, stretch them."

"Can she lick them herself?" Puppy asked.

"Let's find out. Madison, try to lick your nipples."

I knew I could tongue my own nipples, but I normally never did. It just wasn't something I enjoyed when I was pleasuring myself. But doing it for Chino's pleasure, at his command, made it one of the most cheek-glowingly hot things I had ever done. So naughty. His free hand, the one not holding the glass, rubbed up and down the bulge in his leather pants as he watched me.

Bry and Jill came out and pulled up chairs to join the growing group around Chino. "She's a real beauty, isn't she?" Chino said.

"Easy on the eyes doesn't even begin to cover it," Bry said.

"Madison. One step closer, turn around, and bend over to show us your ass."

I did that, my face burning but my arousal just as hot as they watched me like an animal doing tricks for them.

"Legs apart, and reach back and pull your cheeks apart, too," Chino said.

So fucking hot. They were staring at a trickle of my juices; that's how hot this was. I couldn't even process why it turned me on so much. I used to get excited when I first danced burlesque, but it had quickly become a job and I'd concluded exhibitionism wasn't my kink after all.

Maybe I'd been wrong.

"So look at these two gorgeous holes I have to choose from," Chino said. "I've been in the back door but not the front. What do you guys think: Should I try the other one this time?"

The debate broke out immediately. "My daddy always said the pussy is for her pleasure, the ass is for yours," Bry said.

"But he was wrong because I can come from ass-fucking," Jill said with a giggle.

"You can come from Bry looking at you wrong," Puppy chimed in and made everyone laugh. "Personally I'm an ass man myself, not that you would've guessed that."

Faisal took an analytical approach. "Well, if you are trying to maintain a mystery, some depths literally unplumbed, then you could leave her vagina untouched."

"Well, it's not *untouched*, if you see what I mean," Chino said. "I've got no problem with putting vibrators or my fingers or whatever up in there, but no cock yet."

"Ah. Well, the metaphor still stands. If you wish to maintain territory for future explorations."

The pup's master, David, still in his leathers, joined the

group. "I would hold out until she was begging you to do it. That's what I did with Puppy here."

"Four months of pure torture," Puppy whined. "He's like Scrooge McCock. Always making me work for it."

"With women it's different," Jill told him. "It's more like a metaphorical wedding night thing."

Sakura joined the group then. "I never understood that. I'd never buy a car without taking it for a test drive first."

"Oh, no kidding. I mean, the whole female virginity concept is just there to oppress us anyway," Jill said.

"I think," Chino said, clearing his throat a little, "that Madison isn't letting her virginity or lack thereof rule her life. Or her lack of my cock in there."

My insides spasmed with desire and I was sure they all saw it, setting off another wave of heat to my face.

"She obviously wants it," Bry said.

"And you obviously think there's something special about it or it wouldn't be the thing you're dangling in front of her," Jill added, coming around to Chino's other side. "Fucking, I mean; not your cock. Every guy thinks his cock is special."

"My cock *is* special!" Bry and Puppy exclaimed in unison, causing all of them to crack up with laughter.

Chino's attention never wavered from me, though. "I guess you could say by holding out I've turned traditional sex into something special. Plus torturing her is a lot of fun. I think I'll know when the moment is right to give in. Madison, stand up straight."

I straightened slowly, making sure to unlock my knees. Part of me was hoping he was about to tell me to come climb onto his cock. I was sopping wet, hungry for him, and willing to do anything he said. It would be perfect.

"Come over to me."

I walked until my toes were almost touching his. Have I

mentioned that Chino in leather pants but bare feet was sexy as hell? Leaning to one side in his chair he was the very picture of raw sexuality.

"Kneel."

I sank to my knees, focusing on him and him alone, even though nearly all the other party guests were gathered around us now. He took a drink from his glass and then leaned close until his mouth touched mine. I kissed him instinctively and his hand at the back of my head encouraged me. Then his lips parted and his tongue and a heady flood of cognac swept into my mouth. I swallowed reflexively but he didn't stop kissing me, alternately teasing and crushing my lips, suckling my tongue and invading with his.

By the time he pulled away I was breathless and dizzy and not from the booze.

"Can you make her come on command?" someone asked.

"Maybe after I train her," Chino said.

"She seems pretty well trained to me."

"Thank you for saying so, but I think orgasm from voice command probably requires a software upgrade." He stood in front of me looking very pleased. "Pardon me, folks, but the urge to wet my dick is overwhelming at this moment."

For a second I thought he meant he was going to take me somewhere private to fuck, but no, he unzipped his pants and revealed his cock to all assembled.

"Mouth on the head, circle your tongue, lots of spit," he said. His voice was calm, quiet, brimming with confidence that I was going to do as ordered.

Because I was. It was so easy to do exactly as he said. I had stopped worrying about *how* I was doing and simply concentrated on *what*.

His commands kept flowing and I realized he was directing me to give him his ideal blowjob. Interesting. I always thought guys preferred the "deep throat" method, which I'd never been super-good at but could do it if a guy wasn't as large as Chino. With Chino it was going to take some doing, I thought, waiting for the command to take him all the way in, or not to gag, or something.

That command never came. He liked my hand working the shaft while my mouth was busy on the head, and for me to pull on his ball sac firmly but not suddenly. He liked his crown nibbled with my teeth, the slit explored with the tip of my tongue, and for me to coat my lips with precome so he could kiss it off me.

I felt a sudden throbbing in his balls at one point while I was pulling them and working the head with my mouth, and I thought for sure that meant he was coming. But no bitter flood burned my mouth, just another spill of precome. Chino leaned a hand on my shoulder, unsteady on his feet suddenly. "Maddie, I think these folks would like to see me fuck you."

Cheers and clapping ensued.

"I'm reserving your orgasm for me in private, though," he said. "So I'm turning off your ability to come."

Huh, okay, I thought.

"Turn around and place your hands on the chair."

He slipped aside and I put my hands on the patio chair cushion he'd been sitting on. The chair was made of wrought iron, sturdy and probably almost as heavy as me. I gripped the edge as his hands smeared my natural wetness around.

"Okay folks, place your votes. Ass or pussy."

The voting was overwhelmingly for "ass," and someone even brought him additional lube and a condom. I felt a tinge of disappointment, but it was washed away by a flood of desire and sense memories of the last time.

"I'm going to try to make this ass-pounding last," Chino said. "But honestly she's so hot, I don't know if I'll succeed."

He lubed me fairly quickly, and before long he was pushing his way in.

"Making it ache the way she likes," he told them and I couldn't hold back a groan. So good. Exactly the way I liked it. And him telling everyone made me feel like such a naughty girl; my face turned as hot as my pussy.

Once the fucking began I lost track of how long it went on. Apparently not so long that anyone got bored of watching him drill me. Someone even changed the music from the thready techno to a pumping, loud, guitar-driven Nine Inch Nails song. And as Chino transitioned from giving a porn-star-worthy artistic performance—pulling his cock completely free sometimes to slide it up and down and then driving it back in, varying his rhythm and showing off his hips—to going like a steam-piston racing toward the finish line, people started chanting his name louder and louder, faster and faster.

When he came we all broke into cheers and raucous laughter, me included. I just couldn't help myself. It was like Chino had just had sex with everyone here simultaneously and as he came he raised his arms and pumped his fists in victory.

* * *

CHINO

I sequestered Madison into our casita after the scene by the pool. She deserved an orgasm or three after that performance for sure. I lay her down on the bed and kissed her all over, starting at her toes and working my way up her legs, hips, tummy, tits, mouth. "You are the most beautiful, fantastic woman in the world."

She let out a huff but didn't actively argue, still in "sex doll" mode. Good.

"Don't believe me? I'll be more specific. You are the most beautiful, fantastic woman I've ever had the honor of making come." I pulled one of her legs to the side, exposing her glistening folds. "I'm reactivating your ability to come now, but I'm deactivating your ability to move."

She lay perfectly still and I felt that thrill pour through me: she obeyed! Every time this gorgeous, independent spirit bent to my will I felt that power surge. Oh yes.

I moved her other leg and she stayed wonderfully limp. I licked slowly right up the middle of her, dragging my tongue across her clit. A deep shudder went through her but she didn't move. Every part of her was swollen and slick, the most aroused I'd ever seen her, and that included after she'd been wearing the phone-controlled vibrator.

I framed her pussy with my hands and continued my slow licking. Each pass of my tongue was like a kick drum, low and deep. After a while at the end of each lick I added a flutter of the tip, like a hi-hat fill that didn't break the rhythm. I let myself fall into a kind of trance, repeating the motions again and again, measuring time not by seconds but by her breaths, which came faster and faster.

When she began to come she could no longer keep silent, a long, low wail starting in her stomach and rising in her throat as her arousal crested, hung like a wave, then broke and washed all the way up the beach. I doubted she was done either, and slid my fingers inside her, triggering another one immediately. She was wired for penetration for sure. If I hadn't just come minutes before I would not have been able to hold back putting my cock into that pleasure tunnel. Unfortunately, though, I was limp for a while. Probably another half hour at least. Well, something had to feed that hungry pussy, so I handfucked her roughly, sparing her nothing, and she responded with the most wonderfully encouraging cries, changing from screams to the word "yes!" repeated again and again. I made her come until her screams began to sound more exhausted than enthusiastic, and then I let her rest at last.

As before, when I lifted my sloppy fingers to her face, she licked them clean. "You're a better sex slave than the supposed 'house-trained' slaves at the private clubs in London."

"I am?" She licked her lips and lay back, the fitting picture of a ravished goddess, like something from a painting.

"Way better." I didn't want to jump into a heavy discussion seconds after ending a scene, but it was clear to me now that her submissive streak ran very deep. I heaved myself up onto the pillows next to her. "Or maybe you're just more into me than they were."

She blinked and stretched, rolling her shoulders. "Wow. I hadn't realized how much work it would be not to move. I've never done anything like that before."

"A doll scene, you mean?"

"A pure obedience scene," she said. "But wait, what private clubs in London?"

I chuckled. "Come on, Madison. You don't think the Governor's Club is the only place like it in the world, do you?"

"Well, I assumed other groups of people meet in secret but I don't actually know any of them. You've been to ones in London?"

I nodded. "Went to one that's been in the same house since the 1800s. It was pretty wild. People have been hiding their kinks for a really long time."

She snuggled against me. "How'd you get the idea to turn me into a sex robot?"

"Do you really want to know?"

"Yeah."

I snagged the edge of the bedspread with my foot and pulled it over us. "You might not realize this but you have a tendency to resist being dominated."

She poked me. "Quit being sarcastic. I know I resist. I know I . . . top from the bottom sometimes, too. That's why it's surprising you think I'm a better slave than someone trained."

That made me smile. Did she really not know how exciting she was to play with? I guess what some people considered topping from the bottom I considered a fun challenge. "Maddie, you've been-there, done-that when it comes to so many kinks. If I put you in bondage it's like inviting you to resist. But if I make you hold yourself still, that's a whole different story."

"Okay . . ."

"Making you a doll gave you no opportunity to top from the bottom. Because when there's no bondage, no ropes, no blindfold, there's nothing to resist."

"But you like it when I resist," she said, a hint of confusion in her voice.

"I like that *also*. It's exciting when there's a power struggle," I clarified, "but I like it even better when I win."

"Ah." With that one syllable I felt her drop back into subspace, which meant this conversation was no longer on the level—if it had ever been.

I rolled her onto her back. "I think that's what I'm waiting for."

"What?"

"For your total and complete surrender to me. For all the fight to be gone. For your will to be 'one hundred and ten percent' mine."

She chuckled at my imitation of Puppy's voice, but then

asked, "But when I go into subspace, my will is totally yours. What'll be different?"

I kissed her temple so she wouldn't feel these next words were a rebuke. "What'll be different is that you won't hold back whatever it is you wouldn't tell me at TGC that night."

She bristled a little anyway. "I told you there was no flashback. It wasn't like that."

"But something is definitely going on in there. Listen to me, sweets. I'm not scolding you for not being able to tell me. But I think we both know there's something to figure out."

She swallowed, then admitted, "Yeah."

"So that's the key. When we unlock that box, that's when I'll fuck you. Other than in the ass, I mean."

I could feel her considering this idea. "You mean... it's the dom/sub version of a woman not giving it up until he puts a ring on her finger."

"Exactly. Until that commitment's total, yeah, we're not going all the way."

"How's that different from using your cock as a prize?"

"Because this isn't about sex. This is about whether there's more here than just sex. If all the toys and role-playing is just set dressing to spice up sex, then there are plenty of things we can do to get off besides P-I-V." I felt proud of myself all of a sudden. Life of a rock star: I had a steady stream of women ready to be instantly sexual and it had kind of devalued "traditional" fucking for me. But with Madison, I didn't want a quick fuck. I wanted much more. I wanted her. I wanted to own her. Not because she was a meek submissive creature but because she wasn't. Holding back from fucking had given it meaning for me again, and cemented in my mind that what I had with Madison was precious. "It'll happen when you're really ready to submit, completely and totally. When you won't feel like you have to hold back part of yourself."

"Submission is complicated for me," she said, half a whisper.

"That's why it's worthwhile," I murmured, slipping my hand between her legs again. "If it was simple, I wouldn't be interested."

She clamped her legs together. "I thought we were done."

"If you want to be done, say so. Personally, at this moment, I want to put a finger inside you."

"Why?"

"Isn't it obvious, sweets? Maybe it isn't, actually. I'm not ready to stop pleasuring you. I'm not ready to stop torturing you. I'm not ready to give you back your body. "

Her eyes were staring intently into mine as I felt the pressure of her thigh muscles slackening, as she gradually convinced herself to let go. When her knee shifted to give me better access I slid my fingers up and down her wetness. "You tell me which finger to put in you," I murmured into her ear. "Or how many."

"Two," she whispered. "Index and middle finger, please, sir?"

The sound of her voice as she submitted again was the sweetest music. "Oooh, dirty girl." I obliged her, slipping them deep inside and fucking her gently with them. "You see how good it feels when you surrender?"

"Mm yes," she said, her arms around my neck as she arched her back toward more pleasure. "I . . . I think it's because it's you, Chino."

"What's because it's me?"

"I mean, I've never got off from submission before, not like this."

"Oh, and you think it's because you just hadn't met the right dom?"

"I guess. No other guy, or gal for that matter, has ever made me feel like this."

"Maddie, I keep trying to tell you, that doesn't mean you're not 'good at it.' That you can only drop for me is even better." She really didn't seem to understand why that was so perfect—why the fuck would I want a sub who was submissive for anyone and everyone? I crooked my fingers against her G-spot and made her eyes roll back in her head. "Puppy's master was onto something. When you're completely ready to be mine I won't have to put you into subspace for you to feel it. Being mine will be such a part of you that you won't second-guess, you'll do it completely with no reservations."

"But I already feel more deeply about you than about anyone else I've ever been with."

I nodded. "Likewise. But give yourself this test. If I had a tattoo gun sitting right here, would you let me ink my name into your skin?"

She stiffened in my arms. "I'd . . . have to think about it."

"Exactly." I kissed her gently. "Which means we're not all the way there yet. Not all the way to you giving me the gift of your body forever. It's okay, Maddie. I'll accept what you give. You're just not ready to give it all."

"I'm not even ready to come again," she whispered.

"Too bad," I whispered wickedly. "Because I'm going to make you come now."

She made a noise of dismay but didn't protest, didn't use her safeword, didn't fight, unless you counted the way she bucked against my fingers as a fight. Given how hard she came, I wouldn't call it a struggle at all.

CHAPTER ELEVEN

CHINO

We avoided heavy D/s relationship talk again until we were in the car driving back to the city on Sunday afternoon. I exchanged contact info with a bunch of the other partygoers and Bry and Jill asked if we wanted to go to a party with them in a couple of weeks up north somewhere. I told them we'd look at our calendars; I knew the band had some upcoming gigs but didn't know when we'd scheduled the rehearsals.

The drive back was peaceful. I felt good and it seemed like Madison did, too. I wasn't sure if she was taking all the talk about her surrendering to me as just an elaborate mindfuck that heated up our scenes or if she was taking it seriously.

The truth was I meant it very seriously. I could understand why she might want to laugh it off. I mean, come on: become my permanent sex slave? Get my name tattooed on her? I had to be kidding, right?

But I wasn't, not about the tattoo or how I felt about her.

I'd been falling for her right from the start, right from the moment at the Governor's Club when I'd realized what I wanted most from her wasn't a warm place to stick my dick but someone who'd listen. And every time we got together I fell deeper into that hole. I wanted us to be together, and everything we had done so far felt really good, but I didn't think we'd found quite how to fit together. "I wonder how it works with Faisal and Puppy both belonging to David," I mused aloud. "Do the two of them have a relationship, too?"

"I got the feeling it was kind of like sibling rivalry," Maddie said. "They both love their Daddy but their relationship with each other is on a different axis, not romantic but still important."

When she said the word "Daddy" I felt a deep throb in my gut, as if a bass string connecting my balls and my heart had been plucked. "Did they call him that?"

"I didn't hear either of them use the word, but he called them 'my boys' and he had the whole gay 'leather daddy' wardrobe and look down pat. Even if he doesn't use the word itself."

"I think Faisal addressed him as 'sir' even when they weren't in scene. But maybe the whole party was a scene for them."

"He was definitely the service-oriented one."

"Does that make him a slave, you think? Or just a boy, if leather boys are expected to serve."

"Probably depends on what they decide for themselves." She yawned and stretched in her seat. "I've never been totally comfortable with the word 'slave.' I mean, it's fine for other people, and I know a lot of people find the whole ownership idea super-hot, but something about the word just doesn't sit right with me."

I felt a rush of joy. Once again Maddie said the perfect

thing. "It's like you read my mind. I can play master and slave for a night or two but in a relationship? It's like the word's too loaded." *Ha. Like "Daddy" isn't loaded?* I kept quiet about that for the moment.

"So what do you think was going on with Lion and Kittyn?" she asked. Her eyes were hidden behind dark sunglasses as we drove through the desert.

I should've kept my eyes on the road and not try to look at her, but I had to steal a glance or two. "What do you mean? Oh, you mean with the whole thing about how she can never remember to ask his permission before eating?"

"Yeah. Didn't that strike you as kind of weird?"

"You mean the whole asking permission thing?"

"No, that makes sense now that I think about it," she said. "I mean, she's a collared slave, supposed to be his property. Her entire body. Right? The idea is she doesn't eat, shit, breathe, or come without it being like a benevolence from him, am I right?"

"That's pretty much what it sounded like to me," I said.

"So that's the weird part I'm trying to wrap my head around," Madison said. "If she's that into him and into her role as his, how can she forget? I mean, there they are at a play party, the whole thing is kind of like one big scene—"

"If they're into 24-7 play their whole lives are one big scene," I pointed out.

"Exactly. So how does she forget? He even said she never forgets to ask him to come. I'm trying to . . . figure this out."

I glanced at her and couldn't read her expression, but I had the feeling she was trying to process what was going on between her and me. So I tried not to be flip in my answer. "Not knowing them that well, I'm going to make a lot of guesses. But the first is he seems to put up with it pretty tolerably, so maybe it isn't as important as it seems to us?"

"He seemed almost resigned to being embarrassed by her."

"Yeah, you're right. That did strike me as a little odd. Like, if it was me, and I knew my submissive had trouble following an order I think I'd . . . I dunno . . . do more to give them a better chance of succeeding."

"Like what?"

"Like maybe remind her when she went to get the burgers, 'here Kittyn, here's a chance to practice your food restriction.'" *Like you would if you were trying to teach a kid the right way to behave.* "Or maybe punish her swiftly, quickly, when she did it so it'd sink in." I drummed my fingers on the steering wheel. "But maybe they've already tried all those things and they didn't work?"

"Or maybe what he really wants is for her to remember for herself without a lot of special prompting from him," Madison said. "Maybe that's the test. She has to remember it for herself. And he's patiently waiting for the day she gets it right."

"Huh. That's a nice way of looking at it." It truly was. I'd been thinking the guy was kind of weaksauce before that, but perhaps she had a point.

"Just imagine how powerful that scene is going to be when she finally does." Maddie leaned back in the bucket seat with a sigh.

"Yep. And until then there are infinite excuses for punishment and training scenes in between. It's win-win." *And what about us, Maddie? Is that what we're headed for? A long string of scenes where I dominate you every which way until you finally come crawling to me of your own free will?*

I swerved slightly as I realized my daydream was stealing my attention from the road. I hit my blinker to pull off at the next exit to get some coffee.

* * *

MADISON

My phone buzzed with a text shortly before Chino dropped me off. I glanced at it in the car but kept my face neutral. Lawson. I'd been hoping to curl up with my journal and write down some thoughts about Chino and the weekend and whatnot and maybe take a nap, but Lawson had to rear his head. I called Gwen the second I got into the house to tell her about what he was up to now.

"Maddie, where are you?"

"Facedown on my couch. What a weekend I've had. I have so much to tell you."

"Oh? Do tell. A little bird told me you were in Palm Springs with Chino."

"Yes, but there's something much more urgent." I sat up and put the phone on speaker so I could read the text again. "I'm worried about a... potential breach of security."

"Oh."

In other words we probably shouldn't talk about it over the phone.

Gwen's voice remained chipper, though. "Have you had dinner? Maybe we should go grab something and talk about it."

"Sure. Give me a couple of hours to clean myself up. Should I meet you somewhere?"

"Hm. Not sure how cloak and dagger to be about this..."

"Pick a restaurant, text me the address and I'll meet you there at seven."

"Sounds like a plan."

I spent the next hour trying to convince my cat not to be miffed at me for leaving him alone overnight with a small mountain of kibble. "Morris, you didn't even eat it all, and you've even got water in your fountain," I told him when he decided to come out of hiding and march back and forth in front of me, voicing his displeasure loudly.

I eventually coaxed him into my lap whereupon he instantly became a puddle of furry affection. "See, you just had to get over yourself. Sweet kitty."

A few hours later I met Gwen at her favorite sushi bar, a place she and Ricki frequented partly because the restaurant was excellent and partly because the Hamilton security team approved of the place. It was off the beaten path enough that the paparazzi didn't haunt the parking lot and the tatami rooms provided visual privacy.

We placed an order quickly and then the waiter left us alone with an iron teapot and two small cups. Gwen poured for both of us. "Okay, so what's up?"

"Do you remember Price Lawson?"

"The name is familiar. Wait. From the *LA Times*...?"

"*Newsday.* He quit or was fired a couple of weeks back. He was also the guy who bait-and-switched a business lunch for dinner just to hit on me while he was getting a divorce."

"Ugh. Now I remember." She made a face. "Do guys who resort to that kind of shit really think it's going to work? Don't they know it only proves to us they're unsuitable for either sex or relationships? What does he want now?"

"He's starting a new gossip website and magazine called *Pop-litico*—trying to combine all the tawdriness of the celebrity tabloids with the political news, I guess—and that's led to him digging into stuff like the political contributions of the rich and powerful in Hollywood."

Gwen raised one blond eyebrow. "Ricki and I only give to children's and women's charities."

"Not yours. Schmitt's."

Now both eyebrows went up. "Oh?"

"Lawson showed me what looked like pretty convincing

evidence that Schmitt has been funneling a lot of money to Purity Values causes, including a SuperPAC and also a ton of ballot campaigns around the country. I told him who cares, Schmitt probably gives to a lot of causes and I wouldn't put it past him to line any pockets he thinks will boost his influence, right or left wing. But this idiot Lawson actually tailed Schmitt to the mansion."

"Oh." She nodded with understanding.

"And the thing is, he knew I was there, too. So he tried to blackmail me about having an affair with Schmitt."

"What!" Gwen stage-whispered.

"And when that didn't work, he tried to 'rescue' me from the affair by—get this—offering to give me the byline on the exposé of Schmitt."

"What planet does this guy live on?"

"I know. I told him if he needed a big exposé to launch his thing with, he was barking up the wrong tree. I thought I'd convinced him to move on, but then Chino caught him staking out my house."

"Oh man. And it's not like you can tell him the truth about why you were at our place, or why Schmitt was there. But you definitely can't pretend to be having an affair with Schmitt, either."

I sipped from the bright green tea and was surprised when it tasted like rice crackers. "Final straw came today. He sent me a text with a photo." I brought it up on my phone screen.

Gwen squinted. "It's a bunch of numbers."

"I've gotten a little bit lazy about depositing my club salary. Ricki pays in cash, same as your grandfather did, so it's untraceable, but Lawson got hold of my bank statements and it's obvious that the same time every month I'm depositing the same amount. When I first started, Cy told me not to do that, to keep some at home, deposit it in two chunks, vary it up, but since he died I haven't bothered."

Gwen stared into the tiny green pool of her tea. "And Lawson thinks it's either hush money from Schmitt or that you're his kept woman or whatever."

"He's sure it's something very not legit. What should we do?"

"We should definitely fill Ricki in and then, maybe move the date of this month's party? That'd mean contacting everyone about it, though, and that's even less secure..." She pressed her palm to her forehead. "This is going to take some thinking through. Here, let me see if Ricki can join us. She just got back from Silicon Valley today, but I know she had some kind of a meeting in town tonight on her calendar. Maybe she can drop by here on the way home."

While she fired off a text to her sister, I looked at my own phone. I texted Chino: *Did you get home safe?*

The answer came back quickly: *Yes. Just a little while ago. I stopped at the gym first.*

I smiled a little at that. *You mean to tell me I didn't give you enough of a workout over the weekend?*

Ha! You know you did, sweets.

Gwen set her phone down. "She's on her way." She peered through the crack in the sliding door of the tatami booth. "And so is our fish."

The waiter arrived moments later with a beautiful lacquered tray on which sat artfully arranged rice and fish. I tried to eat but now that I had dropped the bomb about Lawson I could hardly taste what was in my mouth.

"You still haven't filled me in about Chino, you know," Gwen said, faux casually.

"Oh, goodness. He's...we're..." I waved my two hands in the air.

Gwen caught them and clapped them together. "Like Velcro. Is that the word you're looking for?"

I sat back with my tea. "I guess so. I'm loving every minute with him. But part of me is still holding back, you know? Maybe I can't believe it could actually be as good as it seems? Or I'm waiting for the other shoe to drop?"

Gwen knew me pretty well. We'd grown close right after her grandfather had died when she'd inherited the running of the club and had very much needed a friend who understood kink while she explored her own kinky side. That meant for most of our friendship I'd been the one giving the advice. I was the older, more experienced, more jaded of the two of us, and it was disconcerting to have her wrinkle her nose skeptically at me. "Is that really it? That seems like a pretty abstract thing to be afraid of."

"Who says I'm afraid?"

Her skeptical look intensified.

"Okay, yes, I admit the D/s has gotten more intense than I expected. And it happened so fast."

"But maybe that just means you're right for each other."

"It's too early to tell that," I said firmly. "After the Velcro stage, once the hormones calm down, is when I'll find out."

"If that's what you're waiting for, though, I'll tell you." Gwen leaned closer. "Axel and Ricki are coming up on their first anniversary and the Velcro stage hasn't let up yet."

"Nor with you and Mal, obviously," I said.

"True." She beamed at the mention of her fiancé.

Maybe a strong bond between dom and sub was the thing all my previous relationships had been missing. Maybe that was the magic that made the Velcro never come undone.

And maybe that was another fairy tale, just a little different from the usual Cinderella story. "I don't know."

"Cynic," Gwen said with a sad shake of her head. "Does he

make you happy? Let him make you happy until he doesn't make you happy anymore. And then we'll reassess. When are you seeing him next?"

"I don't know. I'm the one who invited him to this weekend's play party. I figure it's his turn to invite me to something now."

"Well, if you want to be old school about it, if he wants the relationship to be more than just sex, his next invitation to you should be to a fancy dinner."

"Oh, like he's going to show up at the door with flowers or something?" I made a dismissive noise. "I'm so not into the candlelight-dinners-and-chocolate-hearts idea of dating. Yuck." Come to think of it, Chino wasn't really the flowers-and-hearts type, which I considered a plus.

"Give him a chance," Gwen urged as she picked up a rice ball topped with something golden.

"I am giving him a chance. I'm just trying to slow down, that's all."

"Slowing down can be good if it means you get to enjoy the ride more. Mm, my goodness. Maddie, you have to try this one." She pointed at another one of the things she'd just eaten.

I picked it up with care, and put it into my mouth. Sweet, salty, buttery—she was right, it was amazing once I slowed down enough to savor it.

"D/s can be pretty scary," she said offhandedly. "It forces you to learn things about yourself. Sometimes there's stuff you just don't want to face."

"What did you learn about yourself?" I asked.

"Not to keep trying to squash my dark side. I kept trying to tell myself kink was just good clean fun, like an extreme sport or a hobby. But Mal reached deep into some twisted fantasies. I think that really is why we did this." She held up her engagement ring. "I can't imagine spending my entire life with someone who doesn't know me all the way down to the core, and the only person who can know that is the dom who dug that deep."

That struck a chord. Chino had already dug deeper than anyone else I'd ever been with in my entire life, but that was what he had told me: he wanted to go all the way to the core. "True submission?" I asked Gwen.

"True love," she said with a nod. "That's the proof it's the real thing. There's some limit in your mind you think you can't get past, but when you're with your dom, you *can.* There's no quote-true-unquote love without being totally open."

And us fucking would be total consummation. Him asking for my complete submission suddenly seemed less kinky and more downright...romantic. Almost traditional, in a way. I found myself smiling even as I was asking myself, *could we get there?* He wasn't asking for me to beg for cock; he was asking me for a deeper emotional commitment. Was I ready for that? "What if it's not real, though? What if all I want is some kinky fun?"

"Maddie, I think you passed the 'just kinky fun' stage a while ago."

"Yeah." On the other hand, Chino was holding back some things, too, and I didn't mean his cock. He'd been cagey about where he lived. I still wondered about the female names on his phone. I wasn't the only one who had to open up a bit more for this to become a real relationship.

A little while later Ricki arrived. She moved into the booth next to Gwen and slid the tatami door closed. "I'm glad you called. I'm starved."

"Didn't they have food at the thing you were at?"

"They did, but it was all passed hors d'oeuvres and I was

busy trying to close a deal. I wasn't about to chase caterers all over the place for a scrap of bacon on a toothpick and mess up my lipstick in the process. In fact . . ." She opened her purse, took out a cocktail napkin, and pressed her lips against it to lift most of it off, then wiped them with the clean corner. "There. Enough of that. Bring on the fish, and some celebratory sake."

"Celebratory?" Gwen asked.

"Yes, because between tonight and what I was doing up north . . ." She took the clip out of her hair and let it down, shaking it out in relief. "WOMedia is acquiring some new pieces, including a portal you might be familiar with, Maddie: PlayPeople Network?"

"That's the site I'm doing the sex toy reviews for," I said, startled. "I didn't realize WOMedia was in the business of buying up web companies."

"A couple of the main investors felt WOMedia needed to be bigger to have the right leverage," Ricki said with a satisfied smile. She had started the company only a year ago, when she was fresh out of business school. "So they poured more money in for acquisitions and now I'll be running a company twice the size it was."

Then her stomach growled audibly and Gwen giggled. "The very picture of the young, hungry CEO."

Ricki slid open the door with her foot, waved to a waiter, placed her order, and then sat back while he closed it. "Okay, what fire is it that we need to put out next?"

Gwen started. "Price Lawson is sniffing around Conrad Schmitt. Maddie better tell the particulars."

I repeated for Ricki what I'd told Gwen about how I knew Lawson and what his off-base suspicions were, but with a little extra dose of apology. "Your grandfather warned me not to make those deposits too obvious. I got lax. I'm sorry."

"Don't be sorry because Lawson is a leech." Ricki shook her head. "That's not your fault. The question is what to do about it. Hold that thought. I'm going to run to the ladies' room and wash my hands before my dinner shows up."

While she was gone, Gwen patted my hand across the table. "We'll figure something out. Hey, you haven't told me how the sex toy review blog is going."

"Well, they've turned out way sexier than I expected because guess who showed up to help me test out my cameras and equipment?"

"Oooh, really? Did his manager approve that?"

"I have no idea. I didn't even think about it." I wondered if Chino had bothered to tell management. "I just gave him a model release to sign and he didn't blink. I don't know if he asked if it was okay to do it or not."

Ricki's dinner, a beautiful ceramic bowl of rice with a veritable rainbow of fish on it, arrived and a few moments later she came back. "I knew the food would show up if I stepped away from the table. Isn't that always the way? Now tell me everything you know about Price Lawson."

"Not that much, other than he left the arts desk at *Newsday* to start this new venture," I said. "And the bit I already told you about him hitting on me."

She chewed thoughtfully. "I've been waiting for something like this to come up. One way Grandpa Cy handled problems like him in the past was to sic Schmitt on them. What do we think happens to Lawson if we tell Schmitt he's on his tail?"

"Lawson? What about what happens to Maddie?" Gwen asked.

"One thing at a time, trying to think this through," Ricki said. "In the old days Cy had a lot of people in his pockets. He could make a phone call to the right person—an editor, maybe an owner—and get a story quietly killed. But that was then. These days even Schmitt doesn't have that kind of power anymore. Especially with a new-media guy hot for exposure like Lawson."

"I think Cy used to get away with it, too, by convincing editors our family wasn't 'real' news, so it wasn't against their journalistic ethics to bury a story about our private lives the way it would be something that actually mattered to the public good," Gwen added. "But Lawson's making the attack on Schmitt very political."

"As you know, Conrad Schmitt is far from my favorite person," Ricki said. "What about the other extreme? If we let Lawson go after him, what happens then?"

"I don't like that plan because there's too much we can't control or predict," I said. "We don't know if Schmitt will leak the news about the club, or what."

"Or even if the Schmitt stuff gets handled . . . What if Lawson eventually figures out about the club anyway?" Ricki dabbed a piece of fish in a dish of soy sauce and then popped it into her mouth. "I've been thinking for a while we need a contingency plan for if the club gets discovered."

"What kind of plan?" Gwen poured more tea but was so focused on Ricki that she sloshed some of it onto the table. I surreptitiously swiped my napkin under it as Gwen lifted her cup.

"That's what I'm trying to figure out. Obviously the classic tactic is just deny deny deny. But with anything salacious enough, denials seem like confirmations. Is there some alternate story we could cook up?"

"The problem is that the alternate story might seem even worse," I said. "Lawson already thinks Schmitt's having some kind of affair. If he wrote down license plate numbers the night of the party he might try to claim you're running some kind of brothel in the mansion."

"That would be worse," Gwen said. "I've kind of wondered actually, for us, would it be so bad if people knew we were into kink? Okay, maybe I don't necessarily want to retroactively out every movie star who used to frequent the mansion in Granddad's heyday, but for us? I've been kind of thinking people don't care that much."

"Seems risky, though," I said. Maybe it was different for the two of them: they lived in a mansion and had private security, and they were used to their faces being in the tabloids. But I wasn't. Yes, I was making sexy videos, but I assumed people who watched that sort of thing were cool with it. Having my face printed in the *Los Angeles Times* next to a "Secret Hollywood Sex Dungeon Exposed" article, on the other hand, could be very different. I didn't want photographers stalking my every move and baristas tweeting that they had sighted me getting a latté.

Ricki pushed her bowl aside. There was nothing left in it but rice. "You know, I've been making the assumption we have to maintain secrecy just as a matter of course, but you've got me thinking, Gwen. Look at all this Purity Values stuff going on. They frame everything about sex as being dangerous for women or oppressing women. But it's just an excuse to try to turn back the clock on women's rights. The real oppression is making women think they can't have full, varied sex lives—or that they shouldn't. By hiding, we play right into that. I'm not ashamed of what we do."

"Not anymore. You've changed a lot in the past year," Gwen said with a smile.

It was true. Ricki had been a borderline prude when they'd taken over the club and had been deathly afraid of the family secrets being exposed. I didn't have as much to lose as they did, but I didn't have the protections they did, either. I shifted the discussion a little: "Well, you know I'm never going to be ashamed of being sex positive. But if we 'came out' about the club, what about the rest of the members?"

"The older ones are mostly middle managers at CTC and subsidiary companies," Ricki said. "Their jobs are secure. Plus it's not like we would release their names. But the younger crowd, the actors and musicians and fashion designers we've been bringing in? Most of them would love a rumor that they're members of the most exclusive kink establishment in America."

"I can't imagine that Mal would care, or Axel," Gwen added with a giggle. "Christina will say it's 'on brand' and want to issue a press release about it."

Christina. "Is that the band's publicist?"

"Manager, but she's very publicity-oriented," Ricki said with a nod. "She's a gem. Think about it. Most publicity campaigns fail and are ignored. What if we told everyone and no one cared? Could be a win either way."

They might be right, but I found myself still wondering. "And if they did care?"

"If they care because they think it's awesome, no problem; it boosts everyone's careers. If they care because they think it's awful, well, then the spin machine has to crank up. But that's why it makes sense to be the ones to make the announcement ourselves, to control the spin and introduce it with the message we want."

That was true. If exposure might happen anyway, being proactive was better than reactive.

She tapped her fingers. "I'm not completely sold on the idea we should step so far outside the box. But I want us to consider the idea, really think it through. Meanwhile, Madison, stay in touch with Lawson. Tell him he's wrong about the money but that you might be able to tell him more if he has any further dirt on Schmitt to share with you. Because if it turns out Schmitt is really deeply into Purity stuff, I'm not sure I want him around anymore regardless."

CHAPTER TWELVE

MADISON

I met Price at a different coffee shop this time, one where we could sit indoors, and where the hissing of the drinks being made and the general clatter would keep us from being overheard. I was already waiting at a small table in one corner with an iced coffee drink when he came in.

He didn't even go through the pretense of getting some coffee himself. He made a beeline for me and sat down, peering at me gleefully over the tops of his sunglasses and grinning a shit-eating grin. "Gotcha," he said, like he'd won some playground game.

I didn't lower my own polarized lenses, merely sipped from my straw and then said, "No, don't gotcha. What exactly do you think you're proving here?"

"Someone's paying you off, Madison."

"Someone's paying me. If you hadn't noticed, I have a lot

of sources of freelance income. Some of them pay in cash, some by PayPal, you name it."

"Do you think I'm stupid? Nearly the same amount every month for four years, always around the same time for the deposit?"

"You'll note my mortgage payment is due at the same time every month and it's important for me to add money to my main checking account before that."

His smile dimmed a little. "You don't really expect me to believe that," he said slowly, but his words lacked conviction.

"Believe what you want, but that'd be an awfully flimsy piece of evidence for a sensational news story." I ran my finger nonchalantly down the condensation on the side of my cup. "On the other hand, I may have more to tell you about Schmitt—that is, someone I know may be willing to talk to you about Schmitt. But they didn't believe the deposit record evidence you gave me. There's got to be something more."

Lawson shook his head. "It doesn't work that way, Maddie. You have to give me something before I give you something."

I laughed out loud, which disconcerted him greatly. He whipped his sunglasses off and made a shushing motion, looking over his shoulder as if expecting someone to be sneaking up on him.

"I don't have to give you anything," I told him, "because I don't actually *want* anything from you. I'd be just as happy not to be involved at all."

"Don't be ridiculous. You want...you want a job. You want to be a political reporter. I can help you with that."

"No, thanks, Price. You've done enough to burst my illusions about journalistic integrity that I'm no longer interested." I sipped my drink and regarded him coolly.

"You're going to want my protection," he growled, leaning forward as if that would intimidate me.

"Is this like the mafia's protection? Is that why you were staking out my house with a camera? To protect me?"

"I—That was—"

"Stalking. And now we're getting into extortion. Care to rack up any additional offenses I could bring to the police? Or your new bosses?"

He stood suddenly, as if his chair had become red hot. "Schmitt himself must've put you up to this. What does he want?"

"Don't be stupid. If Schmitt knew you were digging up dirt on him? He'd have already offered to either pay you off, or threatened to run you out of town. I'm not working for Schmitt."

"I... I'll e-mail you." He moved quickly away from the table then, trying to look casual with a fake "good-bye" wave as he crossed the floor, but then he had to come back to grab the sunglasses he'd left on the table.

I watched him flee, thinking *what a piece of work.* He was trying hard to be a chess master but he had hardly any pieces on the board and didn't even seem to know the rules. But when I walked to my car a couple of blocks away, I felt like looking over my shoulder the whole time. This thing with Lawson and Schmitt, the talk with Gwen and Ricki about paparazzi, the importance of managing the exposure if it came... it was all making me paranoid. *You're going to want my protection,* Lawson had said. What had he meant by that? Was he just blowing smoke or was he continuing to dig? Of course he was continuing to dig. That's what he did.

I got in the car and drove toward home, telling myself, *No one is following you, Madison.* But Price had staked out my house that one time... He could've assigned a photographer I didn't know. If he was desperate enough to dig up some dirt he might even make something up that could be more damaging than the truth. I drove all the way to the highway, got on, got off at the next exit and reversed direction, just to confuse anyone who might be following me.

I got off the highway and took out my phone. I had not yet entered Chino into speed dial and had to pull over to bring up his number and call him.

"Madison," he said, "how are you?"

"A little freaked out. You know the reporter guy you scared off from outside my house? He's still annoying as fuck." I put the car back into gear and started driving.

"Are you in the car?"

"Yeah, can you hear me okay?"

"I can hear you just fine. Anything I can do about the annoying asshole?"

"At the moment, no." I sighed. "I just... just wanted to hear your voice."

I felt like a dork for saying that until he said, "I'm glad it's me you called."

I wished he was there with me right that second. I was suddenly tired of slogging through life alone. Independence was great; this was its drawback.

"Are you scared?" he asked.

"No. Well, maybe. I'm just feeling weird about the whole thing. I don't want to be home alone."

"Where are you now?"

"I got off the 101 at Vermont Ave."

"You know..." he trailed off, thinking. "You're not far from where I live."

"Is that so?" I held my breath. He'd been evasive about where he lived and I still didn't know why.

"Do you want to come over?"

"Yes." I said it with more force than I intended, but knowing he was nearby made me suddenly desperate to see him, all the more so because of my questions about his living situation. Maybe they were about to be answered.

"My place isn't much," he said. "Come south on Vermont Avenue and I'll talk you through the directions."

I thought he was being mock-deprecating, after the mansions and modern palaces we'd looked at in Laurel Canyon. But as his directions took me deeper into a not-ritzy neighborhood I began to wonder.

"So have you heard from PlayPeople about whether they liked the kit review?" he asked, as I drove slowly down a commercial strip.

"They loved it. And the bathtub one went over well, too. They're cleaning up the edits a little and going over the written stuff I sent and checking the links. I think the first one should launch next week. They didn't say exactly."

"If you're coming up to the motorcycle detailing shop, turn left. The building right behind that's mine and you can park in the back."

His place was a smallish loft apartment in the back of a somewhat run-down-looking converted industrial building. No wonder he was looking to trade up if this was where his digs were now. He was on the second floor, waiting for me in the doorway. He was wearing cargo shorts, a tank top, and nothing else.

"I told you it wasn't much," he said as he shut the door behind me and threw the deadbolt. He showed me into the main room, where a set of electronic drums stood in one corner. On the coffee table sat a practice pad and some drumsticks.

"Don't you have a big set of drums, too?" I asked.

"The full kit's at our rehearsal studio," he said. "And aren't you forgetting something?"

My cheeks flushed and I turned to look at him. "You mean, a proper hello?"

He clucked his tongue. "At your age I didn't think I'd have to be the one to teach you proper manners. Come here, sweets." He beckoned me to come to him, placed my hands on the hard planes of his chest, then slowly wound his arms around me until our mouths met.

The kiss heated up instantly, one of his hands slipping into the back of my jeans as he pressed our bodies together. I opened for his tongue, sucking in a breath.

And then he pulled back. "Can I get you a drink? Are you hungry?" When I didn't answer right away, he added, "Or are you already slipping so deep into subspace that you can't answer questions about your own needs?"

That jolted me a little. "I'm fine. I just came from a coffee shop."

"Horny, then?"

I sucked in another breath. "Always, when you're touching me, and that's the plain truth."

He gave a slow nod. "Same here. But I don't want to take advantage of you if you're feeling scared and vulnerable. You know, *hey baby, come over to my place.*"

"Um." My brain felt sluggish, like it was partly frozen. It was like being asked something by a teacher in school and knowing the answer was in your head but not being able to think of it on the spot.

He kissed me on the forehead. "Here. I'll give you the nickel tour of the place."

There wasn't a lot to show me: a galley kitchen, the main room with its overhead skylight, and a bedroom with a very small window but another large overhead skylight in one corner, the bed in the other. He had almost no furniture. The closet lacked a door and his clothes were mostly in makeshift shelves of milk crates or scattered in several laundry baskets under a small table. Out in the main room he had two mismatched armchairs, a kitchen table, and a flat screen on top of a trunk serving as a TV stand. A laptop sat on one of the chairs. He moved it to the kitchen table and sat where it had been, pulling me into his lap. "Now you've seen what none of my bandmates have seen."

"Your apartment?"

"Yeah. I got the cheapest place I could stand so I could sock away as much money as possible. Saving up for a house for my mother." He ran his fingers through my hair and I felt relief running through me. Once again Chino wasn't what I expected...and wasn't *hiding* what I expected, either.

You might have to accept that he's actually as good as he seems, I told myself.

His phone rang. I recognized the ringtone and couldn't help but give him a questioning look as he pulled the phone out of the pocket of his cargo shorts. I saw the name on the screen: Flora.

The last time I'd heard that ringtone he'd sent it to voice mail and brushed it off. That nagging fear I had about another woman in his life reared up like acid reflux in my throat. Just when I had let myself think there was nothing left that could come between us other than the crap in my own head.

To my surprise, this time he answered the call. "Hey, Flor. You okay?"

Sitting in his lap like that I could make out the woman's voice, tinny and frantic, if I stayed quiet. "Chino, I'm really starting to worry."

"Where are you now?"

"The parking lot of the grocery store. I volunteered to go out and get something so I could call you where no one can overhear."

"What's going on? Are you okay? Is Mom okay?"

Mom? Was this his *sister*? The knot in my throat started to loosen.

"Listen, I don't want you to think badly of Vincent or me that we didn't do something sooner—"

"Flor, what are you talking about?" Chino's voice dropped as low as I'd ever heard it. "Just tell me."

"I don't know if it's because Vincent's getting married and moving out or what, but he's been more volatile lately."

"He, Vincent?"

"No. Father. He's been getting more and more violent. I mean, maybe I'm reading too much into it, he never raises a hand directly to her or me, you know?"

Oh, no. I leaned closer to listen and felt Chino's arm squeeze me tighter. This didn't sound like a good situation.

"Flor—"

"I don't know. I mean, everyone gets angry sometimes..."

I eased myself out of Chino's lap and motioned to him, pointing at myself and miming holding a phone to my ear. *Let me talk to her?*

He nodded at me, leaned close with the phone tipped slightly toward me, and I could hear her say, "He blames you. He puts the blame on you. He's forbidden us from speaking with you. I had to call to tell you that's why Mom hasn't called you back."

"So you had to sneak away to call me? Flor, is he threatening you?"

"Not directly. Maybe I'm blowing it all out of proportion."

I gestured more urgently. Flora sounded like so many women I'd talked to back when I worked the crisis line, scared but unsure.

"Flor, listen to me. I have a friend. She knows about this kind of thing, okay?" He stood up and paced the length of the room. "I want you to talk to her. Tell her what you think is going on."

I couldn't hear her reply now but I sat down in the other chair, hoping she'd talk to me.

"She counseled women, that's why. Look, if it's nothing she'll tell you."

I watched him pace back and forth like an agitated tiger at the zoo, getting more and more ready to lash out.

"You wouldn't have gone to all this trouble to call me if you weren't worried. Why do you keep trying to talk yourself out of it? Here. Just talk with her."

He thrust the phone at me and I took it. "H-Hello?"

A female voice was at the other end. "Hi. Look, I'm sorry to bother you about this, but I guess it's worth a try. I'm Flora."

"Hi, Flora. I'm Madison."

"Marilyn?"

"Madison. Like the avenue. Call me Maddie."

"Okay. Thanks, Maddie. Look. I don't want you to think badly of our family or our mother."

"I promise I don't. It's okay, Flora. Every family's different. Can I put you on speakerphone so Chino can hear, too?" It had been several years since I'd helped on the crisis phone line, but the training was still there. Number one, don't act judgmental or you'll scare them off. In the early going it was my job to listen, and if possible to try to get them to see—or admit—that there was a problem. Often women who were suffering any kind of intimate partner abuse were sort of brainwashed into thinking their situation was normal—or hopeless, or shameful, or any number of other things that would keep them silent about it. Getting them to see past that was so important. I put the phone on my lap and dug a notebook and pen out of my bag. "I'm not here to judge you or your mom's choices. Can you fill me in a little on your situation? Do you live with your mother?"

"Yes, I live in the same house, but it's a large house. I used to worry, but then things seemed all right. I mean, things got better for a while. After Chino left I started to believe the story that the reason Dad was so angry all the time was because Chino was making him angry. He calmed down a lot after Chino left. But it feels like now that Vincent's finished with college, something's changed."

"That's your little brother?" I motioned to Chino to stay quiet.

"Yes. He's on Dad's side."

Dad's side. Who was on the other side? Chino? Mom? "And you're not?"

"I'm...not so sure now. Mom's been really depressed lately. Dad says it's because her 'baby' is all grown up. He's very...impatient with her all the time now. I just don't know what to think."

I took a deep breath. I wasn't prepared to grill her about whether she'd seen signs of physical abuse, but there didn't have to be punching or hitting for there to be threats or emotional manipulation. "Think about what you just said a second ago, 'things got better for a while.' What were they like when it was worse?"

"Oh, goodness. Dad having rampages where he said he'd put the fear of God into us. Into Chino, mostly."

"Rampages?"

"Oh, he smashed the TV one time—"

Chino couldn't stay silent any longer. "Because he said our minds were being poisoned by it. There was the time he smashed the coffeepot, too. Tell her about that."

Silence. Then Flora cleared her throat and went on. "He...he picked up the glass pot from under the coffee maker, full of hot coffee, and smashed it on the counter, glass everywhere."

"And you got burned by some of the coffee, Flor."

"I did, but he was so *so* sorry about that afterward."

"Was he? I remember him screaming it was Mom's fault for making the coffee too strong and bitter, and forcing her to clean it up."

"I don't remember that," Flora snapped.

"Sure you don't, because he was kissing up to you to make it *aww better.*"

"Chino," I said sharply. "If you want me to talk to your sister you should stay out of it."

He glared at me for a second then shook his head as if suddenly remembering he was looking at me and not his mother or his stepfather or his little sister. He raised his hands then stood silently and went into the hall, either to the bedroom or bathroom.

I picked up the phone. "Sorry about that," I said to Flora. "It's just me now."

"That's all right," Flora said. "It's just... hard. Our stepfather did a lot for us. Our mother taught us to be grateful to him and to be respectful."

"I would never ask you not to be respectful of him if that's important to you," I said. "But it does sound to me like you're describing someone who, at the very least, acts out dangerously at times."

"I... I suppose that's fair to say."

Good. I got her to admit that much; there was hope I could get through to her. "Now, you were saying that the rampages stopped after a while?"

"Yes. After Chino left town. Father... calmed down a lot. For years. I thought he mellowed with age. But lately..." She trailed off and seemed unable to say anything more.

"It's okay, Flora. Can I ask you if you've ever felt unsafe with him?"

"Well, we were always afraid when we were kids, but that's normal."

That's normal, I thought to myself. *Oh dear.* "So what's changed since Vincent finished school?"

"Mom's changed. She's anxious and nervous. I mean, more than usual. But she's depressed, too. Like she's not interested in going to our knitting group anymore. I still go, but the women there treat me funny."

"Funny how?"

"Like they don't really like me or trust me? But they're too polite to say it to my face so they're ultra-polite instead. But it feels weird."

Maybe they're afraid of your stepdad, too, I thought to myself. *Try to be neutral. Try to be neutral.* "Well, if your stepfather is known for his rampages, they might be leery?"

"He's a very well-respected member of our community," Flora said primly.

"Sometimes 'respect' is just another word for fear," I said. "Flora, you're not responsible for how other people feel or how they react to your stepfather. I'm just saying, if they'd ever seen him smash a pot of hot coffee or a television, they might worry, okay?"

"Okay. Yeah."

"But they probably don't want to say anything. So they don't know what to say."

"That makes sense, I guess."

"I think I agree with them that your stepfather could be dangerous."

"He's done so much for us, though. Fed and clothed us, put a roof over our heads."

"Is that what you think or what he thinks?"

There was a long silence before she spoke again. Then her voice was soft. "You're right. That's what he says. When he's angry. That we ought to be grateful."

A wife shouldn't have to be "grateful" that her husband gives her food and shelter, I thought angrily, but now wasn't the time to rail about that. I kept my voice calm. "Being grateful doesn't mean you have to put yourself or your mother in danger, Flora. Let me ask you one more thing. If you tried to leave, do you think he'd be angry?" I used the words she used: "Would he 'go on a rampage?'"

Again there was a long silence, before a single word: "Yes."

"Flora, I want you to take down my number. I want you to know you can call me anytime you need to talk about it, okay?" I could hear rustling as if she were shifting the phone and I gave her my phone number. It sounded like she was writing it down. "And please tell your mother, too? And give her the number of this national domestic violence hotline: 1-800-799-7233." Again the writing sounds. Good. "Tell her she doesn't have to want to leave her relationship to get support. They'll listen. They won't judge."

"Oh, Maddie," she said before she hung up without saying good-bye, "people always judge."

I found Chino boxing his reflection in the mirror in the bathroom. When he saw me he chuckled and shrugged like he'd just been goofing around, but his moves had looked legit to me. I handed him the phone.

"Well?" he asked.

"I'm probably not telling you anything you don't know if I say he sounds dangerous," I said. "But you can't make your mother leave him. If he *is* an abuser then he breaks her down psychologically so she believes she's worthless without him. They typically isolate the victim from their families and other people, and convince them that only the abuser is trustworthy, and to be paranoid of everyone else. Then if someone tries to intervene, it'll look like he was right when he said people will try to split them up. His paranoia will seem justified."

"That's twisted," Chino said.

"Very. But if that's what's going on, you can't make her see it. She has to come to see it for herself. The only thing you can do is try to get her to trust you. To believe that she can tell you anything and you won't judge her for it."

Chino's shoulders slumped. "How am I supposed to not judge her? She's the one who kicked Dad to the curb and then fell for this guy. She's the one who uprooted us from here and moved us halfway across the country to marry him."

I knew those were childhood wounds talking, but I couldn't think of anything to say that wouldn't sound condescending. Instead I put a hand on his shoulder and found myself suddenly pulled into his arms. I wrapped mine around him, too, feeling the quaking of rage deep inside him, helpless about his mother and unable to do anything about it, no matter how deeply he cared for her.

"It's going to be okay," I ended up saying, because I had to say something. "We'll keep trying."

He let go of me as suddenly as he'd embraced me. "I'm sorry. I didn't mean to yank you into all my family's bullshit."

I grabbed a handful of his shirt. "Is your family another thing you don't let people see?"

"What do you mean?"

I wasn't the only one he had kept all this from. "You don't let your bandmates see your apartment. I bet they don't know about your family, either."

He didn't meet my eyes though he put an arm around

me. "They know my family's so religious they don't listen to rock music. That's pretty much all they know." He closed his eyes and his voice was thready with pain. "But you think he's abusing her. You think she's abused."

I tried to keep my voice gentle, but it seemed to echo in the tiled bathroom. "Yeah. I do."

"I can't believe I left her there. No wonder she won't ever talk to me."

"Your mother?"

"I mean, it's obvious now; isn't that what you're saying? That we should've seen it sooner. I was just so glad to get out of there and I blamed her. I actually blamed my own mother for it..."

"Hush, you were sixteen and you were under threat, too." I tried to pull him toward sitting down in the living room but he didn't move, just swayed like a tree rooted to the spot. "Did he ever smash anything else like the TV?"

"It's like Flora said. Because he never crossed the line to raise a hand to her, she can believe maybe it's only things that happened by accident. You don't want to believe that the man your mother loves is going to hurt her." His eyes were still shut and he was practically vibrating with rage. "This is the first time Flora came out and admitted that she's scared."

"Abusers are very good at keeping people on their side and convincing them nothing's wrong." This time when I tugged him toward the living room he let me lead him onto the rug, but then stopped short, clenching his fists.

"I've been so angry with my mother for so long, for choosing that bastard, and then... you know, I try to call her and sometimes she doesn't call me back. Or when she does call all she wants to do is ask me when I'm going to let Jesus save my soul."

"Keeping her from talking to her family or friends, isolating her, that's a classic thing abusers do."

"Shit." He bowed his head. "And here I've been thinking all along it's that... she doesn't love me."

Chino was too much of a tough guy to cry at that admission, but I wasn't. I felt wetness on my cheeks while he sucked in a breath in a kind of dry sob. He looked up at the skylight. "And I left her. Abandoned her. I don't deserve—"

"Hush, no, Chino." I hugged him and he hugged me reflexively, hard. "You didn't know. If you'd stayed it might have only gotten worse."

"What am I going to do?"

"You're going to keep in touch with your sister. She might be able to get through to your mom. Maybe... maybe your mom is getting ready to break away and he knows it, and that's why he's escalating."

"I want to go get her," he said.

"Rescue her, you mean? How, kidnap her? If she's not ready to go, Chino, you'll really make it worse. She needs to trust you."

"How's she going to do that?" He spoke through clenched teeth: "Her devil of a son."

"You don't believe that," I said softly.

"I'm too much like my dad, my real dad," he said, anguish squeezing his voice. "That's what she said. She'll never trust me."

"It's been years, you said. You're a good man, Chino." I kissed his cheek, his ear, trying to assuage his pain with little affections. "Maybe she'll be ready to see the man you've become."

* * *

CHINO

When you've believed something for a long time it's so difficult to see something different. I knew that, but I was counting on my sister to believe something other than what she'd been told all her life: that our stepfather was a saint and that rock and roll was a one-way ticket to hell.

But I had to challenge my own beliefs, too. Some of them didn't even make sense, contradicting each other. Like part of me believed my mom had only married him for the money, because she was tired of being hungry and overworked and sending me to school in the same jeans every day because I was outgrowing them faster than she could afford to buy new ones. Another part of me believed she did it for love, that the only thing that could justify what she'd done to my father, to me, was love. Now to find out maybe it wasn't either of those things, or maybe that it was somehow both? To have it thrown at me like this when I was two thousand miles away—and unable to do anything about it—crisp-fried my brain. I felt simultaneously like I was going to collapse and like I was going to explode. Everything was raw. Everything was wrong.

No, not everything. Soft kisses trailed my jaw. Madison. Madison was everything right in my world. The scent of her shampoo, and the enticing heat of her skin as she sweated anxiously on my behalf, penetrated the fog of rage and hurt clinging to me.

I pulled her closer, bringing her mouth to mine, and was amazed to find her tongue coaxing mine out, gentle licks encouraging me to part my lips and a sinuous tongue tip drew its counterpart out to play. A moment later I had her head in my grip and my tongue fucking her mouth. Yes. Taking her mouth felt right. Here was something I could control, something I understood. I kissed her until my own lips went numb, but when she tried to pull back I held her firmly until my tongue forced lustful moans from her throat.

One of her legs was wrapped halfway around my hip. *Mm.* I pulled back at last to look at her. Her lips were slick, her eyes glazed, her mouth slack and ravished. She blinked at me once, then in one swift motion peeled free of her T-shirt. Her bra was beige and I could see her nipples pressing the fabric.

I gave the barest nod and she reached behind herself and unhooked the bra, then tossed it aside.

Yes, gorgeous breasts, and very much mine. She bared them, lifted them and offered them, and in her eyes I could see the supplication, offering them for pleasure or pain, for whatever my desire should be. I ducked my head directly to one nipple and suckled hard, tonguing the nipple and nipping it with my teeth. When she yelped I moved to the other, biting it first, then soothing it with laps of my tongue.

But my thoughts continued to tumble and fall. What if that bastard hurt her? What if he'd been hurting her in secret all these years? Guilt turned my insides to icicles, fearing the worst, fearing everything that could have happened and which still might. The sixteen-year-old me that had left home wanted to go back and kill the bastard. I took a step back from Madison, trying to take deep even breaths.

Madison looked at me, her eyes searching mine. "Chino, please," she whispered. "Don't pull away from me now."

I shook my head. "I'm sliding down into the darkness."

"Don't." Such a simple little word, and spoken so quietly you'd think I could have brushed it aside. But I couldn't. It was the tiniest grain of defiance—how dare she tell me what to do?—but it caught my attention. "Slide down into this instead."

She slipped her jeans and panties off and then stood there stark naked in my living room, hair loose, skin glowing in the light from the skylight overhead. I drank in the sight of her but tried to act unmoved, as if the most beautiful woman I'd ever known stripping herself naked in front of me was no big deal.

She held my gaze, her eyes blazing with magnetism, as if she were readying herself to say something devastating. But instead of saying another word, her tongue darted nervously to the edge of her lip, and then she slowly sank to the carpet, to her knees, her eyes never leaving mine.

My blood, which had been pounding with rage and hate, now pounded in a different direction. I popped the button on my fly with one hand and twitched one eyebrow.

She got the message. I don't know which was more arousing, that she instantly knew my desire or the way her hands felt as she lowered my zipper, pulled my erection free of my shorts, and cupped my balls in preparation for taking me into her mouth.

She remembered what I'd told her about what I liked, the way to work the shaft with her tongue and the head with her fleshy inner cheek. I pulled off my own shirt to give myself an unobstructed view down my front to her mouth being stretched by my cock.

"Slowly," I told her, because I wasn't interested in coming, I was interested in her working me, in her submission and obedience.

And she didn't falter. Even when I could see her jaw was tired and she needed to wipe her nose and her lips were sore. Her eyes were closed and I could see her lids were shiny with unshed tears. That was when I took hold of her head and pumped my cock in and out, never deep enough to make her gag but kicking my arousal up to the next level. "Good girl," I said, words starting to spill out of my mouth as I let the troubles of the outside world fall away and the world of just us two close around me like a bubble. "Good girl, oh that's it. Yes. Give me your mouth, give me your body. Yes, girl, yes."

When I pulled her up to give her a break, to give her air, her eyes were closed and her mouth was open like she was ready for me to plunge back in whenever I wished. "Tell me what you want now, Maddie."

I was expecting her to beg to be fucked again. I was expecting her to tell me this was as deep as she could go and she needed me that much. We were both as raw emotionally after Flor's phone call as we'd ever been, and I had never felt how much I loved Maddie before that moment. "Tell me what you want, sweets. Time for a reward."

She opened her eyes and said something completely unexpected. "Did you come home with the paddle?"

I knew the one she meant. The leather studded one she'd taken from the Governor's Club and brought to Palm Springs. "Yes, it seems to have made its way into my toy bag," I said. "Wonder how that happened?"

"Paddle me? Please?" Her voice was tentative, quiet, but clear.

I rubbed my palm along her arm since her butt was out of reach. "And why should I paddle you, sweets?"

Again, what she said wasn't what I expected to hear. "Because you love me?"

"You are a delight." I pulled her up into a hug. "Toy bag's in the bedroom. Go get the paddle and bring it to me."

Her leaving the room gave me a moment to gather my wits. Did she know how good this was for me? Just when I'd been ready to slip into a hopeless, dark place—a shadow of my time on the streets, motherless and fatherless, helpless against the power of a man I couldn't touch—here was Madison, reminding me of what power I had, giving me strength. And I needed her strength, too.

When she returned with the paddle, she appeared at the doorway of the bedroom with it and then hesitated. "How should I bring it to you?"

"Oh, you mean, should you crawl over to me with it in your mouth like a puppy? Puppy doesn't feel right, does it?"

"No, sir."

"What feels right to you, Maddie? Do what feels right."

She took a breath, then carried it in two hands and knelt in front of me, offering it up like a scepter to a king. I took it and swung it in the air. "You must want to find out what's going on in your head as badly as I do."

"I want any barriers between us to be gone," she said. "I realized if I don't know myself, I don't know if I can love you the way you need. Or if I can even b-be loved the way I need." Her voice shook a little, as if admitting she needed love had been hard for her.

Maybe this was going to work, then.

"Knowing you better can never be bad," I said. "I want you to be mine, Madison. Wholly, truly mine. Body, heart, soul. Good, bad, and in-between. Maybe we're going to find nothing inside Pandora's Box, but I'm going to try to open it anyway."

CHAPTER THIRTEEN

MADISON

"I think you know the position and the rules." He gestured to a suitable spot on the apartment wall.

"Yes, sir." I put my hands against it and glanced back at him.

"Stick your rump out a bit more, would you, sweets?" Chino said. I bent over further and spread my feet flat against the rug. He rubbed my bare ass with the palm of his hand. "Are you nervous?"

"Yes," I said. Then, "I mean, I'm kind of jittery with anticipation but I'm not, um, using the warning word."

"Good. Points for being clear." With that he began to spank me with his hand, warming me up slowly, intimately.

I was already in subspace, but his touch and the sensual sting of the spanking stoked my arousal. I loved being spanked this way, each swat layering atop the previous in a gradual buildup of intensity.

He paused to shuck his shorts. I stole a look back at him.

His cock strained upward and he was swinging his arms, loosening them up.

He picked up the paddle and rubbed the non-studded side against my bottom. "Here we go, sweets."

He continued with the layering approach, not hitting overly hard, moving the paddle from place to place, the pain beginning to ramp up as he started to hit me harder. In any other dom such a methodical approach would have come across as cold, but with Chino his passion came through: I felt as if it were vitally important for him to claim each inch of skin individually.

And then he switched to a freer swing, hitting harder, knocking me forward with the force of the blows, and sending my mind onto another plane, one where I couldn't sense time passing any longer and I forgot I had any reason to exist other than to be a target, a receiver, to catch what he threw. Knowing that it aroused him to beat me like this made each blow as potent as a kiss, each swat the equivalent of him licking his way up my leg or the deep thrust of his finger. I fell into the rhythm of it the same way I often sank into sex, wholly connected with my partner as our bodies did what they did over and over because it felt right.

When he paused again, to catch his breath, I realized I was out of breath, too. Even when the brain is blissed out on endorphins the body knows it's going through something. This time I forgot I meant to look at him while I spun through the breaths. I felt his bare skin as he molded his body against mine and licked sweat from the back of my neck.

"Turn around, back to the wall," he commanded into my ear. "Hands over your head."

I moved as quickly as I dared into position, careful not to bang my head against the wall. What was he going to do now? Paddle my tits?

No. I felt his breath a moment before his tongue rasped hotly over one nipple. He took his time, licking each nipple until it was jutting hard, and then sucking until it was borderline painful.

I felt his mouth moving south, over my belly button, licking all the way down until he was eating eagerly between my folds. Was he planning to make me come in the middle of this? I didn't feel any closer to knowing what had happened to me that night at TGC, so surely this wasn't the end...

No. Not at this moment, anyway. He brought me to a whimpering height but not all the way to the peak of release, then stood to kiss me, his mouth musky with my own scent, sharing the salt of my sweat on his lips. He pulled back to say, "Hands against the wall again, sweets."

My voice came out a whisper. "Yes, sir."

I returned to the position and thrust my ass out, ready for more.

I knew he'd use the studded side of the paddle now, and I was expecting another ramp up.

I was half-right. The studded side of the paddle struck, but instead of building up gradually this time Chino went straight to brutal pain. I screamed and kicked one foot then the other but I kept my hands on the wall. The blows only got harder and when I instinctively tried to wiggle my ass out of the way, he grabbed me by my pubic hair. *Bam, bam, bam*—the hitting was hard and fast, solid and inescapable.

"No! No! No!" I screamed.

"You know how to make it stop, Maddie," came his voice from below me, on one knee.

"No! No!" I pressed my hands even more firmly against the wall and clamped my lips shut, biting down on the pain.

"I'm going to get to the bottom of your mystery, Maddie. I

just hope you're ready for it." He stood again and sank one fist into the hair at the base of my neck. The next blow was from the paddle but instead of having a big backswing it was short, almost downward, *smack*. I cried out, not from the physical pain exactly but from the message it seemed to convey: *bad girl.*

"I'm trying!" I gasped out.

"Are you?" *Smack*. His voice sounded harsh, disappointed. Smack. "Are you, Maddie?"

A sudden sob broke free. "Yes! I'm trying so hard for you. So . . . hard . . . to be good."

Another sharp smack. Then another.

"Don't be angry!" I found myself crying. "Please don't be angry with me."

"Don't you deserve this, Madison?"

"No!" I was crying full-on now, tears pouring down my face and gulping air as I tried to answer, the words pouring out of me without passing through any of my filters. *Smack*. "I'm trying so hard!" *Smack*. "I don't deserve it at all!"

Smack. "Why not?"

"Because I've been *good*!" I screamed as another swat caught me right at the join of my buttock and thigh. "I'm a good girl! I haven't done anything wrong! I don't deserve to be punished!"

"Are you sure?" he pressed, and this time no blow accompanied the words.

"Yes! I'm . . . you said I was everything you ever wanted! I've been good!" I stamped my foot, tears streaming down my face. "I've been good! Please, Daddy! I've been good!"

The word "Daddy" seemed to echo in the air and I froze, trembling, terrified, disbelieving I'd said it and afraid he was going to walk away from me in disgust or frustration or whatever it would be that meant I wasn't really what he wanted.

That I wasn't good enough. That this had all been a very damaging mistake.

But sweetness and light poured down on me from his answer. "That's my girl."

I felt his body against mine again, the sheen of sweat on his skin cool against the flaming hot flesh where the paddle had done its work. "That's my girl," he said again. "Daddy loves you, sweets."

Now my tears were tears of release, of relief. "Do you mean that?"

"Yes, Maddie, you've been very, very good. And I think maybe we've dug down to what you were holding back." His lips pressed against the top of my shoulder. "Now, tell your Daddy what you want. Good girls get a reward for being good."

Was he asking me now if I wanted to fuck? Hadn't he said I would have to be ready to take his name in ink for that, though? I was way too much of an emotional wreck right at this moment to be able to tell whether I'd regret it or not if I said that, though I seriously wanted to. That's how a script would've gone—*fuck me, Daddy, fuck me now*—and then all the fucking ever, roll credits. But this wasn't a porno film. I was too deep in little-girl-land to be thinking rationally but not so deep I didn't still know it wasn't right to make it happen like this.

"I want to please you, Daddy," I said, my voice tiny but clear. "Please let me please you."

The tightening of his arms around me felt like I was being wrapped in his approval, as if it were seeping out of his skin and into me, the best drug in the world. I felt no pain, not from the bruises, not from the fading fear, not from anything. "You please me so much," he said. "So much. You've been so good, so perfect, Maddie. I love you."

Those words rocketed through me, ears, brain, heart—*I love you!*—and I pressed back against him, sucking in a breath. "I love you, too."

His fingers snaked down my belly toward my snatch. "Are you sure?" A hint of amusement crept into his voice.

"I'm sure." In the back of my mind the thoughts flickered about how I'd been wrong about so many things about him, and how again and again he'd proved himself right for me. The "other woman" had been his sister. The house hunting hadn't been for a rock star ego palace but for his mother. The joking flirtation had been genuine interest in me. His passive manner hadn't been lack of dominance but the patience and confidence of a hunter. I truly was sure now about him, about how I felt, what I thought, and what I needed deep down. I couldn't explain why but that didn't change the fact that the moment I'd called him Daddy I'd felt a restless need in me filled.

His fingers spread me and one of them set to flicking my clit. His teeth explored my back, nipping a few times while his other hand plumbed both of my holes. Mine still had not left the wall.

He made me come like that, both his hands working me mercilessly, making me scream as the orgasm ripped through me. And then a second one, and an even louder scream. I suddenly wondered if he had neighbors who might mind the noise.

"Such a good girl," he murmured, the fingers inside me twisting and making my hips writhe. "Come for Daddy. Show me how much you love me. Come again."

I came again, exhausted and no longer experiencing it as pleasure, exactly, except that the best pleasure of all was pleasing him and feeling that approval wash over me as he praised me. "Perfect girl, beautiful girl, so good. She tries so hard for me."

I panted, nodding because I couldn't quite swallow enough to speak.

"One more, sweets. Come one more time for me."

I shook my head then finally cleared the lump in my throat. "I don't think I can."

"No?"

"But I'll try, Daddy. I'll try. But what if I can't?" The panic flooded in suddenly, sweat breaking out all over my skin. "What if I can't come? Will you be mad at me?"

I felt his mouth against my labia then—a kiss—and I opened my eyes to see him on the floor on one knee between my feet, looking up at me. "I won't be mad if you try your best. But if you really can't, Maddie, you know how to stop the scene."

Right. Drop my arms. That hadn't even occurred to me. "I-I'll try."

"Good girl. Because if you don't come, I won't either." He had two fingers inside me and was gripping his cock with his other hand. "So I really need you to do it for me." His tongue swept up my sore clit and then he sucked it into his mouth, torturing it with the tip.

It worked. It hurt to have my bare, overstimulated nerve endings roughed up relentlessly, but I couldn't bear the thought of disappointing him, of leaving him unsatisfied. I screamed one final time, my legs shaking as I came, clamping my thighs against his head. His breath was hot and sharp against my skin as he must've come himself, but he didn't let up until my aftershocks were completely done.

I don't remember how we ended up lying down on the rug, but there we were, breaths slowing, my eyes opening to see his doting smile. His hand was between my legs, cupped loosely over my flesh, massaging it gently.

"Not ready to give me back my body?" I said with a smile.

His eyes were serious. "Never, sweets. I want this forever. I want you forever."

"Am I your girl?" I was trying to ask what that meant exactly but the words hadn't quite filtered up after the wracking orgasm had taxed my brain.

He kissed me as gently as he ever had, his lips sensuous and full. "Yes, sweets, you are my girl, my one and only girl."

I whispered the word, wanting to taste it in my mouth again: "Daddy."

He kissed me again more firmly, forcefully, and slipped a finger inside me again, his tongue doing the same. When he lifted his mouth from mine he said, "I knew 'slave' wasn't right for you."

"I knew 'master' wasn't right for you," I answered. "But 'sir' still works in scene, you know? When it's time for... discipline."

He nodded. "A girl obeys her daddy, and is rewarded when she does. She's punished when she doesn't."

"And if he's good and fair he doesn't punish her unless she deserves it," I added.

"Exactly right, sweets. You belong to me, but that's because we belong to each other." He wiggled his finger inside me. "There's only one more test my girl has to pass to make it official, I think."

"To make the relationship official, you mean?" I asked, so endorphin high I had to make sure the words were making sense.

"Mm-hm," he affirmed. "To consummate it."

Right. Despite being completely exhausted and deeply sated, I still felt a sharp spark of desire for him where his finger was buried. "Yes, Daddy," I whispered. "But I thought you said I needed your name on my skin before you'd do that?"

"Hm, so I did," he said, nuzzling in my hair.

"I want it," I found myself saying.

"My cock?" he purred, voice rich with amusement.

"Your name. In ink. On my skin." I wriggled against him. "*And* your cock."

"Mmm. My cock won't be ready to go again for a while, though," he said, pulling his hand free of me and lying back to tug on his limp flesh. No response from the organ in question.

I draped my arms on his chest and rested my chin against them. "That gives us time to go get me inked."

"Oh ho, is my little girl impatient?"

"Very."

He thumbed my lips, admiring my face, or maybe searching it for something. "Is it just that your girl persona is impatient or is Madison tired of being strung along?"

"Both," I said. Now that I was thinking about it, Daddy/girl made more and more sense. As a child I had been headstrong and independent. My parents had always been supportive of anything I truly wanted to do—paying for dance lessons, ice skating lessons, clothes I wanted, cheerleading camp, you name it—but they'd been wary of praising too much. I'd gotten most of my validation from my own accomplishments, only a little bit from their praise. And as I'd gotten older, I'd pulled away from needing their approval entirely, choosing my own major in college and deciding where to live and how to work since then.

But had I ever really stopped needing approval? Was the journalism major really my own choice or was it something I thought they'd approve of that I'd also liked? I believed I'd outgrown the need but deep down it was still there. My "girl" role was proof. I'd been keeping her buried for so long, telling myself not only that I didn't need anyone's approval, but I didn't need love, didn't need a man to be happy, didn't need to be subservient to anyone. Guess what? I did need love, I did need approval, I did have a deep need to obey and to be challenged with hard work in order to get that approval.

And with Chino as my Daddy I'd get all that. Love, praise, affection, protection, correction. A perfect match. I could be headstrong and independent in a way I didn't associate with "slaves" or even with "submissives." But I had a place. A role. And Chino would put me in my place when I needed him to. I could feel it. "I don't want to wait. I want to capture this moment forever." I climbed on top of him and leaned down to put my mouth beside his ear and whispered it again. "Daddy."

His hands caught me by the hips and he growled. "Fuck, you are a naughty girl sometimes."

"That's why I'm your girl," I said. "That's why you can't wait to put me in my place."

"Fuck yes." He ground against me. "And put every inch of me into you."

"There's a tattoo place on the corner," I pointed out. "Do they know you in there?"

"They don't, but given some of the art they have in the window, I bet they'll understand what we want just fine." He looked up into my eyes, his dark and deep, misted with lust and love. "I should get inked, too. 'Maddie's Daddy.'"

I ran my hands down his chest, over the designs he had there, all black work. "Where will you put it?"

"At the crease of my thighs, one word on each side." He licked his lower lip. "It'll hurt like hell to get it there, but that's the right place."

I sat up, straddling him. "And on me? Where should your name go?"

"Right here." He drew his index finger across my womb,

parallel to the top of my pubic hair. Then he looked up and I felt pinned by his gaze, by the force of the desire in it. "Maddie."

"Chino." His name felt as loaded as the D-word all of a sudden. As if the heady bond we had while in scene no longer faded when we went back to being our "normal selves." I swallowed sudden excitement. That was exactly it. If we stayed together we were never going to be those old selves again. My tongue touched my teeth for a moment as that sank in. "We're really going to do this."

"We really are, sweets."

"I don't mean the tattoos. I mean, us."

"That's what I mean, too." He reached up and cupped my breasts admiringly. "And I couldn't be happier about it."

"Couldn't you? That's pretty heavy, what's going on with your family."

He nodded. "I know. That only convinces me more that we belong together. You were so good with my sister. And it just feels so right. Like it's fate that brought us together when I needed you most and showed me not to hold back."

"So wrong that it's right," I said with a smile. "Daddy."

"Maddie," he answered, giving my rump a mock swat.

"What's the best part of being my Daddy?" I asked, wetting my lips and giving him a seductive look.

"Besides having your hungry pussy within reach all the time? The right to discipline you—and that means both punish and reward. I love you, Maddie. But if I weren't your Daddy you'd bristle every time I tried to protect you or teach you or correct you."

"You like protecting me." It wasn't a question.

"I do. I also know being overprotective would be a mess. You're still going to work at the club, I assume. I won't always be there. My girl will have to take care of herself sometimes.

Fortunately she's a big girl I can trust. Which means a nice reward when I get home."

"You know a girl only has one Daddy," I said.

"And this Daddy's only going to have one girl. You." He pulled me down for a kiss.

He rolled me over onto my back and ravished my mouth. If either of us had any more words to say right then, they were devoured instead of spoken. I had never felt so complete in my life.

CHAPTER FOURTEEN

CHINO

Madison and I practically stumbled across the street, both giddy from that freefall feeling that only comes when you're falling headlong into love. I couldn't keep my grip on my angst and worry with the flood of sweetness pouring between us. A shower had cleaned us up but didn't dampen my ardor in the slightest. We kept catching each other's eyes, looking deep and thinking, *we're really going to do this. Be together. Yes.*

We walked down to the tattoo place to see if the sign in the window that said WALK-INS WELCOME was really true. A young guy with seven or eight rings running up the ridges of his ears greeted us. He had a tattoo that went all the way around his neck in a slim collar of words. Until he was bent over the counter writing out something I hadn't been close enough to read it. Looked like a motto or saying about submission, though.

That didn't surprise me. Lots of tattoo artists were into other forms of body modification and lots of them were into BDSM, too. I would be willing to bet this wouldn't be the first time he'd be tattooing a sub for a dom.

"Name's Nat," he said. His hair, what little of it he'd let grow, was blond. There was a bigger tuft on his chin than on his head. I liked him right away when he pointed his goatee toward the Bondage Beauty on my upper arm. "Classic Gary, right? You get that done here? I don't recognize you."

"No, had these for years," I said, showing him the one on my other arm.

"Well, if you ever want more..." He indicated the sample wall behind him where there was a section that was all Frank Gary pinups. Nice. Seeing a Gary in the window had been what led me to look on this street for FOR RENT signs last year but this was my first time inside the shop. "So what're you here for today?"

"His and hers tattoos," I said. "We're looking to ink her with my name, and me with... something else"

Nat didn't miss a beat. "What's your name?"

"Chino." I spelled it for him.

"I thought you said that wasn't your real name," Madison teased me while paging through the sample book on the counter.

I laughed. "Trust me, you don't want 'Aloysius' tattooed on you."

"Is that your real name?" She looked unsure whether I was joking or not.

"My given name," I said with a nod. "It's a saint name. I have to guess when I was born my parents were going through an Anglo assimilation phase and a Catholic guilt phase at the same time. Chino's my chosen name and that's what's important."

Nat was all business. "A shorter name'll be cheaper. You want it in a heart or anything?"

"No, no, just the lettering."

"If all you want is black letters, about yea big? Hundred dollars. Hundred-fifty if you want the really heavy black."

"No. The slim letters are more her style, don't you think?" Madison was pointing to an elegant style in the book and I nodded in approval.

"Okay, and upper arm?"

Madison framed a spot under her belly button with her fingers. "No, here."

"Ah, gotcha." Nat looked back and forth between us. "And for you?"

Madison answered, leaning her chin on my shoulder. " 'Maddie's Daddy.' "

"I can take *you* right now," Nat said to Maddie, "but I don't think I can get you both in before my eight p.m. appointment."

"That's fine. I can come back for mine," I said, and Maddie squeezed my hand as she grinned. *We're doing it,* she mouthed silently.

Yes we are, I mouthed back. That phrase could mean so many things and I meant all of them. *We're doing the partner thing. We're doing the tattoos. And we're going to "do it"*—after all, once my name was on her skin, I could make good on my promise to consummate our partnership in the traditional way.

Nat led us into the back of the shop where there were small rooms all along one side of a hall. Some of the doors were open and I could see glimpses of chairs and equipment. Some of the doors were closed and I could hear the buzzing of tattoo guns in use as we followed him into his room.

"Okay, so the panty line. Are you talking about above the snatch, shaving the snatch, or what?"

Madison pushed her shorts and panties down to reveal the very top of her pubic hair. "I think right along the top of there is best?" She traced where my finger had indicated.

From behind her I pushed her panties all the way down to mid-thigh and kissed her bare ass as I stood back up. "Yes, right along there. Don't get any ideas about touching her, Nat."

Nat chuckled. "As if I didn't already have a clue you're kind of possessive. Not to worry, boss. I don't do fish, only meat. Miss, if you'd lie down on the table here, I think that's probably the best way to do this."

He prepped a sample tattoo first, positioning it and then peeling the backing away so that purple letters stood out against her pale skin. That looked about perfect so the next step was to fill it in with black ink. He prepped methodically, laying out tiny cups of ink and testing the tension on the tattoo gun.

While he busied himself with that I slid Madison's pants all the way off her and massaged her pussy. There was a layer of sanitary paper under her on the massage table and I wondered if she was going to leave a wet spot. I grinned at her.

I love you, she mouthed at me.

I love you, I mouthed back.

I held her hand as Nat began to actually apply the tattoo. She squeezed hard. "Oh, fuck that hurts."

"Not a masochist?" Nat asked idly as he worked.

"Well, I sort of am but *ugh*, that feels like you're knifing me in the stomach."

"Breathe," I reminded her. "Breathe and think of me."

Her attempt to smile came out a grimace as she gritted her teeth. After ten minutes of that, I was worried she was going to crack a tooth. "I should've brought a vibrator."

"If you want to, eh, *soothe* her, I don't mind," Nat said. "Just don't get in my way."

I was on the opposite side of the table from him and he was working on the letters upside down, his hands on her belly, leaving her legs free.

I slid my thumb against her clit and saw her begin to relax. "That's a good girl. Don't move."

Her clit grew more and more swollen as the process went on and her breaths became long and deep.

"Hey, Nat," I asked, checking the watch on my wrist. Almost quarter till. "For another hundred would you leave me alone with her for fifteen minutes when you're done?"

"If it's cash, sure," he said with a grin. "And I'm just about done, actually."

He cleaned up, showed off his handiwork to me—the letters stark against her pale skin, my name staring me in the face, permanent and real—then bandaged it over and withdrew, leaving us alone.

Madison was sitting on the table at that point, swinging her feet. "Fifteen minutes?"

"I'm not waiting until we get home." I freed my cock, which was pretty well strained to the limit, and sat down on the chair. "Get on."

She straddled me eagerly, one hand on my chest, the other sliding up and down my shaft. "So hard already, Daddy."

"Get on, girl," I repeated. "Don't make me tell you again."

She rubbed the head back and forth in her wetness. "I'm not on the Pill," she said, and I knew she was serious, not role-playing.

"Then I won't come inside you," I said, just as serious. "Not until we get somewhere with condoms."

We searched each other's eyes. Yes, it was a small risk. But neither of us was going to let that stop this moment from happening. She sank down onto me with a tiny cry.

"Slowly," I murmured against her skin.

"It's hard to hold back," she answered, panting as she pushed herself down further. "You feel huge this way."

"And you feel like everything I ever dreamed of." I meant it, too. She wasn't just warm and tight and pulsating with need; she was mine in every way. I thumbed her clit again and felt her squeeze me. "I'm not coming while I'm inside you," I said. "But you sure as hell are."

She made that tiny sound again, trying to keep quiet, and I put a hand over her mouth to silence her while my other hand worked on getting her off. Her clit was so slippery I almost wondered if maybe there wasn't enough friction with my thumb flicking back and forth, but her hips began to jerk and her breath to come in steam-engine gasps through my fingers, and then her spine went rigid with orgasm. I pushed her to a second one and she pushed herself to a third one, rocking back and forth and banging her clit against my pubic bone.

I pushed her off after that one because I'm not made of stone and I was about as close to my own limit as I could stand without coming myself.

We cleaned up quickly, using the wet wipes Nat had in a dispenser, and put our clothes back together as best we could.

My balls were aching but I had never felt better in my life as we stood at the counter while Nat ran my credit card for the tattoo (and pocketed the other hundred). While he was waiting for the transaction to clear he said, "Hey, I think Frank would love to see your Bondage Beauties."

"Frank. You mean, Frank Gary?"

"Yeah, you didn't know? He's in back doing someone right now but he was almost done last I looked."

"I had no idea he was a tattoo artist. I only know him from the comic books."

"Yeah, he got into tattooing maybe ten years ago. The

work's steadier than comics." Nat pulled my receipt from the machine and handed it to me with a pen. "Sign here, and let me see if he's done."

"An artist you idolize?" Madison asked, as Nat slipped into the back again.

"Yeah. When I was a kid my dad had a ton of magazines with kinky bondage art in them. Frank Gary was my favorite, though."

I could hear Nat's voice as he neared the counter again, leading an older man from the back hallway. "Yeah, what a coincidence, huh? He's just a walk-in, had no idea you worked here." Nat waved toward me. "Frank, meet Chino Garcia. Chino, the inimitable Frank Gary."

He stepped aside to reveal a face made long by the receding of a graying ponytail. Older, but still a face that I knew.

My father.

My real father. "Chino?" he said with a frown on his face—disbelieving, skeptical, but eyes widening as he realized he recognized me after all. "Aloysius Francisco Garcia?"

My lips were numb but I managed to say, "Dad?"

Nat's mouth hung open. I was vaguely aware of Madison closing it with her hand on his chin, his teeth touching with a click.

At almost the same time, my father and I said, "What are you doing here?"

Answering that question was going to take a while.

* * *

MADISON

When the two Garcia men met for the first time since Chino was ten years old, at first I wasn't sure if they were going to hug each other or fight. When they puffed out their chests I couldn't tell if it was because their hearts were so swelled or if it was to see who could dominate the room.

They neither hugged nor fought, physically. The elder Garcia held out his hand across the glass countertop and they shook.

"I live up the road," Chino finally said.

"I've been working here for years."

"How did I not know you were Frank Gary?" Other than shaking his father's hand, Chino had barely moved. They had nearly identical postures: head high but shoulders canted slightly forward. "How did I not know?"

"Even your mother didn't know, until the day she did." He shook his head. "The day she threw me out for being too much of a pervert." He laughed bitterly and then looked Chino up and down. "Didn't want me to influence you kids. But I see the nut didn't fall far from the tree. Who did those?"

Chino patted one of his own upper arms. "Some guy in Cleveland, don't even remember his name."

The elder Garcia nodded slowly in a mannerism that reminded me eerily of Chino. "You're being rude, son. Who's the lady?"

Chino stood up taller. "This is Madison. Maddie, this is my father, Cisco Garcia."

"Gary's a pen name," he said as he took my hand in both of his and bowed slightly. "Charmed."

"Nice to meet you, Mr. Garcia. If you two would like to catch up..."

"No, no, I can't talk long. Got my next appointment coming in at the top of the hour. But what say we grab a beer after work?" He pulled his business card from the holder beside the cash register and handed it to Chino. "Cell phone's on there. Shop closes at eleven. That too late for you?"

"Not too late at all," Chino said. "See you later."

I think Chino was in something of a daze as we left the shop. I made sure he didn't walk in front of any traffic on the way back to his apartment. The sun had set while we'd been inside and the cool night air blew Chino's hair across his face.

In the apartment I sat him down in his armchair and then investigated what was in his fridge. Coke, beer, orange juice, milk... although the milk was basically empty. "You want a drink?"

"Sure," he said, without specifying what. He was staring at nothing.

I poured us both Coke on ice in mismatched tumblers and brought it to him.

He drank to the bottom of the glass and then set it down, ice clinking. "Well. That was unexpected." He looked at me. "What'd you think?"

"Of your father? He reminded me of you."

Chino huffed, a half laugh. "Yeah." Then he shook himself like a dog. "I guess I'll find out more later. But you. You just got inked for the first time. How do you feel?"

I slipped into his lap and put my arms around his neck. "Endorphin high and totally yours."

His smile was blissful and bright. "Which is exactly how you should feel. I'm not done with you yet, sweets."

"Well, given that I'm your girl permanently, I'd certainly hope not."

"Mm. That, too. But come on. Let's do this in the bed. I want to take my time and this rug is hell on the knees."

In the bedroom he shed his clothes as he went around the room lighting candles. He didn't have much in the way of home décor, but he had tea lights on the windowsill, the night table, and the bookshelf next to the crates of clothes.

I undressed myself and climbed onto the bed, watching him as he went. I'd known very few men who were as perfectly comfortable walking around naked as Chino. And I'd known plenty of wild guys in my time.

"What?" He settled onto the bed beside me. "You look like you're having thoughts."

"Just remarking to myself how much you like to walk around nude."

"You should've seen me as a kid. Any excuse to take my clothes off, I would. I'd get the hose and fill up a storage bin in the driveway, fling my clothes off, and climb right in."

"Your parents must've loved that."

"Dad thought it was hilarious. Mom not so much. She was freaked out that not only was I naked in front of the whole neighborhood, I could've drowned. She tried to shame me for showing off my junk but somehow it didn't sink in." He stretched. His cock was much redder than the rest of him, suffused with blood and heat. "When we moved to the Midwest I got naked a lot less often, though. No beach, cold weather, and religion. Brrrrr."

"No wonder you came back here."

"Where I'm comfortable in my skin. That's what the tats are about, too. It's my skin. I'm marking it as my own." He kissed a line down my breastbone and tummy until he came to the bandage covering my tattoo. "Keep it covered for a couple more hours. Wouldn't want to get inappropriate body fluids in it."

With that he dived between my legs and set his mouth to my pussy.

I found myself impatient, though, wanting him inside me. I'd had plenty of orgasms in the shop and although he quickly rekindled my arousal I didn't want to come anywhere near as much as I wanted to be filled, to feel his flesh fill that gap, to feel his body fit against mine. So basic, so simple, but there it was.

But there was no hurrying Chino. Making needy cries only encouraged him to tease me more, and begging, which I eventually broke down to do, only got me his fingers and more Daddy-stalling questions that led to more begging.

And the more I begged, the deeper into subspace I went, and the deeper into subspace I went, the more the begging itself turned me on.

"Please, Daddy, just an inch? Put just an inch into me?"

"Do you want me to suck you? You know I give the best blowjob you've ever had. Let me get you ready to fuck me."

"I need you so much I'll do anything. Anything."

"Please, Daddy, before I go insane."

But he didn't give in. He fingered me and licked me and coaxed me to the edge of orgasm a few times, until I said, "I'll truly do anything."

"I know you will, sweets, because you try so hard to be a good girl."

"I'll even take the blindfold. Blindfold me but fuck me, *please*."

He looked up my body to meet my eyes. "You're serious."

"Very." I felt my heart pounding in my ears, but every word I said was true. Even as my blood pressure rose, though, I felt calm, secured by my submission, knowing I was completely in his care. It was like I could no longer worry, no longer fear, because I had already broken past that fear to become so wholly his in the first place.

"Turn around, sweets. On your knees."

I got to my knees on the bed and turned my back to him. A few moments later I felt his hands smoothing my hair, pulling it into a ponytail.

And then a cloth came over my eyes—awash in the delicious scent of his skin and his cologne. He had made his shirt into a blindfold. He tied it tight and then hugged me from behind, his erection against my spine, his hand over my heart, feeling it race.

"Come back onto me, sweets," he said. "Just to get it good and wet. Then I'll put a condom on."

"All right." I would never have done this—unprotected penetration—with any other man. But with Chino I didn't hesitate. As in the tattoo shop I felt the risk was small and, like the contact, was the ultimate in intimacy. I wiggled my ass back against him and he guided me with his hands until I felt the head of his cock centered between my lips.

His fingers were hooked on my hips and he thrust suddenly, filling me with a burst of pleasure-pain.

"Good girl," he purred. His fingers crept up my ribs, swirled over my breasts, latched on to my nipples. "Now fuck."

I wanted to move back and forth but my range was limited by the fact he was pinching my nipples, creating pure torture as I rocked on his cock.

So good.

Then he let me free and his hands fell onto my bare ass instead. Each time I drove myself back against him he met me with a double spank. Five, six, seven, eight—

He jerked free suddenly, his hands gripping my ass like iron. "I'm getting that condom now."

The bed shifted as he went away and it felt as if the darkness around my eyes was like a blanket, like a cocoon of calm. Like those moments when I had been a sex robot, between orders I could just be, just enjoy being Chino's girl.

I heard the crinkle of the condom package. "Here's a challenge for you, sweets." I felt his hand on mine and then the condom being pressed against my palm. "You put it on me."

He had already opened it. I felt it with my fingertips, figuring out which direction it rolled. I got my tongue good and spitty and loaded up the tip, then felt for his cock with my other hand. Fitting it on like a hat and then unrolling it took a few tries, but once I got it going down his shaft I heard him groan.

"Is that all right? Good enough?" I asked, wanting to make sure it would work.

"Perfect," he said, though I felt him pull away and it sounded to me like he adjusted it somewhat. "Now, if you want it, come and get it."

I reached out and to my dismay he wasn't where he had been. "Where are you?"

"Over here," he said, and I could hear he had backed a few feet away from the bed.

"Chino!"

"It's right here, waiting for you."

I moved to the edge of the bed, my feet on the floor, and stretched my arms toward him but I couldn't reach him.

"Right here," he said again, and I thought maybe he had backed up another step.

I stood slowly, taking a hesitant step toward him.

"You're getting warmer," he said, like it was a child's game. "But if you wait, you'll get colder and colder..."

He was on the move, backing away from me. With my arms out, hands seeking him, I took a few more steps, following the sound of his voice—"warmer, warmer," as I closed the distance, "colder, colder," if he pulled away.

I stayed focused on his voice, on my goal, on the throbbing emptiness between my legs and the heat of him I thought I could detect with the palms of my hands.

"Warmer, warmer..."

I could feel we'd moved into the main room, the air currents moving against my bare skin, my nipples perking up in the cooler temperature. "I thought we moved to the bedroom to save your knees," I commented.

"My knees won't be a problem, sweets." I could hear he was close and then my palm suddenly met his chest and he pulled me down as he fell back into the armchair. Instinctively I straddled him, his cock slipping against my hole but not quite going in until I reached back to guide it.

There. In. He thrust upward into me and it was like my entire inside was being fucked, one huge cavern of pleasure all the way to the tips of my fingers and toes.

I know technically it was all sex but whether it was cultural programming or just the way my vagina was wired this felt the most like sex of anything we had done. There was sex, and then there was sex-sex.

"Do you want to come?"

"No," I said.

"No? Really?" He sounded genuinely surprised.

"Really. I mean, later maybe. Right now I just want this. Just want you. Just wanna fuck."

"We can do that, sweets." He snaked an arm around my waist and thrust upward harder. "Hang on to me."

I held on with arms and legs and the next thing I knew he had picked me up and was fucking me standing up. The breath was knocked out of me as we hit a wall but I didn't care as long as his cock was coring me. I needed penetration more than air.

His voice, words between panting breaths: "This . . . isn't . . . good . . . for . . . your . . . bandage."

He disengaged as I slipped down the wall, my feet touching the floor. He held my hands and led me through the apartment again. "Onto the bed, on all fours," he urged.

I felt the edge of the bed with my hand and crawled into position.

"Now back up onto my cock, sweets. You're going to make me come this time."

Just like that the challenge was set. He steadied himself with a hand so I could impale myself by feel, adjusting my knees so the height was right. "I'm holding the condom, don't worry about that," he said. "Now fuck me, sweets. Fuck me hard. Suck the come right out of me with your body."

CHAPTER FIFTEEN

CHINO

Sometimes when you talk dirty, sometimes when you give your sub an order, you don't necessarily expect it's going to work. You go with the flow, figure out what's working, what's not, change the plan if necessary.

That wasn't the case when Maddie made me come inside her. If I hadn't had a hand holding the condom in place she would've suctioned it right off me, and as it was, even though I was holding it there I had to keep looking to make sure because that's how amazing it felt.

I yelled long and loud when I started to come—her name, praise to the universe, obscenities—I don't even know what else. Listening to myself wasn't high on the list of sensory experiences right then, as my nerve endings and my heart were overloading. But sweet mother of mercy this was everything in life, everything.

Well, okay, it wasn't music and it wasn't food and it wasn't air, which were three things I needed to live, but merging with Maddie—giving her everything I had and taking everything she was—was right up there with the other staple needs of life.

She collapsed under my weight as I made the last few thrusts I could before my cock softened, bliss ebbing gradually, and then I lay there atop her, feeling like I never wanted to move again. I wanted to just stay like that forever, glued to her by sweat and desire, skin to skin, perfect.

But after a few minutes of listening to her breathe, I felt the urge to look at her, to touch her with my hands, to listen to her voice again. I slipped to one side. "You ready to have your eyesight back again?"

"Yes, sir," she said sweetly.

I tugged the blindfold gently upward until it came free. "That's the first 'sir' I've heard since before the paddling." I kissed her temple so she would know I wasn't criticizing. "I thought maybe you'd save it only for when you were being punished."

Her eyes fluttered open. Full night had fallen and the candles gave dim light. "Do you want me to say it more often?"

"No, sweets. I just thought it was interesting."

"I don't want to wear out 'Daddy,' you know?" Her grin would've been utterly lascivious except for the coy way she bit her lip at the end.

"Oh, yes, sweets. I know." I pressed a kiss to her hair. She smelled sweeter and more intoxicating than wine. And she was mine.

"Plus your name means the same thing, now," she said, leaning her head on my shoulder. "I wasn't expecting submission to feel this good."

I was already feeling about as good as I thought I could

imagine, but hearing her say that made me feel even better. "Good in what way?"

"Like everything is... a perfect circle. And like before that I didn't even know it could be a circle. Everything was a square or a triangle, with sharp edges and unfilled corners. And now... everything fits."

I kissed her cheeks, her eyelids, her mouth. "I feel like that, too."

"I'd tried submitting to guys in the past, you know. And it never felt like this. I read about subs who were looking for this... this peace... this inner tranquility, and they wrote about finding it in submission. And I always thought *I'm a bad sub* or not a 'real' sub because I don't feel that way. But it's not submission I find it in," she said. "It's in how safe you make me feel, how loving you are even when you're dominating me. You're what fills the hole, Chino. That's what makes it possible for me to be your girl."

And that's why this is going to work, I thought. "I've had girls crawl to me on their knees and pledge to be my slaves before," I told her. Some just said it to turn me on while others had meant it sincerely, but none had made me want to pledge myself to them for more than an hour of role-play. "I never fell for one of them the way I fell for you, though, Maddie. It just never felt like this. I never wanted to pour my whole heart and soul into dominating them the way I do with you."

"Whole heart and soul," she agreed with a nod. "It's scary, isn't it? I've never felt safe enough emotionally in a relationship to give my whole heart and soul before. Even with some really nice guys. Maybe because they just weren't the right one."

"Or maybe because they were too nice. That's the thing, Maddie." I kissed her again. "You won't just hand over your heart. I had to dominate you for you to open up."

"I guess that means I'm submissive after all." She sounded smugly content when she said it.

"My kind of submissive," I said, my hands searching her skin for the pure pleasure of touching her. My hand looked brown against her creamy white butt cheek. I squeezed. "Do you think we're going too fast?"

"No," she said. "I'm starting to see why all our friends couldn't figure out why it took us six months to get together in the first place."

"You rang my bell the first time I laid eyes on you," I told her. "Six months of waiting to make a move."

She laughed and it was one of the most beautiful sounds in the universe, like the perfect fill topped with a china crash, bright and piercing. "I think I was attracted to you, too, which was why I avoided you for so long. So, see? It's not too fast at all."

"When love happens you just have to go for it."

"Yeah."

Knowing we both felt that way was the best feeling in the world.

I had bacon in the freezer and eggs in the fridge so I made us breakfast for dinner. I was out of butter for the toast so I grilled the bread in the bacon fat instead and served it with the orange juice that had been sitting in the fridge. I'd bought it thinking it would be healthier than soda but I hadn't opened the bottle yet. Sometimes things work out just right.

Madison decided to stay the night and we deferred discussing things like when we were moving in together until the morning. I tucked her into bed, poor exhausted girl, sore from being fucked and tattooed and emotionally drained from everything that day. She was asleep within minutes and then I went out to meet my father for a drink.

We ended up in a dive on the far side of downtown. He ordered two Michelob Lights at the bar without asking me what I wanted and then we went to a booth to sit.

"Let's get one thing straight," he said. "I won't lend you money, I give shit advice, and it's never going to work out between me and your mother so don't even think it."

"That's three things," I said, "and I don't need your money or your advice."

"Good. And one more thing: call me 'Dad' instead of Cisco and I'll belt you. So long's we understand each other." He clinked his bottle against mine and then smiled. "What the fuck, though, you didn't even know it was me and you went and got the Bondage Beauties?"

"I know, right?" I shook my head. "So tell me what happened with you and Mom. Back then. As a kid I thought . . . I don't know what the fuck I thought. That you didn't love us anymore or some shit."

He looked pained, sucking on his beer for a few moments before he answered. "You sure do go for the jugular, don't you? Not that I expected you wouldn't. Your mother basically threatened to get me banned from seeing you if I didn't leave on my own."

"Banned? But you didn't see us anyway. We thought you just up and left."

"Which was what she wanted you to think. She had proof of my fetish art and she had proof that I'd beaten her. Consensually of course, but the courts don't care about that. Last thing I needed was to be a registered sex offender. She wanted to purify your minds of filth." He looked me up and down, like he could see what a kinkster I was. Given my tattoos, he could. "I see it didn't work."

"Not with me it didn't," I said. "But Flor and Vicente—Flora and Vincent, now—they grew up brainwashed."

He shook his head. "That's..." He couldn't even finish whatever he was going to say about that.

"Yeah. She remarried a guy in a Christian community, one of these Bible-thumping throwback, no-TV, no-popular-music types."

"Don't knock the Bible," Cisco warned.

"I'm not knocking the Bible. But they're not even like a real church. It's almost like a cult."

He chuckled, his voice sarcastic. "Like we raised you to love church."

My reply came out earnest. "I remember going to Christmas Mass when I was a kid. In Spanish. I remember the singing." I found myself unable to take a sip of beer because of the tightness in my throat. "Somewhere here in LA."

"*Tch.* You were like five. Probably the last time I set foot inside a church."

"I was seven," I said. "I remember because I'd had my first Communion and I felt like a grownup being able to go up and take Communion for Christmas."

He pulled on his beer and regarded me warily. "Weird when you think about it, isn't it? Here, it's this guy's birthday. To celebrate, his body's the cake, his blood's the wine."

"Yeah," I said. Was Catholicism any weirder than any other religion, though? I didn't think so. "Was that the church where you and Mom got married?"

"Your mother and I were never married," he said, eyes flat and expressionless as he took another swig of his beer. "So. Is she happy?"

"I don't know. She mostly refuses to talk to me, her devil son."

He gave a long whistle, the pitch dropping like hope sinking out of sight. "She can be cold-hearted, your mother."

Here goes, I thought. I hadn't known for sure if I was going to tell him what I knew, but I decided it was now or never. "Flora called recently, though, all freaked out. Told me he's forbidden any of them to call me, Mom included."

"But your sister called anyway?"

"She snuck away to warn me. To tell me she's scared our stepdad's turning violent."

"Well, shit." I could see his fist on the beer bottle, grinding it against the wooden table. "That's no good. What are you doing about it?"

"Waiting. Trying to get through. Trying to convince her to come to LA and get away from him."

Cisco let go of the bottle and pressed his palms against the bald patches on either side of his head. "Listen to me, Chino. You can't always save people from themselves. You can't save them from what they think they know is right. Lord knows I tried."

"I just want to get her away from him."

"Do you want it enough to clean up your act and pretend you're reformed for her? That might be the only way."

Pieces of the puzzle were falling into place. So many things I didn't understand as a kid, or even know were there to be known. "You pretended to be reformed for her?"

"I did." His face was pained, like something inside him was cramping up just remembering. "After you were born, I kept trying to go straight. You know how hard that was when we didn't have food on the table but some editor would call up and want me to draw a Bondage Beauty for him? I couldn't give it up. I would get up in the middle of the night and draw while she was asleep." He sucked on his beer as if it might ease his pain, his eyes drifting toward the TV above the bar but not focusing on it. "And the truth is if you're bent there's no going straight. I tried to get her to see that."

"You think?"

"I know it. People trying to repress what they need is what fucks them up and turns them into monsters." He shook his head. "And what an irony, to end up with a wife-beater, when supposedly me spanking her was a sin? The only thing worse would be if he was one of those types who thinks the Bible gives a man the right to beat his wife."

My blood ran cold. "He beat me a couple of times when I was smaller, telling me he was going to beat the devil right out of me."

He chuckled. "Didn't work, did it. Probably just made you more bent than before."

"You paddled me once, too," I said, but not like an accusation, more like just a fact, a memory.

"You think that's what made you kinky?"

"No. Nothing made me kinky."

Cisco nodded and clinked his beer bottle against mine. "God makes us in his own image and he's the most twisted fucker there is."

I was still straining to understand. "You think that's why Mom's so into this guy? Because his kink's religious?"

He shook his head. "Who the fuck knows. Listen. When I met your mother, she'd only been in the States a couple of months. She was thousands of miles from her family, didn't know where to turn, and was trying to figure out all the shit in life that is hard no matter where you are, much less in a country where you don't understand half of what's going on. She was just a kid, really. By the time she figured out I was an unredeemable mistake, there were three of you. It took a lot of strength for her to leave me and do what she felt was right. I respect her for that. I still think she was wrong, but that doesn't change my respect for your mother."

He tipped back the beer and seemed disappointed that it was empty.

"Let's hope I was the biggest mistake of her life and not this asshole. Ana takes a long time to make up her mind, but once she does, there's no changing it."

"What can I do to change her mind about him? Maybe she's starting to see it."

"Then maybe you have a chance. But... fuck. I told you I give shit advice."

"What should I do?"

"Didn't I just say I give shit advice? You really want to know what to do?"

"Yeah."

"Come with me, then." He stood up. "Finish your beer. Don't waste it."

I chugged the rest of the beer and we left the empties on the table, then got into his pickup truck. He drove me through the city to somewhere I hadn't been before, or at least I didn't remember it. We didn't talk at all as he drove.

It was midnight and I wasn't expecting him to take me to a church. To a locked garden where the wrought iron back gate could be vaulted easily enough. To a statue of the Virgin Mary. In the dark I could hear a fountain but couldn't see it. There was a stone railing in front of the statue.

"Kneel down and pray."

"But—"

"Just do it. I'll never give you the right answers."

"But this statue will?"

"But your *own mind* will if you pray. Pray to her. If you want to say it's the Holy Spirit, fine, but you'll find the right answer if you do it."

If it had been anyone but my own father taking me on such a weird trip I wouldn't have done it. But sometimes you just have to go with the flow.

I got down on my knees and clasped my hands. I pressed

my forehead against them, trying to think how to start. I'd gone through the motions of praying thousands of times before I'd left home but I'd never actually been *doing* it then. I'd been thinking about girls or my homework or band practice, not actually trying to commune with a higher spirit. How was this supposed to go? *Dear Mary?*

I felt my father get down next to me and begin to murmur out loud.

In Spanish. *"Dios té salve, Maria."*

The rest of the words flooded back into my mind. Seven years old and memorizing it in Sunday school. And from there my thoughts took over. *Okay, Maria, help me with my mother. I love her, I can't help but love her even when she's pushed me away, and now I think she's in trouble and I want to help her. I want to help but I don't know how. She's in danger from the man in her life, the man who controls her, who believes he has a right to control her because of what it says in the Bible. How am I going to compete with the fucking Bible? Pardon my language. How am I going to beat that?*

I looked up at the statue. Her stone face was illuminated only dimly by the streetlights along the fence. She seemed to be looking down at me with a kind expression, a sympathetic one.

And it was like she was speaking to me. Like when I would guess what Madison was thinking just from her facial expression. She was telling me to let go of anger and let love rule. Anger would only bring ruin, and love was the only cure. The fears and frustrations of men seemed petty and the source of all the sorrows in the world, and the love of women the one treasure worth guarding.

I think my mouth hung open. I'm not sure how long I stared at her. Until Cisco said, "She give you any advice?"

"Yeah." I swallowed. "A whole theory on heterosexual relations."

"Nice. Usually she just scolds me to be a better person."

"Yeah? Do you listen?"

"Sometimes." He put a hand on my shoulder then, as the sound of a metal door being pushed open reached us. "Shit. Let's go."

"But we're not doing—"

"This is an Anglo church. If they catch us they'll break our fingers."

I didn't question that. We ran for the truck.

* * *

MADISON

In the wee hours of the morning Chino came in, the scent of whiskey and jasmine and smoke clinging to his hair. He snuggled against me under the covers. "My father's a crazy man," he said.

"Does that mean you had a good time?"

He grunted. "I'll explain in the morning. Or, even better. The afternoon."

I guessed if he was out that long that they must have gotten along okay. I wondered if he'd get along with my own father that well. I hadn't brought a guy home in years and at this point my parents didn't really expect me to anymore. They loved me and didn't judge beyond the occasional hints that grandchildren might be nice, immediately followed by an insistence that if I was happy they were happy. I gave them occasional hints about the life I was leading, just enough to make them sure they didn't want to hear a lot more, just enough to convince them I was happy.

And I was happy with Chino. Just plain happy. I snuggled up to him contentedly.

In the morning I slipped out of bed while he was still sleeping and checked my phone. There was a message from Gwen: *Planning for the party. Call me.*

I shut the door to the bedroom and went into the kitchen to start some coffee and call her back.

She picked up right away. "Hey. How'd your meeting with Lawson go? We're getting ready to ambush Schmitt."

"Oh?"

"Yeah, Ricki's been digging into his stuff a bit more and it's pretty gross. Did Lawson give you anything else?"

"He didn't say much, unfortunately." The coffee was right there on the counter where any caffeine-deficient person could find it. Sensible. "I told him he had nothing to go on, that I deposit the amount monthly because I'm getting ready to pay my mortgage, and he at least seemed worried I might be telling the truth. He wouldn't say anything more about Schmitt, though."

"Well, never mind, because we've found enough on Schmitt to want to divest ourselves of involvement with him. Guess who's planning to file for divorce? His wife. We've been hearing some *very* interesting things from her. To keep Schmitt none the wiser, Ricki's planning to pounce on him when he shows up for the party."

I poured the water into the coffeemaker and turned it on. "Which is coming up soon."

"Yeah. I thought you should have a heads up about it."

"Isn't Schmitt such a cutthroat lawyer everyone's afraid of him, though?"

"Apparently his wife found a divorce lawyer with the balls to take him on. We're going to keep the club issues completely separate, though. Which brings up another thing I wanted to ask you about, regarding the club. Why do you think Granddad insisted on paying party hosts in cash, anyway? Why not just add you to the staff payroll?"

The coffee finished dripping and I used the last of the milk in Chino's fridge to prep myself a cup. "You know, I never really thought about it. I figured he didn't want to have to explain it to his accountant?"

"His accountant goes to the parties, though. Or used to. He hasn't been showing up lately. The thing is we've got tons of people on staff. Plus contractors. We've never had to explain any of them."

"I get the feeling it was the way he always did it so he kept doing it." The coffee wasn't a brand I was used to. It was rich and not too dark. "Maybe it made sense in the 1950s."

"Well, it doesn't make much sense now, when the thing that they could really get us for is not filing your taxes. Will it totally mess up your taxes if we give you a 1099 form?"

I chuckled. "Most of my legit jobs pay me that way anyway. When they bother."

"Great. We're going to start paying you by check instead of cash then, too. Trying to legitimize as much as possible."

"Makes sense." They were really preparing for anything to happen.

"Now fill me in on you and Chino. What's been happening with you two?"

I tried to play coy for a second, just to see. "Who says anything's been happening?"

"Maddie—"

"Okay, seriously, I'm at his house right now. I... I think this is the one, Gwen."

"The one?"

"The one I've been waiting for, that I didn't even realize I was waiting for. Mr. Right." I had peeled off the bandage last night before going to sleep and now I peeked under the hem of the T-shirt I'd slept in to admire the tattoo. The ink was fresh and saturated, the skin raised ever so slightly as if the dark, elegant curves of the letters were embossed. *Chino.* I put my hand over it, feeling warm all over and almost dizzy with the rush of feelings seeing it released in me. "I got a tattoo last night, Gwen."

"You did? Your first, right?"

"Yeah." I swallowed, suddenly afraid she was going to tell me I was crazy. "His name."

"Amazing!" she squealed. "I'm so happy for you!"

Okay, so Gwen wasn't going to tell me I was crazy. "It seems sudden, like my whole life took a left turn the minute he touched me, but now I can't imagine anything else. I can't even explain it. When he puts his hand on me I feel whole in a way I've never felt before."

"That's beautiful."

"It's funny. Part of me still says a woman proves her worth by being independent, so what does this mean?"

"Oh, Maddie. You already proved you could be independent if that was what you wanted. You don't have to prove it anymore. Go for what makes you happy."

"It's funny. Words like 'love' and 'devotion' were just words to me before. Abstract concepts. But when we were in a scene together it was like the concepts stopped being abstract, like I could see the love, feel it, believe in it, in a way I never had before. There's a bond. And now we don't even have to be in a scene. I feel it all the time. Every waking moment, I'm his girl. I never knew I wanted that, but now that I have it, it's like I'm complete."

"I never thought I'd hear you say that. I always knew I wanted a dom. I thought I might have to settle for a crappy one, but I always knew."

"But Ricki didn't."

"Haha, no. Ricki didn't want to admit she was kinky. Ricki didn't even admit she had needs or emotions, which was why it took a dom to break through her shell. But that's not you, Maddie. You took care of all your own needs."

"Except for one. He takes me to a place inside myself I can't reach on my own." I watched the reflection of the skylight swim atop the coffee in my cup. "A place where I finally believe everything's as good as I've been telling myself. A place where I stop worrying all the time, where I stop trying to be anything but...me, because who I am is what he wants, what he loves."

"Aw, Maddie."

"And because now I'm just...me...the real me? I feel like I can start fresh, start over. I realized something."

"What's that?"

"I don't want to be a political reporter. I said this to Lawson the other day and it's true. I'm not interested in the bullshit and the compromises that it takes. It would've been a nice thing my parents and my writing instructors would've approved of if I'd done it when I was fresh out of school. But the world that thinks that's the top of the game isn't the world I live in."

"Hm. So what is the top of the game for you now?"

"The top of the game for me now? Helping women—helping people, but especially women—realize how much power they have. I was kind of stupid, wasn't I, Gwen?"

"Stupid about what?"

"For thinking that if I submitted it meant I was weak."

"You thought that about me?"

"No! That's the thing. I don't know any subs, male or female, who are weak, but somehow I still clung to this stupid idea for myself, judging myself by my own standard.

It wasn't until Chino that I realized how strong I had to be to face my fears, how strong every submissive has to be every time they choose to go into subspace. You have to face your own fears about yourself. Your fears that you're not good enough."

"Oh, Maddie."

I took a deep breath. I normally didn't get so intense on the phone, but Gwen was the first person I'd had a chance to talk to since figuring all this out.

"And sex. I'd convinced myself sex was no big deal. Nothing more than another fancy thing I did with my body—like dancing. Like 'people make way too big a deal over this thing that means nothing.' But it doesn't mean nothing. With Chino it feels like it means everything."

"I know what you mean."

"Which brings me to something I guess I need to talk with him about as well as you and Ricki. About working at the club."

"You don't want to work at the club anymore?"

"It's not that I don't want to, it's that I think I need Daddy's permission."

"Ohhh." Gwen drew out that one syllable in total understanding, as my use of the word "Daddy" sank in. "That makes total sense. I can't believe I didn't think of that myself, given how Mal is with me. You'll have to let me know what you negotiate."

"I will."

"I gotta run now, Maddie. Couple more people to call."

"Bye, Gwen. Thanks for listening."

She made another happy sound. "I'm so psyched for you. So psyched, Maddie. You have no idea."

"Submissive Wives Club, that's what we should start next."

"Oooh, that's an idea. Okay, next time." She hung up with

a laugh. Although I wondered, now that I put the idea in her head, if Gwen wouldn't go ahead and do it.

Then I heard a voice behind me. "Is that coffee?"

I turned and saw Chino standing at the door to the bedroom, a pair of gray pajama pants clinging to his hips. "It is." I brought my cup over to him. He had bedhead and stubble and somehow still managed to be the sexiest man I'd ever seen.

He accepted the cup from my hand. "We've got to iron out protocol, huh?"

"Like Lion and Kittyn," I said.

"Mm-hm. I think one of the rules should be no D/s before coffee, though." He blinked.

"At least not after you've spent the night drinking heavily with a long-lost parent?" I suggested gently.

"Hm. Not every day something like that happens, I guess. Still." He took a sip of the coffee, then a bigger gulp. "Okay, girl. Now I've had some coffee. Kneel. Oral."

The commands were delivered simply but firmly and I felt the tug of the bond between us. Yes. I sank to my knees and pulled the pajama pants down to the middle of his thighs. He was hard already, maybe morning wood or maybe that excited to wake up to us.

The first day of us. That's what it felt like. I worked the head with my tongue until his salty precome began to flow and then I switched to taking more of him into my mouth.

"Good girl," he said, one hand on his hip, the other still holding the coffee. "Okay, enough."

He pulled me up into a kiss, my tongue salty from his flesh, his bittersweet with coffee.

"I don't see us turning into protocol nuts with a lot of rules," he said. "Do you? Let's sit."

"There's more coffee," I told him, "but no more milk."

"Bring me some black, if you would?"

I grinned. "Is that an order or request?"

He pulled me close and rubbed my mons with the heel of his hand. "I think it's a reasonable request for a Daddy to make of his girl. If she's a good girl, she'll obey, and if she's a brat, well, I think she can expect to be punished."

"Seems reasonable." I wondered if I'd ever decide to provoke him by being bratty. Right then I couldn't imagine it. I poured more coffee out of the pot for him and refreshed my own. We sat down in the two armchairs and each cradled our cups.

"I've never wanted a servant," Chino said. "I don't even want a housewife particularly, you know what I mean? But if there are things you want to do for me besides sex that would make you feel fulfilled, let's talk about what they are."

"You mean, just because I'm the girl doesn't mean I have to scrub the toilet or cook dinner."

"In the same way just because you're the *woman* doesn't mean that, either. Unless scrubbing the toilet gets you hot."

I smiled. "Not particularly. I wouldn't mind making you coffee in the morning, though."

He took a sip of his. "I wouldn't mind that, either. Especially since I don't know what you did differently, but this tastes much better than usual."

"Maybe when it's made with *wuv* it tastes better," I joked, and then we both made gagging sounds, which caused us both to crack up laughing.

He wiped his eyes. "Next thing. Should we move in together?"

"Yes. You should move in with me until we can buy a place in Laurel Canyon."

He put on a face of mock-surprise. "What, you don't love this place? This palace of mine?"

I smiled at his joking but my answer was serious: "If you want to save up to buy, it'd be even better to pay no rent than whatever you're paying here. I own my place and the downstairs tenant's rent covers the mortgage."

He looked thoughtful. "You know that what I really want to do is buy a place for my mother."

"And your sister?"

"Her, too." His face turned grave. "If they'll come."

I put my coffee down and slipped to the rug at his feet, my palms on his leg. "If I could learn to trust you, they can learn, too."

"I got a piece of advice last night." He swept his hand over my hair. "Let go of anger and petty shit, and treasure love over all things."

I couldn't picture Cisco Garcia giving that advice, but... "That sounds like good advice."

"I love you, Maddie," he said, and leaned down to kiss me once more. "I am so blessed that you're mine."

"I love you, too, Aloysius Francisco Garcia," I said with a smirk.

"Oh, man, no one's called me that since I was seven."

"Not even your mother? Or stepfather?"

"Not even them." He pulled me up into his lap. "If we have kids, and you want saint names for them, promise me we'll pick something people can pronounce and spell."

I wouldn't have guessed he'd be the first one to bring up kids. "Do you want to have kids?"

"I'm open to the idea. How about you?"

"I'm... more open to the idea than I used to be." I had a sudden image of what Chino would be like as a father, and I liked what I saw in my mind's eye. Maybe in a few years I'd be ready to share his attention with a baby. Maybe. "Let's talk more about your mother before we talk about kids, though."

"Okay," he said with a nod.

"Let's try calling her and your sister again. Let me call from my phone. If I need to I can pretend to be someone else."

"Okay. You're in charge of this operation, Maddie."

"Then let's get dressed first."

"All right." He kissed me on the cheek. "We'll figure out the rest of the relationship stuff as we go along."

CHAPTER SIXTEEN

MADISON

We didn't reach Flora or Ana—Chino's mother—that day, but I did get a text from Flora saying she wanted to talk soon. There wasn't much we could do at that point. Chino agreed to move in with me, though, and there was no reason to wait. Neither of us wanted to be apart for even an hour if we didn't have to be. I went home to feed Morris and get the place ready and that evening Chino brought his clothes over—right in the milk crates he had been keeping them in, with the stuff from his closet laid over the top of them in the backseat of his car. He decided not to even rent a truck or get movers; after his landlord agreed to buy his furniture he had only a handful of boxes of books and keepsakes to move, one box of dishes, and not much else. All his musical instruments were at the band's rehearsal space.

Chino moving in sparked a flurry of re-nesting: we decided

to put a new coat of paint into the spare room and change the light fixtures in the bathroom and that sort of thing, which meant a few days went by during which we made slow progress on the renovations because we kept pausing to have sex.

Flora finally called one night when Chino was out at a band publicity appearance and I was filming a toy review video. I was lying in bed, sweat-soaked from trying to come using a vibrator that was simply too weak for me when the phone rang. I scrambled to answer it. "Flora?"

"Madison," she said. "I'm not sure what to do now."

"Okay, talk me through what you've done so far." I lay back and tried to slow my breathing.

"My mother, Ana, I think she's ready to talk to you. She very grudgingly admitted to me the other day that perhaps she views my stepfather as a problem. But I looked up my brother on the Internet."

"Are you allowed to do that?"

"I'm not supposed to, but I'm not supposed to call you, either."

"True."

"Anyway, about Chino. I fear she's going to think he's even worse."

"Worse than your father? Why?"

"Have you seen the videos and photographs of his musical group?"

Oh, dear. "Yes, yes, Flora, I have, but you have to explain to her that what you see in promo videos is not the same as abuse. That's not what they actually do at all."

"Ah," she said brightly. "You mean it's all for show, for an image, because sex sells to the decadent public."

"Not exactly, but—"

"I can tell her that. I can explain that. I think maybe she'll want to speak to him before she makes a decision. We're trying to be careful. So careful."

"I know. Flora, can I speak to her?"

"Not today. Tomorrow, though. I think tomorrow. Around three o'clock."

"Okay. I'll be here. I'll be ready."

"Thank you. Good-bye." Her good-bye was stiff and formal, like most of what she said to me, as if she were speaking in a courtroom. It was weird but at least she was speaking to us.

The next day I finally spoke to Ana. Chino was there, sitting silently at my kitchen table, with the phone on speaker.

"Is this Miss Madison?" She had a slight accent.

"Ana, it's just Madison. Flora told me you were going to call. I'm so glad you did."

"Yes, well, she said you might be able to help." Like her daughter, she spoke very formally on the phone. "As you know I have been married to this man for many years. My goal was always to provide a safe, stable environment to raise my children."

Chino leaned forward suddenly and I motioned to him to stay quiet.

"My youngest has just left the house. I have done what I set out to do. But I made a promise before God that I would be bound to this man for eternity."

Chino opened his mouth but I forestalled him with a stop-sign hand. *I got this.* "Ana, I know your marriage vows are very important to you. But if one partner is abusive to the other? Those who make the home unsafe for their partners or other members of the family, they are the ones who have broken the sacred covenant of marriage."

"*Hmph.* And is that your opinion?"

"That's the opinion of many church leaders, ma'am. In the

same way that adultery would be unfaithful, and grounds for dissolving a marriage, mistreatment and abuse of many kinds are also bad faith. God requires none of his children to remain in situations that threaten their well-being or the well-being of their children. That comes directly from the United States conference of Catholic Bishops."

"Well, smart lady, how shall I deal with the fact that I entered into this marriage in bad faith to begin with, for the sake of my children and not for love?"

Chino looked like a ghost, his mouth hanging slightly open.

"Ma'am, nowhere in the vows is love guaranteed. Does he love you?"

"I am certain he does not. If he loves anything it is the feeling of superiority he lords over me. He expected to make me a slave—do you understand that? By rescuing a desperate woman such as myself—poor, disadvantaged, with illegitimate children—he not only made himself a hero in the eyes of his community, he guaranteed himself a slave for life. Cook, clean, serve him, as a wife yes, but far beyond what the other wives of this community provide to their husbands. No money of my own. No worth. No freedom. Because this is what he wanted. A slave. And this was how he could get it. I was too young and stupid to know what I was getting myself and my family into. I did not love him but I loved having a Prince Charming, a knight upon a white horse who swept in and promised me a castle and education for my children."

"Did Flora go to college?"

"Well, no. She stayed with me because she was afraid for me. She took classes at the community college. She would like to go to nursing school but she has been too afraid to leave me alone with him."

"Thank you for telling me that, Ana. It sounds to me like you're ready to leave him?" I prepared myself mentally for the next step in the call, which was if she said yes, if she was ready to leave him, trying to nail down a few concrete exit strategies. "Is that what you're saying?"

"Yes. But if he knew I was going to do this, well, let us say a man does not let a slave escape easily. You may have grasped by now I am not an impulsive woman. I am patient. I make plans. I will need a divorce lawyer. I will need transportation. I will need shelter. I will need money. I will need a guarantee that Flora is safe, too."

"You'll have all that," Chino said suddenly. "Mamá, money is not a problem. You want a castle? I'll buy you a castle."

"Chino?" All the hardness in her voice suddenly disappeared. "Oh my sweet boy I've missed you."

Chino's hand gripped the edge of the table. "Mamá."

She said something then in rapid-fire Spanish that I couldn't catch but whatever she said filled his eyes with tears.

"Ana, is there a friend or neighbor you might trust if you have to flee suddenly?"

"I trust no one but my own daughter."

"Then we'll need to get you plane tickets, and we'll need to arrange a time—"

"I'll come get you," Chino said. "We'll come get you in a car; I'll have the band's head of security come with me—"

"I must go. I will call again tomorrow at this time if I am able to get away undetected. Good-bye, *mi hijo*. Thank you, Miss Madison."

She hung up and Chino put his face into his hands.

I moved behind him and rubbed his shoulders, trying to get him to release the tension, but no such luck. When he looked up at me it was with distress on his face. "I'm such an idiot."

"This isn't about you," I reminded him gently.

"I know. But, man, what kind of idiot have I been? I believed she loved that guy more than my father. I blamed her for what happened to my childhood. And all along she willingly sacrificed her freedom and risked her health so that we wouldn't go hungry." He swallowed hard. "And she's been pretending she didn't love me so he'd be none the wiser. Because defying him meant punishment of some kind. I'm sure of it."

"What did she say to you?" I asked.

He hung his head. "That if she was regaining me as a son she hoped I'd be a good boy, now."

"Oh, Chino."

"Yeah." He stood swiftly and wrapped me into a hug. "I . . . don't even know what to think. Where did you get all of that stuff about the covenant of marriage?"

"I wasn't kidding. From the Catholic bishops. When I worked the hotline we got women all the time who knew they were in abusive relationships but thought they were required by the Church to stay with their husbands at all costs. That's not true."

"Well, good for the bishops, I guess." He let go of me suddenly and patted himself, looking for his phone. "If we're going to get her out of there, she's going to need a place to stay. Buying something will take a while. I better call my landlord and tell him I'm keeping the place until September after all."

"Your phone's by the bed."

"Thank you." He kissed me on the cheek and hurried to find it. Meanwhile I texted Gwen to ask her for the name and number of the divorce lawyer Schmitt's wife had hired.

* * *

With all the guys in the band back in town, Ricki and Gwen had us over to the mansion for dinner one night. The energy in that room was crackling: three couples, three dominant men with their submissive women, none of us needing to hide who we were or exactly how we felt about each other. It felt a little like the party in Palm Springs except all six of us knew each other so well. Axel and Mal were happy to give Chino a hard time about taking so long to catch up to them.

The Hamilton staff cooked up an incredible meal and wine flowed freely. But when dessert was done and we were taking our after-dinner drinks on the verandah overlooking the pool Ricki said, "Okay, this isn't merely a social occasion. Gwen and I have something really serious to discuss."

Gwen and Mal were sitting together in a swing and Ricki paced back and forth in front of them as she talked.

"I'm getting more and more concerned that the club can't remain a secret. I think there's some chance even if the current tabloid flak goes away that it might end up coming out during Schmitt's divorce proceedings. And if not then, the next tabloid scandal is on the horizon. Reeve thinks he saw a camera drone fly over yesterday. I want us to seriously consider taking control of the narrative for ourselves and, for lack of a better word, coming out."

"You mean, make a public statement about the existence of the club?" Mal asked.

"Yes. And to use it to our advantage, to send a message that BDSM is safe, sane, and consensual, and not something we feel we have to hide. The Rough could use it as a publicity lever, certainly. And I have a few personal and business interests that might be rolled into such an initiative."

Mal tossed his head. "I've nothing to hide."

"And I certainly think we're reaching the point where it's

probably not going to negatively affect my career," Gwen added. "Ever since the whole public proposal thing, people have pretty much assumed about me and Mal. It's really not like it was even a secret what Mal was into before that."

"Same here," Ricki said, gesturing at Axel, who was sitting at a patio table and grinning up at her like he was as in love with her at this moment as he had been when they'd first met.

"What are the personal and business interests you were mentioning?" I asked Ricki from my perch on Chino's lap. He felt tense under my hands, his eyes zeroing in on Ricki.

"Well, personally I want to launch a charity aimed at educating domestic violence advocates that BDSM is not abuse and that those of us who practice consensually have just as much of a vested interest in stopping non-consensual abuse as they do."

"That would be fantastic," I said. "That was ultimately why I had to quit working the hotline. I just couldn't take day after day of having to hear counselors who should have known better telling women that if they liked spanking or bondage and then they got abused that they had 'asked for it' or 'deserved it.' "

"As for business interests, Madison, that deal for PlayPeople is going through. Signed the paperwork today." Her grin was almost sheepish. "So I guess in a way I'm your boss now. Or, again. Additionally. Whatever."

"Cool. The money behind the site was all old porno money."

"It was. The old money was in extorting a shame tax from lonely men. The new money is all in engagement between the site and women and couples." She shrugged. "I can pretty much guarantee that you'll have your toy review blog for as long as you want it. But that's not all."

Gwen tossed a balled-up napkin at her sister. "Okay, who else did you buy?"

"You know that acquisition I told you about when I got back from San Francisco? That was a new media company, too. They've got half a dozen sites with half a dozen more due to launch shortly, including a new political celebrity gossip rag called *Pop-litico*."

"Lawson's baby," I said, my smile getting wider.

"That's right," Ricki said, folding her arms. "Apparently I am Price Lawson's boss now, too. So I think if I want to dissuade him from writing about us, I have the leverage to do that. But we do still have the Schmitt problem. Lawson was unfortunately correct that he's a huge donor to Purity Values causes, which is one of the reasons his wife has had enough. And so have I. We'll have to be careful about what we feed to Lawson, but if we're going public with the club that'll be our spin to control."

"Oooh." Gwen clapped her hands. "Have you thought about this? We could have our own brand of sex toys. The Governor's Club brand."

"They'd have to be better than the gray ones everywhere now," I said. Chino shook his head and I assumed it was because of how terrible those toys were. "We could start filming the vlog here instead of in my bathtub!"

"Yes! And you could have more guests!" she enthused.

"Would now be a good time to tell you I've already had a preliminary talk with Showtime about providing them with some women-focused sexuality content?" Ricki added. "Your toy reviews could cross over to the mainstream, Maddie. If you were interested. I know you said at one point you'd rather be a journalist."

I had one hand on the firm warmth of Chino's chest and I could feel his heart starting to hammer. Was he as excited about all this as I was? "Honestly, Ricki, journalism just isn't what it's cracked up to be. But what would really interest me is getting involved with your domestic violence education charity." I looked at Chino. He hadn't said a word through the entire exchange since Ricki had brought up the subject of going public. "After all, it hits really close to home."

He dropped his gaze with a slight shake of his head. I took that to mean he wasn't ready to tell the guys about his mother yet and I was about to try to change the subject when Gwen blurted out, "Chino, do you know when your mother's arriving?"

He winced, looking back and forth between Mal and Axel. "No. It's tricky to communicate with her. We're trying to get her and my sister plane tickets, prepaid credit cards, whatever it'll take to get them out of there."

Axel looked serious for the first time that night. "Your mother's in . . . a bad situation?"

Chino nodded.

Mal stood, his long dark hair curtaining his frown. "Where is she? Is there a reason we cannot spirit her away?"

"Border of Michigan and Ohio," Chino said. "And we'd stand out like sore thumbs there. It's a small community, everyone knows each other, and if we tip him off that we're trying to help her get away, he might hurt her. Might hurt them both. Who knows."

"Chino's sister is trying to get them both out of there," I explained. "She's got a little more freedom and we're depending on her."

"Please, Chino, Maddie, let us know if we can help in any way," Ricki said. "When they flee where are they going to go?"

"I'm trying to convince them to come to Los Angeles," Chino said somberly.

"Why don't they stay here? We've only got twenty bedrooms not in use," Ricki said.

"Ten," Gwen corrected. "Don't exaggerate."

"It would be nicer than your place," I said to Chino. "That isn't a great neighborhood and I don't know how safe they'll feel there."

"I can't impose on you like this," Chino said.

Ricki and Gwen laughed. "Impose," Ricki insisted. "We need something for the staff to do. Mina loves it when there are houseguests. And there's always, always someone here."

"I'll keep it in mind," Chino said, his brow still wrinkled with worry. "One thing at a time. Still have to get them here."

"Plus now we've got a great divorce lawyer on call," Gwen added.

"All right," Ricki said, like she was finishing a business meeting. "Are we decided, then, that we're all right with going public?"

"Aye," Axel said, raising his hand and looking around. Everyone else raised their hands, too.

Except Chino. He tightened his arms around my waist.

"I can't," he said, shaking his head. "You guys. I just can't. My mother's fleeing a batterer and I'm going to be on Showtime showing off how I like to hit my lover with studded leather? I can't. I can't do it."

"Chino," I said softly. Just his name.

"No, Maddie. I can't. Don't make me choose between what's best for her and what's best for all of you." He got to his feet and deposited me back in the chair. "I can't."

* * *

CHINO

They let me walk away, to stew with my thoughts on the dark garden path on the far side of the pool. I think Axel and

Mal held Madison back from running after me. They knew I needed a little time, a little space, I guess, or I wouldn't have walked away.

You ever have voices in your head screaming at you so loud you can't even tell what they're screaming at you to do? That's what it felt like right then, like the roar of multiple tornadoes trying to pull me in different directions. Madison, my mother, Ricki's media empire, Flora, our manager Christina—it was like I could hear them all screaming at each other about what was right, what was wrong, and what the hell I was going to do about it. I normally wasn't an all-things-to-all-people kind of guy. I was only good at being one thing: me. But somehow there I was, caught in the middle of everyone's needs.

My own father had said it the other night. *You're a man now and you find your own way.* But just because I was a man didn't mean I had cut off all my feelings. You don't just sever your dreams or your hopes or the things you felt as a child like a limb you've decided you aren't using anymore. This close to getting my mother back, I couldn't throw this in her face. I couldn't. She'd left my father because of his bondage art. She wasn't going to take this well.

But even if the club stayed secret, what about Madison? She was my girl now. There was no going back from that. The thought didn't even enter my mind. I guess you could say she was as irrefutably my girl as I was my mother's son. Nothing was going to change that. I'd heard her on the phone to Gwen the other morning and I'd agreed with every word she'd said. This was it. We'd found each other. But how did that fit with the band and the rest of our lives? We were still figuring that out.

"Chino." Axel's voice came from behind me.

Him and Mal. They were standing at a curve in the garden

path where some kind of night-blooming flower climbed a trellis. Tiny lights like fairy pagodas edged the path but didn't put much light onto our faces. I stepped closer to them. "I can't do it, guys."

"It's all right," Axel said. "Chino, we're not here to shanghai you into something you can't do. But you've gotta admit the band is pretty blatant already."

"I know." I scrubbed my face with my hands. "And there's Madison." And the videos I'd made with her, I realized. Well, those weren't likely to be seen by my mother. Were they? I just didn't know what to think. "But this is my mother we're talking about. She's coming out of a bad situation. The last thing I want to do is—what's the word?—trigger her with this. She'll never trust me again."

"Indeed. If you lose her trust before she breaks from her abuser, she may not make the break at all," Mal said, his voice low and serious. "We cannot jeopardize that."

Axel put his hand on my shoulder, his leather jacket creaking as he did. "We'll tell the gals they have to hold off. They wouldn't do anything that would put your mom at risk. But once she's free—"

"I dunno, you guys," I said. "Maybe I can't protect her from the truth, but I can at least try. I can at least stave it off until she gets to know me again, until we can build up a little bit of a relationship before the shock. I don't know if that'll be possible if I'm giving tours of the dungeon on cable TV."

"So keep a low profile. Every member of the club isn't going to be outed," Ax said.

"Yeah, but anyone with half a brain is going to put two and two together from the Hamiltons to you guys to the rest of the band." I looked up into the sky. There weren't many stars visible, only a few shining through the glow from the city. "My mother has at least half a brain."

"The sooner she is safe, the better everything will be." Mal patted me on the other shoulder. "It won't be easy no matter what."

"We're here for you, Chino," Axel said. "Whether she freaks out or what. I just... I wish you'd told us sooner that something like this was going on."

He sounded slightly stung and I didn't blame him. We were supposed to be brothers, bandmates but even closer than just any bandmates, given what we'd been through together—not just the sex parties but the struggle to the top, the days when we slept in our van while on tour, all that. But I'd never talked to them about my family. I'd kept myself a secret from them and now they knew it.

"I didn't even really know myself," I admitted, "until recently. You know, my stepfather threw me out when I was sixteen. I was young and stupid and believed my mother stayed with him because she loved him. I believed she'd kicked my father out and went with this guy because she fell in love. I didn't see it. I didn't see the way he controlled her. He seemed mostly like a threat to me, not her or my siblings who did what he said. I just didn't see it."

"He kept you from seeing it," Mal said darkly.

"I talked to my mother for real for the first time... ever, maybe. First time he wasn't listening in. And she told me she never loved him, that she only married him so me and my siblings wouldn't go hungry. And now that my little brother just finished college, she's done. Mission accomplished. She's ready to leave. But he must sense it. Flora says he's tightening the noose. They need to get out of there."

"Man, that's rough." Axel gave me a man-hug. "But it's all right, Chino. You can talk to us."

"I know. I don't know why I kept everything hidden from

you guys. Old habits are hard to break." Which reminded me. "I may as well tell you about my dad, too, then."

"Your real dad?"

"Yeah. Turns out he's a tattoo artist in Koreatown. He's been there for years and I never knew until recently. He's a bit of a whack job but, you know, not in a bad way. I don't think he's realized I'm famous yet."

Mal cleared his throat. "Perhaps if even your father, who lives in LA and clearly isn't isolated from modern culture, hasn't figured out who you are, perhaps your mother won't make the connection between you and the Governor's Club, either."

He had a point. "I figured I'd tell him at some point. Invite him to a show. I... don't think I'd want to invite my mother and sister to one of our shows."

"Oh, because of the half-naked women suspended from the light rigs, you mean?" Axel said. "My mom was fine with those. She gets that it's performance art."

"She doesn't actually know about your sexuality, though," Mal pointed out.

"No, and I don't think she wants to know the details, either," Axel said. "She knows as much as she wants to know, let's put it that way."

"In the case of my family I am certain they will be appalled at my public connection to the club," Mal said. "They could not give a flying fig about what perversions I practice, but the fact that I would speak about it openly? That is the scandalous part." Mal hated his upper-crust British family and loved any chance to rub their faces in that fact.

"I guess that's the thing. I wouldn't mind being the best-known pervert on the planet if I wasn't worried it would hurt my family." I didn't want Mal to think I was judging him. "You don't have to give a fuck what your family thinks, but I can't just forget mine."

"You walked away from them when you were sixteen," Axel reminded me.

"And I'd like to think I'm a better man now than I was then," I said.

"You are," Mal said, and put an arm around my shoulders.

Axel took my other side. "Now let's get you back to Madison before she gets frantic."

CHAPTER SEVENTEEN

MADISON

The following week was fraught with worry. Ricki was getting ready to confront Schmitt at the party. Ana and Flora were getting ready to leave, but we expected them to make a break next Tuesday, when there was a weekly meeting of the male church elders. Gwen's travel agent had found a direct flight to book them on.

The day of the party, Chino and I had lunch at a local bistro not far from my house where we could sit on the back patio and enjoy the weather. The host recognized him as *someone* but called him "Mr. Navarro"—apparently unclear on who exactly. Chino didn't correct him.

"Does he think you're the guy from Jane's Addiction?" I asked, after we'd been seated at a table for two and given our menus.

"Happens all the time," Chino said. "You'd think people would realize I'm twenty years younger."

"Well, to be fair, Dave Navarro doesn't look like he's pushing fifty." I had seen him on cable TV fairly recently, on a show about tattooing. "Did you know he's got a guitar strap on sale now that doubles as a bondage device? They sell it in the sex toy catalogs."

"Really? Maybe I should market some kinky drumsticks," Chino joked, but his eyes were serious.

"No kidding," I said, putting my hand on his. "I wonder how his family deals with him being out about his kink."

"Maybe they don't," Chino said with a shrug. "I don't know, Maddie. I still can't wrap my head around everyone knowing everything."

I felt his sadness and apprehension like there was a patch cord connecting his heart and mine. The party was tonight but the little jitters I had about that were quashed under heavier emotions. "Maybe everyone doesn't need to know everything. My parents know I do various things and they don't want to know all the details. What matters to them is that I'm happy, that I'm an adult who can take care of myself and that includes the choices I make about my sex life."

"You really think they'd be okay if they knew all the details, though? You think I'm going to ask your father if I can marry you and then . . ." He ran his hand possessively up and down my forearm and turned my wrist over, two fingers holding it as if measuring for a bondage cuff. "Then tell him how I'm going to tie you up on the wedding night?"

"No, and that's what I'm saying." Him holding my arm like that had started my engine revving. *Save it for tonight, Maddie,* I told myself, but that was all it took—a touch, a look, to make desire flare in me anew. "Even if we weren't kinky you wouldn't be going into detail with him about our wedding night. Some things are okay to keep private."

"Except if the chance to do a reality TV show about the

dungeon comes along, Ricki's going to grab it. That's not keeping it private at all," Chino said.

"True. But if that happened, we wouldn't do the show. We'd sign off and let them do it if we weren't comfortable with everyone knowing that much about our business. Speaking of which, PlayPeople just realized you haven't sent them the model release for the videos where you appear."

"I barely appear. You hear my voice twice and you see my hands a couple of times." I could hear the reluctance in his voice. Maybe even regret.

The only thing I knew how to do was forge ahead. "Still. Chino, it's required. Even if we don't use your name in the promo."

He sighed heavily. "I feel like each thing just pushes me closer and closer to the cliff."

I met his eyes over the top of the menu. "Should we skip the party tonight?"

His face was distressed as he looked left, right. "I . . . At the very least, you need to be there to work and to help Ricki with the Schmitt situation if necessary. And if you're going, there's no way I'm letting my little girl go alone." His gaze darkened and I felt a thrill run through me.

"Are you planning a scene for tonight? For us?"

"If you think I haven't been thinking about playing with you in front of everyone for the entire month since the last party, you still don't know me very well." He held in a smile. "But there's always next month if you end up too busy. Either way we are not skipping this party. And that means we should talk over a few things before tonight."

"I was going to ask what rules we should have around being in the dungeon."

He gave an approving nod. "Well, there's being in dungeons in general, and then there's this particular dungeon where you're an employee. I wouldn't want to interfere with your work, but there are things I wouldn't be happy with you doing."

"I want to know what those things are. You're going to tell me, right? Not make me guess?"

He smiled. "Yes, I'm going to tell you. This isn't some kind of test."

I smiled back. "Just checking."

The waitress interrupted us then to take our order. I hadn't absorbed a single word from the menu and found myself flustered.

Chino sailed in smoothly. "I'll take the brunch burger, the one with the fried egg on top."

"Kale chips or fries?"

"Fries. Unless you can come up with a really good reason I should start eating kale."

I realized happily that his banter with the waitress was to give me time to figure out my own order. Being with a man that perceptive was a new experience.

The waitress shrugged. "Kale's the hip thing right now. I'd go for the fries, personally."

"Fries it is. And a black iced coffee."

"We don't have iced coffee."

"Then I'll order a hot coffee and a glass of ice and you can take your chances with me pouring it myself."

"I can probably pour it in there for ya," she said with a knowing nod.

"Thanks."

He kept her occupied enough that I was ready by the time she turned to me. "I'll have the avocado and bacon panini and a fresh squeezed lemonade."

"And kale chips or fries?"

"Kale chips. I'm going to steal his fries anyway."

"Smart woman. Have your kale and eat fries, too. I'll put your orders right in." She collected the menus and was gone.

I took his hand again. "Thank you, love."

He put my fingers to his lips. "I know you don't like looking like you don't have all the answers."

I felt myself blush because that was completely true. But instead of thinking I was annoying for that, he accepted it and had even helped me maintain my cool. And how amazing was it that he realized it in the first place? I'd never come out and said something like that before. "How did you know that?"

He smiled and shrugged. "I know you."

Chino then eased the small round table away from the wall and had me scoot my chair toward him. He did the same. The result was we were sitting on the same side of the table rather than directly opposite each other and now he could hold my hand under the table.

"Now, where were we. Things I wouldn't want you to do in the dungeon unless I was doing them to you. I said I wasn't going to test you, but for the hell of it I'm going to ask you to guess three things and tell me why you guessed them. There are no wrong answers, Maddie."

"Okay." I squeezed his fingers. "Number one, fuck."

"Very good." He gave a slow blink as if the same deep throb of desire that ran through me when I said the word "fuck" also ran through him. "And why?"

"That one's not obvious?"

"Even if it is, I want to hear you say it, sweets."

The rebuke was mild but a blush rose to my cheeks anyway. "Oh. Do you want the sexy answer or the plain answer?"

"Is there a difference?"

"In the delivery, at least."

He chuckled. "The plain answer, then."

"The reason not to fuck is that, as previously discussed, P-I-V is special."

"Do you ever think about the fact that you'll never have another cock inside you, ever? That this one here," he moved my hand to his lap, "is it?"

"Every day," I said, feeling heat with my palm through the denim and a matching heat between my legs. "Unless you suddenly decide to start sharing me."

"I might share your mouth and ass, but not your pussy." He moved his mouth close to my ear. "Your pussy belongs to Daddy."

My panties were going to catch fire, I swear.

"You ever done double penetration?"

"Not yet."

He heard the teasing tone in my reply and teased me right back. "Well, if we find a guy we're both attracted to enough, maybe you'll find out what it's like." He sat back again, his voice returning to a businesslike clip. "Now, two more things. Tell me."

"Well, absolutely nobody is ever blindfolding me but you."

"True. And can you think of a third thing?"

"Kissing. I don't kiss club members either."

"You do realize of course that you kissed me back when I was just a club member." His grin was sly.

"Yes, and look what happened." I squeezed his erection through his jeans. "But I don't know if those are really good answers, since those are three things I never would've done in the first place."

He smiled. "That doesn't mean we don't agree on what they are. Now you want to hear what my actual rules would be if I had my choice?"

"Don't you have your choice? You're the dom."

"I'm the dom, not the king of the universe," he said. "Some

things are negotiable." He moved my hand up and down his shaft with his fingers on my wrist. "But if I had my way…other than the blindfold and kissing, I'd say the rule for when you're in the dungeon should be above the waist you're free, below the waist is for me. That goes for looking and for touching."

"That has a kind of elegance to it." I put my hands above the table again as the waitress came back with our drinks.

"That wouldn't mean a free-for-all, of course. Just that you're on your own to determine who can touch you from the waist up and how. That'd be true if we go to that party Jill and Bry invited us to, too."

"That party does sound like fun." I sipped from my lemonade. The sugar was still swirling around in the bottom, undissolved. "I wonder how it would affect people like them if we were out. If people recognize us as America's—or even the Internet's—perviest couple, how would that affect people like Jill and Bry? Would they have to stop coming to parties with us if they were afraid of being associated with us?"

"I don't know. Part of me's afraid to risk it. And I'm not usually a cautious person." Chino gulped down some of his iced coffee and then pressed the heel of his hand to his forehead. "Ouch. Brain freeze. The least erotic pain in the universe." He moved my hand back to his crotch. "Soothe me, sweets."

I rubbed him and felt his blood pulse in my grip. If we hadn't been in a restaurant I would've said forget the food, all I need is for my Daddy to be happy. The difficult thing about the situation with his mother and sister was there wasn't anything more I could do at this point other than try to be supportive. I couldn't change the facts and I couldn't assuage Chino's fears. All I could do was be with him, spiritually, emotionally, physically.

"Quick," he said then. "Before our food comes. Tell me one more thing we should know about how to be us."

"Hm. I think we're getting pretty good at being us as is."

"Yes, but we're still learning it. Come on, sweets. One more thing. First thing that comes into your head."

The first thing was the one big thing we hadn't talked about yet. It probably wasn't a "quick" conversation, but I did as he asked and spat it out. "What happens the first time you command something I don't want to do?"

"Have you forgotten already that you didn't used to want to do anything I told you?" He chuckled.

"No, no; I mean what happens when it's not just me resisting and needing to be pushed past my reluctance, and it's actually me saying no. Like with Jill and Bry being like 'no fucking way' and then sometimes meaning it? I mean, with them they turn the tables and it works but that would never work for us."

"True. Are you afraid if you refuse me the bubble will burst?"

"Daddy won't be angry at his girl for defying him?"

"I keep telling you, Maddie, within the context of a scene, I don't see disobedience as a failure. I won't be disappointed in you, but you might be in yourself."

"I guess."

"Part of my job is trying to figure out how far I can push you without pushing you too far. But I don't think you're asking about the regular push and pull of power in a scene. I think you're asking about what happens when I fuck up and guess wrong and ask you for something you flat out can't or won't do. Something that doesn't just push your limits but crosses them somehow. You can use your warning word to give me a clue, first of all."

"True. But what if you keep pushing?"

"Then it might be up to you to say, 'Chino, don't be an idiot.' You have to not be afraid to slap me upside the head, even if it's not something you think a good girl would do. A really good girl would keep her Daddy from making a huge mistake if she could. Like I said, I would like to think I'm a good enough dom we wouldn't run into trouble, but I'm not such a fool as to think I'm perfect. We're both capable of making mistakes and we share the responsibility if a scene goes wrong."

"That . . . makes sense." He was saying everything I wanted to hear, needed to hear. Did he know how good that made me feel? Like we had a *partnership*, not just a "relationship," like we were really truly in it together. I felt like there was a bubble around us, a force field that kept the world at bay.

"In a perfect world we'd always be rational and logical. Of course while we're playing logic goes out the window, but at least if we talk about it in advance we have less chance of really wrecking each other emotionally. Don't you think?" He let out a groan as I concentrated my fingers squeezing the head and I felt a spot on his jeans getting damp.

"The important thing, if we have a wreck, is that we help put each other back together," I said. The things we were saying were serious but I couldn't help smiling given how good I felt about his words. And his cock under my fingers.

It pulsed as he said, "Remember I love you. And I want to do what I do to you because I love you. And if I hurt you, tell me, and we'll figure out how to deal with it from there."

"Okay, but likewise. Don't turn into one of these doms who bottles everything up inside and makes the sub constantly guess what's going on in there."

Chino laughed. "Like Mal, you mean? Gwen is an expert at reading him, though. And you're an expert at reading me, sweets. I'm just the large print edition. Easy to read."

I grinned. I was so in love with this man. "Most of the time."

The food arrived then and we moved on to more mundane topics but I felt like we were still so new that every conversation, every meal, every place we went and everything we did was all a part of us learning how to be us.

* * *

CHINO

We'd decided to take separate cars to the party, since Madison needed to go so much earlier to prep the place and so on, but I got restless sitting at home and wondering how much traffic there would be and the result was I got there more than an hour early. I parked my own car since Jamison wasn't on valet duty yet, right next to Madison's. Good thing, too, since her trunk wasn't all the way shut. I made sure it was and then walked up the drive to the main door.

The sun hadn't set yet as I rang the bell. I was surprised when Reeve and not Jamison opened the door. "Mr. Garcia, welcome. Nice to see you again." His eyes were scanning around beyond me, though. Reeve always gave me the impression that he was actually a Terminator and not a human, but without the Arnold Schwarzenegger accent. At least he was on our side. "Did you walk up from the parking area?"

"I did."

"Ah. You may have tripped a motion sensor. Lately there have been some coyotes setting them off, too. Some of them have been coming much closer to the house than they used to."

"They come all the way into West Hollywood these days. I'm not surprised," I said as I made my way past him into the foyer. “Should I go on down or do you think they’re still getting ready? I know I’m early.”

“If you’re not a hindrance to party prep, I’m sure your presence downstairs would be welcome.”

I chuckled. “I’ll stay out of the way. Promise.” Reeve seemed even more on alert than usual. Well, some heavy stuff might go down with Ricki confronting Schmitt tonight.

I tried to imagine being married to someone for decades and then divorcing them. Had his wife been unhappy the whole time or was it only after she found out what a hypocrite he was? Was it sudden or did the relationship erode from happy to hellish bit by bit? I thought about my own mother. *She did it for us.* I felt like an ungrateful heel, a rotten son.

Well, that was out there. In the dungeon I could be the Daddy of Madison’s dreams.

Reeve punched the four-digit code on the door to the downstairs for me and I sauntered down into the club, thinking that I was leaving the real world behind. With me and Madison, we could play anytime, anywhere, but parties were a kind of alternate reality. I felt almost like I was entering a ritual space. Changing my clothes only heightened that feeling, just like changing into my clothes for the stage. Sure, by the end of a show I often had almost nothing left of what I had put on to go out there, but the transition was still important. You prepare yourself to perform, to put yourself out there, and changing what you wear, putting on your makeup (if you do that sort of thing; I’ve been known to put some guyliner on, after all), all prepares you mentally even more than physically.

I’d always liked leather, even before I had a sexual association with it. Or maybe I always knew that association was there underneath and that was why I liked it even though I wasn't totally aware that's what it was. I changed from my jeans to a jock and leather chaps, left my shirt in a locker and put my jacket back on. A second skin.

I tried the door to the toilet from the changing room but it was locked. Bradley or someone must have been in there. I could hear Madison and Gwen's voices as they prepped one of the playrooms. I wondered if Mal and Gwen would do a scene. They were always beautiful together, dark and light, fire and ice. Not as beautiful as Madison, though.

Maybe I'm biased.

I ended up sitting in the main social room on the couch facing the Catherine wheel. I'd pulled a book from the shelf but didn't open it. I sat there thinking, just thinking. Here in this room, on that spot of wall right there, I'd captured the woman of my dreams. It felt like it was important we return here, to this spot, to cement it all in front of everyone. I'd told her if everyone was too freaked out over Schmitt maybe we'd stay low-key and save it for next month. But truthfully I didn't want to wait for next month. I felt like with a BDSM relationship the private consummation and the public one were both equally significant. The whole band would be here tonight; Ford had promised he wouldn't miss it if it meant a lot to me.

It definitely did, which was why it was important that we not try to do it in the middle of some kind of angst fest with Schmitt. We were going to be together forever; so if I had to wait a month, I could wait a month. Patience and biding my time until I had my chance had served me well before. If necessary, it would again.

Maybe I was more like my mother than I had realized. I just hoped I had made better choices than she did. The Virgin Mary's message seemed to be glowing from my heart, though. Concentrate on love and all would be well.

CHAPTER EIGHTEEN

MADISON

Chino startled me just before eight, when I went to make sure napkins and toothpicks were restocked behind the bar and I realized he was sitting on the couch. He was in black leather so he matched it, but still. "How long have you been there?"

"A while," he said, a mischievous smirk on his face. "Everything going all right?"

"So far so good. No sign of Schmitt yet, though he's usually one of the first guests here. Ricki's waiting for him upstairs in her office."

"Smart. No need to make a big to-do down here in front of everyone." He beckoned and I went closer until he pulled me into his lap. "That's my job."

"Making a big to-do in front of everyone?"

"Pretty much. One way or the other." He tucked a hand in the crook of my thigh under the leather tennis skirt I was wearing.

Sakura came in with her sometimes playdate Helene, the same one she'd brought to Palm Springs. They were quickly followed by Mal and Axel, and then a steady stream of other guests that kept me busy for a while—making sure everyone had drinks, helping with their corset laces, and so on. As the regular flow of a party got going I managed to forget all about Schmitt for a while. The rest of the guests didn't know anything was up, of course, so they socialized and began to play as usual. The energy was high and people were having a good time.

"Maybe he's not going to make it tonight," Gwen said at one point when the party was in full swing. "You know who else isn't here? The Palmers. And they haven't missed a party in years and years."

I leaned closer to her so she could hear me over the sounds of people being spanked and flogged, laughing, and the motor of the Rotorvator from down the hall. "Do you think someone could have tipped Schmitt off?"

Gwen shrugged. "I doubt it. I'm just sorry Ricki's sitting upstairs waiting for him. She's missing one of the best parties of the year. Oh, hey, don't look now, but I think someone's waiting for you."

I turned to see what she was looking at and my heart jammed in my throat. Chino. He was standing next to the section of wall where we'd had our paddling scene, the same leather studded paddle in his hand. He was just standing there, hands clasped on the handle of the paddle, face impassive. Patient.

The world seemed to narrow to a tunnel running from me to him, all the noise becoming mere echoes, people fading to the background. He didn't move, but it felt like he was beckoning me. He was obviously waiting.

My feet were moving almost before I could think about it,

putting one foot in front of the other. He was wearing black leather and had put on leather gloves, making the paddle look almost like an extension of him. He was standing directly under one of the lights inset in the ceiling and his hair was as black and glossy as his jacket. He'd pulled it back into a small knot.

When I reached him he pointed to the familiar wall. I put my palms against it and imagined that I could feel the exact spot where they'd been a month ago when Chino had taken charge of my body and soul.

His gloved hand slipped under my skirt and rubbed my bare ass. "I thought we'd start with something familiar before we get into unfamiliar territory."

I took a deep breath. "How unfamiliar?"

"I want you to prove yourself."

"I like proving myself," I said, wiggling my ass back against his caress.

"I know. So you won't mind if the test is kind of hard."

"What, like an essay question?"

He laughed. "No. I just mean challenging because it'll be new territory. Daddy wants to find out how far his girl will go for him."

Something clicked in the way he said that. "You mean, you're going to push me to tell you to stop so you can find out where the limit is, not that you're going to try to break the limit."

I could feel him nodding, his nose in my hair before he answered. "Exactly. I'm not trying to break you, Maddie. You're always a good girl for me, even when you're naughty as hell. Who knows? Maybe I'll reach my limit before you reach yours."

"I'll warn you, I'm willing to put up with a lot if it means your approval at the end."

"Mmm, I have no doubt you'll have that, sweets." And with that he swatted me on the ass with his gloved hand. My skirt was somewhat in the way and he flipped it up and tucked the hem into the laces of my corset.

He warmed me up with a spanking, a harder one than usual; whether that was because of the leather glove or the excitement of being in the dungeon, I don't know. I fell into a half trance as he beat me, the rhythm of his blows matching the pulsing techno currently playing on the sound system. I forgot about what was coming and sank into the moment, connected to him by his hand meeting my flesh again and again.

Then came the paddle. I was vaguely aware of a few cheers and whistles as he brandished it before the flat side came down on my rump. That thing stung! But the beating was arousing at the same time, not from the pain so much as the feeling that it was Chino administering it. My pussy grew swollen and wet as surely as if each swat were a gentle swipe along my clit. The feeling only intensified as he switched from paddling my backside to flogging my shoulders. Soon my shoulders were aglow to match my ass.

I felt the press of his body against mine then. He'd shed his jacket and I felt his skin against my back, the leather of his pants against my inflamed butt cheeks. "You ready for it to get tough?"

"Yes, Daddy," I said without hesitation.

"You nervous?"

He was using that word as a signal, checking my temperature. "No, Daddy." I was ready for anything.

"Good girl. Here we go."

He stepped back and raised his voice. "Madison!"

I flinched at the accusing tone. "D-Daddy?"

"Look me in the eye when I'm talking to you."

My heart rate zoomed like I was really in trouble, like I'd been caught red-handed at something. I turned slowly, barely daring to look up at his face.

He was trying to put on a stern look, but there was a mischievous bend in his eyebrow. Probably only I could tell he was holding back a smirk. I almost smirked in response, but I wanted to stay in character. I folded my hands. "Is something wrong, Daddy?"

"Fix your skirt. Or are you trying to attract attention? You look like a slut."

Oooh, so that's where he was going. I licked my lips. The ball was back in my court and I had to decide what kind of spin to put on it. "O-only for you, Daddy," I said, and my voice came out deliciously shaky.

"Is that so?"

"Yes, Daddy."

"Strip. Show everyone who you belong to." When I hesitated he raised his voice. "I said strip, girl!"

My hands flew to my corset, trying to undo the hooks in front, but I was breathing so hard with excitement that I couldn't get the top one loose at first. Then it finally went and the rest came apart easily. I let the corset fall behind me and undid the button on the tennis skirt, whipping it free.

Chino pulled it out of my hand. "Axel. Come here."

Axel sauntered up, a gleeful look in his eyes. "What can I help you with, my friend?"

"Tell me what it says on her."

Axel made a show of bending down and examining my tattoo—and therefore my crotch—with a critical eye. "I do believe your name is spelled out right here."

"That's right. It's like a KEEP OUT sign for anyone else, isn't it, Madison?"

"Y-Yes, Daddy," I said as Axel backed away.

"Tell everyone here what's allowed in your cunt, girl."

My cheeks were as red and flaming then as my ass. I had to take a couple of breaths before I could quite make my mouth form the deeply embarrassing words. "Your cock, sir."

"Louder, so they can hear you in the back."

"Only your cock is allowed in me, sir," I said, then swallowed hard. I'd never done a scene like this before and much to my surprise I was finding it hot as hell. Instead of humiliation, it was brimming with the same deliciousness of exposure I'd felt when I first started burlesque, before I'd gotten jaded. Except now instead of revealing my flesh, I was showing everyone my kink and our relationship.

"Is that right? Then how do you explain this?" He pulled his phone out of his pants and a video began to play. It was me finger-banging and inserting a mascara tube into myself that day when we'd gone out house hunting. My mouth fell open in surprise. If I'd thought my adrenaline was at its peak before that, I was wrong; it climbed even higher. He showed the video to everyone circled around us. Gwen, the whole band, Sakura and Helene, Dara, Paul—even my two co-hosts were gathered around.

And it was my turn to respond again. "That's because . . . " I realized that the truth was the best answer. "Because you wouldn't give me your cock!" I stamped my foot as I said it.

Chino's eyes blazed, unable to keep his grin off his face now. His smile was sadistic but my defiance had clearly delighted him. "Is that what you want? Is that why you're acting out like a bad girl?"

"It's unfair," I said, crossing my arms. "You promised."

"I promised you could have it if you were good. A good girl takes her punishment without complaint."

Oooh. He was definitely challenging me to find the limits

of my girl persona, making me react to different situations. "Yes, Daddy," I said, pouting a little. "Will you let me show what a good girl I am?"

He spoke to our audience. "What do you think, folks, should I give her a chance to show how obedient she can be?" The suggestion was met with universal approval. "And should I be lenient?"

"Might depend on just how good she is," Axel said with a wicked grin.

"All right, Madison. What would you like to show the people?"

I didn't care if it was a cliché. I dropped to my knees, crawled to him, then undid his belt and fly and took out his cock. Actually it was more like it fell out, heavy and stiff, once his fly was undone. I wasted no time in trying to give the best possible blowjob ever.

When he yanked me off him by his fist in my hair, gasping, I knew I'd pushed him dangerously close to coming. I licked my swollen lips and looked up at him with pure seduction in my eyes.

"Hold her down," he said, and a moment later Axel and Mal had me pinned on the floor, one of them on either side of me, while Chino put on a condom. "Good thing she's wet because this thing isn't." He rubbed the tip up and down where I was wettest. "Okay, girl, what's this hole for?"

"Your cock, Daddy."

"What's this hole for?" he repeated.

"Your cock and nothing else," I half shouted.

"That's right," he said, and thrust into me with a brutal push, just the way I liked it. I let out a scream but it was a scream of ecstasy. Not that anyone but Chino knew it: To everyone else it probably sounded like he had stabbed me with a butcher knife.

He moved slowly, then, a few rolls of his hips to make sure his whole shaft was good and slippery, and then he bucked mercilessly, driving into me with everything he had. His eyes never left mine and I didn't dare close my own for fear it would break this perfect circuit between us, every thrust like a turn of the engine that lit up all my pleasure centers.

"Suck her nipples," Chino said, and his two lieutenants made me gasp, Axel suckling hard, Mal using the edge of his teeth. "Tell me, Madison. Is this against the rules?"

"No, Daddy! You said . . . above the waist is okay."

"That's right. But everything down here is mine." He fucked me in time with the music then, closing his eyes at last and losing himself in the pure heat of where our bodies joined.

But he wasn't done. He pulled free before either of us could come, and tried to resettle the condom but it had gotten wrapped inside itself or something and he yanked it off and wadded it in a tissue. "Do you realize this is the first time we've done the missionary position?" he said to me, his voice quiet and calm, and it felt like we were speaking "backstage," out of the scene.

"If you call being held down by two other doms missionary," I pointed out.

He laughed. "All right. Time for your punishment." Just like that we were back in scene. "Spread her, boys. Ford, Sam, if you'll take her hands."

The other two members of the band held my hands over my head while Axel and Mal each took an ankle and kept my legs apart. I wasn't limbered up but I was still more flexible than the average person, giving me a fairly wide split.

"Gwen, could you bring me a quirt?"

My eyes went wide. The whip. He was going to whip my inner thighs? This was going to hurt like hell.

He swished the single leather tail in the air in front of me, and I could feel the air currents against my lush sex. "Okay, girl. Your punishment. Are you going to take it like a good girl?"

My voice came out breathless. "Yes, Daddy."

"Ten strokes. I'll count them down," he said, going down to one knee and measuring the distance. "Here's number ten."

The whip lashed out and a stripe of fire ignited near one of my knees. I lifted my head to see because I almost couldn't believe I wasn't burned. A red welt appeared instantly.

Chino waited until I'd put my head back down and slowed my breathing before he dealt the matching mark to the other leg. "Nine."

This time I couldn't stay silent, though I gritted my teeth and tried to keep it all in.

Axel whistled appreciatively. "That's gotta hurt like a motherfucker."

Yes, it did. Chino ran the fall of the quirt softly over my legs while he waited for the pain to subside a little, making sure I got the full run of suffering before putting a fresh one an inch or two up my leg from where the previous one had landed. I whipped my head back and forth trying to process the pain. If Mal and Axel had not each had a death grip on my ankles I would have been kicking my feet.

By the time we got to "five" the stripes had progressed up my inner thighs toward ever more sensitive flesh and I full out screamed. The pain had to go somewhere and out my mouth and into the air as sound was the only choice. When I ran out of air in my lungs my throat was raw and I gasped to try to catch my breath.

"Good girl," Chino said. "You're doing great. Four more to go."

I lifted my head again to see the stripes. There was room

for maybe one more on each leg before he got to my pussy itself. I looked him in the eye.

He had his poker face on, not outright cruel-looking, but not giving anything away either.

Was he really going to do it—whip me right on the pussy? Given how the leather felt on my legs, would it cut the more tender flesh of my labia? Would he risk catching me right on the clit and damaging the nerves?

"Such a good girl," he said, lining up the next lash.

"Oh, no," I heard myself say, as if my mouth were in revolt. "No no no, please, Daddy, no . . ." I screamed as he landed another blow on my leg, in the last inch of flesh before my labia. Four, that was four, even if I hadn't heard the number through my own scream.

I didn't hear three, either, as it marked the other side.

He dangled the whip now so that the tip tickled my clit. At any other time that would have been titillating, but knowing now where he was headed the words poured forth again. "Oh, God, please no, no, no, Chino you can't I can't you can't be serious!" He was tugging on his cock with his other hand while teasing me with the fall. I tried to remember what he'd said. That he was going to test me. Challenge me. Make it hard.

He leaned in to lick a wet stripe up the very center of my pussy, leaving my clit glistening and exposed. That really was his target! He backed up and began to swing his arm back and forth, getting ready to strike.

"Please don't hurt me, Daddy, please don't!" I screamed.

He lifted his arm and out of nowhere someone grabbed him. The guys let go of me immediately as Chino fell back. I sat up in time to see him connect with a rather square punch and then land on top of his assailant who was squawking for mercy much less appealingly than I had.

Axel and Mal pulled Chino off to keep him from maiming

the man severely, but in my fury at having my moment stolen I leaped on top of him instead.

Blood ran from his nose but he was easy enough to recognize. "Price Lawson, you unbelievable scumbag!" I spat as I grabbed him by the shirt collar and slapped him as hard as I could. "What the fuck are you doing here?"

He didn't seem to hear me. His bell had been rung too hard.

"Are you all right, Maddie?" Chino asked from somewhere behind me.

"I'm fine." I was endorphin-high and shaking with adrenaline, but that was to be expected. "I'm just fine."

Lawson blinked, catching up with the conversation. His hand flew to his bleeding nose but he gave me a look of outrage. "Thanks to me!"

"No, no thanks to you," I said. "You're an idiot. Don't you know it's traumatizing to be yanked out of a scene before it's finished?"

"But . . . but he was . . . " Lawson sputtered and pointed at Chino, who had come to stand beside me, still flanked by Mal and Axel. "He was about to really hurt you."

Chino laughed. "Are you kidding me? Don't you know a mindfuck when you see one?"

"She was begging you!"

"Yes, she was. Maddie, tell him how the last scene we did in this spot ended."

Even through my rage at Lawson and all the adrenaline and endorphins running through me from the scene, I felt an intense bolt of sweetness shoot through me at Chino's words. We were thinking exactly the same thing! I reached up and felt him grab my hand, but nothing could make me feel more connected to him than that moment, like we were reading each other's minds.

"I was planning to pull the same trick again," Chino said, squeezing my fingers. "Go on and tell him."

"You built me up like the last two cracks were going to be the worst of all and then you just tapped me gently, knocked me over with a feather, so to speak."

Chino bent down and kissed me on the cheek. "I love you, Maddie."

"I love y—" Before I could finish, Lawson tried to struggle out of my grip and caught me on the chin with the heel of his hand. I scrambled out of the way as Axel, Mal, and Chino jumped in again, this time with a set of wrist restraints.

Gwen was on her cell phone. "Reeve isn't picking up, I wonder—"

Before she could finish her sentence, though, I heard the voice that answered the question of what Reeve was busy with. Conrad Schmitt was bellowing from the hallway. "Lay a hand on me and you will find yourself on the receiving end of an assault lawsuit! I assure you, Ms. Hamilton, this escort is entirely unnecessary."

As Sakura lowered a bathrobe onto my shoulders, Ricki answered, "Cy didn't raise any fools, Conrad. I'm allowing you to clean out your locker yourself out of courtesy. Don't make me regret the decision."

Schmitt didn't turn at the changing room door, though. He kept coming straight into the main room but stopped dead in his tracks when he saw the tableau before him: a bleeding man facedown on the floor, Chino sitting on his legs, Mal with a fist in his hair, me beside them with everyone huddled around me. "And is this further shenanigans to discredit me?"

Ricki took one look around. "No, this is some other shenanigans entirely. I'll deal with that later."

"My ejection is entirely improper. The by-laws of the organization—"

"What organization?" Ricki asked. "Oh, you mean the community of sexual freedom and experimentation you've been a part of for fifty years but who you've supported legislation against?" She addressed the room. "You guys want to guess how many millions he's funneled into Purity Values causes? The bill that would criminalize dildo ownership in Texas? The outlawing of oral sex in Michigan? Cracking down on the legal production of porn right here in California? But that's not why you're being drummed out of the club, Conrad. Hypocrisy is gross but it's not against the so-called by-laws. You know what is? Consent violation."

"Consent—" His eyes narrowed. "You can't possibly still be holding a grudge about that one inappropriate pass I made at you, young lady. I apologized and you would not find a court of law that would uphold that as sexual harassment."

Ricki shook her head. "No, not that one. This complaint came from your wife. Would you like me to read the details of the e-mail she sent me to the room? Since you seem to have decided to take this to the court of public opinion."

He paled, coughed, shook. I was afraid he might keel over right that moment with a heart attack or apoplexy. But he recovered from his shock. "My wife is not feeling well tonight or she would be here to refute these outrageous claims."

Ricki seemed bored with his bluster. "Your wife is at your house in Malibu tonight changing the locks." She checked her watch. "You're now officially trespassing in my home. My next call will be to the police if you are not gone in the next twenty seconds."

"You wouldn't dare. And expose all this?"

Ricki could be such an ice queen when she wanted to. She really had him sweating bullets. This time she did not reply but merely kept her eyes on her watch.

"Mr. Schmitt," Reeve said, sensing his moment. "If you'll allow me to accompany you to your car."

Schmitt said nothing, merely preceded Reeve into the hall. None of us said anything either, although Gwen did hand Mal a towel to blot Lawson's nose with. Then her phone buzzed with a message.

Lawson groaned. "I think you broke my nose."

Chino stood and looked at his knuckles. "Well, I did cut myself on your glasses."

"Since when does he wear glasses?" I stood and belted the bathrobe.

"Since he decided to surveil us, it would appear." Mal picked up the broken remains, which looked much like the camera-glasses PlayPeople had sent me to use while vlogging.

Ricki stepped forward and cracked her own knuckles. "Do you think he doesn't realize my company owns his company or is he just stupid?"

"You're the one who always says why choose 'or' instead of 'and,'" I pointed out. I nudged Lawson in the arm with my foot. "Sit up, Price."

"Do I have to? You hit me really hard," he whined.

"Sorry about the lack of negotiation," Chino said sarcastically, "but who invited you anyway?"

"No one, obviously," I said. "He snuck in. Still trying to get his big scoop."

Mal propped Lawson upright and then, with a glare of warning, undid the restraints. Lawson accepted a handkerchief from him sheepishly and held it against his nose. "And I would've snuck out again, but I was trying to film what was going on in here and then got trapped because Schmitt and the security man were arguing at the top of the stairs."

"And then you got suckered into thinking I was actually

doing something horrible to Madison while all these people watched." Chino put an arm around me. "Some crack reporter you are."

"I think Ricki's got his balls in a sling at this point," I said sweetly, pressing a kiss to Chino's cheek. "Let's leave him to her. And we can pick up where we left off."

"Is Reeve back yet?" Ricki asked. "I think perhaps Mr. Lawson and I should continue this conversation in my office."

"Um," Gwen said, "I just got a message from him. There's someone at the gatehouse." She put the phone to her ear.

"One of yours, Lawson?" Chino asked. "Someone coming to pick you up? Let me guess. You snuck here in Madison's trunk."

Lawson held the kerchief against his face. "Yeah. But I've got nothing to do with whoever's at your front gate."

Gwen put her hand on my arm, still on the phone with the guard at the gate. "Chino," she said. "It's your mom and sister."

CHAPTER NINETEEN

CHINO

If I thought when I broke Price Lawson's nose (and I'm pretty sure I did) that was the angriest I could ever get, that was before I saw the black eye on my mother's face. There was nothing I could do at that moment to defend her or avenge her other than run to wrap her in my arms.

She was so much smaller than I remembered, not even five feet tall, her chin high and defiant despite the ugly bruise—or maybe that was just her looking up at me. She also didn't seem as old as I'd expected, her hair still ink black and her eyes only slightly lined. I'd grown a few inches since she'd last seen me, and she fit well under my chin. Once I got her in a hug I didn't want to let her go. Not when she was patting me on the back and telling me, in Spanish, how happy she was to see me, how much she missed me, how sorry she was.

"Don't be sorry, don't be sorry," I told her, my face buried in the top of her hair. "Just be happy. That's all I want. Just be happy, Mamá."

Someone put a soft hand on arm and I thought it was Madison at first. Then I realized it was Flor. I pulled her into the hug, too. "You did it. You got here."

"Chino." She cried a little and I felt the tension leaving her. "Thank God. We were going to wait until Tuesday. We had the tickets booked. But something set him off and I was afraid when he came back it would be worse. He took my phone! So when he went out we ran. First to a neighbor's, and then she drove us down to a motel where we got a cab right to the airport. We had to spend almost everything on the card to change the tickets. Without my phone all I had was what Madison had told me to write down on a piece of paper and hide."

I was persuaded to let go of them and introduce them to Madison. She had hastily put on a sundress and I'd thrown my leather pants and a T-shirt back on, but we were not exactly at our most cleaned up at that moment. In fact, I was certain that I reeked of sex and leather, but there had been no time to get any more prepared. I brought her forward with my arm around her. "Mom, Flora, this is Madison. You talked to her on the phone."

"So pleased to meet you, Flora." Maddie said, and then nodded toward my mother. "Ana . . . ?" she said, as if unsure how to address her.

My mother was no fool. In Spanish she said, "She should be calling me Mamá, too, no?" I nodded and then she hugged Maddie.

"Are you all right?" I asked then, trying to get a better look at her black eye. "Do you need to see a doctor?"

She swatted an imaginary fly to keep me back. "No. I'm fine."

"Although we're starving," Flora said.

"Oh goodness, we have tons of food here. Hi, I'm Ricki. This is my house." Ricki, the only one of us who was respectably dressed, in a sharp skirt suit, stepped forward and introduced herself. "Let's make our way to the kitchen and we can talk more there."

"Oh, and Mom, Flora, these are my best friends, my bandmates Axel and Mal," I said.

Flora suddenly stiffened. "I've seen your photos," she said with a self-conscious nod toward them.

Axel caught my eye as we began moving out of the foyer. Usually when a young woman said she'd seen his pictures the reaction was decidedly different. I shrugged.

Before we could leave the foyer, though, a high-pitched sound came through, clearly audible in the large entryway: Helene's instantly recognizable orgasmic squeals. Apparently someone was finally trying out the Rotorvator.

* * *

MADISON

Axel tried to keep from laughing but couldn't entirely. Ana seemed unperturbed, pretending she'd heard nothing perhaps, but Flora looked around nervously. I tried to come up with something to say to defuse the tension, or any plausible explanation, other than what it obviously was, but my mind drew a blank.

Walking toward the kitchen took us farther from the dungeon area and the sound receded. I had never really thought about it before but the Inquisition Room had to be directly under the foyer, the main room under the main parlor. Ricki had started up a bit of tour guide chatter, describing the history of the mansion and the founding of Coast to Coast Pictures by her grandfather after World War II. Flora continued to look spooked and Ana placid.

They were both beautiful: Flora wide-eyed and Midwest healthy plump, like a dark-haired Adele, Ana trim and deceptively youthful. If she'd had Chino when she was twenty she wouldn't be quite fifty, I realized. Same age as Julia Roberts. Her hair was loose and she was wearing a simple dress and a soft-looking sweater. Ricki got everyone settled around the kitchen table and then began pulling out the post-party food that Mina had prepped and left for us.

"Let me help you," I offered.

"No no, you sit, rest," Ricki said, then made a face, worried that had sounded incriminating. "Er . . ."

"I'll at least get the drinks," I said.

"Okay." Ricki set about putting the mini quiches and other such things into the oven while I got out glasses and a pitcher of fresh lemonade, a bottle of seltzer, a bowl of ice cubes, and tongs.

And then I was out of things to do and I sat down next to Chino, facing his relatives.

When Ricki put a platter of food down in front of us—chicken wings and mini quiches and Swedish meatballs—and proceeded to hand out plates, Flora finally cracked.

"I'm sorry. I can't. I can't eat this food," she said.

"Flor!" Ana said sharply.

"I can't eat the food from a house where such things are going on. I can't pretend—"

Ana silenced her with a sharp whistle and a hand on hers. "What, you think the food's going to taint you? Is it like the magic food in stories you're not supposed to eat?"

"And we're supposed to stay here? To sleep here? How? I'm afraid I'll be raped in my bed."

Chino tried to fix it. “Flora, it’s not like that. We didn’t know you were coming or we wouldn’t have been... having so much fun when you arrived.”

“Fun! You think I don’t see the marks on Madison’s back?”

I sat up straighter suddenly. This dress only had thin straps over the shoulders. I hadn’t even realized the flogging had left any marks. It didn’t hurt and I didn’t think about it.

Chino moved my hair aside and traced one welt gently with one finger, his eyes sad. “This is not like what happened to Mom. Mom, I’m sorry you had to get such a shock. That was never my intention.”

“And you!” Flora continued, pointing at me. “How dare you give advice about escaping battering.”

I tried, too. “Flora, it’s different. What we do with each other, it’s consensual, it’s for... stimulation and, and bonding. Your brother loves me—”

“And my stepfather loves my mother!” She made a disgusted noise and pushed her chair back from the table.

Ana stopped her with an iron grip on her sleeve and said something quickly to her in Spanish. I didn’t get much of it but I thought I caught the word for “virgin” and I doubted she was talking about the Virgin Mary.

Then Ana addressed us in English. “I’m sorry my daughter is so excitable. She’s been raised very sheltered. Not only does she not know your rock and roll, she has a very unrealistic view of sexual relations.”

“Sex doesn’t include hitting. If it did, why did we leave?”

“This?” Ana pointed to her still swollen black eye. “This was not sex. And it was not done for ‘love.’ This was done by a man who wished to do me harm, against my will, because I would not bend to his any longer. Perhaps he had a right to be angry that the woman he had sheltered and supported for years was going to leave him, but he had no right to harm me or to threaten me. And that is why we left. And Chino has no right to harm or threaten Madison, am I right?"

"That's right," I said. "We play. We play with . . . spankings and things like that. But like I said, for stimulation, not because he's actually punishing me."

"I thought you said it was only for show," Flora said to me.

"I never said that, Flora." I clasped my hands. "You're the one who said that. I tried to explain—"

"You said it wasn't real!"

"And it's not real," I said firmly, "if by real you mean abuse and injury. It is real love, though."

Chino appealed to his mother. "I love her. I cherish her. We belong to each other."

Ana made that fly-swatting gesture again. "Yes, of course you do. I know all about bondage, and paddling, and flogging. Did you think your generation invented it? I met your father at fetish night at a dance club." She reached for the serving tongs and moved some food onto her plate and then put some onto her daughter's plate as well. "Flora, I know it's a shock but that's because all your life you've been taught everything about sex by men who know nothing. It's time for you to grow up finally. Forget the petty, sad notions of sex that men put into your head and learn to recognize love." Her voice quavered momentarily while she set down the tongs. "I could never teach you to see it because it took me until now to learn the lesson myself. And it is crucial that you choose love over money, over anything else. If I have sacrificed my best years so that you would never go hungry, the most important lesson you must learn now is to love."

Chino looked like his eyes were about to fall out of his head. "Ma."

"Mi hijo." She smiled, her eyes a bit watery. "If you love

her well and she considers herself well loved, you have my blessing. Now, enough foolishness. Eat. All of you, eat."

We were pretty hungry by that point, and we attacked the platter lustily. Flora looked sheepish at first, but after a few bites began to loosen up. Soon Axel had figured out something in common they could talk about: California beaches. Flora remembered the beach from when she was a child and said the Great Lakes were never the same—too cold, not enough waves, rocky shores. Mal told her he lived within walking distance of the Santa Monica Pier and her eyes lit up.

Shortly after that Ricki took them to the guest wing to get them settled for the night and gave the all-clear for the rest of the party guests to emerge from downstairs. Once it was established that Ana and Flora were okay, Lawson was long gone, and so was Schmitt, there was much laughing and joking about Helene being audible even through stone (and probably air vents) and about Chino's mom being in the know.

Once they were all gone, Chino and I decided to stay the night. Axel and Mal were as a matter of course, and we decided to be there in the morning when the women woke up.

"Besides," Chino said, once we were ensconced in a guest room far from any others, pressing me back against the door with his hips. "We were interrupted and I don't think I'd make it all the way through the drive back to your place without needing to do this." He lifted me up and rutted against me.

"Bed," I said. "My backside and welts are sore and this door isn't helping."

"I suppose the bed might be a good idea," he said and carried me to it, falling down onto it with me. "Although we're both wearing too much."

"Race you," I said, then laughed as he was still getting the fly of his jeans undone when I had pulled the sundress off over my head and slipped my panties off in half the time. Soon enough he was completely bare, though, wrapped only in his tattoos—and a condom.

"Can I come inside you without any foreplay?" he asked.

"My body is yours," I said. "It says so right on the label."

"Mm-hm. And your heart is mine, too. But your mind will always be your own, Maddie. And that's a good thing. So tell me what you think about me fucking you with no foreplay."

"This entire night was foreplay," I said.

"Then I take that as definite consent," he said, and held me down while he rubbed his cock up and down my slit. The dirty talk and that little bit of rubbing were more than enough foreplay for me and although I was at my tightest, I loved the feeling of him wedging in.

So, apparently, did he. "*Nnnghh.* Love to fuck you. This hole especially."

"Was that really the first time we did it in missionary position?" We'd had a lot of sex over the past few weeks and yet I hadn't noticed.

"It was. I was saving it for a special occasion."

I grinned and rocked my hips in time with his as he set about fucking me slowly. At least at first. Once he settled into a languid but steady rhythm, he began to ask me things. "Were you okay with the guys helping out like that?"

"I loved the guys helping out. I loved...being exposed." I tried to explain the feeling I'd had. "I don't mean physically exposed, but it felt kind of like that. Like you bared my kinky soul to everyone there."

"And you liked that?"

"Mm, yes, Daddy."

"That's because my definition of a good girl is a dirty girl who loves sex," he said, dipping his head to suckle at my neck and send pleasure shooting down my skin. "Who loves it when I do twisted things to her."

I wrapped my legs around him, trying to drive him deeper. "Mmm. I don't know which I like better: when you punish me or when you reward me."

"Oh, you definitely like the reward best, sweets. But you like it even better after you've been punished." His mouth met mine and his tongue darted between my lips in time with his thrusts. When he let me breathe again he went on. "You were a very, very good girl tonight. You took everything I dished out, you were super awesome to my mom and sister, and you trusted me. Now I know how deeply you trust me."

I had a sudden shiver, though. "Can you believe Lawson? What a tool. I hope he doesn't press assault charges."

"Ricki seemed to think he won't be daring to show his face in our circles again. Her comment to me was 'he'll have to move to Australia to get a job in the English-speaking world.'" Chino kissed me on the neck, the forehead, the mouth. "Okay, doll, I'm turning off your ability to move now. But you can come if the way I fuck you takes you there."

He proceeded to fuck me for a long time after that, long enough for an incredible, gradual slow-build orgasm to accumulate drop by drop until I was completely brimming, and then when he came I spilled over, awash in sensation and the overwhelming feeling of never-ending love.

EPILOGUE

Six Months Later

We took Ana and Flora with us when we went house hunting in the Hollywood Hills. They both preferred my place in West Hollywood, so our plan was to move them in there and for me and Chino to buy something in Laurel Canyon where there'd be room to put in a dungeon...and a nursery when we were ready to do that. But they liked to come see the houses with us.

We walked up the driveway to a house that looked familiar. So did the agent standing in the kitchen. Her eyes lit with recognition. "Mr. and Mrs. Jones, wasn't it? I believe you visited this property the first day it was on the market. And here you've decided to re-visit now that it's on the market again?"

"What happened to it in the meantime?" I asked.

"Oh, the usual. Buyer and seller took a long time to settle on a price and contingencies, then the buyer's financing fell apart. Lost his job at a website startup or something like that and wasn't able to get re-employed fast enough to satisfy the mortgage company." She did a double-take suddenly as she got a clearer look at my face. "Oh! You're the vibrator advice lady!"

I smiled. "Yes, I am."

"This property has so much great natural light. Have I showed you the upstairs rooms? Suitable for bedroom or office or studio..."

We followed her up the stairs and then also spent a long time looking around outside while she greeted some other prospective buyers.

I sat down on a rock on the hillside with a view over Los Angeles and Ana came to sit beside me. She patted my hand. "Are you troubled, *mi hija*? Is my boy troubling you?"

"Oh, no, Chino is wonderful," I admitted cheerfully. "But I've been wanting to ask you something, Ana. And I never quite know how to bring it up."

"Okay, okay, let me guess, then," she said with a smirk that reminded me startlingly of her son. These days she smiled more and more. "You want to ask me to share my story for your non-profit charity for women, but you're worried it's too soon."

I laughed. "No, that wasn't it, but that's a great guess and if it's not too soon, I actually would like you to become one of our regular speakers."

"Well, what then?"

"I guess I'm still chewing over the question in my mind. If you knew about kink and consensuality, how could you choose a relationship that was essentially nonconsensual? Is all we're doing to educate people wasted if it can happen even if you know?"

"Ah." She patted my arm. "First of all, I was too young when I got involved with Cisco to know right from wrong yet, but I thought I knew. Cisco was young and stupid, too, and we got a lot of it wrong, and I did not like his pornographic art. If I'd encouraged him to pursue that instead of making him promise to stop, who knows? Perhaps he could have earned more. Perhaps if I had been less afraid of my own desires I could have learned to love him for who he was instead of passing judgment on him. I could tear myself apart if I thought about these what-ifs every day. But the truth is that when I made the decision to marry for the sake of the children, I convinced myself of a few things. One, that love would come. Two, that my love of God would be enough to sustain me if love in the relationship did not come. Three, that because I had liked when Cisco spanked me that I could handle whatever might come. I fooled myself on all counts, and it took me years to not only acknowledge that I had fooled myself but then to actually gather up the will to leave."

"I need to understand, though, Ana. If I'm going to be a domestic violence educator, I need to understand how a woman as intelligent and thoughtful as you could get sucked in. I know it happens all the time to very smart women but I still haven't wrapped my head around it."

"Well, you know they are nice at first. And they are nice exactly when they have to be, to convince others that they are harmless, or you. But the dark side begins to show whenever they think you have no choice but them. He had so many things he could lord over me. My immigrant status—he told me if he divorced me I would be deported and never see my children again. When they make enough threats like that, you come to believe you are truly trapped, and that is when the violence begins."

"I'm so sorry you went through that."

"Don't be, *mi hija*. It's in the past now. That's why it's so crucial we teach others. So fewer will suffer what I did." She squeezed my hand. "You are a good woman, and very good for Chino. I can see it. The way you look at each other, the way you turn toward each other like flowers toward the sun."

"Flora is still a little skeptical," I said.

"Flora will find her sun eventually," Ana said. "There is a cute tattoo artist who works in a shop in Koreatown who likes her. He is being very patient. Bringing her flowers. Very old-fashioned. Perhaps it will work." She shrugged.

A tattoo shop in Koreatown? A different one from the one where Cisco worked? Seemed unlikely. That meant Ana had to be in touch with him. But neither Cisco nor she had mentioned it to me or Chino. Curious.

Ana stood. "Christmas is coming soon," she said, and left me wondering what she meant by that.

I found Chino in the room that would become our dungeon if we bought this house. He snagged me by the waist and spun me around. "Hands against the wall," he growled, and then rubbed his hand up and down my jeans until I wiggled back against him.

"Good girl," he said as I twirled in his arms to kiss him on the lips. "Very good, indeed."

A NOTE FROM THE AUTHOR

Although I fully believe in the power of fiction and fantasy, and in the ability of readers to tell the difference between a hot fantasy that breaks consent (Christian Grey, anyone?) and what is acceptable in real life, in this book I wanted to inject one particular element of reality: The domestic violence hotline number that Madison gives to Flora is real. 1-800-799-7233 is the USA National Domestic Violence Hotline, which celebrated its twentieth anniversary in 2016 and answered its four millionth call for help. I wanted to include a real phone number in case it might help some reader escape an abusive situation. The bit about the US Conference of Catholic Bishops condemning abuse and making it grounds for annulment of marriage is also true.

There are also many good local advocacy organizations. In the Boston area where I live, The Network/La Red is one in particular that helps LGBTQ and members of the BDSM community with partner abuse problems. Their 24-hour hotline number is 617-742-4911. Please remember that liking kinky fiction, or even kinky sex, does not mean you support abuse, nor that you should tolerate abuse.

The BDSM community and domestic violence advocates share a goal: consenting partners and consensual relationships for everyone. Be safe out there!

Everyone knows Ricki Hamilton as the icy heiress living in a billion-dollar mansion. But few realize that behind the gilded gates, Ricki is the mistress of LA's most exclusive private club. A place where no fantasy is forbidden and no one goes unsatisfied—except for Ricki. She's ready to leave the business behind, until she meets the one man who changes her mind...

Please see the next page
for an excerpt from *Taking the Lead*

CHAPTER ONE

OVERTURE

RICKI

"Ms. Hamilton. The car is ready."

I turned toward Jamison, who was standing in the doorway with his usual impeccably bland demeanor, his hands folded. "Do I look all right?" I asked him.

"Stunning as always, Ms. Hamilton," he said, his voice low and smooth.

"You didn't even look," I complained. I gave myself one last glance in the floor-to-ceiling mirror in the two-story foyer. If I'd had my way, I would have had one of Sakura's designer friends make me something artsy and avant-garde to wear. But if image is everything, then an expensive, big-name designer's dress was required wear. It was off-white, beaded, classic. If that wasn't good enough for the paparazzi, then there wasn't much else I could do. "Where's Sakura?" Last time I checked, the stylist had been affixing some glass beads in her hair.

"She is already in the car," Jamison said with a slight bow. That was as close to telling me to hurry as he would ever get. When he'd first taken the butler job with my grandfather he'd gone to finishing school. I wondered if that was where he learned to be so . . . polite-pushy? Pushy-polite? Maybe it was a Cuban thing. He had come to the States when his family fled Castro and at first my grandfather had hired his older brother. Jamison wasn't his real name: it was the name he'd picked for himself. It suited him. His wavy black hair was slicked close to his scalp and I felt he was a thousand times more polished than I was. He gestured toward the door.

"Fine, fine." I hurried across the entryway toward the front door, reminding myself not to do anything to dislodge the dress or my coiffure. Members of the staff were bustling about, readying the mansion for tonight. We didn't host this kind of soiree that often anymore, only a few times a year, not like in my grandfather's heyday, when the "Governor's Mansion" was host to a steady stream of Hollywood's elite. Cy Hamilton, the man they called the "Governor of Hollywood," had liked to party.

Sarah—Sakura, I mean—was waiting in the limo, looking as perfect as always. Somehow she managed to rock an Asian style without ever coming off like a parody of a geisha or kung-fu movie courtesan. She was half-Japanese and *all* business when it came to finding the right clothes. Mine just had to look expensive or people would talk. Sakura's had to look unique and yet tasteful and powerful and creatively artistic all at the same time. I took the seat across from her in the stretch and off we went to pick up her date, then mine.

She grinned. "This is like prom night, only better."

I shrugged. "The prom night I never had." Being a Hamilton heiress, I didn't exactly have the standard American upbringing. "It's just an awards ceremony, Sarah."

"Sakura," she corrected.

"Don't worry; I'll get it right when it counts."

"And don't rain on my parade. Maybe this is dull and boring for you, but it's my first time at the Grammy Awards."

"You went to the Oscars last year," I pointed out.

"As official arm candy to a total bore. And he wasn't even a nominee. Axel's band is up for Best New Artist." She drummed her toes excitedly on the carpeted floor of the limousine. "Plus I really like him."

"*Like* him-like him?" I asked pointedly. This wasn't the first time Sakura had mentioned this guy. I admit I only knew him from the entertainment trade magazines where he was, admittedly, one of the only rock stars I thought was cute. It might be really good for Sakura's career to date a rock star.

But she dashed that idea. "Not like *that.* As a friend, I mean." She glanced out the window, not that she could see much through the tinting. "He's really great. A really great guy."

"Didn't he start out a client of yours, though?" I was trying not to sound judgmental about it, really I was.

She sighed. "I'm not doing the professional dominatrix thing anymore, Ricki."

"That doesn't answer my question."

"I met him at a photo shoot if you must know," she said with a sniff.

"The photo shoot where you're in a latex catsuit with a whip and he's in a cage?" Of course I'd seen it. After we learned the terms of the will, I found out that the staff regularly scanned all the tabloids looking for anything about BDSM to make sure our family wasn't being implicated. They regularly showed me anything remotely having to do with kink and pop culture.

She sighed. "Yes, that one. But he is sooooo not a submissive."

"No?"

"Definitely not. In fact, I'd say he's a dom but you wouldn't necessarily guess that from the vanilla supermodel arm candy he's been seen with."

"You don't think he shows his kinky side to the press?"

She clucked her tongue. "You of all people should know most people don't."

"Yeah, yeah." The whole reason my grandfather had built the secret dungeon in our basement had been to give A-list kinksters a private place to meet and spank. Well, and so he could spank them himself, honestly. These days the members were mostly A-list because of their money, though, not their celebrity. We had a lot of presidents and vice presidents of major film studios and entertainment corporations. I know Grandpa Cy had meant well, but I couldn't help but think my main job was to ensure that these entitled executives could get their knobs polished in the most exotic fashion possible. "Hey, wait a second. Is this all a setup so I'll consider him for membership?"

Sakura held up her perfectly manicured hands in surrender. "I swear, I didn't plan it that way. He really has become a good friend, and he asked me to go to the awards, and since I knew you were going, too, I thought it would be a good idea to double date."

"You haven't said anything—?"

"Of course I haven't. Ricki, your secrets are always safe with me. All he knows about you is you're the Bitch Queen of Hollywood."

"I am not!"

"You have the worst case of resting bitch face in the state of California." Sakura framed me between her thumbs and index fingers. "Just sayin'."

I resisted the urge to fold my arms across my chest, which I knew would only make me bitchier looking. Sakura really didn't understand how important it was that I not come off as a frivolous airhead or a flirt. Unfortunately the only other stereotype left for women in the popular media seemed to be "ice queen."

Ice queen had worked for me so far. I had secured a nice job in development at Blue Star that would be a good stepping-stone to eventually running CTC. And other than a few "society" photos here and there I had mostly stayed out of the media, because ice queens weren't actually all that interesting to them. They much preferred the party girls and the fuck-ups, the Paris Hiltons and Lindsay Lohans.

She tried to change the subject. "So tell me about your date. You never told me who you're taking."

"You know Milford Randolph?"

"The president of Blue Star Entertainment? Of course I know him! But he's more than twice your age!"

"Not *him.* His nephew, Grant."

"Oh," she said, much less energetically. I guess she was less impressed with a mere executive at Blue Star Pictures. Or less upset. I had quit trying to figure out Sarah's moods back when we were college roommates.

"Yes." I decided not to try to describe him to her. She'd be meeting him in a few minutes, anyway. "He's a nice enough guy."

"If you say so," she said, sounding skeptical, but she didn't outright contradict me. The only real reason I was going with him was politics, but neither of us was going to say that out loud.

We pulled up to Axel's hotel. I settled back into my seat and took my phone out of my clutch, expecting we'd be waiting for a while until he came downstairs. But to my surprise, Riggs, my chauffeur, opened the door right away.

Axel Hawke alighted on the seat across from me like a cat hopping onto his favorite perch—lithe, sleekly groomed, and self-possessed. He kissed Sakura on the cheek. He had a diamond-stud earring, a barely tamed coif of blond-streaked hair, and a tuxedo tailored to make it look like his arm and chest muscles were barely contained by the fabric. What looked cute on the magazine page was downright devastatingly good-looking up close. He even smelled good. I found myself suddenly wishing I had worn something more interesting, more of a statement, something that might seem worth his notice, instead of the classic-but-boring dress I was in.

Sakura smiled coyly, as if holding in a gleeful grin at seeing him. He took her hand and kissed the back of it. "Good to see you."

"You, too, sweetie," Sakura said. "So this is the 'playboy' makeover you were telling me your image consultant wanted?"

"Yeah. Bad boy isn't good enough anymore, she says. So now I'm a good-bad boy. Or maybe that was a bad-good boy? I don't know."

She gave him an approving shrug. "Suits you, anyway. Axel, may I introduce my friend, Ms. Rickanna Hamilton?"

I held out my hand. Instead of looking at it as he took it, he held my gaze. His eyes were agate green. He grasped my fingers with a gentle surety, lifting my knuckles to his lips and saying, "May I call you Ms. Hamilton?" And then planting an intensely warm, suave kiss on the back of my hand. I hadn't realized my hands had gotten so cold in the air-conditioning of the limo, and the warmth of his mouth seemed to send a wave of heat through me.

"You may," I answered, a little taken aback by the intensity of his gaze and the fact that he surprised me, asking if he could call me Ms. Hamilton, not Ricki. He had been pointedly polite—and yet the force of his charisma was hitting me like a searchlight. It was too much, I had to push back, had to dim that light somehow and take him down a peg. "So are you really a good boy at heart?"

The light didn't dim in the slightest. If anything the beam narrowed to point even more directly at me. "Oh, no, I'm very definitely a bad boy," he said, his voice quiet, but firm.

In spite of myself I felt a little shiver go through me at that sound, that tone. Parts of me very suddenly wanted to find out just how wicked he could be. Little fantasies flashed through my head like sunlight coming through patchy clouds: which part of him was the wickedest? His tongue or his fingers or something lower down...?

And then I thought about what Sarah had said. He was a closet dom?

Ugh. The last thing I needed was another spoiled-rotten man in my life bossing me around. And I definitely didn't need any more BDSM in my life given how hard it was going to be to keep that damn club a secret.

But that didn't mean I couldn't have a *little* fun, did it? She was right. Tonight was for celebrating glitz and glamour, not for showing off resting bitch face. A little flirting would be polite and wouldn't hurt anybody, as long as I kept my hormones in check. I gave him a little "cat-canary" smile of my own. "In that case, should I call you Axel? Or Mr. Hawke?"

I saw his eyes flick toward Sakura for a moment, as if wondering if she'd told me anything. The intensity in those gray-green eyes ramped up again and it almost felt like he was wrapping me in invisible velvet. "Definitely Mr. Hawke," he said deliberately, and it was as if with each syllable the invisible velvet wrap grew tighter and tighter around me. Like I was being pulled into his spell.

No. We're not going there, I reminded myself. Especially not with Sakura sitting right here and my actual date about to get into the car. Time to take things down a notch. I tried to bring the chitchat back to business. "So, Best New Artist nominee? Are we allowed to say 'good luck'? Or is that bad luck?"

He laughed, a deep, unexpected, and genuine laugh, and sat back, resting his hands on his knees. His artfully tousled hair was not as wild or full as a lion's mane, but he still reminded me of a big cat sitting there, languid but alert. "I have no idea. It's my first rodeo. The only 'Superstition' I know is that old song by Stevie Wonder."

Sarah began to sing the song, then, and he clapped his hands and snapped his fingers along with her for a few bars, though she only knew a few of the words, and Axel didn't really know much more. Then they punched each other in the shoulder like playful siblings.

"Oops, careful," she said, reaching a hand up to make sure the glass beads strung in her hair hadn't come loose. "Let's not be rowdy, now."

"Yes, ma'am," he said with another deep chuckle. I got the feeling when he said "yes, ma'am" he meant the opposite, though. I wondered if Axel Hawke had grown up a troublemaker or what.

We pulled up to the Blue Star building then. Under Randolph they'd swallowed up several of the major studios and record companies. I needed a scorecard to keep track of who owned who these days. Riggs got out and I expected the door to open, but it didn't. I peered through the tinted glass: he was standing beside the car, waiting for our last passenger to come out. There was no sign of him just yet.

I turned my attention back to Axel. Let's see. I was curious if Axel Hawke was a stage name or his real name, but it would be gauche to ask. What could we safely make small talk about?

I settled on, "So where are you from?"

"Everywhere, I guess." He shrugged. "My dad was a weapons instructor in the Air Force so we moved around a lot when I was a kid. Japan, Texas, Germany, a couple of years in England. Then when I was a teenager my parents split and my mom and I settled in Boston, so I guess that's the closest thing to an answer to the question. Kind of depends on what you meant by it."

"Just making conversation," I said. "Though I guess that explains why I can't really place your accent."

"Sometimes when I get really tired I forget to speak English," he said. "But I only remember a little Japanese, a little German. My bandmates say I need subtitles at times like that."

That made me chuckle. He sounded so down-to-earth now, so genuine and honest, it only added to his air of self-possession instead of detracting from it. I could see why Sarah liked him. I wondered if the reason they weren't a couple was because they were both dominant in bed. Maybe he would be a fun addition to the "Governor's Club." I had a couple of women on the staff who'd probably enjoy him. He couldn't have been much older or younger than me, and if I was tired of catering to the annoying, middle-aged and older men who were the majority of the club's members, I'm sure the gals were even more so. I imagined him moving through the dungeon like a hungry tiger. A hungry, sexy, bad-boy tiger.

"You're staring, Ms. Hamilton," Axel said, startling me out of my reverie.

"Oh! Sorry. My thoughts were a million miles away." *Oh, thank goodness*, I thought. *Here comes Grant to distract everyone from the fact I was just staring at a rock star while sort of fantasizing about him.*

Riggs opened the door and Grant half fell into the seat I had left for him. He pulled his legs in and shook himself, holding up a bottle of champagne. For half a second I wondered if he'd been drinking from it, but no, it was still corked, and he wasn't drunk, merely a klutz. "Whoops, here we are. Hello, I'm Grant. Alex, is it?"

"Axel," he corrected, shaking Grant's hand. "Like the long thing that connects two wheels."

"Sorry?" Grant seemed unprepared to hear an explanation.

"Or an ice skating move," I added. "The one where you jump-spin in the air."

"Yes, exactly," Axel said, with a smile that was like warm sunshine. God, every time he looked at me I felt a thrill, like I was some kind of giddy teenager.

Grant stared at me for a moment, then back at Axel. "I seem to have arrived in the middle of a conversation?"

"Grant, let me introduce my friend Sakura—"

"Charmed, charmed." He shook her hand vigorously.

"And Axel Hawke, the lead singer of The Rough."

"Yes, yes, a prestigious award nominee! Well, let's celebrate." He opened the bar compartment and popped down the shelf, took out a few champagne flutes, handing them around to each of us before attempting to open the bottle. He wrapped his fist around the cork and pulled. Sakura shied away.

After he had strained at it for a minute or so, Axel said, "May I give it a try?"

"No, no, I've got it. It's just stuck," Grant insisted.

He strained at it for a while more, until sweat was clearly shining in the hollows of his eyes.

"Give it here, Grant," I said. He handed the bottle to me.

I handed it to Axel, who took the handkerchief out of his pocket, wrapped it over the cork so it wouldn't fly loose, and then, while holding the cork still in one fist, twisted the bottle. There was an immediate pop sound, and Axel looked me in the eye as he said wryly, "Happy New Year."

He poured a glass and handed it to me. I found it hard not to let my fingers linger where they touched his. After handing around champagne to the others, he set the open bottle in the holder in the bar shelf that was intended for the purpose. We each took a sip.

Then Axel spoke to me as if continuing a conversation, which I guess he was. "We're up against some stiff competition tonight. Jamie Goode is incredibly talented. Kaptain Krunk are so unique, totally original. I'm a big fan of Duwanna, too."

"May the best band win, then," I said, and clinked glasses with him. "Though I still hope it's you who gets it."

He bowed his head slightly, averting those moss-green eyes and then looking at me again. "Thank you. But why?"

Because you're a sexy beast and I'd better content myself with rooting for you since I know I can never actually have you. "Because I know you, and I don't know any of the others," I said, drawing a circle around the four of us with my index finger. Was I that desperate to create some kind of a connection between him and me? Yes. But I wanted a safe connection. "You're *our* Grammy nominee now."

The look in his eyes said he wanted a connection with me, too, and not a "safe" one at all. My hormones were making me dizzy. But I patted Grant on the arm and felt Axel back off. He shifted his weight back slightly, and he looked at Sakura instead of at me.

"How's the champagne? Is it good?" Grant asked, then continued on without waiting for an answer. "It should be. I stole it out of the caterers' stash where they were setting up for my uncle's after-party. It's not like he'll miss it."

Both Sakura and Axel murmured that it was good. All champagne tasted pretty much the same to me, more like bubbles than like wine.

"It'll go flat, you know, so we better drink up," Grant said, waving the bottle. He drained his own glass and then set to filling them again.

"I've got plenty, Grant," I told him.

"Come on, it'll go flat," he insisted, as if I might not have heard him the first time. "Drink up."

If there was one thing I had learned to do, it was to humor a man when he was in his cups. I was getting an inkling that Grant was not exactly Prince Charming, but better the devil you know than the one you don't, right? I resolutely took a very small sip and Grant splashed a tiny splash into the top of my glass to replenish it.

We were in line with the other limos waiting to pull up to the red carpet for a good thirty minutes, maybe longer, which gave Grant plenty of time to harangue me to drink more. I continued to take tiny sips and he continued to drain his glass and then fill it all the way again.

By the time the door opened, the bottle was empty. Grant stuck it upside down into the bottle well in the shelf with great ceremony. "Ta-da," he declared solemnly.

I caught Axel's eye suddenly. His expression was half sympathy that my date was now this boorish drunk and half disdain for him. At least I hoped the sympathy was for me and the disdain for Grant—my heart sank. Even though I kept telling myself I should steer clear of Axel Hawke, the last thing I wanted was for him to think I was anything like Grant Randolph. Spoiled, drunk, pushy, and an idiot. Maybe Grant wasn't the best choice to be photographed with after all, I thought, even if the Blue Star PR department would have liked that.

A moment later a greeter opened the back door of the limo so we could exit, and Grant sped out like a kid off the monorail, throwing his arms wide as he blew kisses to no one in particular, then tripping over his own feet and landing face-first.

The rest of us could not really keep from laughing at that. It was simply too comical. Sakura and I both hid our faces from the open doorway with our hands. "Omigod," she said. I could hear some cameras clicking and when I dared to peek I could see Grant was still facedown.

"I think my image consultant would say wait a minute before we get out," Axel said.

Riggs, good old Riggs, was helping Grant to get up, then. Riggs was not a small man, a former bouncer as well as a former college linebacker, so Grant really had no choice about the matter.

"Ugh. You guys go. I'll stay in the car and come in the side entrance," I said.

"Don't be silly," Sakura said. "Look, Riggs is dragging him off to the side now. There's quite a distance to go before we hit the actual *public* area of the carpet, you know. Let's just waltz along, the three of us, before anyone really notices we were supposed to be with him."

"Won't it look odd that I don't have a date, though?" I asked.

"No, because you're each going to take one of my arms," Axel said. "That is, if you're okay with helping me play the playboy, Ms. Hamilton."

"Are you sure you want to do that?" I asked, though I was really asking myself whether I was ready to go through with that.

"It'll be fun," Sakura prodded.

Everyone wanted to be out of that limo by then; the handler was peering in trying to figure out what was taking so long, and I really wanted to be away from the cameras before Grant caught up with us. I had a sudden panic that the Blue Star PR department might blame *me* if the two of us—Blue Star's favorite son and their newest hot hire—were photographed with Grant puking onto my off-white dress. "Oh, all right. Let's go."

We joined a queue of others in a staging area, while production assistants managed the line and took names and checked credentials.

Finally it was time to step out into the spotlight, though. An usher gave me a hand around the rope, while shutters snapped wildly. Axel followed, provoking shrieks from the spectators. He'd donned dark sunglasses, which made him look more like a killer in a Hong Kong film than a rock star to me, and he held his hand out for Sakura to take.

As she glued herself to his hip, he slipped his arm around my waist and pulled me snug against his other side. To keep my balance, my hand landed on his stomach. Wow. The tuxedo was hiding how muscled he was, how strong his arms were.

With the two of us attached, Axel made his way through the gauntlet of news cameras, pausing for a few quick interviews. The lights were very bright and I marveled at how he didn't flinch when someone held a microphone right up to his mouth.

"Axel Hawke, so glad we could catch you. The Rough is the hottest new act."

"Thank you," he said with an all-teeth smile.

"We heard that 'The Rough' wasn't the first name of the band?"

"Oh, definitely not. We tried a bunch of things before we

agreed on that. I kind of liked Bandit, but there used to be a band called that. My next suggestion was Ass Bandit, but our manager didn't think that one would fly."

Sakura was trying hard not to laugh out loud.

"Is it true you were homeless as a teenager?"

Axel did laugh briefly, as he joked, "No, I just looked like a homeless teenager in our early photo shoots." Then he spoke more seriously, almost vehemently. "Don't disrespect the actual youth out there trying to survive by comparing it to my situation. Being a runaway is no joke and I'm grateful to everyone who has helped me get where I am today."

A little farther down we were stopped by another one who asked, "'Kidnap My Heart' is at number one in three countries now. What will the follow-up single be?"

"Oh, you'd have to ask the record company but my guess is either 'Razor Sharp' or 'Knockout.'"

I wondered if any of these sound bites were going to make it to air. I just smiled and appreciated how deftly he was able to handle so many different questions in such a short space of time. As soon as he had passed the last interviewer, he let go of Sakura for a moment, whipped off the sunglasses, and tossed them like a Frisbee into the delirious crowd. As we turned to go up the steps into the theater, though, I lost my footing and nearly fell.

That iron-strong arm around my waist kept me from going down and probably saved me a sprained ankle in the process. The heel had broken clear off one of my shoes, as we could all see when Sakura snatched it off my foot and held it up with distaste. "Oh for the love of... and these heels cost more than that bottle of champagne, I bet."

Axel still had not let go of me. He glanced back the way we had come, where I could hear a raised voice I feared was Grant's.

Axel cleared his throat. "If you'll allow me, Ms. Hamilton?" He picked me up before I quite realized that was what he was asking for. He didn't seem like that big a man, but I had already felt the steel strength of one arm—now it was two, one under my knees, one behind my back. With the whiteness of my dress and the blackness of his tuxedo contrasting, we looked almost like newlyweds crossing a threshold. I put my arms around his neck like I couldn't help myself.

In fact, I couldn't.

I laughed as he carried me the rest of the way, Sakura following behind twirling the dead shoe. "My hero," I said.

He just made a hum of agreement, almost a purr, and I might have tightened my grip around his neck when he did. I wanted to bury my nose in his collar and just breathe his scent and imagine he was carrying me somewhere dark and private to do bad-boy things to me. *Enjoy it while you can*, I told myself.

Once we were well inside the lobby, where a massive pre-event reception was taking place, Sakura took my other shoe, too, and Axel set me gently onto my stocking feet. "Surely you can't be the first person this has ever happened to," he said, looking around, then waving to someone.

A woman of some Asian American extraction hurried over to us and gave him a quick hug. "Ah, you made it! Good."

Axel introduced her to me and Sakura as his manager, Christina Pempengco, and she gushed at us for a few moments, then said, "What size shoe do you wear?"

"I'm a seven and a half, why?"

"Wait right here. I have shoes for you."

"Wha—?"

Axel laughed as Christina rushed away into the crowd. He also waved off a caterer coming toward us with a tray of full champagne flutes before the guy even had a chance to get near. "Christina is a high-energy problem solver, which is why she's a great manager," he explained. "It doesn't even have to be her problem and she'll still solve it."

We stayed where we were, my shoeless feet hidden by the fact that without my towering high heels, my dress now dragged on the floor. Axel eventually corralled some non-alcoholic drinks into our hands and ensured a steady stream of catered hors d'oeuvres flowed past us.

"I swear, it's like he has magic eye contact," Sakura whispered to me at one point.

I know what you mean, I thought.

"There's Mal," Axel said. "He's the one over there who looks like he waltzed out of a vampire flick."

I couldn't see who he meant, since without heels I couldn't see over most of the people in the crowd. But then a tall man with long black hair joined us. He and Axel hugged like brothers and the man gave Axel an up-and-down look. "What's the expression? You cleaned up nice."

"Mal, meet Ricki Hamilton, and of course you already know Sakura."

"Charmed, I'm sure," Mal said. He had a deep voice and a mildly British accent, and his tuxedo was subtly piped with silver and green. "Have you seen Chino? I seem to have lost both him and our dates."

"No. You're the tall one," Axel chided. "What do you see from up there?"

"Ah. There he is." Mal waved to someone else, and a moment later a shorter man with black spiky hair and a woman on each arm came up to us. He was grinning from ear to ear, but before I could be properly introduced to him or the women, Christina dashed back.

In her hands she had a pair of pumps miraculously almost the same color as my dress. "Here, try these."

I slipped them on. They weren't quite as tall as my previous shoes, and they were slightly too small, but they would do to get me to and from my seat. "Excellent. Thank you."

"No problem. It's so awesome to meet you, by the way. I'm the treasurer of AWESM, the Association of Women in Entertainment Studios and Media, and I wanted to thank you for your generous donation!"

"My pleasure," I said. "It's a valuable organization."

"Have you heard about the fashion show we're doing before Valentine's Day? We'll have VIP seating for our top donors! You probably have an invite in your mail!"

I smiled at her. "I'll look for it, I'm sure." Sakura had been mentioning the show, too: some of her designer pals were showing in it. Paul, my assistant, probably had the invitation in a file of low-priority things for me to look at.

"Now, Axel, I'm trying to find Errold Rothschild so you can make a good impression on him."

"Remind me who that is?" Axel asked with a skeptical look on his face.

Christina rolled her eyes. "The head of the UK division? I want him to be impressed by how fantastic you all look." She gave me a quick smile. I got the impression she was happy Axel might be seen with me. Interesting.

She dashed off again to find the record company executive but she hadn't returned by the time the ushers were urging us to go into the auditorium.

By the time we reached our seats I was very ready to disappear into the audience. I've never particularly liked being in the spotlight and even though no one was really paying attention to us once we'd left the red carpet, I had felt like everyone was staring at me.

We were in the orchestra section, between twenty and thirty rows back, near the aisle in case Axel's band won anything and he had to go on stage. There were three empty seats next to us, though, that made me wonder. Grant's and who else?

I got my answer when two more guys hurried down the aisle together and were enthusiastically greeted by Chino and Axel. Axel introduced them to me and Sakura as "Samson, our keyboard player" and "Ford, bass." Ford had his blond hair pulled back in a ponytail but shook it free before he sat down. Samson had brown hair, blue eyes, and a quiet smile. They both had firm handshakes even though they looked pretty overwhelmed by the whole setting.

Chino seemed to be the one having the most fun. "Who do you think sat in this seat last time, eh? Madonna? Beyoncé?" He wiggled in his chair. "I'm going to pretend my booty is long-distance time-traveling touching the seat that Beyoncé's booty touched."

Mal rolled his eyes. "Honestly."

But Axel laughed. "How about you, Sakura? Who sat in your chair? You still have that fantasy about David Bowie?"

"Oh, please, he's like three times my age," Sakura said, but she blushed a little.

"Mal? How 'bout you?"

Mal gave his friend a dark glare. "Celebrities are the last people I'd want to fuck."

I teased Axel, then. "What about you? Whose chair do you want?"

Axel drew himself up to his full height. "No, really the question is who wants to sit in *my* seat." It felt like sex god vibes were pouring off him in waves.

Or maybe I was the only one who felt that way. The rest of them were used to being around him, I guess. They shrugged it off when a short while later he made everyone get up and change seats, supposedly to make it even easier for the band members to reach the aisle. But I did notice I ended up in the seat he had been in. It was as warm as if he had rested his hand on my back.

The lights went down then for the start of the show and I settled back as the intro music began to play. Fairly early in the ceremony a category came up that included one of the band's songs and I noticed that Ford held Axel's hand so tight I thought both of their fingers must be going numb. Alas, the song did not win. Axel patted Ford's arm and told him that they'd have to hold out for Best New Artist.

And then a short while later the whole band was spirited away by a handler. I gave Sakura a questioning look.

"They're performing a number," she explained.

Well, I thought, *at least something'll be worth seeing at this show.*

ACKNOWLEDGMENTS

Thanks go to my dear agent Lori Perkins; can you believe we've been together sixteen years? And to my partner in life and love, corwin, with whom I just celebrated twenty-five years together. Meow.

Thanks also to my beta readers and sensitivity readers, who helped with everything from accuracy of domestic violence phone support to Latino and religious cultural elements: Brittany, Linda, Sirius, and Mel. And to the New England Leather Alliance, still the best BDSM community organization in the country.

This book wouldn't be as fabulous as it is without the shepherding of Madeleine Colavita and her willingness to ply me on short notice with olive oil and cocktails. (I promise that's not as kinky as it sounds.) Cheers to her and the whole Forever team—Jodi, Michelle, Alex, Leah, Beth, Elizabeth, et al.—for taking great care of me and my books. You guys make me feel like a rock star.

ABOUT THE AUTHOR

Cecilia Tan is the award-winning author of many books—including the Struck by Lightning series, Magic University series, and Daron's Guitar Chronicles—as well as an editor, baseball historian, and taekwondo instructor. She is also the founder of Circlet Press, publishers of erotic science fiction and fantasy. When she is not gallivanting across the globe in search of great bookstores and gourmet food, she can be found at home in Cambridge, Massachusetts, with her lifelong partner and three rather demanding cats.

Learn more at:
CeciliaTan.com
Twitter: @ceciliatan
Facebook.com/thececiliatan